The Princess and the Wolf

"Why did you kiss me?"

At some length, High Wolf said, "Do not worry. I realize it was a mistake. It will not happen again."

Sierra said, "How can you be so certain that we will never again kiss?"

"How?" he asked. "Because I can control my impulses. To what end do all these questions tend?"

She said, looking away from him, "I am attempting to understand if my life and my . . . feminine person are secure with you."

He grunted. "You are safe with me. Let me assure you that I will keep my hands—and my lips—away from you from this day forward."

"Will you?" she asked, glancing toward him and smiling.

He ground his teeth. "I give up. Tell me, what is it you want from me?"

Facing him fully, she leaned in and grinned before saying, "Mr. High Wolf, I ask a very simple thing. I merely want you to do it again."

Other **AVON ROMANCES**

Coming Soon

And Don't Miss These
ROMANTIC TREASURES
from Avon Books

KAREN KAY

The PRINCESS and the WOLF

AVON BOOKS
An Imprint of HarperCollinsPublishers

Excerpts from *Sonnets to a Soul Mate: 39 of the Most Erotic and Romantic Poems of Our Time* copyright © David Ziff, 2003. All rights reserved.

AVON BOOKS
An Imprint of HarperCollins*Publishers*
10 East 53rd Street
New York, New York 10022-5299

Copyright © 2004 by Karen Kay Elstner-Bailey
ISBN: 0-380-82068-4
www.avonromance.com

First Avon Books paperback printing: May 2004

Avon Trademark Reg. U.S. Pat. Off. and in Other Countries, Marca Registrada, Hecho en U.S.A.
HarperCollins® is a registered trademark of HarperCollins Publishers Inc.

Printed in the U.S.A.

10 9 8 7 6 5 4 3 2 1

This book is dedicated to some very special people, who not only inspired me, but helped get me through what I am referring to as the summer from . . . Well, perhaps we shouldn't go there.

For Thomas Lechner and Arlen Lieberman, who together inspired the image of the prince.

For Lokesh Bharadwaj and Kalbana Bharadwaj, loan officers extraordinaire.

For Arlene Richards, a friend for almost thirty-four years, and an incredibly competent financial advisor.

For Donna-Gail Wilcox and Caroline Veech, who both listened and helped.

For my daughter, Trina, who also helped.

For every single person in the Advanced Organization, III FLAG, and in particular to Betty Stafford. What would I have done without you?

For David Pomeranz, whose musical genius humbles me.

For Diana Venegas, who is probably one of the most beautiful women of my acquaintance.

For Bob and Joyce Bailey. How fortunate I am that you are a part of my family.

And for my husband, Paul Bailey, who continues to set my senses afire. Our love is truly a spiritual awakening.

Acknowledgements

Special acknowledgement is due the following people, whose works have documented—luckily for us—different aspects of the life of the scout:

Tom Brown, Jr., *The Way of the Scout*. This book introduced me to "the water dance of the scout."

Frank R. Linderman, *Plenty-Coups, Chief of the Crows*.

L. Ron Hubbard, *Buckskin Brigades* and *The Philadelphia Doctorate Course Lectures*.

I would highly recommend reading them all.

Note to the Reader

∽∾

THE SCOUT: Traditionally, North American Indian tribes called their scouts wolves. These scouts were the most trusted individuals within the tribe, belonging to a mysterious medicine society of their own. Upon their trusted word stood the well-being and safety of the tribe and every member in it. Even chiefs bowed down to the wisdom of their scouts. These men were warriors, trackers and trailblazers, but most of all these were men of incredible skill and pride. This series honors them.

THE STORY: The year of 2004 celebrates the bicentennial of the Lewis and Clark adventure. And so, perhaps it is fitting that this story is inspired by the youngest member of that exposition, Sacagawea's baby, Baptiste Chareonneau.

Baptiste Chareonneau led an extraordinary life. Capturing the admiration of not only Captain Clark of the Lewis and Clark expedition, he also charmed a European prince, who endeavored to befriend the lad.

In 1823 Baptiste and Prince Paul of Wurtemberg, Germany, set sail for the European continent, and for six years (from the age of sixteen to twenty-two), Baptiste lived in a royal castle and betook a classical education, which included speaking, reading and writing the languages of English, French, German and Spanish.

In late 1829, Prince Paul and Baptiste returned to the

Americas. Here, somewhere along the route, Baptiste and the prince separated, and never saw one another again. Baptiste went on to become a mountain man and a scout for various private and governmental parties. Why the two friends parted remains a mystery, as none of Prince Paul's published works mention the affair. It is, however, speculated that their separation was less than amicable.

The mystery of Baptiste became highly enigmatic, since he never again corresponded with Prince Paul, nor did he keep a diary. However, because Baptiste went on to be one of the best scouts the West has ever known, we have learned of him from the writings of travelers at that time.

Perhaps one of the most interesting aspects of Baptiste's life is that he neither married, nor produced heirs, and this in a land where a man could easily have taken more than one wife or mistress.

What happened? Why did he suddenly cut all ties to the prince, to Europe?

This story, although the characters and events in it are the product of the author's imagination, is a supposition as to what might have happened and, were this a more forgiving world, what could have happened . . .

Chapter 1

Southern Germany, The Black Forest Region
Baden-Baden
A Royal Estate and Castle
1824

"Maria, come quickly," Princess Sierra called to her English maid-in-waiting. "There is not a moment to be lost."

"Yes, Your Highness," said Maria, stepping into Princess Sierra's bedroom chamber.

"We must hurry."

"Yes, Your Highness. We?"

"Yes, we two. I will require you to pack as much clothing as you can into a very light traveling bag . . . and with all due haste. No, not the chest," she instructed, "a simple satchel that even I could carry. That will do."

"Yes, Your Highness," said Maria, as she abandoned the chest and hurried toward the wardrobe. But no sooner had the maid thrown wide the wardrobe door than a knock came on the princess's chamber door.

Sierra straightened away from the desk where, though standing, she had been busily scribbling out a note. Head held high, shoulders back, she gazed at the door as though it might bear tidings of misfortune. Her countenance, usually clear and bright, was unnaturally pale and frozen; her eyes were wide.

"Please see who it is, Maria," said the princess in a whisper, "but do not let them enter. You must make some excuse. After all, 'tis a very late hour."

"Yes, Your Highness," replied Maria, quietly closing the wardrobe and treading toward the chamber's door.

"Wait," whispered Sierra. "Slowly, slowly," she instructed, as she herself rushed toward the bed on tiptoe and quickly threw back the bedcovers.

Mid-stride, Maria paused for a moment, glancing toward her mistress; Sierra looked back at her. Indeed, so strong was the connection between them that for a moment the maid started for the bed, as though to help the princess. But Sierra waved her away, putting a finger to her lips. "Sh-h-h."

Maria nodded, and turning away, stepped toward the chamber's door and opened it, but only a crack.

Maria spoke. However, from Sierra's position across the room, she could decipher nothing of what was being said, unhappily confined to hearing no more than muffled voices. Within moments, however, Maria closed the door and, spinning toward her mistress, approached the bed.

"Beg pardon, Princess," said Maria, "but there is a note for you from Prince Alathom."

Sierra visibly gulped, pausing. Then nodding, she placed her hand out for the letter. "I hope," she murmured softly, as though to herself, "that there is not more trouble than that which we already have."

Silence was all that met this declaration, while Maria remained quietly by the bed. Quickly, Sierra scanned the contents of the note, the loose curls of her dark ringlets easing forward against her temples, making her appear younger than she was. At sixteen, her countenance was usually transparent and impossibly carefree, but for the moment, her face was marred by a frown. At length, she folded the paper and absentmindedly placed it within the folds of her chemise.

" 'Tis not bad tidings," said the princess, her gaze caught unseeingly on some object across the room, "but our plans have been changed, I fear. And though it seems not unsatisfactory, I do not like it."

The princess glanced up briefly at her maid. However, when Maria remained mute, Sierra went on to say, "Though I realize that in the past you have given me your vow of silence, Maria, I must beg it of you once more. For I fear I have need of someone to talk to."

"Yes, Your Highness, you have my word."

Sierra nodded, sighing. "We are to escape together, tonight, the three of us, Prince Alathom, High Wolf and myself. But this note tells me that Prince Alathom has decided that we must devise our own escapes, each separately. Otherwise he fears our scheme will be discovered.

"Both High Wolf and myself are to meet as planned, in our usual spot, but Prince Alathom himself has gone on to the ship to prepare the way for us. There he will wait for us. It seems simple enough . . . Yet I don't like it."

Maria inclined her head, as though in agreement.

"The prince also begs me," continued the princess, "to send notice of the change in plans to High Wolf. Maria, you must do this for me, for I cannot leave the castle until I finish the note I have begun to Papa . . ."

"Yes. Of course I will do this for you."

Sierra nodded absentmindedly. "You know the spot of which I speak. You are perhaps the only other person besides the three of us who is aware of our secret meeting place. High Wolf is to be there at the midnight hour, but he is expecting both myself and Prince Alathom. You must take a note to him so that he understands what is now to be. And then you must come back here in all due haste, for I fear that I will need your help in leaving this palace."

Maria nodded.

"Do you think you can do all these things I ask? You have little time to accomplish it."

"I do, Your Highness; I will. But may I ask where are the three of you destined to go?"

"To Scotland," said Sierra, standing up, away from the bed, her feet still encompassed in satin slippers. But no sooner had she found her footing upon the floor than she was hurrying toward the desk, her steps practically flying over the lush carpet of her bedchamber. " 'Tis in our minds to leave here quickly, and we plan to set sail tonight. High Wolf and I will be married there, and once that is done, we will return."

" 'Tis a bold thing the three of you plan."

"That it is, Maria. That it is. Yet it is what I must do, what the prince must do—and High Wolf, too, for a marriage between myself and the prince would be a most unhappy affair. I do not understand why our parents have done as they have, for they have gone against our wishes this night. You must know that we were expecting quite another announcement at the ball . . ."

"Yes, Your Highness, that I do."

"Still, all things considered, I believe the plan the three of us have conceived is a good one, for it will force my parents to see that I am an independent creature who knows her own heart. Plus, it will do much toward establishing the idea of independence amongst our people. It is Prince Alathom who suggested the scheme, for I fear that High Wolf and I were too stunned by my parents' announcement of my engagement to Prince Alathom. On my honor, I believe that at that moment, neither High Wolf nor I was able to envision more than an uncommon hurt."

"As well you might," said Maria. "And do you think His Royal Highness, your father, will accept a marriage between yourself and Mr. High Wolf?"

Sierra sighed. "It is our hope that he will. But if he will not—if he banishes us—then we shall set sail to the Americas, a land where people are free to marry the person of their choice; where people have a voice in what happens in their government and particularly where the people have a say in their lives. It is not an unattractive alternative, Maria, since I have heard that America is the place where the ideal of Greek independence still lives."

Sierra smiled, her look reflective, but it lasted a moment only. With haste, as well as with a grace befitting her station in life, she sat down at her writing desk, and taking out a clean sheet of paper, began to write.

"How long do you intend to stay in Scotland, Your Highness?"

"Only a fortnight, that is, if the ship's sail is what it is said to be."

Maria nodded. "I will pack accordingly, then."

"No, Maria, I will take very few things with me, for I must pretend that I am going nowhere. There, done," said Sierra, holding up the paper and fanning it in the air, that the ink might dry more quickly.

At last, however, it was done, and she set seal to the letter. Standing up, she folded the paper and placed it urgently into Maria's hands. "Hurry now," she said, "and carry this note to High Wolf. Take my seal with you, so he will know that it comes directly from me."

"Yes, Your Highness."

At that moment, a heavy knock fell onto the chamber's door. Both women jumped at the sound. Surprised, they both glanced at one another, as if seeking comfort from each other.

"Go see who it is," whispered Sierra, "but let me reach the sanctuary of the bed first."

Maria nodded.

"Sierra Morena Colheart," came a loud, male voice on the other side of the door, the voice of her father. "I know you are awake."

Sierra swallowed hard. What bit of bad luck was this? She was not in any mind to confront her father.

Earlier, she had been scratching out a note to her father, informing him of her reasons for running away. At present, that note lay within her drawer, awaiting only her signature, for she had hoped to leave it with Maria, along with instructions to give it to her father. But not until she and the prince and High Wolf were safely away.

Certainly, such was an act of cowardliness on her part. But what other choice did she have? Were her father to discover what the three of them planned . . .

But now he was here at her bedchamber, allowing her no option but to confront the man on her own, without the aid of either one of her friends. It would be a most difficult task, for in the past Sierra was prone to confide her troubles to her father.

Taking a deep breath for courage, and gaining her place once more in the bed, Sierra pulled the bedcovers up to her chin. This done, she gave a nod to Maria, mouthing the words, "Go to High Wolf while I speak to Papa. And Godspeed."

Again Maria acknowledged her mistress with a quick nod and paced slowly toward the chamber's entrance. Opening the door, Maria curtsied, saying, "Good evening, Your Royal Highness."

"Good evening, Maria. You may leave us now."

Maria arose slowly, and with a quick look sent to her mistress, backed out through the door, shutting it without even the tiniest of clicks. And then she was gone.

Sierra's father paused awkwardly for a moment before coming directly to the point. He began, "You and Prince Alathom are to be married tomorrow morning."

"Tomorrow?" Throwing a quick glance toward the entryway, Sierra could see that His Royal Highness, the grand duke—her father—was ill-at-ease. But at the moment, she was beyond giving consideration to his discomfort, and she said, "Papa, how could you?"

"Very easily. But come, there is not a moment to lose. Now that your engagement has been announced, all eyes will be turned to you, watching anxiously."

"But—"

"Come, dear, Father Junipero assures me that a quick marriage in such circumstances is for the best. And, alas, I fear that morning will be here all too quickly."

"But Papa—"

"I know that this is not what you three had envisioned, but you both—nay, the three of you—are expected to do your duty."

"Yes, Papa, but—"

"My dearest daughter." The grand duke paced slowly toward her bed, as though uncertain of himself. Clearing his throat, he continued, "You must know that our two countries, ours and Prince Alathom's, are engaged upon hard times. The marriage between the two of you will give our people the stability they are seeking, while strengthening the defenses of both countries. Let me assure you that all look to you to do your duty."

Instead of answering, Sierra stared down at the covers she held so tightly to her chest, though eventually, she said, "Yes, Papa, but—"

"Come, now, Sierra. I know that you and the prince are good friends. And it will all turn out well in the end, I suspect. You are too young yet to realize that in time, your friendship with the prince will blossom into a love, true and full."

The grand duke paused, while Sierra remained silent. And truth be known, she couldn't have spoken at that moment, had her father required it of her, so large was the knot in her throat. Luckily, the grand duke seemed disinclined to pay heed to her silence, and he went on to say, "High Wolf will grasp the situation for what it is, as well. He has been educated by the prince himself, and by your own tutor, and I'm certain he understands our customs, our duties, yours. Yes, Sierra, I have every faith that he will come to see that his suit for your hand could not have been looked on with favor. Though it be true that His Serene Highness, Prince Eric—Alathom's father—has adopted the boy in order to give him title, you must still ask yourself, as I did, if an American Indian could ever be in line to inherit the crown, if such a match could give security to our people."

His Royal Highness, Grand Duke Colheart, bestowed his daughter with a sympathetic, tolerant look, while he took his seat beside her on her bed. "Besides," he continued, "there are legalities to weigh in such an instance as this."

"Perhaps," said Sierra at last. "But Papa, you could have told me about what you planned beforehand. As it was, learning about the engagement between myself and Prince Alathom—and in front of all our guests— was so much of a shock, I don't know how I managed to get through the rest of the evening."

The grand duke coughed, appearing, for a moment, as though he might be struggling with a call to conscience. However, when Sierra made no overture to say more on the subject, he again spoke. "And you would have argued with me. No." He held up his hand when Sierra would have interrupted. "You know you would have done so. So would Prince Alathom, I imagine. But understand, the three of you were allowed a free hand only because your outings with the prince and High Wolf were looked upon as necessary. We believed, both his parents, as well as your mother and myself, that you and the prince were becoming closer because of this allowed freedom. Never did we dream that you and that Indian . . ." His Royal Highness paused, running a finger under the stiff collar of the uniform he still wore, as though his next words were either to be swallowed or, perhaps, to be momentous. He continued, "Understand, Sierra, High Wolf was looked upon as the prince's companion during those outings, a common servant . . . and no more."

A common servant? High Wolf? Surely not. She said, "But he was adopted by Alathom's father. He is part of their family. Surely that is not the position of a servant."

The grand duke shook his head. "The adoption makes no difference in the end, my dear. High Wolf is still an Indian. He might be more than a servant to you; a friend, perhaps, but a prince . . . never . . ."

Sierra's chin took an obstinate, upward turn. She said, "I see little difference between High Wolf and the prince . . . even myself, except in skin color perhaps, and High Wolf's is only a shade darker than my own."

"Descent, my dear. Descent." The grand duke squared his shoulders before going on to say, "Oh, what rebellious times we live in, for the world is changing rapidly around us. Though you have studied well Greek, English, even the newly emerging American cultures, I fear your early education has failed to teach you the true value of royal ancestry. And it is that ancestry, after all, that is important."

"I disagree, Papa."

The grand duke merely shook his head.

"I fail to understand," said Sierra, continuing, "why, if you truly believe this . . . this theory of descent—then, why, all this time, did no one tell me what you planned this evening? Why was I allowed to believe that . . ." She paused, looking down at the bedcovers as though they were of the utmost interest. "I thought you truly liked High Wolf."

"We did. We do. How could anyone not share some affinity with a young man so amicable? So eager to please? But as a son-in-law?" The grand duke shuddered.

But Sierra sighed. "And so, if I understand you correctly, what you are really saying is that, although he is fine in every way, but one—that of royal blood—he is not good enough for me?"

"That is exactly what I am saying."

"Does our lineage really create so much difference?" Sierra spoke almost to herself. "I fail to understand you, Papa, for I refuse to believe that the color of one's skin, one's heritage, one's chance of birth, makes for a good or a great man. Only a person's heart, his kindness and his sympathy for the afflictions of others make a man great."

The grand duke harrumphed several times before saying, "Yes, yes, so it is said these days, and yet a monarch must at all times be ready to use force in order to protect his people."

"I fail to—"

The grand duke held up his hand. "Perhaps you are right, my dear, perhaps you are right. Times are changing, and a wise monarch must change with them. But you misunderstand, I think. Prince Alathom is all kindness and goodness."

"Yes, he is. But I'm not in love with him."

"I understand, my dear, but whatever your feelings, your inclinations; whatever are mine, mean nothing."

"This is incredible. Surely I must have a say in whom I am to marry. I must. Otherwise . . . Papa, this contradicts all I have been taught . . . my studies of the Enlightened Age in Greece—"

Her father flushed. Even in the candlelight, she could see it was so. And he said, "You were, in the past, given too high a regard for that country and too free a rein. I ask you, where do these ideals fit into our lives?"

"Very easily, I think."

Her father shook his head sadly. "Ideals are for dreamers, and that is all. They are not for the practical world we live in, and they are certainly not for a sovereign. You must know—Father Junipero assures me that he is doing his best to instill this principle in you—that a princess is not free to bestow her favor wherever she may wish."

"Yes, Papa, but marrying High Wolf would do so much to enhance our country. He is a fine man, and

I'm certain he would bestow upon the role of prince consort great honor."

The grand duke did not answer. Instead, a long, stretched-out silence filled the atmosphere, until at last, the grand duke inhaled deeply. "Your mother and I have spoken on this; we have counselled with others in high places on this. After much discussion, know that we have all come to the same decision. And that is, an Indian must not sit close to or on the throne."

"But—"

The grand duke held up his hand. "I will hear no more talk on this. I am beginning to understand the problems that Father Junipero has related to me regarding your earlier education, for you speak your mind quite plainly."

"Yes, Papa, but—"

"No more, Sierra, no more."

Sierra lowered her lashes, saying again, "Yes, Papa."

"That's a good girl. Now, I shall call for Maria once again, and she will help you dress. I know the hour is late, but Father Junipero wishes to speak to you. He, not Prince Eric's priest, will be performing the marriage ceremony in the morning. In truth, I fear that you may have little sleep tonight, for the hour of your wedding is set at nine o'clock."

"But Papa, please—"

"Sierra, you must learn to speak only when you are spoken to. You try a man's very patience." Thus said, the grand duke arose, his countenance stern, ungiving. Still, before he left, he glanced down at his young offspring, gazing at her as though he might have a bit of sympathy for her, though he remained quiet. In due course, however, he said, "Marriages, even for a commoner, are rarely a matter of the heart, my daughter. It is a hard lesson to learn at such a young age, but I assure you that your infatuation with the Indian will diminish with time. In a year or so, you will probably not even remember his name."

Sierra gulped, knowing that what her father said would never be so. But for the time being, she restrained herself on the subject. Besides, to argue with her father further might arouse his suspicion as to her own plans. Odd, her father's lecture tonight had only strengthened her resolve.

"And now it is time," said the grand duke.

"Time, Papa?"

"Come, my dear, there are wedding arrangements to be made, and Father Junipero wishes to have a few words with you. Shall I ring for Maria to help you dress?"

"No, no," Sierra spoke quickly, fully aware that Maria would no longer be in the castle. At least she hoped not, for Maria's errand would have taken her outside the castle walls. "I . . . I wish to be alone. If there is to be little sleep this night, please grant me a few moments to myself before I must meet with Father Junipero . . ."

"Ah, yes. Of course, my dear. Of course. Take as long as you wish, but do not make it overly long. Your duty awaits you."

Sierra nodded. "Yes, I know . . . and thank you, Papa."

Briefly, the grand duke leaned over to press a kiss

upon the top of Sierra's head. "I know this has been a shock for you—all three of you—but, trust me, it will pass. Yes, my dear, it will pass."

Sierra raised her lashes, sending her father a quick, glance, attempting at the same time to smile at him. But she feared that, with her heart momentarily crushed, all she accomplished was a crude sort of smirk.

Her father must have sensed her discomfort, however, for he went on to say, "You will see. It will all be for the best. Now, I will set someone outside your door to bring you to Father Junipero as soon as you are ready. Do not worry. It will all turn out right." And straightening up, the Grand Duke Colheart, Sierra's father, took his leave.

Chapter 2

He waited at their sacred place
He stayed 'til way past noon.
But when she reached that meeting place,
'Twas nothing there, save the moon.

Anonymous

"**M**aria, at last you have returned. Did you succeed in carrying the note to High Wolf?"

"Yes, Your Highness, I believe so. But it had to be accomplished with the aid of the priest."

"Father Junipero?"

"Yes, Your Highness."

Sierra frowned. "How did Father Junipero come to be involved in this?"

For a moment Maria looked discomfited. At last, however, she said, "The entrance to and from the castle is blocked, even for myself. I could not leave, and not wishing to bring notice to myself, I tried to use a servants' entrance in order to sneak away from the castle's inner sanctum. But Father Junipero caught me and asked me what I was doing, and I could not bring myself to lie to him."

"Of course not. What did he say?"

"When I told him that I was on an errand for you, he wished to know what it was. When I related a little of it, that I needed to bring a note to a friend, Father Junipero listened carefully and said very little. In truth, Your Highness, at first the father frightened me, he looked so stern."

Sierra nodded.

"But then I pleaded with him to help me, and taking pity on me, he said that he would."

"That is good," said Sierra. "And how did he help you, Maria?"

"He wished to read the note I carried."

"And did you show it to him?"

"Yes, Your Highness. I'm sorry, but I had no choice in the matter."

Sierra sighed. "Of course you did not." She frowned. "And so now Father Junipero knows of our plans."

"Yes, Your Highness. Please accept my apology."

"Do not worry over it, Maria. I am certain that Father Junipero can be trusted."

"I hope so."

"And so, am I to understand that you both went into the forest together?"

"Yes, though once there, Father Junipero dismissed me."

"He dismissed you?"

"Yes, Princess."

Sierra frowned. "I think I begin to understand why you said you *believed* High Wolf received word of the change."

"Yes."

Sierra arose from the chair where she had been reclining, taking the necessary few steps to bring her face to face with her maid-in-waiting. But seeing the look of concern come over Maria's countenance, Sierra's anxiety quieted.

Taking Maria's hand in her own, she said, "Do not worry. You did the only thing you could do. I am certain of it. Everything will be fine. Father Junipero has always been friendly toward myself and High Wolf. And I believe that he is not one to carry tales."

"Yes, Your Highness. I, too, believe in his honesty, although . . ."

"Although what?"

"He often frightens me, I must say."

"Yes, yes, I can understand why. He sometimes does that to me." She paused. "But once he learned of your purpose, he was more amicable?"

"Yes, Your Highness."

"There, you see?" As she stood up straight, Sierra tried to lighten the situation with a smile. "I begin to believe that the time has come for me to quit this castle. But," she said, turning away, "if *you* had difficulty leaving, I am certain that it will be quite impossible for me."

Maria bobbed her head in agreement. "There are two sentinels standing watch outside your room, Your Highness."

Sierra's frown deepened. "I had no idea that Papa would go to such extremes," she said. "I am afraid, Maria, that I have not done well in foreseeing this. None of us did. Although perhaps this is why Prince Alathom is attempting to change our plans."

"Yes. It might likely be so."

"But tell me, Maria, with the priest's help, were you able to come and go without great search?"

"Yes. No one paid me notice." Maria's eyes became suddenly bright. "Perhaps, Princess, we might . . . I mean you could . . ." She cleared her throat. "Might we not trade places?"

Sadly, Sierra smiled. "Maria, what a good friend you are to me. I praise the day my father made arrangements to bring you here to be my lady's maid."

"I am, too, Princess," said Maria. "With both my parents killed, and with me left in the care of an indifferent uncle, my plight looked hopeless."

"Yes," said Sierra. "I remember. On my honor, what your uncle did was terribly unjust, seizing hold of your father's title and all of the family's wealth, leaving nothing to you. What did he expect you to do? You, an aristocrat, a lady of gentle birth? I am glad, however, that things turned out as they did, and that you thought to seek employment. Otherwise, I would have been denied your company."

"I am glad also." Maria grinned. "And so, shall we trade places?"

Sierra drew in a deep breath. "Oh, no, Maria. We must not."

"But why not?"

"Ask yourself," said Sierra, "what would be your fate if you were discovered helping me escape?"

"Humph! Do you think I care about that? It is my duty to help you."

"Assist, yes. I need that. But duty? How tired I am of that word, I must say."

Maria remained silent.

"No, Maria, though I shall always remember your loyalty to me, I cannot do it."

"But—"

Turning away, Sierra paced back and forth to the window. At length, she came back to stand before her maid-in-waiting, and taking Maria's hands into her own, she smiled before saying, "You have been the best lady's maid a princess could ever desire. In truth, Maria, I believe you are my only friend."

"Thank you, Your Highness," said Maria, a gentle blush stealing across her cheeks. "You pay me a great compliment."

" 'Tis not a compliment, merely the truth."

At that moment, a knock sounded at the door, causing both young women to gasp and to cling to one another.

"Go see to it, Maria," whispered the princess. "But beg them not to enter."

"Yes, Princess," said Maria, and sending her mistress a fond smile, she turned toward the door.

Sierra could hear the murmurings, and once again it goaded her to realize that she would have to wait.

At last, however, Maria shut the door, and spinning around, paced back toward her mistress. She said, "Father Junipero wishes to see you, Your Highness."

Again Sierra frowned, although the exact reason for her worry escaped her. She said, "Do you suppose that Father Junipero might help me?"

Maria shrugged. " 'Tis worth trying."

"That it is, Maria. That it is."

The Royal Chapel

"Ah, Princess Sierra, my child," said Father Junipero. "Come."

The princess trod quickly forward, looking as

though she might likely run away if he, her mentor and confessor, were to give her any reason to do so. But fleeing was next to impossible. Though her Swiss guard—the soldier who had escorted her there—had faded back into the shadows, he would not leave. Not until the princess was safely married would anyone in the castle relax.

And so Father Junipero began, saying, "Feel no fear, my dear. I think that you are shocked because of the evening's announcement concerning your future. But do not fret. I understand now that you had hoped for something else."

"Yes, Father, that I had," the princess said, her countenance downcast.

"And you think I should have prepared you more aptly for what was to come?"

"No, Father. 'Twas not your responsibility."

"Perhaps not, my child, yet here you are. Now, please. Come." He beckoned her forward. "I would have you pray with me."

"Yes, Father."

Father Junipero bowed his head as did the princess, and from afar, it would have appeared as though the father was in deep contemplation with his Maker. However, at the moment, Father Junipero's mind was caught up in other, more pressing contemplations.

Placing a hand over Sierra's head, the father said, "Continue with your prayers, my child, while I retire to my study."

Sierra nodded.

Slowly, Father Junipero backed away from where the princess stood. And silently gaining his study, Father Junipero carefully took a seat behind a large, wooden table. Folding his fingers under his chin, he frowned as he carefully assessed what would be his next course of action.

He must wield extreme caution in this matter of the princess. Indeed, if he were to fulfill his destiny and become a power behind the throne, he must make each move quite warily.

With care, Father Junipero turned a page in the book that always remained open upon this table. Quickly, he scanned the written words that stood out upon the page, reading them reverently, stroking the page at the same time as though it were a living thing.

And perhaps that wasn't quite so farfetched an idea, since this was not a usual sort of book. This particular treasure had been passed down from monk to monk through a span of practically four hundred years, if the book's legend were to be believed. A legacy from Tomas de Torquemada, of Spanish Inquisition fame, the book was purported to be made of human skin, a fitting effigy; plus, if myth were true, he who held the book might possess—for a moment only—the power to damn anyone.

In the name of heresy.

If only the princess were guilty of that. But she was not . . . although she *did* keep and hold opinions that were dangerous to the well-being of the state: ideas of free speech, of frankness of mind, of enlightenment. Indeed, these were hardly beneficial to his own ambition, an ambition that had thus far been nurtured by the cleverest of deceits.

And make no mistake, Father Junipero, out of necessity, had been resplendent in his deceptions. And why not? Who better to rule than he? He, who knew best for the country? He, the only man who understood what to do to those who did not, or would not, repent.

Thus far his ambition had gone undetected. No one suspected him to be the power behind decisions of state.

Was he now to let a mere wisp of a girl undermine all his good work? A mere child fell him from power? And all because she had fallen in love with an Indian . . . an American Indian, who insists on keeping alive ideas of freedom, of self rule, of individual rights.

It had not been an easy task to attain his current position, for Father Junipero had begun his work in a lowly capacity, having come into the royal family as no more than a tutor. Yet he had worked diligently, seeking royal confidences until at last he had gained the position of the royal family's confessor. And from there, the rest had been easy: a choice statement here, a carefully worded threat there.

Certainly, if he were to retain his royal influence, the princess's ideas must be squashed, even though it might prove to be a difficult task. For he feared that at an early age—before Father Junipero's more recent tutelage—the princess's governess had been English, the young lady influencing the princess to believe in the tradition of the Enlightened Age of the Greek philosophers. For good or bad, the princess had cut her teeth on the work of Pericles, a reformer and believer in the rights of the people.

Thus, from the start, the princess had been led to behold the power of her own mind, had even been taught to trust in her right to reason and to think for herself. Furthermore, of late she had taken to voicing her opinions without any regard to Father Junipero's convictions.

Ah, undoubtedly, the princess's ideals must be squashed, and she must be brought to heel . . . quickly. Would marriage be the answer? Was Prince Alathom the man to coerce her?

It was doubtful, much too doubtful to trust to chance.

At least Prince Alathom was easy to control, even if the princess was not.

Stroking the book before him, Father Junipero glanced down toward the open page; a page filled with images of the damned, of fires, of sacrifices. Could the book be an answer?

Perhaps. Perhaps.

Carefully, he rubbed the parchment and under his breath decreed, "For your 'goodliness,' to an unworthy, my dear princess; for your open defiance to me, your unwarranted and untimely devotion to a heathen; I place a vex on you. Not to kill you, no, but rather to frighten you should you do something that defies me. Yes, yes. If such an event should come to pass, may those things you fear most materialize, and those things you love most elude you." In his excitement, his fingers lingered over the images of fire.

And then he smiled, but the look could hardly be called joyful. Alas, such was the look of great evil.

And perhaps it was not in the father's mind to curse the princess so utterly. Mayhap he did not realize his power, and like a spoiled child, simply wished for the demise of one who might defy him. Perhaps . . .

"Father?" The princess's voice carried even to his study.

He arose at once, walking toward her. "Yes, my child."

"I must go. My maid awaits me in order that we prepare for tomorrow."

A light of artifice entered into Father Junipero's eyes, his duplicity of mind carefully hidden by the poor lighting in the chapel. He said, "Yes, Your Highness, of course you must. Are you aware that I have seen your maid this night?"

"Have you?" the princess whispered, though she suddenly cast her gaze toward the ground.

"Yes," said Father Junipero. "Only an hour past. She begged for my assistance in helping her leave the castle, that she might deliver a note to someone . . . a letter from you . . ."

"Ah, yes," said the princess evenly. "That is right."

Father Junipero took a step closer to her. "I granted your maid's request."

"That was kind of you," said the princess, though she did not raise her gaze to meet his.

Father Junipero paced another careful step forward. "I delivered the note for you."

"Did you?"

"Yes, my child."

The princess paused significantly, then said, "And did you read it?"

"The note?"

She nodded.

Father Junipero smiled. "I would not presume to read a note not meant for me."

"Of course you would not, Father. Please forgive me."

"There is nothing to forgive, my child. You have every right to question me."

Again the princess nodded, her head still bowed.

"But I should tell you that High Wolf, after reading your note, became quite upset and left."

Father Junipero watched closely as the princess looked up at him. "Excuse me, Father?"

"High Wolf is gone."

"He is gone?" Princess Sierra's eyes went wide. "I . . . I don't . . . I'm afraid, Father Junipero, that I don't understand."

"He told me to tell you that he sends you and the prince his blessings."

The princess frowned. "I . . . I . . . ," she stammered. "I cannot believe it."

"Yet believe it you must."

"I cannot . . . there must be some mistake."

"I assure you there is not one. High Wolf demanded money from me, to be repaid by your father. He seemed to feel that he should be repaid for his time spent with you."

"He demanded . . . money?"

"Yes, Your Highness. He requested and was granted a sum of three hundred gold dukaten, in order that he quit his claim on you."

"Quit his claim on me? Excuse me, Father, but are we speaking of the same man?"

"It is easy to see how the boy deceived you, Princess."

"He did not deceive me. He is in love with me."

Father Junipero shook his head. "Oh, yes, I am sure he told you that. He seemed quite amicable. Almost believable."

"No, it was real. Real—"

"Come now, my child, do not despair."

"I do not despair. I simply do not believe you."

"You do not believe the word of your priest?"

"I . . . I—"

"Come now, my child. I know it is a hard thing to accept that one's friendship should be repaid in such a way, but I, for one, have always thought that High Wolf might do as much. It is lucky for me that I had the forethought to bring some finance with me as I followed your maid into the woods."

"Show me, Father. Show me your ledgers that I might understand it. For without such evidence I will not believe it," she said, and then under her breath, "I must not believe it."

"Very well," said Father Junipero. "Though it pains me to learn that you do not trust me. Rest assured, Your Highness, that High Wolf is well satisfied and is probably en route to the Americas as we speak."

The princess said nothing until Father Junipero had shown her the ledgers. Clearly, three hundred gold dukaten had been taken from church's coffers, disbursed to a man named High Wolf for services rendered. It was all there, carefully written. For Father Junipero—knowing that no living person would dare to dispute the church's system of accounting—was nothing if not thorough.

At last, however, she spoke, but all she said was "Thank you, Father, for indulging me. However, I am positive still that there has been some sort of mistake."

"Oh?"

"High Wolf might have thought you offered him finance for an entirely different purpose."

"A different purpose?"

She nodded.

"Yes, yes, perhaps you are right," said the priest. "And yet, I remember High Wolf asking for safety in leaving the country. And I was quite specific when I gave him the money, that it was in payment for his services to you, which were no longer required."

The princess fell silent.

"Of course it could be I, who is in the wrong, but it appears," said Father Junipero, "that the young man had his eye on your fortune, and your fortune alone. Becoming a prince, sharing in your responsibilities meant nothing to him. Apparently his was a facade, a pretense of interest in you, in your country, even in Prince Alathom. But I must say that this, however, is only apparently so."

The princess rubbed at her temples. "Forgive me, Father, but this is too much for me to comprehend all at once. I must go to High Wolf and speak to him myself. I believe I know where he has gone, and the way is not far."

"Your Highness. You must see that it is impossible to do so. You are to marry Prince Alathom in a very short while."

"But the prince does not wish to marry me, nor I him. Nor is he even to be found in the castle, if you were to look for him."

"Is he not?" Father Junipero stiffened. *What was this?* Carefully, he inquired, "And where might he be?"

"If I am correct, I believe the prince might be elsewhere."

"Ah," said Father Junipero, "and that place is . . . ?"

"May I have your word, Father, that you will not repeat what I am to tell you?"

He gave her a look of much disappointment. "You must ask?"

But she was firm. "Your word, Father."

He nodded. "You have it, my child."

And though the princess's countenance clouded with uncertainty, she said, "He awaits us on a ship, Father. It sails one hour past midnight."

"Ah, I see. Then we must go there at once."

"No, Father. First I must seek out High Wolf and speak to him."

"But my child," said the father, "would he not also be aboard the ship, having obtained that thing most precious to him?"

"No, I . . . I . . ." She hung her head. "It is possible, Father."

"It is not only possible, it is most assured. But come, let us make haste. The prince must not be allowed to slip away."

The princess frowned.

"And, of course, if you need to speak to the Indian, you best accompany me."

"Yes," said Sierra. "Perhaps you are right."

And without further conversation, Father Junipero hurried the princess from the chapel, obtaining a coach and a guard as quickly as if their services had been awaiting them all evening.

But alas, too much time had been consumed in talking. And quite unhappily, they were late, much too late. For all that could be seen of the ship when the two figures arrived, was nothing more than a speck upon the ocean, as though it were but a toy that had been set adrift in a stream.

"They are gone," said the Father.

"Gone?" repeated the princess, as though she were incapable of placing meaning to the obvious. And she trembled.

Exhaling deeply, Father Junipero placed his arm around her shoulders. "Yes, they are gone. But take heart, my child. Remember, there is always marriage by proxy. Yes, indeed," said the father, as though the thought had only occurred to him. "Marriage by proxy. I believe that His Serene Highness reserves the rights in such matters. Yes, my child. Trust me. I will determine the facts of the matter at once."

Wearily Sierra watched the ship—out in the distance—until even the tiny speck of it disappeared from view, leaving nothing to see but ocean and the moon-bathed waves. And gradually, as a tear found its way onto her cheek, she said good-bye to the two people she had loved most in the world.

Her heart broke, yet instinctively Sierra knew that more than her heart had been taken from her this night. Her trust in the character of her fellow man, her belief in the loyalty of friendship, were both cast into as dim a light as possible.

And there, beneath the wavering beams of a full moon, Sierra vowed to herself that she would not forget this treachery. Neither High Wolf's, nor the prince's own. Not ever.

Chapter 3

" 'Tis said she is a black widow," whispered one of the
kitchenmaids.

"Yes," agreed a housemaid. "And did ye know that
'tis rumored that this is the reason why His Royal
Highness, Prince Alathom, our wonderful, lonely
boy, has never, in all these years, returned to her
side."

> Gossip between servants at
> Prince Alathom's castle

Ten years later
St. Louis
June 1834

She was going to kill Prince Alathom. Simple,
pure, straightforward murder ... unless he
agreed to act as a responsible adult, something he
hadn't done in ten long years. After all, the rumors at
home would be set right. Too, she hadn't defied her
parents, crossed an ocean and endured the thunder-
ous swells of the Atlantic for this ... this ...

What was this port of call dubbed St. Louis?

"Why, it's nothing more than a silly, overrated village of . . . of . . ."

"Colonials?" Golden-haired Maria grinned cheekily. "Your Highness?"

"Yes," agreed Princess Sierra after a moment. Turning slightly to her right, she bestowed a smile upon Maria, her maid-in-waiting. "Colonials to be sure, but also savages, I think. Savages in an untamed, barbaric land."

"Yes, Your Highness. If you say so, Your Highness."

"And do you find it otherwise?" asked the princess.

Maria cocked her head to the side, her look serious as her eyes—as golden in hue as a summer field of wheat—took in her surroundings. "No," said the maid at once. " 'Tis a savage land at best, I think. And yet, it has its own beauty, too."

"Yes, Maria. If you say so, Maria," Sierra mimicked, grinning at her maid before returning her attention forward, facing west. From her position atop the highest deck of the steamboat the *Diana*, Princess Sierra Morena Colheart, daughter of His Royal Highness, Grand Duke Frederick Colheart III, gave St. Louis another scathing glance.

Below her lay a village that could only be described as primitive or savage, no more than an outpost. On the dock, laborers of all different types, clad only in what might have been the worst in homespun wear, busily rushed about here and there, intent, it would seem, upon their own individual tasks.

Raising her sights for a moment, she espied, there in the distance, a swarm of hogs, roaming about the town.

"Pigs, pigs and more pigs. How weary I am of seeing them, in most all of these western villages."

"Yes, so am I, too, but I suppose they serve a purpose."

"Yes, I am aware of it, Maria, having been told several times of their use in hindering an overabundance of snakes. And yes, I am also cognizant of how it is said that the pigs keep the streets clean of debris—better than any man could."

This last was voiced in unison by both maid and princess as they glanced at one another and smiled.

Said Maria, "And they are also owned by families who can use them as food if the need arises."

"Yes, yes. I know. Still, I find the sight of them rather tedious, do you not?"

"Yes, Your Highness. On this I must concur. I find them tedious, indeed."

Inhaling deeply, Princess Sierra let the subject drop, and training her gaze back onto something closer to hand, she stared out over the muddy waters of the Mississippi, noting that not even the sun could brighten the river's turgid character. True, the air in this place was clear, unfettered by the tarnish of burning coal, by soot which marred a good part of the continent. But the earthy scent of humidity in the air, the odor of the mud, the fishy smell of the water and even the fumes from the burning of the cord wood used to produce steam for the ship did not bring her comfort.

And never would it. Never. For Princess Sierra was determined to hate America, the frontier, the West; hate it as much as she disliked the two men in her life who loved it.

She moaned, and taking out a handkerchief, dabbed at the moisture on her face.

"It is very hot here, Your Highness. Do you wish me to go to your quarters and lay out a change of clothing for you?"

Princess Sierra grimaced. "No, Maria, as you well know, the humidity in this place is not to be borne, and changing clothes would only cause me to soil several dresses instead of one. And would only lead to taxing your talents with the laundry."

"That is true, Your Highness. That is true."

Princess Sierra nodded. "And goodness knows, it is difficult enough for you, in such quarters as these. It is simply too small a space and too hot and humid an environment. And as long as we are aboard this boat, with its steam exhaust constantly upon us, any attempt at keeping cool is but a dream, I fear. In all honesty, I can only hope for a speedy accomplishment of what I must do, so that we can take our leave of this place soon . . . very, very soon."

"Yes, Your Highness. I must admit that this would please me, as well. Would you like me to fetch a fan? One for you; perhaps one for me, too?"

"Yes, Maria. That would be a grand gesture."

"Yes, Your Highness."

Although, Princess Sierra thought, as she watched Maria's retreat, little good a fan would do her in this sort of climate. Witness the fact that her clothing stuck to her, both in her present situation and during the past few weeks aboard the steamship. And no amount of fanning, either by herself or with Maria's help, seemed to give relief . . . ever.

Wap!

What was that? The princess gazed toward the direction of the sound, witnessing a very large bird, as it ascended into the air. The sound, although somewhat loud, had been a mere flap of the beast's mighty wings.

She watched the bird closely. Gently, regally, the fowl circled in front of her, once, twice. It even spoke, its screeches filling the atmosphere—which was already saturated with too much noise—with an odd sort of song. Strange, she thought, how the voices from the humanity on the dock, even the clamor of the steamship's cannon as it belted out notice of the ship's arrival, dimmed in comparison to that majestic, native song.

What kind of bird was this? she wondered.

Certainly it was no seagull or any other kind of water bird, for that matter. At least not any with which she was familiar.

Sierra narrowed her gaze, staring at the bird as it circled about her once more, before, with another powerful stroke of its wings, it disappeared from view.

What an extraordinary sight. Had it been an eagle? A large hawk?

And if it were one of those creatures, had it been bringing her a message? For, as a man from out of her past had once told her, these creatures speak to human beings in such a way.

Sierra blew out a short breath.

Nonsense. What utter nonsense. That man—she wouldn't dignify the thought of him by even thinking his name—had also lied to her in a most horrible way; had betrayed her, humiliated her.

Still . . . Sierra shook her head.

Had she made a mistake in coming here? In leaving all she'd ever known?

Possibly.

Lost in thought, Princess Sierra set her lips, unconsciously thrusting forward her jawline. No, she was correct in what she intended doing. She was certain of it. After all, hers was a mission of vengeance, a mission of discovery, a move to set the score right.

After all, she was *not* to blame for the incredible number of mishaps that had befallen her country and Prince Alathom's. *She* had been the one to set things right. This, she would prove. And no matter how unconventional, how foreign . . . or even how barbaric a place this might be, she would never regret her decision to come here. If need be, to accomplish her purpose, she would force herself to learn about the American West, coming to know it as well as those who roamed the land.

Yes, that was it. Such a greedy place as this would not hold sway over her, the grand duke's daughter. And this *was* a greedy land—to have taken so much from her . . .

Turning away from the water, she swallowed down the turbulence of her thoughts, glancing once more toward the dock. It was then that she espied a team of four white horses, drawing an emerald green coach, which, in a flourish of color, had pulled up toward the dock, stopping in front of the steamship.

Sierra caught her breath.

"Such a beautiful carriage, Your Highness," said Maria, having returned to her position next to the princess. Together, they peeked over the railing, while Maria proffered Sierra a fan.

"Yes, it is," said Sierra, a bit more enthusiastically.

"It quite reminds me of home." *Of home, though not of happier times,* she added to herself. "Although there are many differences, are there not? For instance, have you ever seen a footman and a driver wearing buckskin?"

Sierra nodded toward the servants in question before glancing at Maria. Cheerfully, she grinned at the maid, as though to share a confidence.

And Maria grinned back. "Buckskin? I think not, Your Highness."

"Or witness the height of those ponies drawing the coach."

"Yes. What extraordinarily small specimens of horseflesh they are."

"Quite. I must admit, too," continued Sierra, "that the red and gold uniforms of my father's estate are a much more beautiful sight." She sighed. "Yet, still, that carriage's grandness is not to be mistaken or put lightly aside. Perhaps these Americans are not as badly mannered as we have been led to believe."

"Perhaps."

At that moment, an elderly, red-headed man poked his head out of the coach's door, a door he had evidently opened himself, something no person of title would certainly do. Nevertheless, Princess Sierra sighed with relief.

She said, "That man must be Governor Clark."

"Governor Clark?"

"Yes, the same Mr. Clark of the famed Lewis and Clark adventure. You do remember me speaking of him, don't you? He and another man led an expedition into the interior of America. They were the first white men to see many of the native tribes."

"Oh, yes, I believe I do remember you speaking of him. So that is he, do you think?"

"Yes, it must be the same person, since I have been amply informed as to the color of his hair, even despite his advancing years."

Maria nodded. "His hair is quite red. And his dress is certainly not that of buckskin."

"Thank heaven for that," said Sierra. "At least he is good for his word, for he had promised to meet me at the dock."

Again Maria nodded, but when she offered nothing more to be said, Sierra, too, fell silent. Had Governor Clark, she wondered, also procured her a guide, the one she had requested?

Unwillingly, that specific speculation came accompanied with a nervous sort of anticipation. One that set her stomach to twisting.

The princess squelched the feeling as best she could, trying to ignore it. However, it took many deep breaths before she regained a bit of relief. But then, as if on cue, the thought occurred to her that she would have to include that guide—the one she had requested—on her two-name list of men who deserved to be shot. But not until the "guide" had led her to the prince.

No, not until then.

Prince Alathom could not be dead.

After ten years of silence, ten years of wondering, ten years of frustration—to be suddenly informed of the prince's death?

Well, it was not to be borne.

No, the prince was not dead. It was all a lie. Of this Princess Sierra Morena felt quite certain. After all, her acquaintance with the prince went back quite far, and she knew him well enough to realize that the prince loved the West too well, loved it too much to have lost his life here.

If what she suspected were true, his death was a ploy. For no sooner had His Serene Highness—Prince Alathom's father—announced that he had at last found his son, than word had come of Prince Alathom's death.

Princess Sierra furrowed her brows and compressed her lips, as though her thoughts were burdensome. In truth, she was tired of this business, tired of being blamed for the prince's wrongdoing, tired of carrying on the prince's responsibilities, tired of pretending all was well when it wasn't.

But that was in the past now.

She, a royal princess, was not going to allow Prince Alathom to shirk his responsibilities—not anymore. She would find the prince; she would confront him, and she would treat him as he well deserved. All she needed to do now was to find the man she had once known well enough to have thought herself in love, he, the only man who could lead her to the prince . . .

All at once it struck her. Was *he* waiting for her even now? Had he accompanied Governor Clark?

Sierra gulped unconsciously, placing a hand, which suddenly shook, over her chest. Narrowing her eyes and glancing downward, she tried to scrutinize the interior of the carriage.

Reaching out, she touched Maria's hand with her gloved one. Nervously, she swallowed. "Maria, please," she said. "Can you distinguish any forms, any faces, there within the carriage? Is there another person inside?"

Maria squinted. "I cannot see inside the carriage, Your Highness. I am afraid the glass windows of the rig are too fine as to allow me the opportunity of seeing easily into it."

"Yes," agreed the princess. "Yes, indeed. Although I also think we are hampered by our high position atop this boat."

Maria nodded. "Yes, Your Highness. But do not be anxious," she said. "I am here, as well as Mr. Dominic. When the time comes, you need not confront *him* alone."

The princess opened her mouth, perhaps to refute her maid, but unbidden, a question came to her: What would *he* look like after these past ten years? Certainly, the man she had once known as High Wolf would not have changed overly much. His hair would most likely still be black, as would be his eyes. But no longer would those dark, dark eyes look at her with the longing she, and she alone, had once been treated to . . . ten years ago.

Without willing it, the princess felt her pulse rate race, while simultaneously the sweep of life-giving blood pumped more furiously through her veins. Within a small space of time, without full knowledge of why, she felt curiously alive. Alive again, as she had not been in . . . well, in ten years.

Sierra blew out a quick breath.

Ridiculous. More alive? Because of thoughts of *him*? He, who had so thoroughly betrayed her? He, who had left her with nary a word? And at a time in her life when she had needed him most?

Sierra jerked her head to the left, staring away from

the carriage. The truth was, she hated him. She had to remember that; hated High Wolf almost as much as she did Prince Alathom . . . perhaps more.

"*Once betrayed, a wise sovereign never bestows confidence again. Not ever.*" So had said her father, repeating a warning passed down from generation to generation, one monarch to the next.

Unwittingly, other words came back to haunt her as well; words that had been uttered to her in confidence by a man beyond reproach, Father Junipero: "*If he had truly cared for you . . .*"

Sierra had been sixteen when those words had been spoken; sixteen, very innocent, utterly naive and very much in love.

Well, she was certainly none of those things at present.

And she, for one, was glad of the change in her. Indeed, she celebrated her departure from naivete, for she was entirely aware that, had she known the truth about High Wolf all those years ago, heartache would never have been hers.

No, the events of the past had sobered her. But then it hadn't taken a great deal of stiff, uncompromising reality to do so.

Friends, the prince and High Wolf had once called themselves, High Wolf claiming to be more. Ha! Both had abandoned her without explanation, leaving her—and her alone—to explain the unexplainable, not only to her own parents, but to the prince's mother and father as well. And all the while, in the interim, the two of them had shipped off to the Americas . . .

No, she told herself, she wasn't nervous because of

this prearranged meeting. She was enraged; deeply, dreadfully enraged. And she intended to take it out on somebody . . . very, very soon . . .

"It's 'cause of a woman, I hear tell."

"A woman? We're supposed to escort some dang-blasted royal 'n' his woman inta Injun country, an' all fer nothin' more than a hunt?" The old trapper jerked his head toward the ground and spit. "Gov'ner Clark didn't say nothin' about a woman. They's bad luck, I tell ye. I seen one once. And she smelt funny. Yep"— he shook his head—"it's as my pappy once said, they's bad luck. Terrible bad luck."

Dusty, the younger of the two trappers, nodded, as though these observations were golden truths, carefully gleaned from lofty, mildewed texts. He said, "Nothin' good ever came from the mouth of one of 'em, thar's fer sure." He snickered. "Heard we're also supposed to kowtow it to this here Injun, says the Gov'ner." He pointed, quite impolitely. "Supposed to be one of them expert trackers. Cheyenne."

The two men glanced in Ho'neoxhaa'eho'oese's direction while Ho'neoxhaa'eho'oese looked quietly away.

To stare at either of these two, as they were staring at him, would have been the height of bad manners, something no well-brought-up Cheyenne man would do. Besides, Ho'neoxhaa'eho'oese, or High Wolf in the English language, had been scrutinizing the two men as well, his single glance ascertaining more about them personally than either of the men would have imagined, or liked.

For instance, from reading their tracks alone, he

knew that the one called Dusty suffered an old injury to the knee, that his bowels hurt him and that he was probably suffering a headache at this very moment. The other trapper, the one called Jake, had already imbibed too much liquor and was playing a dangerous game with his heart.

It was all there in their tracks, easily read.

Not that High Wolf's eyes had missed reading their character traits, either. In one quick glance, he had concluded that both men had been a few months without a bath, that from the condition of their rifles, the two men were inexperienced hunters, which probably accounted for the undernourished pallor beneath the top layer of their skin. Neither man would look at him directly, either, except to glare at him for a few seconds. Then their eyes would dart away, as though each man were fearful of detection.

Untrustworthy. Capable of lies. It was all there. All one had to do was look.

Although perhaps he should be more generous. After all, a trained scout, or wolf, as the Indians called High Wolf's clan, could tell all this about a person and more—in no more than a sweeping glance. If a man only knew what could be read from the condition of his clothes, his body and his weapons, he might have more care.

But, in truth, it was only this last observation that troubled High Wolf. Had Governor Clark—or Red Hair, as he was known to the Indians—honestly thought that he, High Wolf, would lead a danger-filled journey with these men acting as guards?

The idea was ludicrous; it also presented him with a slight problem, for although he wished to show Red

Hair the utmost respect, High Wolf realized he could never travel with these men. Not when he knew well that upon the state of a man's weapons rested that man's fate, his very life.

It was one of the first lessons any good scout learned—perhaps the hard way. To leave one's defenses—and that meant his weapons—in ill repair was to court disaster. It was something no man of good character would ignore.

Not that High Wolf would have journeyed with these two men or any other man, for that matter. Even if a gentleman might be the most pristine, pure human being alive, with a reputation as unvarnished as virgin wood, High Wolf would still refuse.

He worked alone. He preferred it that way.

Still, it seemed remarkable that these two men should natter and carry on like some old woman dissecting a beetle, at the expense of the character of women in general. When was the last time either of these two had laid witness to the fairness of the female form?

Years. Perhaps tens of years, he reckoned.

Well, it hadn't been so long for him. He had enjoyed the sight of many of the women in his tribe, his sister being perhaps one of the most renowned beauties in the entire Cheyenne nation. Of course, there had been another; one who had once held his heart . . . all those years ago.

The princess. For a moment, Ho'neoxhaa'eho'oese could almost hear again the strains of the violins, the cellos, the pianoforte, as the step and sway of slippered feet had pattered over the marble floor of the ballroom, in what was to be their last dance. In faith, if he'd let himself, he might have even rocked back and forth as he stood here now; maybe he would have even smiled at the memory, had he given himself full rein to do so.

But the enchantment lasted only a moment. For in truth, an instant, and an instant alone, was all he could allow.

He didn't hate her; no good scout hated anyone. In sooth, he understood why she'd done as she had.

But betrayal was betrayal all the same. And a trust, once forsaken, could never be renewed. Never.

Of course, he understood that she couldn't have done anything other than what she had and still remain true to her duty to her family. But understanding was a shabby substitute for the pain of loss.

He leaned against his rifle as he watched the steamship, the *Diana*, come into port, cannons blasting out the news of her arrival to the scrambling humanity on the dock. But even this much noise dulled in comparison to the tragedy of his thoughts.

The truth was, he seldom thought of the princess anymore. Soon, perhaps sooner than he could allow, he wouldn't remember her at all.

No, that wasn't right. For good or for bad, he would carry her memory with him to his death. Perhaps in time, his loss would fade. Perhaps . . .

Still, there were times when he wondered if she were as happy with the life she had chosen as she would have been had he—

"Hey, thar, Injun. Do ya speak any English?"

"Don't bother him, Jake. Cain't ya see he's got better thin's ta think about?" This last was said with as degrading a snicker as the man was capable.

But nothing they said or did could bother High Wolf. A scout, above all other things, understood the weaknesses of others, if only because he could see reflections of their afflictions within himself.

No, High Wolf simply didn't answer and, turning his back on the two men, he stalked away. It was enough that he knew that he could produce more stimulating conversation than these two would ever be capable of, and in any language known to the civilized or the savage world, as well.

Why bother with them? He'd made his decision. He would do this job alone, or not at all.

Chapter 4

"The housekeeper tells that 'tis well known the prince would divorce her, were he here," said the kitchenmaid.

"Aye, that he would," replied the housemaid. *"And good riddance, says I. It was she that drove him away. That she did."*

Gossip between servants at
Prince Alathom's castle

"Do you wish anything else before we go ashore?"

"No, Maria," said Princess Sierra, watching from her perch high above the dock, as Governor Clark stepped from the carriage, accompanied by an Indian maiden. "I do not require anything else at the moment. You've done quite well, my friend, despite the demanding conditions of this vessel." She gave Maria a brief smile. "Would you please find Mr. Dominic and inform him that I am ready to leave this ship?"

"Yes, Your Highness. At once. Do we go to greet Governor Clark, then?"

"I believe so," said the princess. "And for this task,

47

I will have need of you both to accompany me."

"Yes, Your Highness," Maria said, curtsying before she turned to do as bid.

Sierra smoothed a white-gloved hand over the blue and white muslin of her very full skirt, pulling the lace that bordered her walking dress into place. Straightening her shoulders, she settled her blue and white-lace mantle over the double bouffant of her sleeves, buttoning the mantle's closure at the neck. Briefly, she touched her wide belt, which was made of the same light blue color as her dress, pulling it a little more tightly around her waist so as to accentuate its most tiny aspect. A white straw bonnet, adorned with ribbons of blue and tied at the neck, completed the image of the fashionable royal that she was.

Opening her blue and white parasol, Sierra narrowed her eyes, placing a hand gently over her forehead as though it were an extra shield from the sun. She frowned.

From her view of it, there seemed to be no sign of the man she had instructed Governor Clark to hire. Had she needlessly tortured herself over this first meeting with High Wolf?

Perhaps he hadn't yet arrived.

Or maybe, she thought on a grimmer note, he wasn't coming. Had he perhaps learned that it was she behind the request?

For a moment, she worried over the possibility. As absurd as it might appear, such a thing was possible: He might know of her coming. He'd always seemed to have ways of gleaning information about things— ways that she had never understood. Perhaps he had discovered her scheme well ahead of the fact.

At that thought, Sierra tried to swallow her disappointment.

It wasn't that she was looking forward to seeing him again. No. It was only that he, and he alone, could lead her to Prince Alathom, and it was Prince Alathom she needed to find and challenge, Prince Alathom whom she would repay in kind . . . if need be . . .

Squaring her shoulders and setting her features into as delightful a smile as she could, Princess Sierra pulled unconsciously at her mantle, noticing as she did so that her fingers shook with the effort.

It was then that she caught sight of something in her peripheral vision . . . something familiar. She turned her head carefully to the left, her eyes colliding with and staring hard at a pair of dark eyes looking directly back at her.

Her stomach flipped over twice before it at last performed a dive toward her toes. She inhaled swiftly to try to quell the reaction.

It was he, High Wolf. He had come, after all.

As impossible as it might seem, she stared back at a face that she had once thought never to see again. Yet, there he was; there, across a very short distance.

And unable to curtail it, she was suddenly awash in nearly palpable relief.

Relief? Nonsense. It was probably more to the point to say that she was glad that her scheme now contained the element of possibility, the possibility of success.

But if he were to be caught looking up at her, she would be staring back down at him as well, almost as though she were hungry for the sight of him . . .

although, she corrected herself, this last thought was ridiculous.

Again, she reminded herself that he, as well as the prince, had betrayed her. In different ways, perhaps. But betrayal was certain treachery after all, regardless of the circumstances. And faith, once lost, could never be restored.

Still, despite the intervening years, an all too familiar pain shot through her, and without her conscious will, she found herself scrutinizing the man she had once thought herself to be in love with . . . a man who had left her for no more than three hundred gold dukaten.

He looked much the same as he had ten years ago, yet different. Whereas High Wolf had been little more than a boy then, he was now very much a man, and he looked bigger somehow, though he was still extraordinarily slim. Perhaps it was because his chest was wider, larger . . . or perhaps he was more muscular.

He looked . . . better, more handsome, more virile.

Sierra grimaced at her thoughts and decided to scrutinize something else less potent . . . his manner of dress, for instance . . .

Gone were the fashionable trousers and high leather boots that she remembered him wearing in the past; in their place were buckskin leggings, breechcloth and moccasins. Gone also were the carefully stitched linen shirt and cravat so precisely tied, supplanted now with a long buckskin shirt, fringed, with the bottom of it hanging down almost past his breechcloth. An ornament of what looked to be a concatenation of beads and bone, in the shape of a breastplate, hung down over his chest. It was a sight she had never beheld until this moment.

Instead of a hat, however, he now wore feathers on his head—or at least there was one feather sticking straight up behind him. And his hair . . .

Relegated to the past was the fashionable haircut she recalled so well, displaced now by long, black hair that hung well past his shoulders.

He looked . . . Indian, alien from all she had ever known and loved. Yet his countenance was, contrarily, as familiar to her as a well-rehearsed play.

And she wondered: Despite their past, would he help her?

Not if he knew her purpose.

Only too well, she recalled that High Wolf considered the prince to be more than a friend. To him, and perhaps rightly so, Prince Alathom was a brother, a brother in fact as well as in deed. Besides, High Wolf would hardly condone her murderous plan . . . a plan she fully intended to execute if the prince refused to return to the Continent, whereupon he would take up his responsibilities.

Indeed, she would be satisfied.

Those at home thought she knew nothing of their wagging tongues; they believed their whispered insults were discreet. But Sierra *did* know. She *did* care. And he *would* pay.

Oh, yes, he would pay.

Which meant, she realized, that the real reason for her journey must remain a well-guarded secret; from Governor Clark, from her guides and especially from High Wolf.

She only wondered if she could successfully hide her motives from High Wolf. After all, as she had already surmised, High Wolf was an extremely perceptive man. Might he guess?

Well, it was up to her to keep her secret well hidden. She only hoped she was up to the task.

He stared at her as though he had come face-to-face with his worst nightmare—or maybe his best fantasy. Princess Sierra? Here? Now?

His heart skipped a beat, then picked up its pace, pounding onward in triple speed. High Wolf caught his breath before forcing himself to breathe in and out. In a daze, he stared up at her, feeling as though he were caught in an illusion.

Had she come for him? Had she traveled all this distance to reach out to him, realizing after all this time that she could not live without him, as she had once proclaimed?

Or was she a mere mirage, the same sort of image that haunted his dreams?

Without warning, the desire to run to her, to take her in his arms and embrace her, was almost more real than the solidness of the ground beneath him. Of its own will, the memory of the taste of her, the scent of her, the sweetness of her embrace, overwhelmed him.

And he knew he needed, he wanted to kiss her. Now. In truth, so strong was the desire, he had taken a few steps toward her before he became once more fully aware of himself and stopped.

The prince. How could he have forgotten the prince—as well as her duplicity—so easily? Where was the prince?

Odd, he thought, how the mind could forget the pain, the anguish, the loss. For a moment, all had been gone, replaced by the simple joy of seeing her again. Odd, too, how his body was even now reacting, that most manly part of him pulsing with every pounding of his heart, remembering, anticipating . . .

. . . What could never be.

He groaned. He had to bring himself, his thoughts, his body under control, quickly.

Concentrate on her faithlessness, he cautioned himself. Hers and Prince Alathom's.

He glanced to the side of her and all around her. Where was the prince?

And then, as though it came through the fog cluttering his mind, a thought came to him. Governor Clark had hired him, had told High Wolf that he was to escort and protect a royal party, one that was coming to the Americas for a wild-game hunt.

It was the prince and princess. It had to be.

Had the two of them asked for him, personally? For old time's sake? Was that why Clark had sent for him?

Or was this mere coincidence?

Coincidence? He sneered. High Wolf knew there was no such thing.

Had the two of them no compassion? No pity?

Surely they were aware of what the mere act of seeing them again—together—would do to him.

Or did they think that they could renew friendship? That he would have forgotten?

Well, he had *not* forgotten; he could not.

Breathing in deeply, High Wolf calmed himself. He was letting his emotions take control of his mind, even of his body. It was possible, he conceded, that he was not thinking clearly, putting elements together that did not necessarily go together.

Besides, he didn't have to take the job at hand. He had not pledged his word.

And it wouldn't be as if he were deserting the prince and princess, either. After all, there were these two disreputable trappers that Clark had hired as well.

Wearily, High Wolf glanced at the two shabbily dressed men. Yes, let them have the assignment . . . while he, High Wolf, quietly disappeared . . .

Surely, that would be best. For indeed, if this were his initial reaction to the princess—and at this great a distance from her—what would be his fate if he were to witness her beauty closer to hand?

At that thought, a rush of desire swept through him that was as uncontrollable as it was unwelcome. In truth, so swift was his reaction, he rocked back on his feet.

The response shocked him as much as it excited him. And High Wolf knew he had best renew his intention to leave—quickly . . .

Yet he didn't budge so much as an inch. In faith, he could not have turned away from her now had he been a saint. Not yet.

Contrarily, another part of him reasoned that little harm could come from feasting his sights upon her for a while longer. Perhaps the image gained could serve to fuel the fire of his imagination in the lonely nights ahead of him.

Make no mistake, Princess Sierra had always been the most beautiful creature he had ever seen, and it appeared she had changed little, except to have blossomed. More curves, more womanly features.

As he stared, his heart warmed to his subject. Dark curls bounced around her face while her bonnet hid the rest of her coiffure. Oval face, high cheekbones, eyes that he knew were as green as a prairie in spring. Even from this distance, he could attest that her skin still glowed with health and vitality. It was one of the things he remembered most about her. Her skin had been luminous, clear; had shone with a radiance even under cover of darkness, as though she might be lit by a fire within.

How he had loved to run his hands over her face, her neck, those curves . . .

Cease this, he cautioned himself, letting out his breath.

Yet the mind was often a mysterious thing, and despite himself, his thoughts rambled on. At five foot four, she had always been a slender little thing. He recalled that he had once spanned her waist within the outstretched grip of both his hands. They had laughed about it. All three of them. Himself, Prince Alathom and the princess.

Odd, how close the three of them had once been, so close they had shared most everything.

High Wolf sighed.

Perhaps it was the way of the world that some things—even good things—were destined to end. Maybe that was why one should reach out for all the happiness he could have, while it still lay within his grasp.

Taking a few steps away, High Wolf at last turned his back on the sight of her. Best to disappear now, as quickly as possible. For of one thing he was entirely certain: He would not escort the princess and the prince. Not now. Not ever.

He took a few steps away.

"High Wolf!"

His insides plummeted at the sound of her voice. Yet he remained steadfast in his decision and kept walking, ignoring the call.

"High Wolf, don't go!"

Don't listen to her, he counseled himself. *Go now, before she has a chance to weave her spell around you. Go at once.*

But even as he thought it, an odd music, a rhythm perchance, began to pound through his mind, reminding him of other places, other times . . .

Chapter 5

Step, sweep, sweep; up, up, back. Hands locked together, step apart, meet. Smile at her, she at him; step, sweep, sweep. Hands held, turn; up to the toes; down again. Shoulder to shoulder, change position. Step, sweep, sweep. Hands touching; smile . . .

High Wolf could practically hear the strains of the violins and cello in three-quarter time. It had been a different time and place; a different environment. In truth, it had been like a different life.

A hand clapped him on the shoulder. "High Wolf?" It was a male voice.

Sighing deeply, High Wolf put the memory from him, while at the same time he glanced around behind him, casting a look over his shoulder, espying the well-dressed, yet massive gentleman who stood behind him. Pivoting slowly, he came to stare at the man, who was, perhaps, the tallest human being High Wolf had ever seen.

Silence reigned until at last the other man said, "Princess Sierra Morena requests that you await an audience with her."

High Wolf squinted at this giant, rendering him with as condescending a look as he could muster, though inwardly an ugly emotion ripped at his innards. Aloud he asked, "Does she?"

"Yes, sir. If you will wait a moment."

High Wolf turned aside. "But I won't wait," he said, feigning a foreign accent that was all too natural, at least for his own peace of mind. "Please give my regards to the princess." He bowed slightly, more out of a long-ago habit than in deference, a habit, he realized, he hadn't used in ten long years.

A hand came up to clasp his shoulder. "The princess wishes to speak to you now."

High Wolf paused as he considered his options. He could leave. It was probably what he should do. After all, there was no man alive who could keep him here; not if High Wolf desired to walk away.

He cast another glance at his opponent. No, not even this big, brawny man could keep him if he truly wished to flee.

But did he?

Would she look different up close; would she be different? Would her marriage to the prince have matured her? Or would she still be the sweet, young girl he had once loved so very, very well?

High Wolf rocked back on his feet. He was caught. Truly caught. Not by his own honor, but by his curiosity.

Later, he would take his leave of this party, and in particular, of the princess. But not now.

No, for now he would wait. He would observe. And then he would leave, quickly, and as silently as he had done ten years ago.

Inured to his fate, he gazed upward, watching the princess depart the steamship, scrutinizing her progress down the ramp as closely as if he were reading a track marked upon the earth. He caught her smile as she grinned at Governor Clark, saw her speak a few words to Governor Clark, scolded himself for wishing he might be the man on the receiving end of her smile.

And then gradually, so very, very slowly, she turned toward *him*, raising her sights to meet his.

And High Wolf stared back, his gaze, for all that he was aware of her faults, still hungry for the sight of her. And for a moment, time distorted. There was no past, no present, no future. There was only she . . . and he, the rest of the world diminished, as though it were no more than their own personal backdrop.

He sighed, recalling too well his loss. And the magic of the moment faded.

In vain he awaited the shy downturn of her eyelashes as she stared at him, the flirtatious one he remembered so very well.

It never came.

No, the princess gazed back at him boldly, brazenly, and try as he might to find it, there was nothing coquettish about the look she gave him. In faith, if he were to examine her appearance at this moment, he would have to conclude that she was beautiful. Yes. Beautiful, but hard—as though time had extracted all the softness from her.

So, he thought, the princess, too, had changed in many more ways than those of a physical nature.

As he took note of her approach, time passed quickly, and yet in a way it seemed to drag. Leisurely, he watched her, knowing that hidden deep within him, there was an impossible hope that perhaps this was all a mistake, a horrible ten-year-old mistake.

It was remarkable, he thought as his gaze drank in her beauty, how the princess could appear so severe, yet still innocent in countenance. As though she bore no shame, no regret; as though she had never been the cause of an injustice.

Saaaa. He used the Cheyenne expression which stood for many things, including astonishment. It was as though *she* might be the wounded party from all those years ago . . . not he.

High Wolf nodded a silent acknowledgment, even if the movement of his head was a slight one. Then, leaning his weight upon his rifle, he awaited the "angel in blue" as she approached.

"Ho'neoxhaa'eho'ese," she pronounced his name in Cheyenne as soon as she stepped within a few feet of him. "It has been a long time."

She did not offer her hand, and her words, softly spoken, cut through him, as though the sound of her voice were blazed in steel. Yet High Wolf simply nodded, trying to shake off the feeling of being ill-at-ease.

In contrast, she seemed all poise and assurance; she even smiled. However, he took careful note, no happiness reached those green eyes before she said, "How have you been?"

"I am well," he replied, his voice, usually full-bodied, no more than a dull monotone.

She seemed unaware of any problem with him, however, and replied, "That is good. That is good, indeed."

"And you?" he inquired politely.

Again, she grinned up at him, before saying, "I am well, as you can see."

High Wolf inclined his head toward her, catching her eye before he said, "And your husband?"

She flinched as though he might have dealt her a blow, and oddly, her face drained of color, her eyes becoming suddenly dull. Hurriedly, she glanced away.

Strange.

Frowning, High Wolf ventured further, "Is he in company with you?"

However, the princess did not deign to answer; her gaze looked instead out upon the dock as though it were of great interest—a dock that was streaming with people. "Mr. High Wolf," she said at last, "over there, due west of us"—she nodded toward the spot—"there is a patch of level ground that looks fairly well deserted of people. I would very much like to take a turn in it, if you would be so kind as to accompany me."

Take a turn. He hadn't heard that phrase, hadn't spoken that phrase in well over ten years. Hearing it again, unfortunately for him, had the effect of turning back time.

Politely, out of a habit from long ago, he bowed at the waist. "I would be happy to join you, Your Highness," he said, "at some other time. But I am afraid that I have . . . other business that calls my attention at the moment."

She acknowledged him with a delicate dip of her head. "I understand," she said. "I am assuming this business relates to Governor Clark and his hiring you as a guide?"

High Wolf said nothing in reply.

"And I am sure you have already surmised that I am to be the party you are to accompany into the interior."

He blinked at her, his only acknowledgement.

"And you are considering declining, now that you know more of the facts?" She might have asked it as such, but he knew her words were no question.

He shrugged, saying, "As you say."

"Very well," she acknowledged, "although I find it monstrous ill that you can turn so easily away from a promise."

He raised an eyebrow.

"For you see," she continued, "I am calling in a favor you once granted me. A favor, you had once said, that would send you to me in a moment of distress. If I remember correctly"—she gave him a sly look—"you promised to come to my aid if I did no more than call upon you."

He didn't blink—not even a single eyelash—as he countered, "All such promises came to nothing, Your Highness, on the day you became Prince Alathom's wife, by the very nature of that act."

When she frowned, he went on to observe, "Did you not vow to forsake all others? That would include me, would it not?"

"Perhaps," she said, then grinned up at him, while High Wolf suddenly found himself at odds, disliking her, while all the while longing to take her in his arms. Instead of doing either, however, he stepped back, away from her.

But she continued, "If I remember correctly, there were no restraints upon your favor when you made the vow, although I do admit it was a long time ago. You merely said, 'Ask, and I will come.'" She smiled at him flirtatiously. "Perhaps your favors expire with time if not used?"

He shrugged off the insult. "It was the heartfelt promise of a boy from long ago. You have a husband now to attend to your needs."

"But that is precisely the reason for my visit, Mr. High Wolf," she said, her expression suddenly modest. "For you see, to all the world, I no longer have a husband."

High Wolf went very still, his outward demeanor showing little of his agitation. Instead he watched her watching him; saw her scrutinize him, her glance perhaps hoping to find some weakness in him. But High Wolf was too well versed in the ways of a scout, and much too observant to be affected by such an overt contemplation, and with ease, he carefully hid the sudden quickening of his heart.

But she was continuing to speak, and said, "Now, please, Mr. High Wolf, let us take that turn." And sweeping her skirts with a grand gesture, she stepped toward the place she had earlier indicated, though shortly she turned back. "Mr. Dominic," she called over her shoulder, "please inform Governor Clark that I will join him soon. I shall be only a moment."

"Yes, Your Highness," said Mr. Dominic, and bowing, turned away.

Slowly, Princess Sierra pivoted around, her gaze capturing *his*. "Now, Mr. High Wolf," she said, "shall we?"

And High Wolf, bound by an imprudent oath from his past, had no other option—at least none at the moment—but to hear her out. And though he wished himself somewhere else—anywhere else—he followed her lead.

Oh, how she wished things were different. Oh, how she wished she could turn back time.

But events were as they were, and not even God in His heaven could change the past.

Princess Sierra sighed and, as she stepped lightly toward the spot she had earlier indicated, she wondered what she could say to this man that would sway him to her cause, trying to recall her well-rehearsed speech.

It was one thing to determine and practice such things in the privacy of one's quarters, quite another to confront the actual man. Plus she hadn't counted on the increased rate of her heartbeat, or on the weakness which came over her limbs. And despite herself, Princess Sierra was experiencing a desire to throw herself into High Wolf's arms and beg for his mercy.

She snorted instead. She? Beg this man?

Never.

Still, she must do something to solicit his help, and all without allowing him to perceive her real purpose. Could she do it? Could she fool this very insightful man?

Oh, if only life, past events could be different. For within her, and increasing with every minute, was a sensation of old, a desire to purge herself of her troubles—as she had often done with this man in their not-too-distant past.

But she could hardly afford such a luxury and remain true to herself. Indeed, not only must she remain steadfast, she daren't forget that this was the same man whose treachery had broken her heart . . .

Sierra inhaled deeply once again. There were some things that, once done, could never be taken back. And make no mistake, this man's offense had been such a one.

Well, so be it. Squaring her shoulders, the princess turned to face him and said, "The prince is dead."

High Wolf frowned. "Dead?"

"Yes, apparently so."

"Apparently?" As High Wolf's frown deepened, his stare became piercing.

Ignoring the look, she continued, "Prince Alathom was not home when the event which took his life happened, as you might already know."

High Wolf raised one single eyebrow. He repeated, "Already know?"

"Yes," she said. "It was a hunting accident—here in the Americas. We received word of the incident only a few months ago."

"We?"

"Our families." Sierra swallowed, and inhaling a deep breath, took a plunge, when perhaps it might have been more prudent to tread water. However, she continued, "Come now, High Wolf, I'm certain that I'm not telling you anything of which you are not already aware."

If he detected the note of censure in her voice, he overlooked it, for all he said was, "Why would you think that?"

How dare he pretend to be innocent? Did he mean

to insult her intelligence? Did he honestly think she would not be able to piece together the facts?

Well, perhaps it was time to show him that she could play any game that he chose to play. And, determined to put him in his place, she began, "I would think that, because the accident that took his life happened here . . . in the West, you would be well versed in it."

High Wolf narrowed a glance at her. "Meaning that you think he and I were together when it happened?"

"If the shoe fits . . ."

"And you think I was responsible for his death? Is this what you're insinuating?"

"No," she denied, momentarily thrown off guard by his question. In vain, she tried to ignore the confusion his question brought her, for despite her anger at him, she never would have thought this man responsible for the prince's accident. He and Alathom were simply too close.

No, the truth was that she simply did not believe such an accident had taken place.

If she were correct—and there was no reason to assume she was not—the prince and High Wolf had conceived the deceit together, had planned it as deceptively as they had once planned another escape.

But she could not very well tell him that.

However, he was frowning at her, staring at her in a way that brought her to understand that he was reading every nuance of her reaction . . . something he was quite adept at, and a little too breathlessly, she continued, "I . . . I would not accuse you of having caused his death. I know you would never do anything to intentionally harm the prince. It's only that . . ."

"You think I should have died in his place?"

"No."

"Then what?"

Then why, when you had a reason to do so, didn't you come back to me?

No, that wasn't right. She couldn't have actually thought that—not about this man.

High Wolf, however, as though ill-at-ease, crossed his arms over his chest before repeating, "Then what? What are you accusing me of?"

"I'm not accusing you of anything except perhaps being more friendly toward the prince than you have been to me."

This last appeared to baffle High Wolf, and even he could not subdue the look of bewilderment that settled across his features. In truth, so honest was his perplexity, had she not known better, she would almost have believed in his innocence—almost . . .

And she said, "Come now, High Wolf, we were always friends, weren't we? You, the prince and myself?"

High Wolf visibly stiffened, though all he said was, "We were—once."

"And so all I am asking of you is that you give me as much deference as you would, or more correctly, as you have, the prince. I would like to go into the interior for a hunt, perhaps to ease my mind from my 'loss.'" She emphasized the word. "I would request that you guide me there."

Sierra glanced up to see, not the countenance of a man who had been caught out in a lie and was quietly ready to admit it, but rather she was met with indisputable contempt.

Oddly, it was this look that gave her courage. For it was she, not he, who had a right to indignation.

He stirred, moving away from her, and said, "I will not lead you into the interior of this country."

Instantly, a feeling of disdain swept over her, returning to her a presence of mind. And she said, "Stay where you are. I have not yet given you permission to leave."

He stilled. "No, you haven't, Your Highness," he said, pivoting around and coming face-to-face with her once more. However, with a leer on his countenance, he added, "But perhaps you should look around you."

In defiance, she kept her glance glued to him.

"And maybe, if you did so, you might examine your environment even more carefully."

Sierra stared straight ahead, still training her gaze on him and him alone.

He continued, "For, Your Highness, if you were to do this simple act, you might discover that you are no longer in Europe. Now look at me closely."

"I already am."

"More closely than even this."

She blew out her breath, refusing to do as he bid, and glanced away from him instead.

But if her reaction bothered him, he seemed not to show it. Indeed, he said, "Do you see that I am not one of your subjects?"

Even as he uttered the words, the sneer in his tone, the curtness of his very manner, could not have been mistaken for anything other than what it was: disrespect. In response, her chin lifted high into the air, and she declared, "One does not need to be a subject of a particular country in order to exhibit proper manners," she scolded. "And there is nothing that I have said that gives you leave to mock me. Indeed, I ask a simple thing."

If she had hoped to make him more propitious, she had certainly failed, for within his glance was pure defiance, and he said, "True, the request is simple, but I suspect that the entreaty which is so sweetly given is yet filled with venom."

She sucked in her breath.

And he continued, "I am not for hire by you." He spun about, ready to leave.

Goodness! *The man hated her.*

For an instant, the realization caused her to sway from where she stood. And for another heartfelt moment, she felt as though every single drop of blood in her body had become frozen.

She had certainly not anticipated this man's hatred. After all, by what right did he dare show her ridicule? *She, and she alone, possessed leave to seek revenge.*

Yet he was retreating from her, without her leave, without her approval and with as much ill-will as she had ever witnessed. Worse, his departure was not something she would or could permit.

Reaching forward, she grabbed hold of his sleeve, the rough leather of his shirt feeling oddly soft against her fingers, a softness, she noted, that was not reflected in his countenance, or in any other part of him. She said, "What did I ever do to you that you feel compelled to treat me like this?"

He stopped, he stiffened, he inhaled slowly before he

at last rocked back on his feet. Then swallowing hard, as though he were not as confident as he might like her to believe, he shut his eyes, letting go of his breath.

It was a show of minor weakness, but it was also the advantage she wanted, and she said, "You, sir, deserted me. It was not the other way around."

"Was it not?"

"What do you mean?"

He let out his breath. "Try to understand, Your Highness, I am a different man now than I was when you once knew me. Ten years can bring about a great deal of change in a person."

"I see," she said dumbly, as yet another thought struck her. Aloud, she asked, "Are you married?"

She held her breath. It was a reasonable question, given their situation. It was also one she should have asked herself before now, if only to soften any surprise. After all, High Wolf was nothing if not a handsome and virile man. And being such, he was probably much sought after as a husband.

Her stomach dropped, and unreasonably, she felt defeated.

He said, "Does it matter if I am?"

"Of course not. Not to me."

"Then why would you ask, I wonder?"

She shrugged. "Curiosity. Is this, then—your marriage—the reason why you will not guide me?"

"Could be."

"I see." She gulped in air. "You could bring her with you. I would not mind." It was a lie; even as she spoke the words, Sierra knew she would rather die than meet this man's wife.

It was an odd thing to become aware of, and she

trembled with realization: Did she still care about this man?

Impossible. It simply could not be.

She glanced up to catch him grinning at her. But his good humor was far from a pretty sight. In truth, his grin was simply a movement of his lips, with no inclination to mirth whatsoever, a mere shadow of what she remembered.

However, he was speaking, and he said, "Well, I, for one, if I did have a wife, would mind bringing her along, although I realize you might not share my scruples on that."

If he had a wife . . . ?

"No, Princess," he continued, "you are wasting your precious time on me. Go home. Leave me to my own thoughts, and let me grieve for my friend in private, for I meant what I said. I will not lead you anywhere in this country."

The words had no more left his mouth than he had spun about and was doing exactly as he had threatened: He left, without so much as a by-your-leave, and with no deference to her whatsoever.

But this time Princess Sierra barely noticed. In truth, she was frowning, thinking . . .

Had High Wolf always harbored such antagonism? And if he had, how had she missed seeing it until now?

Sierra closed her eyes, inhaling and exhaling slowly. Well, this was a fine mess. Should she have confided her own doubts about the prince? That he might still be alive? And if he were, that she wanted nothing more than to have a council with him? Would that have persuaded High Wolf to her cause?

No, she had already made up her mind on this account, and she was certain: High Wolf and the prince were in one another's confidence, as they had always been. And little good would come from her pleading.

But, dear Lord, what was she to do now?

Chapter 6

> "'Tis said she threatened to bite him; lest 'tis what
> her maid said."
>   "And did she bite him?"
>   "She would have if he would have been here. 'Tis
> said she is like a vampire, that she is."
>
> Gossip between servants at
Prince Alathom's castle

*T*he sun shone brightly on the trio as they rode
through the lush woodland valley of southern Germany. Laughing, the three friends stopped at a brook, both
gentlemen dismounting to help the princess to the ground.

As they led their horses to water, Prince Alathom, the
shortest of the three, said to High Wolf, "I have spoken to
my father about you and Sierra." He paused.

"And . . . ?"

"And?"

Both the princess and High Wolf asked the question at the
same time, smiling at one another. As they came to realize
what they had done, and that their minds had, perhaps,
tended in the same direction, they laughed.

The prince grinned back at them, as though he, too, understood. "I think that my father looks with favor on the match, for I have told him my wishes on the matter. And as he has declared his intention to adopt you, my friend, you most certainly will have the title to court Sierra officially."

High Wolf grinned. It was more than he had dared to hope. Turning toward the princess, he found her smiling, and reciprocating, he took her hand in his own, and led her to a private spot.

Ah, how he loved this girl, and staring down into her eyes, he became so filled with emotion that he knew he must say something or die of pleasure.

Bending toward her, he gazed down urgently at her, and said, "I give you all of me, my Sierra. Know that my heart is yours. There is nothing in this world that can change that; not time, not distance, not even the test of the flesh. Know that if ever you have need, you have only to ask, and I will attend."

"You do me honor, sir, I am sure."

High Wolf smiled. "Perhaps. Or maybe it is simply true, and you are the most beautiful princess in all of Baden-Baden."

Again she blushed.

High Wolf breathed in profoundly, unable to remember a time he had ever been so happy. Gently, he took Sierra's chin in his hand, turning her face up to him, that he might see her properly. And he said, "From this day forward, my dearest, I shall endeavor to court you in a fashion most suited to your position. And now, tell me, do you love me as much as I do you?"

"Oh, yes," she replied at once. "And thrice more in kind . . ."

* * *

High Wolf had, of course, countered with the taunt that he loved her four times as much as she did him, leaving her to quip back that she loved him five times more. Thus had begun the pleasant argument.

In the end, the prince had found them and had proclaimed that he admired them both more than either of them did each other. And that had solved it.

How silly. They had all laughed at the joke.

However, the argument had never resurfaced.

Of course, there hadn't been time for it to do so. The magic of that evening had ended too shortly thereafter.

"You have only to ask . . ."

High Wolf froze in his retreat, as though by ceasing all physical movement, his thoughts could be as easily contained.

It was true . . . too terribly true. He had pledged his word to help her.

But he had been a mere boy. Or was that merely a trick of his mind, seeking to justify the abandonment of a promise? Unfortunately for him, it did have that ring to it. For his was an honorable life, a life of duty— to his people, to his clan. And whether he liked it or not, he feared that duty would demand he pay homage to his words.

Duty.

"Saaaa," he hissed out the word to himself. What an incredible situation life had suddenly thrust upon him. He was damned. Utterly damned, condemned by his own integrity. Doomed by his own inclinations toward the princess—tendencies he should ignore.

Duty.

Odd, how duty had separated them long ago. Was it

also to be duty that, years later, pushed them unwillingly together?

He glanced skyward, his gaze sullen, intent. He was trapped. Truly, utterly trapped.

Shaking his head, he stirred uneasily. He needed to think: now. But first he required distance from her . . .

To this end, he broke into a run, sprinting through this swarming outpost—which the French had dubbed St. Louis—as quickly as possible; darting on and on until he reached the wooded wilderness that bordered the village.

As he stepped into the woods, his spirits calmed. Here were things familiar, an environment where the sounds and echoes to be heard were those of the wild. It was here, in the realm of nature, where he felt as much at home as he might in his own lodge, which lay farther north.

Quickly, he scanned the forest's depths and valleys, looking for a shelter, someplace that would remain hidden from the untrained, as well as the trained eye of the scout. What he desired was a spot where a man might rest for a while, rest and think through his thoughts. A place where he might grieve for his friend.

He found refuge easily enough in an old burned-out tree trunk, the tree long gone, the trunk still standing. And though it was doubtful he would be disturbed there—for few Indians and hunters loitered around this village—a good scout left nothing to chance.

And so he began the preparations of making his camp—though only temporary—invisible.

This he did easily and quickly, accomplishing the camouflage with the products of the earth. Soon done, he settled down within the hollowed-out tree, built a small smokeless fire, and pulling his pipe out from his parfleche, lit it and smoked, paying homage first to the four directions and then to the Creator.

At last he was ready to come to terms with his thoughts. Closing his eyes, he was surprised to find that his memories turned, not to the princess, but rather to his brother, Prince Alathom.

"Would you like to test your prowess with mine?" asked the fifteen-year-old prince, conveying his meaning with sign.

High Wolf, an "ancient" twelve-year-old, nodded and, handing the prince his spear, indicated that Alathom should throw it out onto the prairie.

One throw, two, three. On and on. It was a tough match, and though the prince was the elder by three years, he could not quite manage to make his spear fly farther than that of High Wolf.

"Perhaps we should wrestle," suggested the prince, on what appeared to be a rather futile note.

And so they had turned to wrestling, with much the same result.

"Why am I not beating you at any of these things, for I should. I am three years older . . . and a prince."

But High Wolf had laughed, saying, "Maybe it is because you are not any bigger than I am. And what does being a prince have to do with it?"

"It has a great deal to do with it," said the prince at first. But then, as though realizing the absurdity of such a statement, he laughed.

Thus had begun an incredible friendship. And while the adults had stayed in conference the day through, the two lads had grown closer. Although, even then, there had been things that High Wolf could not share: those secrets and rituals of the clan, for instance. For like the wolf of the plains, a scout's best defense was his obscurity.

Then came the time when his whole life changed.

It had occurred on a day such as this; sunny, bright, cloudless, though of course it had been on the plains farther north. The adults had been hunting buffalo that morning, having spotted a small herd. And though a buffalo hunt was not out of the ordinary for High Wolf, any buffalo chase was not without its danger.

And so it had happened.

High Wolf wasn't paying attention. In truth, he had been off on his own, tracking an antelope, which looked as though it had been injured.

His Serene Highness and the other hunters were stationed more than a mile away from where the prince and High Wolf had wandered. And no one had seen the bull, a dangerous animal with an arrow sticking out of its ribs.

The bull was angry: It was looking for a good target. It found one in the prince.

At first it had snorted, and perhaps that was the first alert given to High Wolf. He glanced over his shoulder.

And that's when he saw it.

The huge beast was pawing the earth, head down, horns pointed.

And the prince hadn't seen it; he had been busy chasing a butterfly.

High Wolf didn't think. He ran for all he was worth.

And then the bull charged. The prince turned, his countenance startled, and then nothing: He froze.

The bull hadn't seen High Wolf, and leaping forward in a lunge, directly into and over the bull's path, High Wolf toppled the prince to the ground, rolling over and over, one boy tumbling over the other.

The bull kept running, but turned posthaste. However, that allowed High Wolf to crouch down amid the tall prairie grass.

"Do not move," he whispered to Alathom. "A bull does not see well, although he might smell us."

But luck was with them that day, for the wind changed directions, blowing away from the bull and toward them, effectively erasing their scent.

But the buffalo bull wasn't finished, and it prowled the grounds around them, looking for its target. However, alert, High Wolf kept himself and the prince well hidden and downwind.

Still, neither boy had mustered the courage to stand up again until the adults had found them, though the bull had long ago trotted away.

And then came the celebration, and a coup for High Wolf . . . and more . . .

An invitation—to go to the prince's home—to live like the prince did, in his castle in Baden-Baden, a beautiful country, a beautiful land.

High Wolf's father and uncle, pleased with what High Wolf had accomplished that day, had been more than willing to grant him his wish. And off High Wolf had gone, on to the adventure of his life.

Educated and treated like a prince, High Wolf had come to know the advantages permitted the royal class, though at first High Wolf had little understood or even agreed with such foreign principles.

Still, the royal lifestyle was not without its rewards, and High Wolf was often glad that he had made the journey. Indeed, the beautiful and serene Black Forest region of Baden-Baden had become his home, the prince's family his own, His Serene Highness even adopting High Wolf.

And then, there had been Sierra . . .

Yes, Princess Sierra.

Saaaa, but she was beautiful—had always been so, with her dark, dark, hair, green eyes and pure, clear complexion. Yet he had been right in observing from the start that there was something sterner about her now, something that had aged her, if not on the outside, then on the inside.

It was as though her spirit were sick, as though the softness in her manner—the one that he recalled so well—was missing. Why? Hadn't the prince nurtured that aspect of her personality?

Ah, the prince . . .

Why had Prince Alathom been in the Americas? And without her?

How long had he been here? And why hadn't he tried to contact his old friend? Unless the prince, unlike his lady, had been too embarrassed by the turn of events that had taken place.

Unfortunately, these speculations and questions led High Wolf far afield, since the prince was not here to either answer these questions or to field them. Which led him back to the matter at hand:

Why was the princess here? Yes, why, indeed?

From the first moment he saw her, High Wolf realized that he should have asked this most intriguing question—and demanded an honest answer—for he was certain that "hunting" was of little interest to her. She, who in all his acquaintance with her, had never once held a rifle?

Had she come to renew her relationship with him?

He snorted at such inventiveness on his part. Ten years was a little long to wait to do that. Besides, he had watched her closely enough to know that her manner had been too distant, too reserved and too arrogant for that to be true.

Looking back on the entire matter, he realized that when Red Hair had originally written him, he had mentioned that the Europeans who would be arriving were anxious to hunt. And contrary to what High Wolf had related to the princess, this sort of event was not something objectionable, or even unusual. In truth, these excursions usually turned out well: The royalty gained the excitement they were seeking, and the tribes acquired free meat.

But for the princess to endure the rigors of a sea voyage to do nothing more than seek a diversion from her loss?

No, she wasn't telling all. She couldn't be. Not unless she had changed so much as to acquire traits and tastes in sport that were normally considered masculine.

But if not that reason, then why *was* she here?

Because she was free?

At this last thought, High Wolf's heart tumbled over itself, as though anxious to make itself known.

But as quickly as it came, he stifled the feeling, for that sort of response betrayed him as much as it excited him.

He breathed out slowly. That she had specifically asked for him was without doubt. That she must have envisioned some design for doing so was also a given.

Did her presence here have anything to do with the prince? That is, besides her avowed need to forget her loss?

As High Wolf turned this thought over in his mind, it occurred to him that the prince's death might not be . . . *It might be a lie.*

Stranger things had happened here on the plains. People sometimes did deeds they might not normally do.

For a moment, High Wolf experienced a perception of old—that of being of one thought with Sierra and the prince. And he wondered, did she, like he, sense that the prince's death might be too fantastic to be true?

That he had merely staged it?

Oddly, this last thought brought on a calmness of mind that was as welcome to him as a warm day. And for the first time since espying the princess, High Wolf felt as though he stood on more solid ground.

Yes, if she were the same person he had once known, he could envision Sierra venturing west to investigate the report. Discard the fact that she was female, it was not so farfetched an idea, especially since it would be exactly what he would do.

Thus, in coming here, she had asked for him, hiding her identity until the very last moment.

Haa'he, yes. Though these were mere suppositions, other facts fell neatly into place.

But still, the real question was this: Would he help her?

Did he have a choice?

Damn, he cursed to himself.

There was none. No choice. Absolutely none.

He hunched his shoulders forward and shuddered. His thoughts had brought him once again full circle, having decided nothing—a circumstance that usually resulted from lack of information. Which left only one thing for him to do: He would seek out Red Hair and ask for a council, because, if what he suspected were true, Red Hair knew more about the princess's reasons for being here than those he had revealed.

And so it was that High Wolf broke camp, and rising, trod off toward the home of General William Clark, governor of this territory, and the same man of the famed Lewis and Clark expedition. And it was there, perhaps, at Red Hair's home—a place that sat high on a bluff above the Big River, or as the white man called it, the Mississippi—that High Wolf hoped he would glean the information he sought.

Chapter 7

"Why, she cannot rule the country without him, and with him gone these long years," said the kitchen-maid. "'Tis unrest in the streets . . . and all because of her."

"Aye," agreed the housemaid. "One can only hope His Royal Highness will return forthwith."

Gossip between servants at
Prince Alathom's castle

Red Hair and High Wolf never counselled.

Sierra was there before him, and not wishing his presence to be known, at least not yet, High Wolf kept to the shadows of the trees that clustered around the western rim of the house. The princess and Red Hair had taken their seats out upon the open veranda, where the two were enjoying a cup of tea.

And he couldn't help but hear . . .

". . . You cannot go into Indian territory alone," said Red Hair.

"I will hardly be alone," the princess responded. "I have Mr. Dominic, my steward, who will protect both myself and Maria, my maid. Now, Governor . . ." She smiled. "Would you tell me, sir, which name you prefer that I use when I address you? Am I to call you Superintendent, Governor, General, or simply Mr. Clark?"

"Any of those will do, Your Highness. We don't stand on ceremony here."

She nodded.

"But to your needs, Princess. I feel it my duty to inform you that Mr. Dominic will not be enough protection. Though he is certainly a big man, he doesn't know the lay of the land out here on the western frontier, nor is he familiar with the various Indian tribes and their customs. And these things are imperative to ensure your safety, Your Highness. I beg you to consider this, as it has become very concerning to me. Not only do I feel compelled to see to your welfare myself, but only this morning, I received a letter from your father, who charges me with this duty, as well."

"My father has written to you?"

"Yes, my dear. Now, rest assured that I will find you another guide."

Princess Sierra sighed. "My father promised that he would not interfere in this."

"Parents sometimes worry."

"Yes," she agreed. "Sometimes they do. Now, Governor Clark, how long might it take to find another guide?"

"I'm certain that I can obtain the goodwill of another gentleman very shortly. There are several trailblazers right here within this territory. I will send each of them a letter at once."

"A letter?"

"Yes, it is a fast means of communication."

"I see. Ah, thank you, Governor. But time is of the essence, as you might well comprehend. How long will all this take? As you know, the steamship is due to leave by dusk, since we are making up time. And I wish to be on her."

"You are planning to leave tonight?"

"Yes, sir. I believe there is only one trip made into the north country each year. I cannot afford to miss this chance."

William Clark was rubbing his chin as though deep in thought. At last, however, he said, "Tonight. That might be a little difficult, but not entirely impossible. And there still are the two men whom I already procured, and they are ready to—"

"I have seen those men and have spoken to them. They will not do."

"But, Your Highness, they know the countryside as well as the various tribes who roam this land and—"

"On this I must be firm. They simply will not do."

He paused. "Yes, Your Highness. Well, if you would only be willing to wait a few days, I'm sure I could—"

"I cannot wait, Governor. As you might understand, my mission is somewhat timely, and it is imperative that I leave on this boat, as there is no assurance there will be another one for some time."

"But a few days will not matter in the least. I could procure some men and you could rejoin the ship somewhere a little farther north. You see, once the Missouri River is forded, the steamers tie up each night, since it is too dangerous to navigate all the snags and such in the dark. You would have ample time to catch up."

"Thank you, but no, that will not do, either. I have

too much luggage to cart with me and I am unused to traveling on anything less than a well-driven road, or a river, as the case might be."

The governor frowned. "Well, this does present a problem. You are entirely certain that the Indian I originally hired, High Wolf, will not accompany you?"

"Yes," she said. "Yes, I am."

"How strange," said Clark. "He may be Indian, but he is a very educated man and has worked for me on this sort of excursion before. I wonder why he's refusing now?"

"Perhaps he had a dream."

"A dream?" Governor Clark paused and stared at the princess as though she might have suddenly grown scales. He asked, "How do you know about an Indian's dreams?"

The princess blushed. "I . . . I have some knowledge of the Indian tribes myself. You see, I once knew a man who had been brought to the Continent with a friend—and that man was American Indian. He used to speak to us of many things. And I know that if a man has a bad dream about a particular journey, he will not feel compelled to continue that expedition, and he is never thought of badly for quitting it altogether."

"Yes," said the governor. "Yes, that is true. Although I must admit that it seems strange to hear knowledge about these things from a member of the royalty, someone so removed from these cultural taboos. A man, you say, who was brought to the Continent? That sounds exceedingly familiar, as this is what happened to High Wolf."

"Is it? How strange."

"Yes, yes. But I don't understand this urgency. Let me be very clear on a subject of some delicacy, Your Highness, if you would be so kind as to permit me."

"Do not think to spare me, sir, for I assure you, we should speak frankly to one another."

Governor Clark nodded. With care, he cleared his throat before continuing, "Your Highness, I have made inquiries into the matter of your late husband, and I can assure you that there is nothing remiss in the report which was sent you and your parents. The prince was killed by a wandering band of Sioux Indians. There were several trappers who saw it, as well as a few members of a Crow party who survived the attack. He was traveling with these Crow Indians as well as the trappers. And all of these men confirm that they saw him fall."

The princess stiffened. "And did they bury him?"

"I would assume so."

"Good, then they can show me the grave, for I will not be satisfied until I see it."

Governor Clark shook his head. "You must have loved him dearly to have come this far and to be so persistent."

The princess cast her gaze down, and with a hand over her mouth, coughed before she admitted, "It is true that my feelings for my husband are very strong, indeed."

Governor Clark reached out and patted her arm. "I understand. Be assured that I will make the necessary inquiries for a guide with all possible speed."

"Yes, please, Mr. Clark, please do so at your earliest convenience. And if you do manage to find such a person, send him to me at once. In the meanwhile, I am prepared to leave when the *Diana* lifts anchor. If you have obtained no one by then, but you do so later, please send him after me with a letter, that I might know him."

"Yes, Your Highness. That I will."

The princess smiled, the gesture warm and friendly when compared to the smirks she had given High Wolf earlier this day. And yet, High Wolf noted, there was still little joy to be found in her expression.

But if Governor Clark noticed these little nuances, he must have overlooked them, for after a time, he said, "And now I have a surprise for you."

"A surprise?"

The governor grinned. "I have a feast planned for you and your company—a gesture of goodwill— before you leave our humble village."

The princess smiled once again, a mirror of her earlier gesture. In due course, she said, "That would be splendid, Governor. Simply splendid."

Except for the crickets' serenade, the puffing of the engine's two blackened smokestacks, and the occasional squawk of a hawk, all was silent on the river. The boat still lay in anchor, but was in readiness to leave.

Would she ever see him again?

The thought was quite involuntary. Nonetheless, a sort of melancholy had overtaken her, and she could only imagine the cause being that she had counted on obtaining High Wolf's help. Of course, there had been some doubt about his cooperation, but she had been fairly certain that her reminder of his promise would have swayed him to her cause.

After all, until that very last day, he had never denied her anything.

The princess raised her chin at an angle, looking every bit the regal monarch, as she realized quite sadly how much she didn't know or understand him.

Shaking her head, she sighed softly while the *Diana* slowly pulled away from the dock. And high atop the boat's upper deck, Princess Sierra watched as the shoreline crept farther and farther away. Tediously, and quite without her will, a tear streamed down her face, but it was not from the sadness in her heart, she thought, as much as it was from the wind, which was stinging her eyes.

She gazed outward. In the distance, and to the west, the sun was announcing its departure from the day in pinkish red and golden hues, the dimness of the light blurring the shoreline so that her ability to distinguish figures was greatly hampered. She blinked in quick succession, placing a hand on her forehead as though the pose might give her better vision. Leaning forward against the ship's wooden railing, she stared, hoping for a final glimpse of *him*.

But it was not to be. Indeed, she had fairly well believed that he would not be there. He was, by now, probably a good distance from the village of St. Louis. In truth, remembering his reaction, as well as his cutting words to her, she decided that he had probably set out upon a journey away from her with all possible speed.

He hated her.

The thought came to her again out of nowhere, and

Princess Sierra silently scolded herself. Why could she not stop remembering that, or what had prompted it? Or better yet, why could she not put the entire meeting with him behind her?

It wasn't as if she had to worry about him liking or disliking her. He had made it abundantly clear what he thought of her.

Nevertheless, it did bother her.

Why?

Because he had once loved her?

She took in a quick breath. Supposedly, it was as Father Junipero had once said: High Wolf simply didn't care about her. Perhaps High Wolf's motive, all those years ago, had been selfish, taking only his own interests into account, and not those of her or her people.

For better or for worse, it was certainly what she had come to believe.

High Wolf had been mercenary, as well. Although if that were true, he had certainly chosen an odd lifestyle to show it.

She frowned, and placing her fingers over her forehead, she rubbed at it. Why did remembering these things make it so difficult to think clearly?

Well, of one thing she was certain: She had done nothing to him. Nothing whatsoever. Nothing to regret.

Still, she sighed. As eager as she certainly was to seek revenge on the prince, she had felt equally justified in including High Wolf in that same category. Odd how, since her arrival, she now felt on the defensive, as though *she* should explain herself to him.

It was strange, too, the way she had reacted to the sight of High Wolf, for her pulse had accelerated and she had definitely felt her lifeblood stirring, as though

.

she hadn't been living these past few years, merely surviving. Perhaps, she thought, there were some awarenesses of life that never died, despite the travails of a love affair gone wrong.

"May I be of any service to you, Your Highness?"

Sierra turned her head toward that voice, bestowing her maid with a smile. She said, "No, Maria, although perhaps you could turn down the bed. I do plan to retire soon."

"Yes, Your Highness. It is a pretty sight, isn't it? The dusk, the sunset. How glad I am that you asked me to accompany you."

"Are you, Maria? You don't curse me for taking you away from the Continent? Away from your home in England?"

"Not at all, Your Highness. It has been many years since I was in England. Your home, I think, is now my own. Besides, one is seldom offered an opportunity to experience such an adventure as this. Think of it. You and I might be the first white females ever to see this West."

"Do you really think so?"

"I do. After all, look around you. 'Tis only men who staff these boats. 'Tis only men that we saw on the docks, men in the town, men on the outskirts of town. I would like to think of myself as a female adventurer. And Princess, you have given me the chance."

"What a wonderful thing to say, Maria. Even if you are only trying to set my mind at ease."

"But I do mean it."

"Thank you."

The two women fell silent then, until at last Maria ventured, "Was it difficult to see him again?"

"Him?" asked Sierra.

But Maria didn't answer, merely sent her mistress a look.

And letting out her breath, Sierra glanced away. "Yes," she admitted. "It was quite wearisome."

"I should think so," said Maria. "Has he changed much?"

"Not much," said Sierra, "except that he hates me."

"He? Hates you? By what right?"

"I don't know, Maria. I honestly do not know. Though I must admit I, too, found it rather shocking that he should feel so. Worse, however, is our present predicament. For we have no one to guide us."

"Yes," said Maria. "That is most unfortunate. Tell, me, do you have an idea where we should go? Where we might begin our search for the prince?"

Sierra shrugged. "A little. There is a fort I am told that is deep in Crow country. Perhaps we might start there."

Maria nodded.

"Maria, please, would you see if you can find Mr. Dominic and ask him to come to me? I know he has been reading as much as he can on subjects regarding the Indians and the West. Perhaps he might be able to help me plan our next step on our quest."

"Yes, Your Highness," said Maria, "that is a very good idea. I will leave at once to find him." And curtsying, she sped away to do as bid.

The twilight of dusk was finally settling down as the boat chugged its way into the deepest part of the river. It was slow going, and yet a breeze tugged at the tendrils of Sierra's hair.

She turned her face into that wind, bewailing her present situation.

Was he watching her, she wondered, even now as the ship pulled away? And if he were, did he, too, feel this gloomy sort of ache?

Probably not, she determined. After all, he had his hatred for her as a cold bedfellow. And if she were to be honest, so did she . . .

Divested of his clothing, except for a breechcloth, moccasins and his weapons, High Wolf basked in the retiring rays of the sunset. A scout traveled lightly, and with no more than his parfleche bag over his shoulder, High Wolf hid himself within the panorama of nature, invisible to even the most discerning eye.

He watched as the steamboat pulled out of port. He even surveyed the princess as she leaned against the upper deck of the boat, and despite himself, his heart fluttered in his chest.

She looked like some distant cameo, so beautiful, but so completely out of place, here in his home. And yet . . . Hadn't he dreamed of her coming here? Hadn't he wished it too many times to even count?

He supposed he was afraid of her in a way, and rightly so. If she had ruined his life so thoroughly in the past, what was she capable of doing now? Now, when they both were of an age to understand the physical allure of attraction?

Nevertheless, despite his misgivings, his purpose had at once been determined as soon as he had heard that she planned to seek the truth concerning the prince. It was interesting to think that both of their minds had been of the same set, neither of them believing the report of his death. One would almost think that both she and he were still very much attuned to one another's thoughts.

But of course they weren't.

However, her love for the prince must be very great, he thought, if she were this determined to discover his whereabouts.

Oh, if only she had ventured as much for him ten years ago. But, he reminded himself, he must not dwell on the past, for it was clear to him now that she had loved both of the men in her life at that time. What he hadn't realized was that she had been physically attracted to the prince.

Strange that he had never observed it in either her or the prince. But perhaps that sort of physical love hadn't materialized until after the marriage. After all, nearness was said to breed bodily love. Even his mother had once ventured to say as much.

High Wolf swallowed, hard. These thoughts would never do. More than anything, they troubled him further.

Shifting his weight, he surveyed the steamboat closely to determine its speed before he endeavored to set out his own trail. He would steer his path as close to the shoreline as he dared, so that he might keep a constant eye on that vessel. For yes, High Wolf would help her. But he would not go near her again.

This he vowed to himself.

Chapter 8

" 'Tis said she howled at the captain of the guard, and for nothing more than a tavern brawl. 'Tis little wonder that the prince stays away . . ."

"Aye. And 'tis rumored this is what started the war . . ."

Gossip between servants at
Prince Alathom's castle

It was high noon and the sun, bright on this warm day in June, beat down its heat upon the top of her bonnet, warming her head unnecessarily. The scent of smoke from the steamboat's engine filled Princess Sierra's lungs as she hung over the upper railing of the boat. Beside her, and secured to the deck with ropes, sat a white wooden lifeboat, looking as though it were in readiness to attend to any emergency. Glancing downward, she espied the churning water from the *Diana's* sidewheel, the noise from the wheel, as well as the spray of water attendant to it, having long ago become commonplace. She said, "I am told that the Missouri has been aptly called a river of sticks by Mr. George Catlin."

"Yes, I believe it has, Your Highness," said Mr. Dominic.

She paused. "It's quite easy to see why," she observed, strolling forward, along the deck and toward the bow of the ship. Once there, however, she paused to look ahead and down, staring out into the wild, seething and cloudy waters of the Missouri River, where there was nothing to be seen but one constant stream of current and obstacles, the hindrances composed mostly of tree limbs.

She stirred uneasily. Not even an eddy or a calm pool was to be found in any part of the river; nor was there anyplace where a vessel could rest or take leave of the unending flow, if only for a moment. With a sweeping gesture of her hand out in front of her, she continued, "Our journey was smooth and somewhat of a more pleasant nature until we reached the Missouri, but now it has become more difficult and, I must admit, more frightening."

"Yes, Your Highness, it has."

"Sometimes I wonder about our safety aboard this ship."

"One can understand that, Your Highness," said Mr. Dominic, her steward, as he followed her and stood to her left, though slightly behind her. "But be that as it may, these steamboats have travelled this river on several other trips and have made the journey to the various trading posts unharmed. Perhaps there have been a few incidents that I have read of, but none of a serious nature."

"Yes," she said. "Please refresh my memory, if you would, Mr. Dominic, and tell me when was it that Mr. Catlin made a similar journey to ours?"

"It was in 1832," said Dominic, "and he was a passenger aboard the first steamboat, the *Yellow Stone*, which made the journey all the way up the Missouri to Fort Union."

"Ah, yes, so it was. And where is this Fort Union, to be exact?"

"According to Mr. Catlin and our captain's statement, it is at the headwaters of the Yellow Stone River and the Missouri, very deeply situated in Indian country in the north."

"I see. And now, the most important question, Mr. Dominic: Do you think we'll find Prince Alathom there?"

"I cannot venture to speculate on that, Your Highness. But it is there where we will have a better chance of determining what we should do next. From what Governor Clark told you, it appears as if the prince was travelling with a band of Crow Indians, which means those Indians may have knowledge of him. And in Mr. Catlin's notes, he makes mention that he met Crow Indians at this fort."

Princess Sierra breathed in deeply, while she dabbed at a patch of perspiration on her brow. "Yes, Mr. Dominic. I only wish I knew these tribes a little better than I do. How are we ever to gain their confidence, in order to determine if they have knowledge of the prince? How are we even to communicate to them?"

"Perhaps we might hire someone at the fort to do it for us."

"Yes, perhaps." A light breeze, carrying a spray of mist, flew into her face, causing the princess to hold up her parasol, opening it wide. From this position, at the bow of the boat, the effects of the sun were not as persistently felt. Nonetheless, it did little to allay the effects of the heat. She said, "Perhaps we should retire to our quarters where we may read over that map which was given to us by Governor Clark."

"Yes, Your Highness."

"Though it is certainly hotter in our cabins than it is out here, even considering the sun."

"Yes. At least out in the open, there is some hope of a breeze, Your Highness."

"That is true. As long as this wind keeps up, the trip is perhaps a bit more bearable. I only hope that we do not get caught in yet another snag, as we did yesterday. Not only was our trip delayed, but the heat, without the chance of a draft, was almost too much to endure."

"That it was, Your Highness. One can always hope that we are delayed no further, but the river is cursed with fallen debris from the shores, and the trees' roots and limbs mar the way."

"Yes, I know. It is monstrously wild, this place. And yet . . ."

She gazed out toward the shore. "How large these cottonwood trees are that guard the shoreline, and how cool their shade might be if ever we could stop and partake of it."

"Yes, I believe you are right, Your Highness."

She fidgeted and looked away, glancing forward once more. "But such is not to be, since there is no spot on this river to rest . . . and all because of this incessant current." Sierra raised her head up at an angle as she said, "Did you inquire of the captain when we might be able to set ashore?"

"Yes, I have, Your Highness, but he forbids it at present. Although the captain did say that once we reach the northernmost regions of the river, the sticks and snags should not be so numerous, and the journey should be made more easily. I believe that at that time there might, therefore, be a chance to set ashore."

"That would be well, Mr. Dominic, very well, indeed, for I would love to walk among those cottonwood trees. They quite remind me of a park, so regal do they appear."

"But that appearance is deceiving, Your Highness. They are very dangerous."

"Dangerous?"

"Yes, Your Highness. I have been told that Indians often hide themselves in groves such as those, and some of the tribes are hostile to us."

"Yes, yes, of course. So I, too, have heard." Sierra turned her attention onto other things, and said, "Tell me, did the captain say anything else about the river, once we reach its northern outlets?"

"No, Your Highness, he did not. But Mr. Catlin has many things to say about it in his notes, I believe. Would you like me to relate to you what he writes about that region?"

"Yes, do go on, please."

Mr. Dominic cleared his throat. "I believe, if I recall rightly, that Mr. Catlin observed that the northern shores of the Missouri River were the most picturesque of all, and he compared them to a fairyland."

"Did he?"

"Yes, Your Highness. Perhaps we have only to endure these snags awhile longer and pray that we reach those more enjoyable parts of the river as quickly as possible."

"Yes," said Sierra. "Perhaps we should do that. Mr. Dominic, did you see that?"

"What, Your Highness?"

"There, on the shore. I saw a movement." She pointed toward it. "Do you see it?"

Her steward gazed in the direction she indicated and squinted at the place. However, at some length, he observed, "It is no more than a wolf, Your Highness. And though it might do damage to us were we on that shore, it is surely no threat to us here. Look, there above it." He pointed to a cliff that overlooked the shoreline. "There are mountain goats and antelope atop that bluff. Do you see them?"

Sierra squinted. "Yes, yes, I do."

"They seem quite unconcerned about that wolf below them. And I daresay, if they have no fear for their own safety, I believe that we are in no harm, either."

"Yes, Mr. Dominic, I'm sure you're correct, though we could hardly be likened to mountain goats." She grinned. "It's all very strange, isn't it?"

"Strange, Your Highness?"

"There's a beauty to this place. A beauty so unlike anything on the Continent that one can hardly compare the two. It's a wild sort of charm, to be sure, the stuff of which I've never seen until this moment, and yet . . . Look before us, in all directions, there seem to be hundreds of rolling hills and valleys and ravines to please the eye. And they are so green. Alas, they look as though Nature herself is a caretaker, for the hills look manicured. Tell me, Mr. Dominic, is this what is called the prairie?"

"Yes, Your Highness, I believe that it is."

"Fascinating, isn't it? Have you noticed that here and there are patches of blue, pink or yellow amongst all the green? What do you suppose they are?"

"Wildflowers, Your Highness?"

"Yes, yes, of course. They would have to be wildflowers. I had no idea flowers would bloom in such profusion, and without extraordinary care."

"It is something to behold, is it not, Your Highness?"

"Hmmm. And yet, look, over there, before us is another sight. Is that cliff there made of clay deposits, do you believe? Look at all the colors in the soil."

"It is quite something for the eyes, that is to be sure. I read of this in Mr. Catlin's notes, too, but I never thought to behold it myself."

"Yes, and over there." She pointed. "Do you see it? There, amongst all the rocks? It could be a castle. And over there, a fortress."

"Yes, Your Highness. If my studies are correct, I might venture to say that these formations have been formed by the constant stress of the river's current, and also by frosts and rains. These 'ruins' that we see are perhaps thousands of years old."

She paused for several moments before at last muttering, "Thousands of years old. Amazing. And to think we are amongst the first white people to see them."

The observation must have alit upon some truth, for both parties became silent, as if lost in thought. At length, however, Princess Sierra spoke up again, saying, "The scenery is quite something, but come, let us retire to our rooms that we might peruse that map once more. I would desire to have some knowledge of where it is that we go."

"Yes, Your Highness," said Mr. Dominic, bowing slightly at the waist as his mistress turned and took a few steps forward. But before she could go too far away, he said, "Perhaps I could find some refreshment for Your Highness while you read over the map."

"Ah, refreshments. Yes, Mr. Dominic, that would be quite in order, I believe. Thank you."

And as Mr. Dominic retreated to the kitchens, Princess Sierra found her step to be a bit more lively as she strolled toward her room. Perhaps there was something to be said for the beauty of this land.

Perhaps . . .

A shadow crept over the water, moving steadily forward. It was looking for something, or someone. But what? Or rather, who?

Albeit, such a romantic opinion of the land was short-lived, to be sure; a mere illusion. By evening, Princess Sierra was once again to be found on deck, leaning against the railing, gazing down into the depths of the muddy and frightening waters of the Missouri River.

The boat was in readiness to move into position for its nightly mooring, and every voyageur was involved in the process of maneuvering the *Diana* through the heavy currents of the river. Perhaps that was why the air was heavy with smoke, much more so than usual. Or perhaps it had something to do with the wind, which had shifted from the west to the north.

Dusk had yet to fade into darkness. Indeed, it was still quite light out, despite the fact that the sun was ever so gradually setting. Odd how the land picked up the pink and golden hues of the sky at sunset, the land magnifying the sunset's intensity by creating the illusion that sky and land were one and the same. It gave a body the feeling of space, as though a person's troubles gained room, moving away and dissipating.

But Sierra's problems were far too large for the simple act of gaining space to solve them. The rift between herself and the prince, between herself and High Wolf, was too immense to make the grievance so easily resolved.

Still, glancing away from the sunset, she brought her sights back to the water, noticing how even the river mirrored the sky; the pinks, the blues, the golden hues. For a moment, if a moment only, these sights gave her peace.

Leisurely, she glanced toward a large stick, which had become caught up in the current, the force of the river itself spinning it, making the stick look as though it were dancing . . . as though it might be a dancer.

It reminded her of another place, another time . . . a happier time. And without consciously wishing it, she remembered . . .

Wide-eyed, Sierra Morena Colheart watched the toy ballet dancer spin in time to the tinkling strain of the music box. She stared at the miniature dancer, fascinated, until the music at last slowed and the dancer stopped. Glancing up at herself in the mirror, the sixteen-year-old princess smiled at her own image; her grin, young and fresh, was full of vigor. Indeed, it was the giddy gesture of a young woman in love.

Ah, she thought. Tonight was the night. Tonight it would happen. Dreamy-eyed, she stared out her window, only to witness the reddish rays of the setting sun.

Goodness, how long had she sat here, lost in thought? What was the time? Was it already half past six, the scheduled time she was to meet High Wolf? Was he even now awaiting her in their own secret place?

Glancing at the grand, old clock in the corner of her room, she realized she was "going before herself again," as High Wolf had often said of her, which meant, she supposed, that she was living in the future instead of the present. The clock read only a quarter to five.

Still, she had much to do to prepare for the evening. Where was her maid?

Arising from her seat at the vanity, Sierra felt the urge to run to the rope that would summon Maria. But instead, she cautioned herself into taking steps that were as precise and dignified as her anxious heart would allow. But even then, a silent voice reprimanded:

"A monarch never hurries. Others will wait. You must learn, Princess Sierra," purred Father Junipero, "to sweep into a room as though you own it, and everyone in it."

But sometimes, thought Sierra, she wished to simply let go of convention and formality. Wasn't that what High Wolf often did? And if there was one thing Princess Sierra desired more than anything, it was to do everything that High Wolf found exciting.

Still, the habits of the last sixteen years could hardly be ignored, and she walked as calmly as she could to her door, where she rang for her maid.

Almost at once, Maria knocked gently at the door.

"Yes, Maria, do come in."

Maria did as bid, bowing as she came farther into the room. "May I be of service, Your Highness?" *she asked.*

Sierra grinned. "Yes, you may, Maria. I need to dress for this evening, for it is to be a very special evening."

Maria nodded. "Yes, Your Highness. That it is," *she said.* "Have you thought of what you might wear? The yellow gown always looks well on you, as does the blue. Although since this is to be a special night, you might think of wearing the new gros de Naples gown. What do you think?"

"Hmmm. The gros de Naples, I think, but not the brown one. The pink one with the satin flowers and pearls. And of course I'll need my long gloves, the pink pair."

"Yes, Your Highness. The pink pair."

"Oh, Maria, think of it," *said the princess, holding up a pelisse robe to her bosom while she spun about in place.* "This is the night my engagement is to be announced. It is to be the best night of my life. I just know it. I can feel it."

Maria grinned back happily. "Yes, Your Highness," *she said matter-of-factly, and stepped to the closet, where she extracted a pair of white slippers.*

"The pink ones, please, Maria."

"Yes, of course," *said Maria, replacing the white pair.* "And your hair? Would you prefer ringlets at the side of your face, as you usually wear, or curls?"

"Ringlets, I believe, as well as . . ."

"Pearls?"

"Ah, yes, pearls. Pearls to ornament my hair tonight instead of a coronet or tiara."

"Yes, Your Highness. It will be beautiful. You will be beautiful."

"Do you really think so?"

"I do."

"But we must hurry, I think. I'm to meet with High Wolf and the prince before the ball, and I don't wish to be late."

"Heaven forbid, Your Highness."

For a moment, Sierra stopped, glancing askance at her maid. And then, without a word being spoken between the two of them, both females broke out in laughter.

Maria said, "I think the gentlemen will wait, do you not think so, also?"

"Yes," said Sierra. "I believe they would. But still, I would not cheat myself of a single moment that I might spend with High Wolf."

Maria smiled. "Ah, to be so much in love. I wish it were I."

"Someday it will be, Maria. But for now we must hurry."

"Yes, Your Highness. We must. Now, if you would be so kind as to be seated, I will begin work on your hair."

"Yes, Maria," said the princess, dutifully taking her place at the vanity. "Anything you say, Maria," she said, grinning widely and catching her maid's gaze before both young women succumbed once again to a fit of giggles . . .

"Princess Sierra? Your Highness, shall I turn down your bed?"

Sierra jumped, startled. Maria's voice, so close at

hand, awakened her from out of the past, but none too gently. She took a moment to compose herself before saying, "Ah, no, not yet, Maria. I think I may watch the sunset for a while tonight. For in truth, you caught me deep in thought."

"Did I?" said Maria. "I am so sorry. And yet, it is a beautiful sunset. I can easily see how one could get lost in it."

"Yes."

Maria hesitated, as though waiting for her mistress to say more, but when Sierra remained silent, Maria said, "If you don't mind, I believe I will go on below and prepare your bed anyway. Perhaps an early bed will refresh me."

"Yes," said Sierra. "That would be most advantageous. In the meanwhile, I think I'll go topside and have a talk with our captain about this journey and when we might at last arrive at our destination."

"Ah," said Maria, "that would be most opportune."

"Thank you, Maria."

"Yes, Your Highness," said Maria, and curtsying, she retreated.

But Sierra never did seek out the captain, nor did she change her position from against the rail. Too many thoughts had been brought back to mind; too many recollections were close to hand. And without consciously willing it, her mind replayed that most memorable night . . .

"My father said he would be announcing your engagement tonight," said Prince Alathom.

Both Sierra and High Wolf grinned at each other, while

High Wolf took her gloved hand in his, bringing it to his lips, where he pressed a kiss upon it. He said, "You are the most stunning creature in all the world."

Sierra blushed, then grinned and looked shyly away. She said, "There are many more young women who are prettier still than I. Many."

"Where?" said High Wolf. "Show them to me, for I do not think they exist."

Sierra merely smiled rapturously up at him while Prince Alathom groaned aloud, saying, "I'm going to have to teach you some new forms of flattery, my fine friend, for I tire of hearing the same things said over and over."

"Tire all you like," said High Wolf. "You may go elsewhere if you don't like it, for I speak only the truth as I see it."

Despite all her upbringing to the contrary, Princess Sierra giggled. Just then, as though in accompaniment to the merry sound of the three friends' laughter, the strains of violins and cellos reached out to them.

"Oh, High Wolf, Alathom, the dance begins," said Sierra. "And I am so very anxious to dance. Shall we go?"

"We shall," said High Wolf as he linked her arm with his, leaving Prince Alathom to follow along behind them, a circumstance to which the prince had never given objection.

"Alathom?" the princess called out over her shoulder.

"Yes?"

"Please, come up on the other side of me, that the three of us may enter into the room together and be announced at the same time."

And without another word, Prince Alathom did exactly as asked . . .

* * *

Loud bells rang out unpleasantly, interrupting her reminiscence. "*Fire!*"

What was that? Fire? Here? Now? Was that why there had been a smoke-heavy odor in the air?

"All hands on deck," rang out the call. "All hands on deck. Fire!"

Without further pause, what had once been a calm evening turned riotous. Men rushed by her, below her, above her. Horses whinnied in the haul, while the hogs shrieked.

Sierra stood still, frozen, watching, barely able to comprehend the danger as being real. It had seemed so quiet only a few moments previous. Where was Mr. Dominic? Where was Maria?

She needed to find them . . . now. Turning, she backed up from the railing, intent on running away. However, she did no more than set herself into the path of a voyageur, who had suddenly come upon her. Inadvertently, she knocked him to the deck.

"I'm so sorry," she said as she threw herself forward and out of the way. Quickly, she clung to the rail as the man jumped to his feet and sped away, all without uttering a word.

"Your Highness."

It was Mr. Dominic. Somehow he had found her.

"Your Highness, you must come this way." Taking hold of her elbow, he gestured toward his left. "I will see you safely into the lifeboat."

"A lifeboat?" Abruptly, the panic of those around her took substance, became more of a reality. Still, "Surely that's not necessary, is it? These men are undoubtedly able to put out a fire."

"That they probably are, Your Highness, but there is still danger in staying aboard. If the voyageurs do manage to put out the fire, you can always reboard. But first you must be safe."

"Do you know what has caused this?"

"Yes, Your Highness. The cotton being carried up-river caught fire, and has nearly consumed the lower level. It has been discovered too late, I fear. Now, come. There is no time to lose."

Taking her arm, he propelled her along with him as he fought his way toward the lifeboat, shoving through the hurrying crowd of voyageurs. Confusion reigned supreme, and men rushed by them with little regard to what they did, more times than not pushing Mr. Dominic and Sierra out of the way.

Within moments, although it seemed to Sierra to take a lifetime, the two caught a glimpse of the lifeboat. Through the haze of smoke, they could see that several other passengers were scrambling toward it.

Sierra stared around her, coughing as she inhaled soot and smoke. "Where is Maria?" she asked.

"I don't know," answered Mr. Dominic, "but I am certain she will find her way here on her own."

"Find her own way? . . . Mr. Dominic, do not lie to me. If she could easily come here, she would be here. Why is she not?"

Mr. Dominic didn't answer.

"There must be trouble, I fear. Please, you must go and see to her."

"I cannot, Your Highness. My first duty is to you, and we must get you quickly aboard this lifeboat, while there is still room aboard her."

"Yes, you are right, I must, but," said Sierra, "you will not stay with me a moment longer. You must go and find Maria."

"Your Highness," pleaded Mr. Dominic, "you must not ask me to desert you. It would cause me great alarm, for not only are you my first concern, I am duty-bound to your father, having promised him that I would not leave your side."

"Mr. Dominic, how could you promise my father such a thing?"

"It seemed little enough to ask."

"Yes, well, you can ease your mind, Mr. Dominic. You have done your duty. My father could not have foreseen all situations that would arise on this trip."

Mr. Dominic didn't answer.

"Do you not see? I cannot leave this vessel until I can determine what has happened to Maria. What if she has fallen somewhere? My mind would never rest easy if I saved myself and deserted her."

"But Your Highness—"

"It is either you go to see about her, or me."

Mr. Dominic looked uncertain.

"Man the lifeboat!"

Eyes wide, Sierra grabbed hold of Mr. Dominic's sleeve. She said, "Tell me, is there another lifeboat aboard this vessel?"

"No, there is not, Your Highness."

"Then you must leave this instant. You must find Maria, stay with her and keep her safe. Do you hear me? I will gladly step into this lifeboat, but not until you—"

Suddenly, Mr. Dominic bent over and picked her

up, setting her into the boat. Then, straddling one leg over the side of the boat, he began to climb into it.

But Sierra would have none of that. She jumped up from her seat, straddling the boat herself, her pose an obvious dare. She said, "I command you to find Maria this very instant. I would be of little help to her, as I cannot swim, but if you do not go, I will."

"Your Highness, please, I beg you. I . . ." Mr. Dominic trailed off his objection, looking, for all that he was big and muscular, as though he might wail. But at last he appeared to capitulate, releasing his straddle from the lifeboat.

"Now go!" It was Sierra commanding. "Before more time is wasted, go! I promise that I will ride this lifeboat to shore. Do not worry about me. I will await you both from the safety of the shoreline. Go quickly!"

Mr. Dominic looked as though he would raise yet another objection, but, as the flames climbed higher into the smoke-laden sky, and with little choice other than to obey his monarch, Mr. Dominic turned and fled in the direction of the maid's cabin.

Chapter 9

" 'Tis said she is the cause of our own prince's death."
"Aye," said the housemaid, "that she is. 'Tis ru-
mored as well that he died rather than return here to
her side."

Gossip between servants at
Prince Alathom's castle

At the first hint that something had gone amiss, High Wolf immersed himself in the waters of the river, and in doing so, became a part of the river, so much so that not even a swirl could be seen in the water to indicate his progress. Cautiously, he floated toward the ship, practically invisible. He didn't swim, nor did he float, but rather he executed what could only be described as a dance with the river's current. Never did he fight the river's power, but rather he moved with it, letting the water propel him closer to his target.

At last he came up close to the boat, himself a calm influence in comparison to the turmoil aboard the *Diana*. He could feel the terror there, sense the smoke-induced delirium of the boatmates, but it was not in his mind to aid these men. No, *she* was the reason he was here; he would find her.

Quickly, he perused the voyageurs, as well as the passengers who were still aboard the steamboat. Some of them were already jumping from the burning remnants of the boat, an action that could bring sorrow, unless a person either knew how to swim with the river's flow or was strong enough of body to fight it. But perhaps these men were that hardy, for these white voyageurs, who worked the boats, were sometimes admired for the physical marvels they could perform.

Alas, however, High Wolf saw nothing of *her*.

Making a quick circle around the boat proved to be a waste of time, for he still had not seen her. And so it was that he found himself with little choice but to board the boat. Quickly, he hoisted himself up to the main deck, coming down flat-footed and at a run, aware as he did so that the steamboat was sinking, and with the majority of the *Diana*'s body enveloped in flames, there was little to be done for her. As it was, her lower deck was flooded, and in places already half submerged.

Still, without losing more than an instant, he found his way around the decks, until as he rounded a corner, something large and heavy fell into the water, creating a terrific splash. But the gray mist of smoke hung heavy over his eyes, and High Wolf found he could see but little.

Swiftly, he trod closer, and looking toward the spot, High Wolf recognized the cause at once: a smaller boat; one he knew to be a lifeboat, had been thrown into the rushing current.

Suddenly, things became worse: A piece of wood from above, engulfed in flames, broke off the *Diana*'s main hull and fell, streaking, toward the water. And before anyone knew what it was about, the wood, now a flaming dagger, struck the lifeboat. In moments, the boat tipped off balance, catching fire.

A feminine scream split the air, its intensity piercing High Wolf like a knife. Bodies dove off the life boat, but not one of these people was female. Where was she?

And then, through the soot-induced haze, he saw her, still aboard the blazing lifeboat, her countenance oddly composed. For she didn't move, not even to save herself.

What was wrong with her? Was she frozen in place from shock and fear? Although it seemed impossible, he knew that sometimes these things could happen to a person.

Or was the problem something else? Was it her outrageously full dress? Was she afraid, with so much weight upon her, that she might sink, becoming entangled in its mass?

But if that were true, she was surely acting in a poor manner to solve the problem, for she did not remove any of her clothing, or take any action to save herself. Instead, amid the ballet of diving bodies, the princess slowly sank along with the boat.

Quickly, High Wolf plunged into the Missouri's depths, then came up for breath and caught his bearings. But she was gone, swallowed up by the muddy, swirling waters of the Missouri. That's when it occurred to him:

Could she swim?

It seemed amazing to him that he had no answer to that; he, who should know her well. Instinctively,

High Wolf swam toward the place he had last seen her, and diving deeper into the water, hunted for her, but not with his eyes, for the murky waters of the Missouri did not allow sight for more than a few feet.

No, he searched for her intuitively, spiritually, and in doing so, found her within seconds. But he had no time in which to experience relief. Grabbing hold of her, he kicked out hard, bringing her up with him to the river's surface, forcing her head above water, where he heard her gasp for breath. She struggled, and down they both went once more.

He kept hold of her with one arm, while with his other hand, he took out his knife, and then he did the unthinkable. As quickly as the water would allow him, he cut off her dress.

In response, she mustered a formidable response. Whereas before he'd seen little life in her, she now fought him with renewed strength, as though he were some sort of madman, or perhaps she, a madwoman. But High Wolf didn't have time or even the ability under water to explain his actions, and despite her best efforts, he continued cutting away until the dress was removed and the danger had passed.

The weight of her dress fell away. That this left her in nothing more than her calf-length drawers, hose and corset was hardly discreditable, for she was still almost fully covered.

But their commotion under water had sunk them too low, and an undertow grabbed hold of them. Quickly, he seized her around the chin, and with mighty strokes, fought his way to the surface of the water, not stopping until he heard her sputter.

At least she was still breathing.

He caught his breath, feeling somewhat safer, now that their heads were above the water's surface, and he called out, "Do not fight the river's current, or me, because if you do, this river will claim us. You must become composed." He spoke loudly, but calmly, as though the two of them were taking a stroll, instead of fighting for their lives. He continued, "You must become one with the water, for if you do, it will protect you."

But she appeared to be beyond listening, and she fought him with revitalized vigor.

Once again, he called out, "Cease your struggles, or you will force me to bind you, so that you do not drown us both."

But she was obviously unused to the water, and in the end, he had to use brute strength against her, holding her arms and legs with one each of his own. Meanwhile, he kept afloat, lugging her with him and letting the water carry them back to shore.

After a few moments, she came suddenly alive and howled at him, "I can't breathe," and she struggled once more. "You . . . you're drowning me."

"I am not drowning you; you are doing it to yourself. Cease your struggle and merge your body with mine. I will not let you drown."

"And who will keep you afloat?"

"The water, of course. I have no fear of the water, for I become as one with it. Only those who fight the river's power ever come to harm in it."

"But—"

"Do you see that you are talking? That you have energy enough to yell at me?"

"I . . . I . . ."

All at once, she ceased her struggle. In truth, his words must have had effect, for she at last let her body meld with his, allowing him to repeat his earlier dance with the river's current, shoving off here, letting the stream take him there, forging through the water as easily as if he were picking his way across lily pads.

It took little time before they were set ashore, appearing, to anyone who might have been looking, that the river had lovingly placed them there.

At once, High Wolf left the water, and with her tucked under his arm, crept into the protection of the bush, where he granted her a moment to catch her breath.

But, alas, a moment was all he could afford.

Staring out toward the vestiges of the boat, at the brightly burning embers, Sierra thought for a moment she saw a hooded figure, cloaked in black, moving through the smoke. Warily, she rubbed her eyes. But when she opened them, it was gone.

It must have been a figment of her imagination, a result of her near brush with death.

But, if not that, if she were here, alive and well, what about her friends? Her maid and servant? *Dear Lord, were they safe?*

Glancing toward High Wolf, she ordered, "You must go back!"

The command had been spoken more harshly than need be, but at present, Sierra could hardly consider such things.

But High Wolf did not deign to answer at once, and in a voice louder still, she once more commanded, "You must save the others!"

But if he heard her, High Wolf ignored her, except to indicate with hand signs that she should cease talking.

How rude! Cease to communicate at a time like this?

How dare he pay her no heed. Did he not remember who she was?

Unused to her wishes going unfulfilled, she charged him again, only this time she practically yelled the words, "You are to go back, Mr. High Wolf! Now!"

But instead of sending him into action, her words acquired his anger instead, and without another moment to be gained, he took hold of her arm, and with one hand, jerked her to him impolitely. Then, with no ceremony whatsoever, he clapped his other hand over her mouth. His warm body pressed up against her own caused a degree of pleasure to shoot through her that was simply not to be borne.

The strap of his parfleche bag bit into her chest and Sierra squirmed. She attempted to scream, too; even tried biting that hand, but without any success. He held her so tightly that she could not even kick him.

How impertinent. How demeaning. How close he was to her . . .

She ground her teeth together in frustration. Why would he not let her speak? Surely, there was little need for silence. After all, there was noise enough from the effects of the fire, from the struggles of the men. Indeed, that clamor alone would drown out the sound of her voice, if that were truly a concern.

However, High Wolf seemed loath to share her viewpoint, and, rough-handling her to keep her quiet, he effectively gagged her with one hand, freeing his other hand momentarily to motion her again to silence.

What nerve! What daring! He, thinking to command her?

It was not to be endured. Thusly, taking advantage of his loosening grip, she bit down hard on that hand, gaining a moment to command, "I charge you to get back to that boat, Mr. High Wolf! Do you not understand? My maid, my steward are still there!"

However, her antics produced the wrong kind of effect, and he not only frowned, but worse: She gained his utter contempt. His lip curled, his eyes spit indignation, and in his regard was disgust.

Sierra, however, little cared what he thought at the moment, and her own reaction was to stick her nose into the air.

But at last he decided to speak out, and though his voice was no more than a whisper, he managed to utter, "If you say another word aloud, I will gag you. Do you understand?"

She opened her mouth, but when he leaned over her, leering at her, she closed it.

"The steamboat under fire will attract attention from neighboring tribes," he continued in that same low, mocking voice, "and some of these Indians are not friendly toward either you or me."

"Do you think I care about Indians at a time like this? How can I sit safely ashore, while my friends and the others are in danger? And you shall not thwart me, Mr. High Wolf. If you cannot be coerced to save them, then stand aside, that I might. For I, at least, shall do all that is within my power that I might save them, and now."

High Wolf rolled his eyes. "An enlightening speech, to be sure. But no, you will not. Nor will I," he said. "Your steward is strong enough to fight the current.

You will not embarrass him by sending me to save him, or going after him yourself."

"But—"

It was all she dared utter, for with a devilish grin, High Wolf increased his hold on her with one hand, while he reached into a pouch tied to his side with his other, producing a wet strip of rawhide. Merrily, he waved it in front of her.

Sierra snorted, tossing her head to the side to keep from looking at him. However, she kept wisely quiet.

But High Wolf seemed to have missed the point altogether, and before she could inquire as to what he was about, he fell to his knees, bringing her with him.

She opened her mouth to utter a protest, gaining a mouth full of mud for her efforts. But no sooner had she started sputtering out the unsightly dirt, than he shoved her onto her stomach. At the same time, he, too, fell forward, onto his forearms and stomach, and then, without so much as a by-your-leave, began to belly crawl through the bush, clearly expecting her to do the same.

"Argh!" The sound escaped her throat quite involuntarily. Nevertheless, at the noise, High Wolf sent her a glance, and she would have had to be dead to miss his opinion of her. Contempt—most passionately displayed—was emblazoned upon his countenance. Again, he motioned her to silence, sending her as stern a look as he had yet to muster.

She opened her mouth, but High Wolf, sitting up, turned around and, taking hold of her, jerked her to him, hauling her forward. And whatever she would have said was lost to the grass and dirt beneath her. She came up onto her elbows choking out mud, and would have gladly told him exactly what she thought of him. However, the words died in her throat. Once more, he was leaning over, waving that silly rawhide in her face . . .

. . . And didn't stop waving it until it became evident she would remain mute. Only then did he face forward once more, coming back onto his belly, and crawling over the loose soil and tall grass. Slowly, inch by inch, using only one forearm and his chest to propel him, he kept his other arm thrown around her waist. He pulled her along with him, forcing her to move in the same way as he was. And, make no mistake, there was no pleasure to be had in either her position or in his embrace.

Pleasure? She sneered. How could there be such a thing as pleasure, when sand tore under her fingernails? When plants and sticks pricked and scratched her as he tugged her along? When her clothes, wet and cold, hindered and chilled her until her flesh had become a mass of goose bumps?

Trembling, she became acutely aware of the earthy odor of mud, soil and sand under her nose, as well as the aromatic smells of the river and those of the prickly bush. And heaven help her, all these scents clung not only to her, but to the air around her, making her feel as though she might surely swallow the odious stench.

Her hair was another problem, her coiffure having long ago come loose from its pins. It was at present hanging down over the front of her shoulders, hindering her. But her arms were not free to take care of the problem, and alas, each movement pulled on the length of it, sending shooting pains through her.

"What are you doing?" she finally spit out at him, though she was careful to speak in no more than a harsh whisper.

"Keeping us alive."

"I don't see that—"

He turned back to her, and twisting around, whispered harshly, "If you say one more word, I will silence you in a way you will not like."

"Is that a threat? How dare you speak to me in such a high-handed—"

She might have protested more, had she had the leisure to do so, but before she could say another word, he was pushing her backward, his body coming down to spread entirely over hers. She gasped, but the sound was lost beneath his hand. And then he did the unthinkable: He rolled over her, bringing her up and on top of him. Then again he rolled, and she was on the bottom; then on top, the entire process repeated until he had managed to maneuver them both into a small gully. When at last they lay still, he was once again positioned over her—that darned hand of his still covering her mouth.

She gagged. Muck and grimy sand clung to her clothes, her lips, the inside of her mouth, her hair. But this was the last detail that seeped into her consciousness. In truth, at this moment, Sierra forgot to breathe.

And though High Wolf immediately rose up on his elbows and set to work, pulling branches, leaves, small shrubs, anything available, over them to give them cover, he was much too close to her. In truth, he was so very close, she could witness every single pore on his face and breathe in the masculine scent that clung to his body. And despite herself, she swayed in closer.

Her heartbeat quickened, her eyes went wide, and she stared up into the dark depths of High Wolf's regard, feeling as though she were a rabbit in this man's lair. It was an agonizing moment, for she was more than aware that there was scarce clothing between them; she, in the thin material of her drawers and corset; he, in little more than breechcloth, moccasins and his weapons. Except for the strap of his parfleche, which angled over his chest, she could feel the hard angles of him fitting perfectly into her own soft curves.

A shiver took hold of *his* body, and conversely, she felt it to the depth of *her* being. Her heart pounded loudly in her ears, and slowly, so slowly that she barely noticed it, his grip over her mouth slackened, and a softness took hold of his expression. It was a look she remembered well: a demeanor that said he adored her.

Unreasonably, she felt as though she were an adolescent again, an adolescent with nothing on her mind but this man.

His hand fell away from her mouth, an action that brought too clearly to mind the fact that they were much too closely bound, and that she could too easily feel every motion of his chest. Even the simple act of breathing in and out became seduction. And they stared at one another, as though each one were hungry for the simplest of things: a mere touch, a passionate look. In truth, despite the chill in the air, Sierra felt so suddenly warm, she became certain that a fire had been lit within her.

No. This could not be. How could she react this way?

Yet, despite all logic, Sierra felt as though her spirit met with High Wolf on some mystic level that belied their physical existence. In truth, if she were to be honest, it had always been like this with them.

At that moment, something stirred in the bushes above them, and though it was barely perceivable—for High Wolf did not take his gaze from hers—Sierra sensed his attention shift away from her, to be centered on their environment. Illogically, she felt the loss of his regard as deeply as if she were losing the man all over again.

She wanted it back. She wanted him back.

The realization startled her, and she mentally scolded herself. This was not right. It could not be right.

Sierra exhaled forcefully. If these were her reactions to High Wolf, in so short a space of time, she must be careful to wield extreme caution with him in the future, and she must command herself to think and to respond more exactly as she had planned when she had first conceived the idea of venturing into the American West. For of one thing she was certain: She could not, she would not, allow this man back into her life, back into her heart.

Warily, she watched High Wolf draw in a breath as he lifted a hand and brought it down to her face. Lightly, he touched her chin, and she closed her eyes against the sensation sweeping over her, willing herself to feel nothing.

But alas, the attempt was in vain.

And she wondered, what sort of magic did High Wolf possess that he could start afresh with her? As though the last ten years had never been?

Well, she wanted nothing to do with it. What was more, she would ensure she had nothing to do with it, and opening her eyes, she tried to release her chin from his grip. But he held on tightly. And slowly, he commandeered her attention, turning her head and forcing her to look up toward a spot he was indicating. Unwillingly, because she had no choice, she lifted her lashes and gazed off where he pointed. And she gasped.

There above them and on all sides were Indians!

Sucking in her breath, she would have screamed aloud from shock alone, but the cry never had a chance to take form. High Wolf's head had come down to hers and his mouth covered her lips before a sound ever issued forth. Alas, he was there, kissing her, silencing not only any noise she would have made, but also any attempt at protest at what he did.

But would she have objected?

Perhaps at first. However, when the kiss lingered, her body reacted against her will, and a surge of energy swept over her, weakening her . . . making her feel giddy. For a moment, if a moment only, her world rocked off balance, changing her conception of time and space, distorting it. And whereas before she had been viewing this man from the present moment only, her past came back to engulf her unmercifully. And despite herself, she melted into High Wolf's embrace.

It was as though time had turned back on her, and she was again sixteen and he, eighteen. Of their own will, her arms wound around his bare neck, drawing his naked chest closer to her. Forget the past. Forget the present. For a moment out of time, he was hers to love, to nurture, to adore all over again.

Perhaps he was experiencing the same effect, she thought, for even as she surrendered to him, his lips prodded hers open and his tongue swept into her mouth, where he took what was given so very, very gladly. Indeed, whatever thoughts there had been of betrayal, of disloyalty, whether hers or his, were forgotten. It was as though none of it had ever happened. And for a very short space of time, her world, perhaps his, too, was as it used to be, as it should have been.

Swish! Thunk! Swish! Swish!

The sounds of arrows being let loose filled the air above them. Even still, it took them both a moment to recover. True, he drew up and away from her slightly, allowing them both a tiny bit of space. But his gaze still lingered over her, his eyes passionately boring into hers as if the two of them had been disturbed in the act of making love, not merely kissing.

And Sierra would not have been female had she not responded in kind. *She wanted more.*

She parted her lips, not to speak, but in open invitation. And he gazed at them, at her, as though he were a man demented.

And then something changed between them. It was a very fine alteration, to be sure. But whereas before he had appeared to be unable to withhold himself from her, he now couldn't put enough distance between them.

And it didn't take a genius for her to realize that *he had not meant to kiss her.*

All at once, the past fell back into place, while Sierra plummeted into the present, and in doing so, she swallowed hard, closing her eyes.

How could it have happened? How could she have

let it happen? It wasn't as though the conditions surrounding them invited a renewal of their love. Far from it.

Danger encircled them. Not only in the form of the fire from the boat or a watery grave, but from Indian warriors.

Yet passion had found them, as though only their love and the two of them were real, not their environment.

Slowly, she released her breath. It changed nothing, of course. She still hated him, and if she were honest, she would admit that within his look dwelt what must surely be a hardy degree of loathing for her.

And yet . . . deep within her was a memory . . . a memory of a love that had once been so powerful, she had been willing to throw away most everything dear to her: her family, her friends, even her life as a princess.

But, as she had done in the past, so, too, did she come to understand that High Wolf could not have experienced the same feeling for her. Obviously. He had left her, completely, utterly, and with total disregard.

She must never lose sight of that fact. Not now. Not ever. As long as she lived.

Chapter 10

I hold you in my arms and whisper this:
You are my one true love. And then we kiss . . .
Excerpted from a poem by David Ziff
"Sonnets to a Soul Mate"

All was quiet until, off in the distance, came a blood-curdling scream, followed by the clash of knife against knife, the swish of arrows, the thrashing of water, the thud of an arrow finding its target; grunts, groans, even hysterical laughter.

Coming up, onto his knees, High Wolf peeked out cautiously from his position within the coulee. Quickly, he glanced around the environment. The enemy had moved out, swarming into the water and swimming out to join the fight. At the moment, both he and the princess were hidden by the branches and the scrub brush he had placed over them. But it would afford them precious little cover against the enemy if the princess should speak out again. Or worse, if she should cry out in alarm.

For the time being, however, they were safe. Horrible as it was, the fight gave him a few moments of reprieve. Moments he should use to his advantage.

Sierra shivered, and sitting up, High Wolf took her in his arms. But even this seemed to bring her little comfort, and he began to fear that there would be little he could do to disguise her fright from any perceptive warrior.

There was only one thing for him to do: He must secure a better hiding spot immediately, one that might mask Sierra's alarm, were she to make some unknowing error. For if there were a scout with that war party—and High Wolf knew that chance was high—a scout would sense her panic and would not rest until he discovered its source.

Saaaa, he had little time, which meant he must work fast, securing them a place before that fight ended. Swiftly, High Wolf squatted back down into the coulee, and motioning to Sierra, gave her to understand that they were to leave—at once. Crawling out of the shelter first, he ensured it was safe before pulling Sierra up next to him. And even then he held her body down, close to the ground, until they were both lying flat out upon their stomachs. With another series of small, quick hand motions, he let her know that she was to do whatever he asked of her.

She opened her mouth, as though she might protest, but High Wolf sat up and reached out, and taking her lips between two of his fingers, closed them, effectively silencing her.

Shaking his head, he swept his right hand out in an arc to the right, the Indian gesture for "no." And then he fell to the ground, where he proceeded to inch forward, toward the river. However, she held herself away from him, tapping him on the back. And sitting up, she refused to go forward, expressing herself with a series of gestures. To that end, she waved her hands in the air. A mistake. Quickly, he reached out to halt their movement.

Though he knew she could little understand it, a good scout would be able to sense such wild motions, and had it not been for the skirmish all around them, she could have betrayed them.

There was no time to explain, if, indeed, he ever would. For the secrets of the scouts died with the scout.

No, he would have to force her to do his bidding, at least this once, if only because their lives depended on it. Later, perhaps, he might try to bring her to understanding. Maybe . . .

Wrapping his arm around her waist, he held her to the ground, and using his forearm alone, forced her to scoot along with him toward the river. For it was the river, he realized at last, that would be their escape.

They had no more than reached the shores of the Missouri when the battle stopped. Suddenly all became quiet.

High Wolf paused. He had hoped to float some distance from the scene while the fight was still in progress, thus masking their exodus. However, that option ceased with the ending of the battle, for, although alone he could have easily slipped away from the enemy, the princess did not know how to disguise her movements. Not only would her awkwardness alert the very perceptive scout, but also any warrior, as well.

What he needed was a different plan. Glancing

around, he could see that there was little but scrub brush for cover, except for an old, dead tree stump that was half submerged by the river. It stood perhaps seven feet tall and was about four feet across, being of the large cottonwood variety. High Wolf could easily discern that it had been hit by lightning, perhaps as long ago as five years. The force of the natural blast had split the tree in half, with part of its body falling off to the left, while the other section had dropped into the water, remaining there to rot.

But the center of that tree still stood and might be large enough to house two people—at least temporarily. The only problem was that the tree was partially immersed in the river. And while this might be of little consequence to High Wolf, he doubted that the princess would appreciate it.

Still, it afforded them a good cover, for the trunk of the tree would filter any movement, perhaps mask any sound that she made, also. Grabbing her again around the waist, he slunk toward the tree, and bringing her in close to him, whispered, "We will hide in that tree, but once inside, you must not make any movement, none at all. For anything you do will be carried by the water in concentric circles. It will also be sensed by their scout, and we will be too easily discovered, I fear."

"What tree?"

He pointed.

"But it . . . it's half flooded. There's no telling what animals have nested there, and I'm afraid of—"

"It is our best cover," he said. "And I will be there with you. Now, quiet, we must not speak again, for the erratic motions made by the battle have almost disappeared, and any other movement will be sensed."

"But—"

He placed his hand over her mouth before returning to the ground, and as quickly as possible, while still gripping her around the waist, he slid toward the tree. At the river's edge, he stopped briefly to pick her up in his arms, a necessity, since he did not trust her to leave no imprints in the sand.

Thusly, stalking much like a heron, he trod toward the tree until he could position himself on the side that faced away from the battle. Next he squatted down, sliding his arms and hands entirely around her buttocks, and without a word being said, he hoisted her up, over the highest part of the trunk and into the hollowed-out base, leaving no imprint of a climb into the tree.

"Stay here and do not move," he said softly. "I will go and erase our tracks."

"But there might be animals in here. High Wolf, please I—"

"I will be but a moment."

"But—"

"If you are afraid, stand toward the middle once inside the trunk."

"Yes," she said, "All right."

And then he was gone, heading back through the brush, erasing all signs of their progress, his mind half on what he was doing, half on remembering the impression of her soft and rounded rump within his grasp. Indeed, his hands still ached with the feel of her, his body wanting more.

But he suppressed the desire. This was not the time or the place, and she was not the right woman.

Or was she?

It took him little enough time to erase their tracks and to return to Sierra, and in less time than it takes to tell it, he had already climbed into the tree.

There was barely room for the two of them. She was standing within the center of the tree, and she was shivering. However, he was glad to note that the water rose only to knee level, and squatting down, his back against the trunk, he let out his breath, relieved for the moment. In faith, he had been apprehensive that the water would be too deep, forcing the two of them to either cling to the sides of the tree, or to tread water—both scenarios would attract attention.

Feeling a trifle more secure, he at last gave the princess his full attention, only to become alarmed. She trembled violently, an action that might send out waves in the water, or worse, motion waves through the air that would be sensed by the war party's scout.

Coming up onto his knees, he reached out toward her and did the only thing he could think of: Slowly, he turned her around, and taking her in his arms, he pulled her back against him, placing her body between his legs while he squatted down, his rear and backbone against the tree. He let her crouch down so that her knees lay flat against the river bottom, supporting her weight. Then he brought his arms around her waist, while her head fit into the crook of his neck.

It was an impossible situation, an impossible position.

She was literally flattened against him, and he was

wet; she was wet. Worse, the thin material from her clothes did little to hide her rounded curves, not only from his gaze, but from his touch. Alas, the two of them might as well have been sitting there together, entirely nude.

Against his better judgment, he noted little things about her. Her skin was as soft as doeskin; her nipples were hard, rounded peaks that thrust out away from him as though begging him for a touch. And how he longed to satisfy them.

But he could not.

Her scent filled his nostrils, while her hair tickled his nose pleasantly, and his head spun with longing. How long could he endure this?

Forget that he was a scout, a man who could survive hardships that could send another man into insanity; forget that he could best a raging river, a blizzard, a natural disaster, with little or no discomfort. All these were as nothing when compared with the control required to simply keep his hands away from her.

But perhaps this state was only natural. For despite the treacherous nature of this woman, his dreams had been filled with her image these past ten years. And, truth to tell, he was finding that, to his utter shame, his dreams had done her beauty little justice.

Worse, of its own accord, his body was answering her unspoken allurement, even to the extent that the frosty nature of the water had little effect on him. Alas, the gradual stiffening in his groin was becoming more of a problem than it should have been.

However, his only choice at this time seemed to be to sit still and endure it . . . and above all things, keep his hands to himself. But it was a difficult thing to do, particularly when her backside was thrust up so intimately against him. Alas, had his discipline been any less, he might have succumbed to her charm. Strict training, however, kept him quiet, and in control.

At that moment, she moved slightly, snuggling even more deeply into his embrace, her head coming back to rest on his shoulder. And without thought, he pulled her in closer.

She was either freezing, frightened or both. Her body still shook, and he realized it would be his task to urge some heat into her, lest her trembling lead another to them.

And so it was to this end that he gently kissed the top of her head, one more kiss, then another, all the while cradling her to him as a mother would for a child, or perhaps as a husband would for a wife.

A wife . . .

The thought was alarming, not because of the nature of it, but because at one time, he had so much wanted this woman to be exactly that.

Quickly, he put the thought from him. He could ill afford the kind of reaction that idea might likely bring him . . . not at a time like this.

He needed to think of something else. But most of all, he needed to *do* something else. And so it was that he concentrated on what he should have been doing all along. Ignoring his physical difficulties, he tuned his senses in to the environment, and as he did so, he felt the disturbance in nature, for the war party was headed back to shore.

Discipline had his body stiffening without his conscious thought, preparing him for a fight, and in consequence, his hold on Sierra became tighter still. Now would come the test. Although their hiding place should keep them invisible, it might not escape notice from their scout.

Would they go free? Or would they be discovered, the princess captured and himself killed . . . ?

Holding her securely, he said a silent prayer.

Sierra felt something swim by her legs, and startled, she trembled. But her fear was misplaced. It was only a fish. Her action, however, earned her a tighter embrace from High Wolf.

But make no mistake, she was frightened. There was no need to tell her that their chance of survival this night might be slim. Even *she* could hear the warriors' retreat, as they passed them by on their way to shore.

Closing her eyes, she turned her face into High Wolf's shoulder, afraid, as she had never been afraid in her life. Although, oddly enough, High Wolf's embrace did offer some comfort. At least enough solace so that she was able to think of something else besides death, and she listened intently for any clues as to what might be taking place outside the tree stump.

But alas, once the main party of warriors had passed by them, the only things she could sense were the different sounds that were common to the night. The crickets, the river as it rolled steadily along, as though it were oblivious to the fate of man.

And then the night became quieter still. Too quiet.

Had the Indians gone? Or were they still out there, lingering, waiting?

Sierra's heart pounded in her ears, her breathing fast, hard. She didn't speak, she didn't move, though she did cling to High Wolf. For good or for bad, this man had become her only stable reference point in this volatile chaos of silence.

And a thought kept occurring to her: *It could have been she. All too easily, she could have been a victim; here, tonight.*

For the first time since coming to the American West, the precariousness of her situation became suddenly too real, and Sierra plummeted to a realization: She was out of her depth, alone with a man who had shown her open dislike, thrust into an environment she little understood.

And though it appeared that she had been saved from the same fate as the others on the *Diana*, it was hardly cause for joy. For one thing, though she needed him, she distrusted High Wolf. For another, she could hardly feel relief when others this night had lost their lives.

But even these thoughts diminished, as something stronger and more powerful grabbed hold of her attention: She felt something for this man.

She might hate him, she might suspect him, she might even detest his past actions toward her. But alas, she felt something for him; something warm, something exquisite, something sensual . . .

Truth be told, she became suddenly all too aware of this man physically, and chancing a quick glance down at herself, she was appalled to see that she might as well be sitting before him naked, for her wet corset and drawers left nothing to the imagination. Worse, this man *was* completely naked from the waist up. Not only that, she had become aware of a rigidness in him that pushed against her backside.

And dear Lord, though she might be incredibly embarrassed by what was transpiring between them, she liked it . . .

Her response startled her, and she shivered, but instead of the action sending High Wolf away from her, he pulled her in even closer yet.

And then it happened.

He kissed the top of her head, once, and again, hugging her against him as though he might never let her go. And despite their circumstances, past and present, such an act of tenderness shot straight to her heart. Alas, she was helpless as the memory of what this man had once meant to her came back to haunt her. And she recalled again his love, his humor, his laughter, his understanding, his incredible smile—those and many other reasons why she had loved him so much.

She sighed against him, her only response to his open display of affection. To have done more would have spoiled the moment. Instead, she savored it.

Undoubtedly, if she lived to see morning, she would still distrust him, and truly, she might never let him into her life again. But his actions tonight had exonerated him in her opinion, and she was coming to realize that because of tonight, she might never hate him again . . .

The wind, which seemed incessant in this far western land, suddenly picked up force. Surreptitiously, she quivered.

"They will soon leave. Remain calm," High Wolf whispered into her ear as he held her to him, his chest against her back.

"You are speaking?" She drew her head to the side that she might also whisper the words against his ear.

But quickly, he caught her activity and held her. "Do not move," he said.

"But I thought—"

"If we whisper, the wind will wash away our words, but we must speak softly. And if you move, it must be done so slowly that it leaves no ripple in the air. Do you understand?"

"Not really," she said, "but I will try." And then, "High Wolf," she began, her voice a low murmur. "Thank you for being here, for rescuing me tonight."

He didn't respond.

"If you hadn't come when you did," she continued, "I would most likely be dead." *Most likely?* she thought. It would have been an assured fact.

Again, he said nothing.

"Why is it that you are here?"

A long pause followed the question, and she wondered if he were even going to answer. At last, however, he said, "I have been following the steamboat."

"You have?" she said, careful to make no movement at all, though she noted that she could feel his chest rise and fall with his breathing. "But I thought—"

"You were right," he said, and then stopped.

"Right?"

"*Haa'he,* I gave you my word to help you, and now, help you I have."

"Yes, and thank you," she said again. After a moment, however, she queried, "But will you give me the assistance I need most? Will you guide me?"

He didn't answer.

"High Wolf?" she prompted softly.

"We will talk about that later."

"But—"

"Later."

She fell silent, until at length, she said, "Very well." But Sierra couldn't stay mute forever, and she murmured, "When this war party leaves, what will we do?"

"I will ride the currents of the river until I find a safer place to camp. There I will let you sleep while I backtrack and see if I can discover the fate of your friends."

"You will?"

"*Haa'he*, yes."

"Then you never did intend to desert them?"

"*Hova'ahane*."

"What does that word mean?"

"No," he said simply.

"I see. Is that 'no' in the language of the Cheyenne, then?"

"Yes."

"How did you say it again?"

"*Ho-va'a-ha-ne*."

She repeated it, going on to say, "I like it."

But when he remained silent, making no response, in due course, she said, "Do you think that you will find my friends?"

"Yes."

"I am happy to hear it," she said. "And after you find them, what will you do?" she whispered.

"I will take you all back to St. Louis."

Sierra stiffened, and had she been allowed to move, she would have sat up, away from him. As it was, she was left to do no more than mutter, "I am not going back there until I accomplish what I must, so you might as well save yourself the bother."

"You will do as I tell you to do, and we will discuss this later."

"Will we? Will I?" she countered. Had he always been this tyrannical? "You are awfully certain of yourself, Mr. High Wolf."

"Perhaps," he said.

"I would escape, if you try to take me there."

"I would find you. Do not forget, Princess, that you are in my country now."

"I do not forget."

"Then you should remember to do as you are told."

She bit her lip in frustration, although after a while, she said, "You treat me as though I am a child, unable to take care of myself."

"In my country, you are, perhaps, exactly that."

"How demeaning," came the instant response. "Do you mean to insult me?"

He didn't answer.

"Very well. Do as you see fit. Take me back to St. Louis, and leave me in the care of Governor Clark."

She could practically sense his disbelief. However, all he said was, "You would give in so easily to me? I thought you were made of sterner stuff."

What was this? Another insult? And though she whispered, her voice was mocking as she said, " 'Tis strange. I have thought much the same about you."

He paused, as though he were letting her meaning take hold. Within an instant, however, he said, "Did you? Then perhaps we both overestimated the other. Let me be quite clear: I will wait in the village of St.

Louis until you are safely aboard a ship that will return you to your home."

"Will you? And you are certain you will watch my every movement until I am aboard ship?"

"There is little that escapes me."

She grinned.

"You smile," he said softly. "Do you think you can elude me?"

"Perhaps," she said. "One never knows, I might be that 'little' something that manages to get away from you."

Suddenly he stiffened. "Quiet!"

Sierra instantly bit off whatever else she was going to say. Instead, she froze.

Wasn't the danger past? Hadn't High Wolf intimated as much?

But then she heard it, the sound of someone moving slowly through the water, as though searching for something . . . or someone. Closer and closer came the danger, and Sierra shut her eyes, backing up against High Wolf as though he would shield her from it. And in response, he slowly changed position, his back shifting away from the edge of the tree, his weight coming forward onto his feet, his legs outspread. And she knew, he was now poised for action.

His hands came down above her breasts, to rest on her chest.

It was an intimate position, and despite the danger to her, to him, she was more than aware of the familiarity of his touch. However, conversely, it seemed the right thing to do, for if attacked, he could better protect her.

Had something gone wrong? she wondered. Had their whispered words been overheard?

Oh, how she wished she hadn't been arguing with him. What if those were to be the last words between them?

Would it matter?

Perhaps. However, she had no time in which to ponder the thought, for she heard something or someone stop next to the tree trunk. That same someone or something trod around the stump, had started climbing the tree trunk . . .

Sierra swallowed hard, and waited . . . wondering if each new breath were to be her last.

It was a strange thing, to confront death. And oddly, in that instant before expected discovery, she became aware that she felt little fear. Indeed not. No, rather she had become profound, her philosophizing hurling her toward a self-realization.

She loved this man, who held her in his arms, and had done so from her first acquaintance with him. And despite all reason not to, her love for High Wolf had never died. Forget that he was the worst sort of prospect, a treacherous liar. Once bestowed, her love had caused High Wolf to become a part of her, as he still was.

The truth stung, and yet curiously, the knowledge calmed her. It changed nothing, of course. She didn't want to love him; indeed, she wished she had never done so.

And yet, there it was in all its simplicity: She loved him . . . still . . .

Perhaps, she thought, she had been wrong in identifying her true mission in this land. Perhaps there was more to it than simply finding Prince Alathom and committing justifiable murder—if the need arose, of course. Rather, it might be asserted that she had hoped to discover the whereabouts of High Wolf and in finding him, put to rest, forever, her infatuation with the man.

Possibly. And if this were so, maybe, if she lived to see another day, she would embark upon this new mission with as great a vigor as she had shown the other. For of one thing she was entirely certain: To let this man back into her heart could hurt her as she had never been hurt before.

Still, kneeling there as she was, practically naked— and he, too—and held tightly against him, she felt that this new task seemed an almost impossible feat. Alas, deep within her, she craved exactly this . . . only more . . .

And so it was with some trepidation that she realized she was in trouble. Deep trouble . . .

Chapter 11

Had we indulged ourselves when we first met,
When love charmed us and made us feel its might,
Would we be looking backwards with regret,
And wonder how we fell from such a height?
Excerpted from a poem by David Ziff
"Sonnets to a Soul Mate"

Saaaa, their voices had drawn attention, and High Wolf silently chided himself for such foolishness. She might not know better; *he* did.

Still, there was nothing to be done but to wait. Slowly, High Wolf shifted his position so that his weight was on his feet, a pose that would allow him to spring into action. Unknowingly, also, he tightened his arms around the princess and brought his hands up to rest over her chest. True, being a scout, his usual tactic was to avoid a fight. But that didn't mean that he, or any other scout, was not fully able to defend himself, if the need arose. Quite the opposite. Alas, a scout could make a most formidable opponent.

As the danger drew near, High Wolf vowed that he would defend this woman, give his life if need be to save her. Not that he loved her—for who could love a woman who had proven herself to be so treacherous? But she had once been a friend . . . more than a friend . . .

But wait. Someone was climbing the tree trunk.

High Wolf tensed, straining in preparation. But he did no more than wait—and listen.

And then it happened. A wolf howled, a nighthawk squawked, a cricket chirped ever so sweetly, and the warrior who was scaling their tree stump halted long enough to answer those calls, giving back his own signal with the hoot of an owl. Someone farther away spoke softly, another man answered. And then there was a scraping sound, followed by a plop in the water.

The war party was leaving.

Of course, it could be a trap. Whoever it was who had started to clamber up the tree stump had sensed High Wolf's presence. That particular warrior might not leave so readily.

It meant that High Wolf would have to bide his time, would have to stay in position if need be all night, all morning. The only problem, if there were one, would be Sierra.

She was unused to the control needed to stay in one physical position for hours on end. Which meant that he would have to prop her up, keeping her awake and on guard. For her tendency would be to nap, and of course he could not allow it; people were known to do strange things in their sleep.

He could take her attention off the danger if he perhaps kissed her again. After all, that had appeared to bring her some relief from their immediate situation. Although this, too, might provide a greater risk . . .

no doubt from himself. For he, too, had become caught up in that kiss, becoming himself unaware of his environment.

Clearly, there was only one thing left to do.

Taking hold of her hand, he brought it up to his face, placing her fingertips over his lips. He sensed her bewilderment, but to her credit, she moved not at all; plus, she kept wisely quiet.

Silently, he mouthed words against her fingers, and he said slowly, "We must wait until I am certain it is safe to leave."

She readily understood what he was doing, and taking his hand in her own, placed his fingertips over her lips, Then, silently she mouthed, "Why? The Indians have left."

"There was one—he knows we are here. He will not leave—easily."

"But—"

"I must be certain."

He felt her swallow, hard. Nonetheless, she said, "Very well."

And once more they returned to silence while High Wolf again leaned back against the tree. How long they sat as such, within that hollowed-out tree trunk, High Wolf couldn't have said. But during that time, he became convinced of one thing: He would require the comfort of a widow . . . and soon. Being this close to a woman, holding her, inhaling her heady fragrance, feeling her softness, her breasts achingly pert . . .

Perhaps at the Mandan village he might find relief . . .

Slowly, she moved, taking hold of his hand, and pressing his fingertips over her lips, she said, "I am cold."

He knew this; he could feel her shivering within his arms. In sooth, he had hoped that holding her would help warm her. But obviously, that wasn't enough.

Reaching down, he brought her fingertips to his lips, as he said, "You must will yourself to be warm."

"What?" she mouthed. "I do not understand."

"You must 'will' warmth into your body."

"What? 'Will' it?" she mouthed. "What does that mean?"

"Exactly what I said. It is easy enough to do. You must pretend you are so warm, you would remove your clothing if you could."

"What? How? I still don't understand."

And he repeated, "With your mind, build a fire around us."

"But—"

"Do this, build this fire, until you are warm."

"High Wolf, I—"

"Did you try to do it?"

"You know I have not."

"Then you wish to be cold throughout the night?"

He felt her slight sigh. "You know very well that I don't."

"Then you must try."

"Very well," she mouthed.

"Good, now, when I tell you to do so, with your mind, build a fire which surrounds us."

He waited a moment, then queried, "Did you do it?"

"No, and this is silly. How can I build a fire when water surrounds me?"

"Then pretend the water has dried up."

"But—"

"Did you pretend?"

"No."

"Well, do so. Pretend the water is gone. The sun came out and dried it all up." He waited. "Did you do it?"

"Yes."

"Very well," he said silently. "Now pretend you are building a fire." Again he waited. "Did you do it?"

"Yes."

He smiled. "Now warm your hands on the closest ember."

"High Wolf?"

"Yes?"

"I cannot. Within that fire, I see a cloaked figure. One which I saw earlier tonight in the fire."

"Humph. Then leave him there and build another fire next to that last one." He waited. "Did you do it?"

"Yes."

He felt her smile. "It's odd," she said, "but I do feel warmer."

"Of course you do," he mouthed. "You can control any aspect of your body with your mind alone, for, as Grandfather has often told me, it is the mind that rules the body, not the opposite."

"Grandfather? Who is Grandfather?"

"He who taught me the ways of the wolf clan."

"The ways of what?"

"The wolf clan. The white man calls those of our clan, scouts. Did you know that a scout can survive and flourish in any terrain, hot or cold, freezing or boiling?"

"Can they?"

"*Haa'he*. And how do you think it is accomplished?"

"I'm sure I don't know."

"By practicing," he told her. "By learning to control the body with the mind alone. Now, build this fire, and keep it burning until you feel so warm, you determine that you must remove your clothing . . . and then I will help you to do so . . ."

He said it so matter-of-factly, he was certain she did not readily understand the implication. However, at length, he felt her smile.

It was a simple enough gesture, that smile, nothing more than a mere grin, but somehow, the knowledge that they both shared a fantasy, no matter how slight, created such a frenzy within him, he was surprised that she did not comment on the rapid beating of his heart.

Silently, he berated himself, for she was too close and there was no manner in which he could hide his responses to her, particularly one very masculine reaction.

But she said not a word. Alas, she pulled back into his arms until she was closer to him, and High Wolf thought for a moment that perhaps he had gotten lucky at last. Perhaps she wanted him after all.

And so it was without any thought to the future that he threw himself into the magnetic pull of her embrace, certain that this action alone had to be the sweetest of tortures.

And of one thing he was entirely certain; he would have no need himself to build the image of that fire this night . . .

A scout's movement in water could not be accurately described as floating, or as swimming, either, for he used the water's own energy to propel him, riding currents and whirlpools effortlessly, dancing back and forth from one tide to another, gliding over obstacles with ease. In truth, to an outsider's eye, a trained scout's efforts in the water might have looked more like a water ballet than an effort to swim.

Morning had dawned gray and dreary as a cloud cover marred the rising sun. Sometime in the wee hours of the morning, the danger from the night before had passed on by them. High Wolf had sensed its absence at once. Perhaps, he had reasoned, the enemy's scout had reason to hurry home, or mayhap, recognizing the skills from another member of the same clan, the man had decided to allow sanctuary to the two refugees and had left.

Whatever the reason, High Wolf had welcomed the chance to leave the half-submerged tree stump. Traveling by waterway, he had begun his search for a safer place to pitch camp.

At present, the river surrounded him like a friend, for High Wolf had merged his mind with the water. In his arms he still held the princess, afraid to let go of her, lest she be swept away by some unruly draft.

And though he was acutely aware of the princess beside him, his perception was extended well past their own location, for a scout must never lose sight of where he was, which included the environment for several miles around him. And so, having sensed no immediate danger close at hand, he let his mind drift onto other things.

The warriors tonight had been from the Pawnee tribe, and he wondered what was occurring in their country that they should be so far north. Had they some grievance? And if they did, was it possible they had set the boat afire?

It was entirely possible. The Pawnee were, at present, in an undeclared state of war with the whites. At first friendly and open to the newcomers in their country, the Pawnee had welcomed anyone to their village, only to find themselves sick with the dreaded diseases of the white man.

Their numbers had now been so reduced that those left in the tribe had declared open war on any white persons, be they male or female.

It was not a sane response, thought High Wolf. Even Grandfather, who rarely commented on anything, had gone on to say that "he who would fight another with anger, and anger alone, becomes that other." Therefore, it was only to be expected that at some point, the Pawnee would again be friendly toward the whites.

But what were they doing this far north? Perhaps they were looking for another wife for the Morning Star, a ceremony that always ended in the slaying of that "wife." Or perhaps they had come on a simple mission to visit their sister tribe, the Riccarees, whose country they were now in.

Or was there something else afoot this night? The princess had said she'd seen a shadow in the fire. And though she might doubt her own mind about such things, High Wolf did not.

Had something else stirred up the Pawnee?

Tomorrow, when he had at last attained a safe camp for the princess, he would return to this spot to look for survivors and to see what clues he might find from Mother Earth.

In any case, he would do well to watch the princess until he could return her safely to St. Louis.

Briefly, High Wolf glanced toward Sierra as he danced his way through the river's currents. It seemed remarkable to him to discover that the princess did not know how to swim, since even the youngest person in his tribe learned this skill at an age when they were beginning to walk—sometimes before even that. Albeit, even more astonishing was the fact that *he* had not known that she could not.

He would have to teach her.

Teach her?

High Wolf frowned. She was not his woman that he should take on that responsibility. And yet, if he did not show her the basics of staying afloat, he could never trust her near the water.

It was not his problem, came a voice of reason.

Or was it?

"High Wolf," she spoke to him softly. "Tell me. What kind of swimming is this that you do?"

"I do not swim . . . as you think of it. I ride the river's currents and use the power of the river to propel me through the water."

"But it looks so easy when you do it," she said. "And yet I can see that we have skirted around many obstacles and obstructions—sometimes long before these things even present themselves. Does this have something to do with you?"

High Wolf grinned. "You are observing the way the scout behaves in water. It is something that every scout learns at a young age."

"Oh? Really? Please, do tell me about it."

"There is no easy way to relate it," he said. "It is better if I show you how to swim and how to blend your mind with that of the water."

"Yes, that would be quite in order," she said, sending him a surreptitious glance. "Then, do I take it that you no longer intend to force me to return to St. Louis?"

"I do."

He saw her frown as she said, "But you just said—"

"I will have to teach you to swim so that you might be safe in the water. You must understand the power of the water and its rules, for if you do not know them and if you do not understand them, and you choose to fight the water, you will find it a formidable opponent, a battle you have little hope of winning. No, I will show you how to swim before we return to St. Louis. How else can I trust you when I am not with you?"

Again, she sent him a warm glance, only this time she appeared slightly confused, and she asked, "You would care?"

How did he answer that?

With the truth, he decided, and he said, "Of course I care. You were once to be my wife. As Grandfather has often said, 'A man does not change his attitude toward a thing simply because that thing bites him.' No, a wise man understands why the thing bit him and makes allowance; a wiser man does all this, and never makes the same mistake again."

The princess turned her head away from him, although he heard her mutter, "How can you make it seem as though I treated you so monstrously ill, when you know that the opposite is true?"

When you know that the opposite is true.

The comment caught him off guard, and though he

let go of his concentration for only a moment, the water grabbed hold of him and spun him around, slipping them both into a waiting eddy.

High Wolf recovered easily enough, returning his attention to the water and to the matter at hand, "dancing" his way back into the stream. Still, in the back of his mind was a question. Could it be true? Did the princess believe he had treated her badly?

How was that possible? It was *she* who had left him; *she* who had betrayed him. He remembered it well . . .

"*Come out, my son, and show yourself, for there is much for us to speak of.*"

High Wolf listened to the words of Father Junipero, but remained where he was, for, in his own mind, to show himself was little more than an act of betrayal. After all, hadn't he, the prince and Sierra found this spot, relegating it to secrecy? Hadn't they each taken pains to make it disappear in the landscape, as High Wolf had taught them both to do?

"*Come out, son. I know you are here. Maria, Princess Sierra's maid, has brought me here, and although Maria has left, I have strict instructions from the princess. Princess Sierra has also given me a note to bring to you.*"

Though tempted to do as asked, High Wolf hesitated. Instinct kept him quiet.

But Father Junipero was not finished, and he said, "Come now, my son, and talk to me, for I know you were expecting to see the princess tonight. I have come in her place."

High Wolf stayed where he was. Something didn't seem quite right. And it would do the Father no harm to imagine that he spoke to nothing more than the wind, at least for a few minutes.

"So it appears that you have flown away, after all, my fine, young friend. And you, who thought yourself to be soon made a prince," spat out Father Junipero, with what appeared to be dislike. *"You, who questioned me at every turn; you, who brought ideas of freedom to Princess Sierra's mind; you, who dared to oppose me. Have you known how much I have hated you?"*

Though High Wolf said not a word, the father's outburst suddenly validated all those times when High Wolf had looked upon the man with much confusion, seeing friendliness in his countenance, but sensing only hatred.

"Come now, my friend," said Father Junipero more urgently. *"I know that you are here. For I have sources that tell me you await the princess."*

High Wolf kept himself hidden. In truth, so undetectable was he that even the most aware scout could not have found him.

"Ah, I see. You refuse to show yourself to me. Embarrassed to be in the presence of a man of God?" said the father, glancing cautiously into the forest that surrounded the clearing.

A man of God? High Wolf knew, at last, that in this, the father lied. Only he, who would walk the path of enlightenment and righteousness, was a man of God. This man, Father Junipero, was proving himself to be no more than a charlatan.

Silently, without disturbing the forces of nature that breathed in and out all around them, High Wolf crept from his hiding place, which had been high in a tree. Coming down noiselessly onto his feet, High Wolf stalked to an area in back of the father, for here was true scout warfare—that of the mind . . .

Slowly, High Wolf stole up behind the priest, and with-out betraying so much as a breath, touched the man's ear.

"Who is that?" Father Junipero immediately swung around, clawing at the air, but he grasped hold of nothing, for High Wolf had faded swiftly, easily and noiselessly back into the shadows.

"Did you know that the princess has sent me here with three hundred gold dukatens? And do you know why?"

Gold?

"To pay you off, my good friend," said the father, answer-ing his own question. "She told me to tell you that, while she considers you a friend, she could never seriously consider marrying you. You, no more than an American Indian."

Lies. These were lies. High Wolf would no more believe them than he would stop breathing.

"You may as well go away from here, for she will not be coming to meet you tonight. She marries the prince in the morning. But in the goodness of her heart, the princess could not see you leave here with nothing."

Sliding slowly, silently back to the priest, High Wolf took hold of the hem of the man's frock, pinning it to the ground with a sharp stone. Then touching his sandaled foot, High Wolf faded unobtrusively away.

Startled, the priest jumped. "Here, here, now, come out and confront me face-to-face. For you do not scare me, my friend. Nothing can frighten a man such as myself."

He lied. High Wolf knew it was so, for though he might deny it, Father Junipero's eyes darted about the dark and deserted clearing frantically. It was not the act of a man who was in possession of himself.

Calmly, High Wolf picked up another stone, and aiming it carefully, threw it into the north side of the forest.

"Here!" said the priest, as he started to strut toward the spot. "You thought to hide from me, did you?" But Father Junipero was going nowhere. He could not. His frock was caught upon the ground, and instead of moving forward, he tripped, falling to his knees.

Meanwhile, High Wolf faded back into the shadows, slipping off to the west of the clearing, where he made a howl like a wolf.

"I know that is you, High Wolf," said the priest. "And these little games do not frighten me."

Nonetheless, the priest trembled.

Slipping to the east, High Wolf again howled, then set off toward the south and finally to the north, repeating the same process.

"You think to confuse me and frighten me by pretending to be a wolf. Well, I know you are little more than such a creature. Certainly you are worth no consideration to a man such as myself."

That decided it. High Wolf vowed he would rather be a wolf than a creature such as this man. Nonetheless, once more High Wolf crept up behind the priest, untying the father's rope from around his waist and pulling on his cloak. The garment fell away, leaving Father Junipero standing in no more than a full black surplice.

"What's that? Where are you? Again, you think to frighten me, but I believe that it is I who might shock you. For I have come to tell you what the princess truly thinks of you."

Skirting around to the side of the priest, and skulking silently upon him, High Wolf undid the clasps that held the man's surplice and cassock together, and with a single pull, left the man standing in no more than his sandals and the cap upon his head.

This seemed to be too much for the priest, and with an

ugly shout, he threw the sack he'd been holding into the bush, a sack of something that clinked as it hit the ground. And shivering from either fright or the cold, Father Junipero turned, picked up his frock, and fled.

However, once the priest had gone, High Wolf retraced his steps and trod to the spot where the sack had fallen. Picking it up, he found, to his horror, that three hundred gold dukaten did, indeed, fill the satchel. That it also contained Princess Sierra's personal seal brought him a great deal of confusion.

High Wolf frowned deeply, and taking the satchel with him, crept back through the forest, toward the castle.

Only she could make sense of these things he had heard and seen tonight. He would await her no longer, but rather he would seek her out in her own lair.

Toward this end he crept to her room in the castle, where he waited and waited and waited.

But alas, the princess never returned to her room. Not to sleep, not to eat, not even to dress for her own wedding.

Chapter 12

How fortunate for me our paths converged,
That when we met our separate futures merged!
Excerpted from a poem by David Ziff
"Sonnets to a Soul Mate"

And so it had been.

High Wolf had stayed in the castle, had roamed the corridors looking for the princess, only to arrive at her room having accomplished nothing. Deciding he might have missed seeing her, he vowed to keep to her room, abandoning it for no more than fifteen minutes, perhaps twenty, at a time.

All through the night, he had endured the tiredness of his body, as well as an urgency within his soul that demanded he find the princess . . . now. Still, he had waited, stalking the halls, the nooks and crannies of the castle.

The dreary hours of the "darkness that descends before dawn" came and went, surrendering to the steel gray sky of morning. Nonetheless, he held fast to his own counsel. In his heart, he knew that his friends would not betray him.

But when daybreak unfolded and the princess had yet to return, High Wolf knew the anxiety in his heart to be real. Should he continue to scour the castle for her?

Deciding this was his only option, he once more left her room. That was when he heard the music from the chapel, and slowly, moving in such a way as to fade into the shadows, High Wolf stalked toward the chapel, which should have been the most sacred of places.

It had been dark inside the chapel when he had slid into the shadows of the room; too dark to see well, for the day outside was overcast and cloudy, and the room itself was lit by nothing more than a few candles.

But High Wolf would not leave. In his heart, he could not.

That was when he saw them. There, in front of the chapel, the forms of a man and woman, both of them kneeling before a priest. Was it the princess taking her wedding vows?

High Wolf could not hear what was being said, nevertheless, he had stayed through the long hours of the ceremony; waiting, watching the woman, if only to ensure that she was indeed the princess.

Slowly, the woman moved, and High Wolf thought he recognized the princess, for only she stirred with such grace.

Though he had thought himself to be prepared for the worst, the shock of seeing her shook him, spiritually, mentally, physically, and though he knew he should, he could not look away from her. He trembled, and falling back, he grasped for the wall behind him as though it might steady him.

But it was not to be. The pain was not physical; it

was a sickness of spirit. And he had stood there in the shadows for a moment, transfixed, unable to take a step backward or forward, if only to raise a protest—if, indeed, such an action would have any effect.

Deep in his heart, he had never believed that the princess and Prince Alathom would obey the wishes of their parents—not when the matter at hand was marriage. True, he had known that a prince and princess were bound by rules and forms of conduct that he had never quite fathomed. But not until this moment had he been aware of how these rules might affect him personally.

He understood it now.

Be that as it may, he had lingered there in the darkness, waiting for what must surely come: a protest. He waited in vain.

And then it was over, the multitude of people pouring out of the chapel and into the corridors of the castle, a false gaiety in the air that belied the heaviness of the chapel itself. But High Wolf did not stir.

No, he, and he alone, stayed behind, as though the physical location itself might steady him. Indeed, he thought, how could he leave this place when its emptiness echoed the hollowness of his soul?

How long he stood there, he was never quite certain. But it had been dark by the time he had managed to prod himself into action, and with the loss so raw that he physically ached, he had slipped out of the castle as quietly as he had come into it, leaving behind a satchel of gold and the princess's seal in his place.

He didn't think to seek out the prince and princess

with congratulations. What could he say? How could he react?

No, they had done their duty to their families, to their countries. It was best that he, High Wolf, simply fade away.

Within days, he had located a ship headed for the Americas, and had boarded her. And to this day High Wolf recalled vividly his thoughts as he stood aboard that ship's deck, watching the shoreline taper slowly away.

And with the wind beating on his face as though it would tell him of something important, something he should attend to, High Wolf swore that he would never trust again, never love. In sooth, that day he lost a gentler, kinder part of himself.

And as the land disappeared unspectacularly from view, High Wolf had said good-bye to the land, to the six years he had spent at this place and to those two people, who had once been his dearest, most beloved friends.

But friends they could be no more . . .

Like a ghost, a dark shadow lingered over the water, moving slowly, as though it were searching for something, or perhaps someone . . . But unable to find that which it sought, it shifted its position slowly north.

Sierra had never felt so miserable or been so cold. Several hours later, sitting next to a small fire in a makeshift camp, which consisted of a large chasm that High Wolf had dug out between two large stones, she tried to envision an enormous fire, while at the same time, she attempted to determine her next course of action. But it was difficult to imagine it, especially since she could barely think of anything other than High Wolf, his presence beside her, the overwhelming hint of power the man exuded.

Somehow, somewhere, during their watery escape, with her body pressed up close to his, she had become more aware of this man physically than she had ever been of anything. And at this present moment, she was painfully conscious of the masculine aura he emanated.

Truth be told, she was all too sensitive in that regard. For one thing, he wore little clothing. There was his breechcloth, moccasins, weapons of bow and arrows and a knife. True, a parfleche bag fell to his side, with the strap thrown over his chest, and his quiver of arrows hung over one arm. But that was all!

Of course, there were little things about him, too: like the look of his long fingers as they fiddled over a piece of wood; the sharp angles of his features; the wide width of his chest, completely unmarred by body hair; the piercing stare of his dark eyes, when and if he chose to look at her.

And she wondered: Had she noticed, all those years ago, these little things?

If she had, she certainly did not call them easily back to mind. Why not?

Had she been too innocent at the time, too unobservant; or was it, perhaps, due to the fact that she had never, before this night, experienced a brush with death? Indeed since that incident, her senses seemed greatly heightened.

She rocked back on her rump, deep in contemplation. What good would any ultra-sensitivity do her, however, when the man beside her seemed curiously unemotional? Completely unaware of her?

Nonetheless, under the cover of her lashes, Sierra decided to look her fill at him, and she let her gaze roam up to his face, committing to mind his look of maturity. She shook her head, amazed at herself.

How could she have forgotten the little things about him? Like the unusual quality of his eyebrows, which were thick, yet sparsely populated with hair? Alas, how could she have neglected to note how high were his cheekbones, how slightly aquiline was his nose, how stubborn was the tilt of his chin? Although she had to admit that she had always been aware of the sensual quality of High Wolf's lips, a promise of passion that belied his stern exterior.

Why, she wondered, continuing her line of thought, had she never remarked upon how truly masculine this man was? Was it because she had been too young at the time? Or had she simply been too full of her own royal status?

It was true that other than High Wolf, she had never known or even had much to do with the more "common" man. In truth, her life had been filled with studies of history and lineage; with decorum, pomp and circumstance; with dinners, obligations; with meetings of only the best and most royal of people.

In truth, seen from her present state, it began to appear as if she had spent the majority of her life in an ivory tower, unaware of what went on in the world, outside her tiny speck of manicured lawn.

But these thoughts, though insightful, were disturbing, and Sierra fidgeted.

However, her antics caused little more than a quick glance from High Wolf. Alas, this and this alone was the most she was coming to expect from him. Since entering into their camp, he practically did little more than ignore her.

Reluctantly, she tilted her head to one side, and since there was nothing else to be done at the moment, she studied him further. Why didn't he talk to her? Was he sorry that he had kissed her within the heightened beat of a war-induced moment? Was he ashamed that he had shown her a grain of kindness?

The thought was distressful, and in an effort to divert her attention, she glanced above her, staring at the sticks and the large evergreen boughs that High Wolf had found near the water, having placed them over the top of their camp for camouflage and beneath them, as well, that they might both be cushioned as they sat. And all around her was nothing but dirt and stone; fresh earth to be sure, but dirt, nonetheless.

Which brought another question to mind: Why were they not camping in the open spaces of this land? Where a person could breathe more easily?

It was on the tip of her tongue to ask this and many other questions, but she found herself reluctant to speak. High Wolf seemed so distant, so uncommunicative. Indeed, she felt loath to make an attempt at conversation, lest he bite.

She shivered, an action that drew his eye to her at last. But he said nothing, just as she was beginning to expect from him.

In a manner of speaking, Sierra wished she hadn't asked High Wolf earlier if he still cared for her, if only because since that time, he had been unusually quiet, answering her questions with no more than a curt reply.

With a shrug, she brought her attention back to what she had come to refer to as their pit, their camp, watching him whittle away over a stick—a piece of wood he had gathered.

She needed to talk to him; albeit, she required his attention to an important matter. However . . .

She bit her lip; it was a bad habit, but one she was far from taming, particularly at the moment. And she wondered, what would it take to persuade this man to help her find the prince? Communication? Feminine wiles? A promise of her charms?

Whatever was to be done, however, she knew she would have to be the one to initiate conversation. And at last, she could stand the silence no longer, and clearing her throat, she said, "Thank you very much for bringing me here and for setting up camp." Again, she cleared her throat. "But, High Wolf, I am cold."

He made no answer.

She tried again. "This fire does little to warm me, and thoughts of three or more gigantic fires, all blazing before me, does not help the matter. High Wolf, could you not build a bigger fire?"

He shrugged, and after a time, responded, "A large fire is easy to see, easy to smell. We are not in safe country yet that I might make a better fire. Be content that you have even a small one, for it will, in time, warm you."

"I beg to differ in that opinion."

He simply raised his shoulders and glanced away.

Staring at him, at his complacency, she decided to change her tactic, and taking a deeper plunge, she came directly to the point, saying, "Why did you kiss me?"

She watched him carefully, noting that he visibly stiffened, that his fingers faltered over what he was doing, and that he cut himself. Furthermore, the very air around them became suddenly stifling.

But he otherwise remained quiet.

However, she knew him well enough to know that she had at least captured his attention. And she waited . . .

At some length, without looking up, he said, "I kissed you to keep you quiet and to calm you. You were about to scream, and there were enemies all around us. Do not worry. I realize it was a mistake. It will not happen again."

"I see," she acknowledged, keeping her eyes trained on him. "And you thought that by sweeping your tongue into my mouth, I would become calmer?"

He paused; he coughed, as though startled that she might say such a thing. However, after a slight pause, he began, "Perhaps I did believe it might," he said, as a gleam came into his eye. "Although maybe I wanted you to notice what you have missed all these years without me."

All these years without him. The thought made her eyes sting. Also, she realized on a note of some reluctance, he might very well have accomplished exactly that.

But Sierra was in no mood to give him quarter, and she said, "I beg to know, Mr. High Wolf, do you think the lesson is complete?"

The question earned her a hard look, although all he said was, "The lesson?"

"Yes, the lesson I'm supposed to learn—the one that makes me realize all I've missed these past ten years."

He shook his head. "Hardly learned, I should say."

"Is that so? Then I suppose that is why later, when we were in the tree trunk, you held me in your arms and kissed me again."

To this, he gave her an incredulous, although a rigid look. Only this time, when he gazed at her, he placed the wood he was whittling to the side. Turning toward her and leaning forward, he brought up a hand to brush aside a strand of her hair, as he said, "There is another reason I kissed you, I think. Perhaps you should know it, too, although this one will not make you happy."

"Oh?"

"*Haa'he*." He nodded.

"And that is . . . ?"

"I fear that I have been away from my true love for too long, and you were"—he pulled a face—"there . . ."

Ouch! With a start, Sierra drew back away from him.

But if he noticed her reaction, it was hard to say, for he turned his face away from her to pick up that darned wood once more. Over his shoulder, he said, "But do not worry. I have my wits about me now, and it will not happen again."

"Oh?" Sierra sat up straighter. "Really?" Her chin shot forward and up. "And you can, I assume, be certain of that?"

"As certain as I am that the sun comes with the day."

"Really?" Seeing red, she gave him a wide-eyed stare, wondering what it would take to break through this man's nonchalance. She said, "How can you be so certain that we will never again kiss?"

"How?" he asked, all without looking at her. "Because I can control my baser impulses."

"Ah, now I understand," she said. "Then if I am to comprehend you completely, I am to believe that I am a baser impulse?"

He looked up to her at last, turning slightly to face her before giving her a considering glance. "I did not say that. You put words in my mouth. I was referring to the urge to kiss."

"Hmmm." She raised an eyebrow at him. "Then you admit you felt . . . ah . . . urged to kiss me?"

He raised an eyebrow at her. "I suppose I did. Now, to what end do all these questions tend?"

"To nothing, I daresay," she said, looking away from him. "I am attempting, however, to understand, after these somewhat diverting incidents, if my life and my . . . feminine person is secure with you. That is all."

He grunted. "You are safe with me. Let me assure you that I will keep my hands—and my lips—away from you from this day forward."

"Will you?" she asked, glancing toward him and smiling. "Even when we are in the water?"

He sat up straighter. "You know that I must hold you close to me then because you don't know how to swim."

Looking as innocent as possible, she said, "Then you should teach me."

Looking sullen, he gazed over to her, giving her his full attention, and he said, "I will. But until then, I will hold you to ensure your safety when we are in the water."

"I see," she said. "And what other excuse do you have?"

He frowned. "It is not an excuse."

"Is it not?"

He ground his teeth. "I give up. Tell me, what is it you want from me? A letter stating my unlecherous intentions? I am sorry, but I am fresh out of parchment."

"I don't wish a letter."

"Then what? An apology?"

Facing him fully, she leaned in toward him and grinned before saying, "Mr. High Wolf, I ask a very simple thing. I merely want you to do it again."

At these words, High Wolf sat so stiffly, he might as well have turned to stone.

And pressing advantage, she said, "Here I am before you. You may try again now."

He moved not a muscle, not even to contain the slight twitch in his cheek. At some length, he said, "Do you think I am afraid to do it? Is that what this all tends toward?"

"Maybe."

"I am not afraid of you, or your touch."

"Aren't you?" She scooted forward, and reaching out to him, trailed her fingers over the wayward muscle in his cheek.

He caught her hand. "What game are you trying to play with me, Princess? I know that whatever it is, what you want from me has little to do with kissing. That is only a ruse. Do not think that your flirtation with me will work as it used to? I am no longer the same young boy whom you could all too easily bend to your will. And I warn you, if I ever again kiss you, you will not want me to stop."

"Try me."

"Do not tempt me, Princess, you, who are a married woman."

"Am I? To the world at large I am a widow."

"Do you think that makes a difference?"

"Yes," she said. "I do."

"Whether you are a widow or not, you are still a married woman."

"If that is so, then kiss me again, that I might remember the role I'm supposed to play."

He sighed, and leaning away from her, said, "Forgive me, Princess, but I find these games tedious. It has been many years since I was at court and subjected to them. Out here in the States, a man—or a woman—says exactly as he or she thinks. Do not dally with me. Tell me what it is that you want forthwith, and I will inform you if it is within my power to help you."

"So I am to be honest with you?"

"Yes."

"And you will be honest with me, as well?"

"Yes."

"Were we ever really truthful with one another, do you think?"

Beside himself, he moaned, "I was sincere with you, Princess."

"Were you?"

"Princess?"

"Very well," she said, sitting back against the dirt-covered stone wall. "If you must know, the real reason I have come to the States is to find Prince Alathom."

High Wolf remained silent.

"I do not believe the reports that reached us overseas, and so I have come here to discover the truth."

Folding his arms over his chest, High Wolf sat back, saying, "Why?"

"Why what? Why don't I believe the letter that came to me and to Prince Alathom's parents? Or why am I determined to learn the truth?"

"Both questions should be answered, I think."

"Very well," she said. "I don't believe the reports because I think that news of the prince's death came too close to our discovering his whereabouts. It is my conviction that the prince is once again trying to shirk his responsibilities. And I must warn you that I am determined to learn the accuracy of the reports sent us because . . . well, because I would simply know the truth." She sent him a quick, though evasive glance. "Do not tell me that you would not do the same."

"*Haa'he*, yes, that I would. And why have you contacted me? Because you knew I once promised you a favor?"

She glanced away from him. "That is true, but only partially. Actually I believed, and I still do believe"— she shot a coy look at him—"that you have knowledge of where the prince is."

If the statement startled him, he showed it oddly, for all he did was say, "So I had assumed from something you had told me earlier. But I can't think of why you would assume this."

She snorted. "Isn't it obvious? The two of you left the Continent together. The two of you have probably been together all this time."

He stared back at her oddly, as though he might be struggling to understand something, and his frown deepened. At some length, he said, somewhat reluctantly, "We left together?"

"Obviously."

"And when was this?"

Again, she snorted, tossing her head. "Mr. High Wolf, I don't have the time or the patience for such a pretense."

"Pretense?"

"You know as well as I what happened ten years ago."

The atmosphere in their small crevice became suddenly stifling, though High Wolf moved not at all. At some length, however, he said, "Are you telling me that you think the prince and I sailed away together? Ten years ago?"

"Obviously."

"I don't see that there is anything obvious about it."

"Well, there I was alone, and neither one of you was present. It was plain to my way of thinking that you both deserted me."

"Deserted you? I saw you marry the prince."

"How could you have done so when he wasn't even there? . . . And neither were you."

"Wasn't even there? But I—" High Wolf frowned. "Princess, are you telling me that you did not marry him?"

"No," she said, her voice rising by a slight notch. "I did. By proxy. And only because the both of you had left the country without me. And . . . and you . . . You dared to ask for money from me."

"I what?"

"How can you sit there and pretend that you did not require three hundred gold dukatens in order to quit your claim on me?"

"My what?" Suddenly High Wolf sat up straight. "You married the prince by proxy?"

She nodded.

"And when he returned—"

"He never returned."

"Not in ten years?"

"No."

"*Saaaa*. Princess, what have you been doing for ten long years?"

"Attempting to help run both his country and mine—or do you forget that I am a princess?"

At last High Wolf sighed. "I took no money."

However, Sierra's reaction was a curt snort. "I know better."

"How can you know better? I left the money and your own personal seal in a satchel in the chapel. Whether you believe me or not, I was there at your wedding. I watched you marry the prince."

"I have already told you. He was not there—it was another man who stood up for him. Besides, if you were there, why did you not step forward?"

As though suddenly drained of energy, High Wolf sat back against the dirt wall. After a few moments, however, he said, "I was too shocked to do so. Princess," he continued, "this may come as a surprise to you, but I am beginning to believe that we were betrayed."

"Humph! So you say now."

"Believe me, Princess. I assure you that I would not have left your side until I was fully satisfied that you had married another. Only then did I leave. And I did not set sail with the prince ten years ago, and I do not know what happened to him, for I made my own passage without giving him any further thought."

"Huh!" she uttered. "You must know that I don't believe you." She glared at him. "This is a country with very few white men. How can it be that you have been here all this time without knowing of the prince's whereabouts?"

He grinned at her. "It is a good question. Perhaps answered only by the knowledge that the prince has been in camp with an enemy tribe. I believe that Red Hair said he was with the Crow."

"Red Hair?"

"Governor Clark."

"And how is it you came upon that information?"

"I listened to your conversation with him at his home when we were both in St. Louis. I wanted to know your real purpose in being here—and I thought he would know it. I learned many things that night, including who was last with the prince."

"But . . . I didn't see you there."

He smiled. "Of course not. It is the way of the scout that he makes himself invisible to others. Only if I had allowed you to see me would you have done so."

She gave him a considering glance. "Very well," she said. "Then you have known all along why I am here, and still you did not seek to help me."

"I followed the steamboat, did I not? I was there

when she sank, and I led you safely away from an enemy tribe. I believe I have helped you."

"Yes, you have helped me, but at what a cost."

"Cost? What cost? What have you paid me for my help?"

My heart, she thought. Aloud, she said, "Too much, I fear," although the words were barely whispered. Then more distinctly, she changed the subject, saying, "It is very easy to spout words—particularly those that you know another wishes to hear. But realize this, I am the one who found that satchel which you claim was filled with money—shortly after my marriage. Nor was it found in the chapel, where you say you left it. But rather I discovered it near the spot where the three of us used to meet. And when I found it, Mr. High Wolf, it contained only my seal . . . no gold . . ."

"Then you think I am lying."

She shrugged. "Yes, I do."

"I am a scout—"

"Yes," she said, interrupting him and holding up a hand. "I know. I have heard you say it often enough. Scouts don't lie."

He sat in silence for a short time, his attention centered upon the ground. But then, raising his gaze to hers, he said, "Think . . . If I am right and we were betrayed, do you not know that it would be easy enough for someone to take the money and leave it somewhere else?"

"Mr. High Wolf, I discovered this 'treasure' at our meeting place . . . there in the woods. No one else knew about that place—only the three of us."

At this, he paused, but only for a moment. "Your maid knew, as well as Father Junipero."

"Maria?" said Sierra, glancing up at him sharply. "Maria would never stoop to do such a thing. No, Mr. High Wolf, I would trust her with my life."

"*Haa'he*, I am sure you would." Then more softly, "But not me."

She made no response.

"But your maid, Maria, led Father Junipero to our rendezvous spot once. And if I am correct in my assumption, I believe it is Father Junipero who is accountable for leaving that satchel in the woods."

A scathing look was her reply, before commenting, "Father Junipero, his word and his name, are beyond reproach. Now, I will hear no more talk that maligns his character."

High Wolf said nothing to this, though there was cynicism in his look.

And Sierra, seeing it, turned her head away, saying, "Mr. High Wolf, I believe that you promised to seek out the whereabouts of my servants; perhaps you had better leave now if you are to keep your word." Quite deliberately, she stuck her nose in the air.

But if he were affected by her attitude, he said not a word. Instead, he offered, "I will say this only one more time: I tell you the truth. I took no money."

"Yes, and maybe pigs will someday fly—" She stopped whatever else she'd been about to say, her gaze coming down as though to inspect the dirt beneath her. However, in due course, she raised her glance to stare directly at High Wolf, and said, "I will tell you what I will do: I will think on it."

"You will think on it? What does that mean?"

"It means exactly what I said, that I will think about it . . ."

"How kind you are," he uttered sarcastically. But when Sierra had nothing more to say, he at last arose, coming up onto his knees. "Very well," he said. "But think on this as well, Princess. Why should I lie? What have I to gain by it?"

"My good wishes, perhaps," she said. "And maybe a renewal of my favor."

"A renewal of your favor?" She heard him use a curse word—something he had never done in her presence in all their past. And she stared at him— hard—as though by a look alone she could censure him. However, he ignored the look, going on to say, "I think, Princess, that if you examine the facts, you might come to realize that you grossly overestimate the worth of your charms."

She opened her mouth to retaliate, but was left speechless, having no option but to watch his Adonis-like body as he rose to climb out of their concealed camp.

And truth to tell, though she might be the last to admit it, she very much liked what she saw . . .

Chapter 13

A dark shadow hung over their camp.
    What was it? A man? An animal? A ghost?
   And then it was gone, as though it had never been there. And yet, it had . . .

   Silently, stealthily and at first light, High Wolf crept back toward their camp, which was situated under a ledge and between two large rocks. Because it was landscaped so as to remain undetected from the eye, one would have to know it was there in order to see it.

   He pulled a face as he came up close to it, dreading what was to come next, for he did not have good news to offer Sierra. True, he had discovered the trail left by her maid and her steward, but the two of them, along with a few of the men, had been taken by Indians; Mandan Indians, friendly to whites, to be sure, but there was a problem . . .

He shook his head as though the action might clear it. However, it did not.

There were simply too many things on his mind, and High Wolf knew he had need of consultation with an elder from his own clan. He must seek to do this before deciding what course to take with the princess.

But that would involve taking the princess with him farther into Indian country.

Should he do it? Over dangerous territory? Or should he act as instinct demanded, and escort her back to St. Louis, where she would be safely lodged? Thus, he could pursue the trails of her maid, her steward, and her wayward husband—if the prince were still among the living.

But she would not go back there willingly, and the desire to fight her was quickly waning from him. In truth, he was beginning to believe that he had little fight left in him when concerning the princess.

True, he had told her he believed she was overestimating the worth of her charms, and at the time, he had meant it. But as he replayed their most recent conversation, he was beginning to admit that he had been in the wrong.

For years.

In truth, each time he thought back to this morning's conversation, he knew shame. To think that he had misidentified the person at Sierra's wedding; the result being wasted years . . . years that might have been spent in happiness.

Indeed, he could barely think of it without chiding

himself. How could he have made such a mistake? He, a scout, prized for his ability to observe?

Worse, he now realized that neither the princess nor Prince Alathom had betrayed him. The prince had probably caught wind of what was occurring and had attempted to thwart it, had most likely left on the ship they had all hired together, thinking that High Wolf and the princess would most likely follow.

But something had gone wrong: No one had foreseen the trouble that could be made by a very vindictive man. A man who hid his evil character behind the cloak of goodness.

Ten years. Ten years . . . wasted unnecessarily. Worse, Sierra didn't believe the truth; plus, his chance to prove his innocence had expired the moment he had left the country.

In faith, the whole affair left him feeling as though he had been set adrift. For years, he had nurtured his righteousness, so certain was he in his reasoning.

But to learn that such piousness was based on no more than a series of falsehoods . . .

It was a sobering fact. And he could only think: Had he taken a closer look; perhaps had spoken up at her wedding, things might be different.

But he had felt helpless at the time; one against an entire nation . . . no, two nations.

Unfortunately for him, in the here and now, no amount of self-recrimination could erase the past. He could not go back and relive it, much as he wished he could.

However, the truth did provide a means to perhaps right this wrong. In sooth, if he looked at it from a different perspective, he might see that only by learning this truth could he now have a chance to right himself with the princess.

Make no mistake, she might be legally married, but in deed, she could be as innocent as she had been ten years ago. And whether the prince were alive or dead would make little difference to High Wolf. He recognized no such marriage—one in which the groom had never lived with the bride?

No, the princess was free, he realized. Free, to love him . . . if he could only make her believe in him.

And yet, why should she? From her viewpoint, not only he, but the prince as well, had deserted her.

Could he ever atone for doing such a thing to her? Especially since, unintentionally, it had been true.

He could try. No, that wasn't strong enough: He *would* try to make it up to her. He didn't know how; he didn't know when but somehow, in some way, he would make reparation.

Oh, how her heart ached.

Confusion, disbelief—alas, ill-will—waged a battle with the deep-seated love that had found its way back into her heart. And she thought that perhaps watching High Wolf go, without so much as a kind word from her, was probably one of the hardest things she had ever had to do. *Dear Lord, help me*, she cried to herself.

She wanted to believe him. *She truly wanted to believe him.* Yet how could she? How could she betray what she knew as fact?

And yet . . .

Deep within her was the desire to forget the past. To leave it alone. After all, what good was it to her now? People change. Situations change.

Still, how could she forget what he had done? *"Once betrayed, a wise monarch never overlooks it, nor does he ever forgive."*

So had spoken a man of wisdom. Her mentor. Father Junipero.

And yet, she remembered happier times. Times when there was no recrimination, only laughter . . . and the newness of first love . . .

The violins sang out in harmony, so very sweetly, while the cellos serenaded the assembled guests with one melodious note after the other. The bass, always low and rhythmic, kept the beat to a constant and invariable meter, allowing the dancers certainty in their steps.

Step up, back, hands linked together. Turn, bow, step, back together. High Wolf smiled at her as the dance led them up close to one another, and in his smile was so much affection, Sierra thought she might surely burst with happiness.

As it was she was loath to restrain her delight, and her gay laugh filled the ballroom, causing several pairs of eyes to turn her way.

But what did she care? Tonight was the night. Tonight she and High Wolf would announce their engagement. At last, she thought, she would be able to start her life.

"Are you as excited as I?" asked the princess, as they stepped in time to the music.

High Wolf smiled, executing a turn, walking away from her to the rhythmic beat. However, soon the step brought him up close, and he said, "I am probably much more excited than you are, my love. For I have never known such happiness."

"Nor I."

The music ended, the partners bowed and curtsied, and taking a step toward her, High Wolf accepted her hand as he led her off the dance floor and onto the balcony. He took her to a corner, where, leaning against a banister, they were able to gaze out onto the countryside, which was laid out before them there beneath a starlit night. And then, swinging his attention around to her, he said, "Do you feel the excitement in the air?"

Sierra did, indeed, and with a single nod, she smiled up at him.

"Good," he said, "then for a moment, let us close our eyes and memorize every detail there is about this time, that we might always recall it, even in our old age."

"Yes," she said eagerly, for this was a kind of game that the two of them had, of late, been playing. A game that excited her very much.

Being a very perceptive young man, High Wolf had initiated her into a few specialties of the scout, had drawn her attention to things in their environment—causing her to look at people, at objects, as she never had before.

He grinned at her. "We have been practicing this skill for several weeks. This time, however, why do you not tell me what you want me to concentrate on, instead of the reverse?"

"Yes, all right," she said, nodding. "I will. Now let's see . . ." She glanced around her. "Here is one: Do you feel the heaviness of the air, the moisture in it? The knowledge that a storm may be pending?"

"Ah, this is a good one," he said. "Yes, I do."

"Good," she said. "Did you know that I have always been afraid of storms?"

"No, but I would like to learn all these things about you."

"Well, it's true. The thunder scares me and the lightning makes me want to hide my head."

He bent toward her. "I would never have you hide your head so long as you are with me. If I could, I would make you strong like the war eagle. Perhaps in the future, when you hear the thunder and lightning, you will remember our talk and will think of me and recall that I love you. And this you will have, instead of your fear."

She grinned. "Yes," she said, "Yes, that would be better, would it not? Now, I have another one: Do you smell the fragrance in the air?"

He turned his head, sniffing. "I do."

"I think the air is scented with the perfume from perhaps each lady present. It is a pleasant odor, is it not?"

He nodded. "It is pleasant. And I think that from this moment on, whenever I smell perfume, I will think of you."

She could feel herself blushing. Nevertheless, she said, "This is great fun, Mr. High Wolf. Now it is your turn."

"At your command, Your Highness," he said, bowing slightly at the waist. "Ah, let's see . . ."

"Yes?"

"Do you feel the pressure of your hand in mine, as I take it into my own? Do you sense the light tension as I hold it?"

She nodded.

"And do you feel how wonderful it is to touch?"

"Yes, yes," she said. "I do."

"And so it is that when I touch you, I will always feel wonderful. And I hope you will feel the same. Do you?"

She giggled. "You know that I do."

But he barely heard her, for he was continuing to talk, and he said, "And as I look at you, under the lighting of a

*multitude of stars, I am reminded of a painting, a painting
of a beautiful, young lady."*

Sierra felt the blood rushing again to her cheeks, although she protested, *"But I am not a painting, sir."*

*"No, you're not. And for this, I am most thankful. Now,
look above you, my loveliest one, at the starlit night; and below you, do you feel the solidness of the marble floor beneath our feet, can you hear the soft sway of others' feet
upon it?"*

"Yes, yes, I do."

*"And as they move, do you hear the swish of a lady's
dress? The solid clicking of the gentleman's boots?"*

"Yes."

*"And when you recall these things, will you remember
them and me, and think on this night pleasantly, as will I?"*

"Always, my love. Always."

"And yet, my dearest," he said, bringing her hand to
his lips, *"there is a most vital perception I have not yet
mentioned. I think it is because it is more subtle. Do you
know it?"*

"I . . . I'm afraid I do not."

Stepping to the side, he brought her into the shadows on
the veranda, and as he did so, he placed her hand over his
heart, and whispered, *"Do you feel my heart's steady beat
against your palm?"*

"Steady?" Sierra asked, glancing up at him with a smirk.
"My dear wolf prince, your heartbeat is racing. Are you ill?"

She watched as he shut his eyes, watched as he shook his
head. *"No, no, I am not ill; I am merely in love with you.
And when you are near, my heart aches most strangely, and
beats most furiously. If it is illness, my sweet, beautiful
Sierra, I am certain that I never wish to recover."*

"Oh, High Wolf." She fell into his arms. "How happy I am," she said, as she took his fingers and placed them gently against the pulse at her neck, letting him feel the effect he had on her. She said, "My dear love, I do promise you that even in my old age, I will recall these things you have pointed out so cleverly this evening. And I will remember them along with my love for you . . . always."

High Wolf inhaled swiftly, as though he could hardly utter a word. However, when he did speak, all he said was "Yes, I, too, will always remember."

And then he looked down at her, and, with his gaze trained softly upon hers, he brought two of his own fingers to his lips, where he kissed them, before placing those same fingers against Sierra's own. And murmuring in her ear, he said, "I love you so very much."

"And I you."

Deep inside the ballroom, the music had ended, but it was only a temporary affair. For within moments, the orchestra struck up a chord, and Sierra's spirits took flight. Gazing back into the room, Sierra observed His Serene Highness, Prince Eric, and His Royal Highness, Grand Duke Colheart, her father, step up onto the orchestra platform, which sat high above the crowd.

She heard High Wolf's breath catch, while her own heart pounded in double time. The time to announce their engagement had come at last.

Excitement flooded her nervous system, and as she placed her hand in High Wolf's extended one, she felt herself shaking.

Gently, High Wolf pressed his lips to her hand before saying, "Do not worry. All will be well. You will see."

They smiled lovingly at one another, and stepping back

through the balcony doors, they took their places within the crowd.

The rest was not worthy of recalling, she decided.

Sierra lay down, resting her head for a moment upon her arm. In the distance, a whisper of thunder coursed through the air.

Was there to be a storm?

"Whenever a storm threatens, I will be reminded of our love . . . "

So she had promised herself. Had she meant it?

Perhaps she had. For at the moment, though her eyelids drooped sleepily over her eyes, *he* and he alone filled her thoughts . . .

Chapter 14

Was this a sunset? This a moon's bright glow?
Was this a lake? A vase of roses unfurled?
I saw first with your eyes till I could see,
Discovered first through you reality.
                Excerpted from a poem by David Ziff
                        "Sonnets to a Soul Mate"

She was asleep, sound asleep, he realized as he carefully removed the camouflage from above their camp. With an easy jump, he squatted down into their shelter, replacing the camouflage at once.

Seating himself beside her, he gazed at her fully now that she was asleep, taking his time, filling his mind with her image, wondering at the same time if she had always been this beautiful. And what a tantalizing sight she presented, her softly rounded curves amply displayed, since she wore only corset and drawers. Her dark hair, usually caught up in ringlets, had long since fallen from its pins and was, at present, hanging over one shoulder, softening her look.

Carefully, so as not to awaken her, he ran his fingers over the silkiness of those waves, adoring them; his gaze lingering over her luminous, unblemished skin. So beautiful, he thought. So incredibly beautiful.

And he knew in that moment exactly what he would do: He would take her with him. For, as Grandfather had once said, "Do not leave your woman behind, but rather, keep her at your side. Though you may believe she could not long endure the hardship of the trail, she will fare better by your side than if you left her behind."

"*Your woman*," Grandfather had said. How he wished that were true.

At that moment, she stirred and, opening her eyes, stared straight at him. Sleepily, she smiled.

"You are back," she said.

"Yes," he replied.

"And did you find any trace of my maid and steward?"

"I did."

She waited, as though expecting him to continue, but when he remained silent, she went on to say, "Did you find them well?"

He hesitated, then, "They are well, I believe."

"And . . . ?"

"They are safe for the moment."

"For the moment? Then they are in some kind of danger?"

"No, at present, they are well."

He heard her breathe out a sigh of relief. "Good. That is good," she said sleepily.

"I have brought some berries and pemmican if you would like some food."

Again, she smiled lazily. "I am quite hungry, but I'm afraid I am too sleepy to do anything about it directly, my wolf prince."

Instantly, High Wolf's attention caught her words, and his stomach dropped, while an overpowering desire to take her in his arms overwhelmed him. He hadn't heard her speak that name, and with that particular endearment, in so many years . . .

He closed his eyes against the onrush of longing, wanting, hoping . . .

But it all came to nothing. Within moments, she was fast asleep again . . .

. . . Leaving High Wolf to consider doing the same.

Alas, he might not be able to kiss her, to make love to her here and now as he would like, but he could settle down next to her, take her in his arms and hold her.

And so, as he surrendered to the toil of physical exhaustion, he curled his body around hers. And with his arm draped protectively over her, he fell asleep at once.

She awakened with a dead weight over her stomach. Was something wrong with her?

Her eyelids flew open, and she stared straight up; pine boughs and branches were her ceiling, as well as her bed; mud, dirt and stone, her walls. Plus, there was an odd, earth and pine sort of smell all about her. Where was she?

And whose arm was this thrown over her?

She started up, but fell back with a grimace as the previous day's events came flooding back to her: a narrow escape from a burning boat; a near encounter with a hostile war party; the loss of her companions. Briefly, she shivered, reminding herself that it was over. Her servants were safe; as was she . . . for now. But safe from whom?

Gazing to her side, toward High Wolf, she took a moment to wonder: Had she jumped from one dangerous situation into another? Traded one predicament for another?

Because her feelings for this man had never died.

Her response to that thought was a deep, sincere groan. And she wondered, how could this be? Hadn't enough time intervened between the past and now? Shouldn't her affection for this man have died?

Yes, most definitely. Yet it had not.

And if that weren't shock enough, to come to realize that she was still harboring a passion for him was staggering.

Indeed, she thought with more conviction, there was great danger here. But it was a danger not from the rampages of the wild Indian or from the perils of a more natural force.

Alas, the danger was from within herself. And if she were wise, she would run from High Wolf, his influence, his charm, as fast as she could.

And yet, had she made this dreadful journey only to give in at the first hint of risk? Was her character not more steadfast?

Of course it was. Besides, she had a score to settle with Prince Alathom. Make no mistake, he would either do as she said, or . . .

No, returning home with her mission unaccomplished was unthinkable.

She could not, however, go on without High Wolf.

Briefly, she turned her head toward the object of her thoughts, watching him as he slept, studying him as though his sleeping form might give her some clue as to the best inroad past his defenses.

Odd, in slumber, he appeared harmless, looking much like a little boy. His long hair had been pulled back, out of the way, throwing his face into prominence.

And it was the handsomest of faces, she decided. His eyelashes were unusually long and straight, creating shadows over his cheekbones. His breathing was even, relaxed; his bare chest rising and falling in a regular rhythm as his body curled in toward hers.

And despite herself, she wanted to touch that chest, his face. Indeed, the urge was hard to suppress. After all, he was asleep . . .

She raised her hand, inched it forward, but let it drop to her side. She dared not do it. What if she were to awaken him? How would she explain herself?

And so she did the only thing to be done in the circumstances, and picking up High Wolf's wrist, she placed his arm, which was draped so possessively over her, to his side. And rolling away from him, she came up onto her knees.

Her stomach growled.

"There are pemmican and berries in my parfleche."

She gasped. "You are awake?"

"No," he replied. "I am talking in my sleep."

The statement made her smile. "You speak well for a man who is out of his senses. Where is your parfleche?"

"Over there." He pointed. "Eat to your fill," he said as he came up onto his side, extending his arm beneath him. And bending that arm at the elbow, he placed his head against his hand. "We are in good game country. I will be able to hunt for our supper this day."

"Will we be staying here, in this camp, then?"

"Only through the rest of the day. When evening comes, we will leave here to follow the trail of your maid and steward."

"We will?"

He nodded.

"We wander by night, then?"

"It is the only safe way to travel when one is in enemy country. The plains offer little cover during the day, making it too easy to be discovered by a hostile war party."

"I see," she acknowledged, grabbing a handful of pemmican as they spoke, and holding the bag out to him, she proffered some of the food. Quietly, he accepted the gift, his hand lingering over hers as he took the parfleche from her.

At that touch, pure ecstasy rushed over her nerve endings, the shock of it reverberating through her body. In sooth, she felt the urge to swoon toward him, inviting more.

What madness was this? she wondered, and retrieving her hand from him, she asked, "Where did you obtain this food?"

"I carry pemmican with me always." Softly, he smiled at her before taking a handful of the stuff.

"Really? It is tasty, I must say." Her voice was breathy, but she calmed herself enough to comment, "I am hungry, however, and I think that at present, most anything would taste good."

He nodded.

"What is it made from?"

"Dried buffalo meat, ground fine; bone marrow fat, as good as butter; and chokecherries. It will sustain you throughout the day."

"Chokecherries?"

"They grow on bushes by the thousands. They are slightly bitter, except in certain seasons."

"I see," she said, and looking toward him, she noted that his gaze practically caressed her. She swallowed, hard, before saying, "Y-you have b-berries, too?"

Again he pointed. "They are in the parfleche that was sitting next to this one."

She grabbed hold of that one, a little too quickly, her nervousness a palpable thing.

But he made no comment.

And so, after a time, when he remained silent, she relaxed enough to ask the question most pertinent to her present state. She began, "Will I be able to bathe today? I am afraid I am in need of one . . . quite."

He nodded. "When night comes. I will then take you to a stream."

"Yes, yes," she said. "And of course you won't look."

"Of course."

She caught her lip between her teeth. Then, inhaling deeply, she said, "But evening is a long time away, is it not?"

"Yes, it is."

"And I suppose in the time between then and now, you are willing to overlook my appearance?"

"If you will overlook mine," he replied, though she noted he said it with a smile.

A quick nod for an acknowledgement and then she said, "That is fair enough, though I would dearly love to wash the odd taste from my mouth."

He pointed out yet another bag that was hanging from the three-pronged sticks that stood over the fire.

Dubiously, she gazed at it. It looked as though it were made from the innards of some animal. Not exactly the most appetizing way to store water, she supposed. Yet, when she reached her hands into that bag, the water was deliciously wet, cool and tasted wonderful.

She sat back, picked up the other parfleche—the one that contained the berries—and began nibbling on fresh, wild strawberries. A silence descended over them, though in truth, it was most comfortable, as though they were each perfectly at ease with the other. At last, however, her curiosity would be satisfied, and she asked, "Where are my maid and steward?"

"They have been taken by the Mandans."

"The Mandans?"

"They are a tribe of Indians who live on a bluff overlooking the Missouri River. Because of where they are situated, they serve as a trade center for all the plains tribes."

"Ah. And are they friendly Indians?"

He nodded. "A bit too friendly sometimes. The women have been known to welcome the white man in a very friendly fashion. But you may discover this all on your own. There is a white man's fort that stands beside their village. Your maid and steward have undoubtedly been brought there, where they will be well taken care of."

"That is good," she said, bestowing upon High Wolf a most leery glance. After a moment, when he did not volunteer any information, she asked, "And do you intend to leave me there, also? Or—once we find Maria and Mr. Dominic—do you intend to take us all back to St. Louis?"

"No."

She hesitated. "Ah, does that mean no, you don't intend to leave me there? Or no, you don't intend to take us back to St. Louis?"

He shrugged. "Both will do."

Cautiously, she gazed at him, her eyes staring straight into his. "Does that mean that you have changed your mind? That you will guide me further into Indian country?"

"Yes," he said. "I will. But for a price."

"Ah, yes, a price. Of course. I should have known." Her voice was laced with sarcasm. "And what, Mr. High Wolf, is your price? I must tell you straightaway that most of my gold was lost on that boat."

Nonchalantly, he picked up a piece of wood and his knife and began to whittle, as though he hadn't heard her. Although after only a short pause, he said, "I do not want your gold."

"You don't? Then what do you require?"

He shrugged. "A kiss might do."

"A kiss?" She raised an eyebrow. "Now who's talking about kissing whom?"

Still he didn't gaze at her. "Perhaps a hug would be good, as well."

"A kiss and a hug. Singular. One of each only?"

"That will do for these next few minutes."

"For the next few minutes? How many of these kisses and hugs do you expect me to give you?"

"Twenty a day, I think, should be payment enough."

"Twenty? A day . . . ?"

Briefly, he gazed up at her and winked. "Is that too many?"

"You know it is."

"Shame. It is an easy price to pay, and I'm afraid I would enjoy it much."

"Yes, I'm sure you might. However, the price would be deadly for me, I think."

"Deadly? I have never heard my kisses described in that manner. Do you mean to say that I might make you faint?"

"Oh, please."

"Then what do you mean?"

"I don't think I need answer that."

He grinned. After a moment, however, he said, "If kissing bothers you, perhaps you might massage my back and my legs, for my legs sometimes cramp."

"A massage?"

"*Haa'he.*"

"You want me to touch your body?"

"That is generally how it is done."

"I think I would prefer the kissing."

"Good," he said. "Then you may start now."

"Now? But—"

"Have I not already saved you?"

She grunted.

"Am I incorrect in my reasoning? If I am, you must tell me the error. For, if I have saved you, and if a kiss is the payment, is it not due?"

She frowned at him. "Very well," she said, placing her hand to her lips where she kissed it, and extending it out palm upward, she blew the kiss in his general direction.

He grinned. "That is not exactly what I meant. And I do not understand you, Princess. Were you not the one begging me for a kiss earlier? And now that I wish it . . ."

She grimaced. "How quickly you change. And the kiss is not due you. I have not agreed to the price."

"Then you wish to massage me instead?"

"I will do neither. You must know that I was only teasing you. You said so yourself. No, I will pay you in gold when we return to St. Louis."

"I wish no gold."

"And I will not kiss you—or massage you. At least not now."

He shrugged. "Then I suppose you will have to cook for me."

"Cook?"

"If you expect me to help you, you should give me something in exchange, shouldn't you? You do not wish to give me what I would like, and I do not desire to take that which you offer. I know of nothing else you can do, then, but to cook and clean for me."

"I've never cooked anything in my life, and I'm not about to start now."

"Princess, Princess, do you wish to find the prince?"

As an answer, she crossed her arms over her chest and glared at him. At last, a thought occurred to her, and she asked, "Why have you changed your mind? You were set against kissing me earlier. Has something happened?"

At her words, he relaxed, lying back onto the ground, where he commenced to stare up at their "ceiling." At length, he sighed. "Yes, something has happened."

"Yes? What?"

"We talked. That is what happened."

"Yes? And . . . ?"

"I realize my mistake. Had I been more astute ten

years ago, our lives might be different. I thought you married the prince, not some stand-in. I was certain of it. Had I stayed . . ."

What was this? A form of apology? Well, if it was, it was ten years past due. And she said, "You expect me to believe that?"

He blinked, his look unruffled. "It is the truth. Because of our talk, I have changed my mind about you, and I will take you to your servants, and will help you to find the prince. Is that not enough?"

"No," she said. "That's not enough."

He nodded, as though he understood her perfectly.

"Do not do this," she said into the silence created. "Do not tell me things like this."

"Why should I not?"

"Because it makes me like you a little, and I do not wish to like you."

"But—"

"Don't you understand? I have hated you these ten years past. That hatred has sustained me through some difficult times. I wish it to remain so."

He came up onto his side. "You cannot possibly wish to give in to hatred. Do you not know that it will eat away at you?"

"Yes, I know."

He paused. Then, as though only now understanding her, he said, "Did I hear you correctly? Did you say that you like me a little?"

She moaned. "I . . . suppose so."

"Liking is not bad."

"Isn't it?"

"I, too, have felt hatred," he said, reaching out toward her to straighten back a lock of her hair.

"Though I have done my best to try to understand you and the prince, I, too, have felt the tug of war that enmity casts. I have avoided it only because of my scout training. But I can understand why you might feel as you do." He came up onto his knees in front of her, and bending toward her, he said, "Princess, I once loved you beyond all other things."

She turned her head away. "Do not say these things to me."

"Why should I not? They are words of truth."

"A truth from the past. I do not wish to live in the past."

"I do not ask it of you," he said. "You are here now; I am here. For the first time in ten years, we are together, we are talking, and I find, Princess, that I need you as much now as I did back then."

"No. It cannot be."

"It is."

Sierra turned her head to gaze at him, at his dear face so close to her own, and she said, "Do not say these words to me, High Wolf. Ten years ago I died a little. I am no longer the same person that you once knew. And I am glad of the change. I do not give my confidence nearly as easily as I once did, and I bestow faith in no one until I am certain they can be trusted."

"And yet there is no way to learn to trust, unless you give a person a chance."

"I gave you that chance," she said, leaning away from him.

"And I failed to take it, is that what you're saying?"

"Yes. And once betrayed, I can never give that person my trust again. Never."

"Never is a long time, Princess. And I think you will

find, if you look around, that 'never' is a hard resource
to find. In all the universe, there is no perfection. All
of nature has its flaws. And yet the very word 'never'
would have you believe there is such a thing."

She remained silent.

And he said, "Sometimes people deserve another
chance."

"Not if they—"

He held up a hand to silence her, and he said, "I am
sorry that I let you down ten years ago. Know that I
have come to realize that I failed you."

She stared down at the ground, saying, "Yes."

"But I never stopped loving you."

Baaa, she thought, though outwardly, she remained
silent.

"I would like another chance."

She turned her face away from him. "How can you
say this when only yesterday you told me that you
have been away from your true love for a long time?"

Shaking his head, he grinned. "That I have, Princess," he said. "That I have. Ten long years."

Stunned silence filled the air, until, at last, she said,
"I don't believe you."

"I know."

She gulped, then said, "Then you are not married?"

He shook his head.

"No serious commitments?"

"No."

"But I thought that Indian men could take more
than one wife. Surely—"

He held up a hand. "My heart was given to one
woman long ago, and with her it still remains."

She brought her gaze up to his and stared at him,

scouring his features for the truth of his words.

"I'm afraid I have been guilty of teasing you, Princess, for it is completely my intention to help you find the prince, and the truth is that you owe me nothing. I will do this because you were once one of my dearest friends, and because it is I who owe you."

"You? You admit it?"

"Gladly."

She frowned.

"Think, Princess. Do I not owe you some happiness? Weren't we going to live forever? Be in love the rest of our lives?"

"Do not say these things to me."

"But it did not happen," he continued. "And had I not made a very grave mistake, it might have had a chance. Do you not see this as true?"

Sierra said nothing, simply stared at the ground.

"I think," he said, "that for the time we have together, I should do all I can to give you some happiness. Do you not think this is the least I could do?"

She stared at him; it was all she could do. What did a woman say to such a man? If, indeed, anything needed to be said.

Instead of uttering a word, she swept forward, across the distance separating them, and placed a kiss upon his cheek . . .

Chapter 15

I miss your kindness and your decency,
Your touch, the fun we have, the jokes, the talk;
I miss your smell, your skin and how it feels,
Your smile, your arms and all your robe reveals.
Excerpted from a poem by David Ziff
"Sonnets to a Soul Mate"

But Sierra didn't expect him to turn his head into the kiss, and before she knew what he was about, his lips met hers.

Ah, sweet, sweet wonder. It was like nothing she had ever experienced. Was this love? Was this ecstasy?

Was this what she had missed all these lonely years?

The kiss deepened, and Sierra lost a little of herself to him. Knee to knee, thigh to thigh, they collapsed into each other. One of his arms reached around her, and placing his hand on the small of her back, he pulled her in even closer.

And Sierra went willingly.

His tongue swept into her mouth, and Sierra met the advance. And they kissed; once, again, over and over, as though with their lips alone, they would commit the act of love.

She couldn't get close enough, realizing that what she really wanted was to crawl into his skin, and the limits of the flesh seemed suddenly too much to bear.

She needed, she wanted more.

Her stomach had long ago betrayed her, the first to fall victim to the magic of this man's embrace. At present, she felt as though a whirlwind had been let loose within her, cascading over her nerve endings, reminding her that her body wanted so much more than this . . .

She needed no such reminder. What she required was a moment of sanity.

In faith, how could she make love to this man? How could she surrender so easily?

She broke off the kiss, inhaling air as though it might be the most precious commodity on earth. And she said, "I can't do this."

He nuzzled her neck, saying, "If you say so, but I think that you can . . . you are . . ."

"No," she said. "You . . . you're still the man who betrayed me."

"Am I?"

"Yes, you know it is so."

He shook his head. "I admit no such thing. I admit to a mistake that made me believe that *you* had betrayed me. There is a difference."

"No, High Wolf, I—I . . . You must let me go."

"Must I?"

She nodded, although her head still nestled against his shoulder.

"Very well," he said, as his arms dropped from

around her. Yet, still, neither one made the move that would put distance between their bodies. Her curves still fit neatly against the hard planes of his chest. And leisurely, without holding her, he bent down to kiss her yet again.

And beside herself with longing, she welcomed him. In truth, she moaned aloud, so precious did it feel.

"I want you as a man wants a woman," he whispered against her lips.

"I know."

"But I will not take from you unless you agree to it." Bending, he made a trail of kisses from her cheek to her ear.

She whimpered, and that place on her body most personal began to throb, responding to this man as though it recognized him as her life's true partner, even if she did not. But Sierra was nothing if not strong-willed, and she said, "How could I ever agree to a love affair with you? What would come of it? We are from different worlds, and eventually, I will return to my home, while you . . ."

"And I would not fit into your world?"

"You would not," she agreed. "Remember, you tried it once. It did not work."

He nodded. "Then we should reach out for all the happiness we can gather to us here and now, that we might remember it for the rest of our lives."

She closed her eyes as she bit down on her lip. "That sounds very well, indeed," she said, "but I think in practice it cannot be."

"Why not?"

"Because," she said, opening her eyes to stare at

him, "I might never recover if I were to lose you again after . . . after we had . . ."

He groaned. "Then you admit you felt loss when I left."

"Of course I did," she said. "How could I not? Just as you say you gave me your heart, so, too, did I give you mine. It was, however, a mistake, and one that I am not anxious to repeat."

"Even if I promise that I will not leave you again unless you force me to do so?"

"Will you not?" She backed away from him, far enough to cast him a dim view. And she said, "Did you feel forced into leaving me ten years ago?"

He muttered something beneath his breath.

And she continued, "No, I cannot step into that same trap again . . . not willingly. I must always remember my purpose in being here—and you do not fit into that."

"Purpose?" he asked, his head coming forward, toward her, where he nuzzled a spot on her neck.

Sierra threw back her head to give High Wolf better access, all the while mentally chiding herself. Had she truly said that? What was wrong with her, that her tongue was running away from her?

And she said, "Y-yes. My purpose in finding Prince Alathom."

High Wolf's head came up, and face-to-face, nose-to-nose, he said, "Let us forget about Prince Alathom. Let him remain dead and buried as far as his relations at home are concerned. For if he is not dead, there must be some reason behind his attempt to stage his own death. And so, let us abandon your search for him, and instead, explore each other."

She shut her eyes. Why did he say all the right things? At the right moment? And why did she want so much to do as he suggested?

But her journey here could not be for nothing. No, she had not endured the past ten years to let go of the sweet taste of revenge—not so easily. Make no mistake, in regard to the prince, she would have her way.

She said, "I cannot abandon my search. How would it be if I made love to you, only to discover that the prince still lives? For if he lives, I will take him back home with me. Married by proxy or not, we are still married."

"No," said High Wolf. "You are not married to him. If he has not claimed his right in ten years, he has lost the chance. You must let it go. You must let him go."

"I will not."

But he wasn't listening to her, and he went on to say, "Do you not see? We have a second chance. Let us live here, the life that we should have lived."

"No, I cannot. You simply don't understand all that has taken place. You don't know what it was like, what I had to endure, the talk, the gossip, the accusations."

"You are right," he said. "I know little of all that has occurred in your life since I left, but is it necessary that I do?"

"Yes," she said. "Yes, it is, I think."

"Then explain it to me so that I might understand."

"I—I cannot. It is too degrading, too personal."

He nodded. "Very well. When you are ready, I will listen," he said. "But do not throw me away without considering what we once were to each other."

"High Wolf, please. Don't you see? You do not fit into the scheme of my life, I'm afraid. Not anymore."

"Do I not?" he countered.

"No."

"Then what am I doing here with you now, while the prince . . . who knows where he is, or if he is still alive? Was it not I who saved you? I who rescued you?"

"Yes, yes, but surely you would not hold that over me?"

He exhaled deeply before saying, "It is wrong of me to do so, yes. But I find the urge to remind you of it is stronger than the need to retain my honor . . . if it means I have to live without you."

These were heady words, strong words, good words. And she let out a deep breath, realizing that she was once again beyond her depth with this man. Worse, when seen from her present viewpoint, revenge seemed to be quite a shallow thing, at best.

Alas, was it more important than discovering love again?

But ten years . . . ten years. Could she put heartache aside so easily? The pain? The distrust? The knowledge that the two people most dear to her had fled? And then there were the rumors, the innuendos, the gossip, the degradation.

No, she could not do it. She had come here with a mission; she had her reasons for it. And, by goodness, she would complete it.

Thus decided, she sat back, breaking bodily contact with High Wolf.

But he followed her forward, and placing his hands on her thighs, he leaned in to kiss her chin, her cheeks, her neck, first with his lips, then with his tongue. And as he kissed her over and over, he muttered, "You are my woman. You have been so since the day we met. I seek only to make it so in deed."

And though she arched her chest and threw back her shoulders in acquiescence, she said, "I am not your woman."

He shook his head. "We both know differently." He cupped her breasts with the palms of his hands, and the thought of stopping him didn't even enter her head. Indeed, Sierra swooned backward.

How could she talk? How could she argue with this man, when every ounce of her strength demanded that she surrender to him? And as naturally as if he'd done this every day of his life, he picked her up, letting her legs drape over his arms and then he lowered her to the soft cushions of the pine boughs. And bending over her, he said, "Do you notice that you do not fight me? Take note, Princess. And consider, is this your way with other gentlemen of your acquaintance?"

Sierra gasped. "Is it your intent to insult me, sir?"

He grinned. "Not in the least. I wish only to point out that you allow me these privileges. This, and this alone, marks you as my woman."

"Perhaps," she said at last, reaching up to brush her fingers lightly over his cheek. "But someday, I will have to leave this place, and when that day arrives, there will be no room in my life, nor in my heart for you. If you would love me, then you must do so knowing that this day will yet come."

He gazed at her, simply looked at her, and the silence that stretched out before them was as quiet as a tomb. However, at length, he said, "Very well. Consider me forewarned."

She drew in a breath, saying, "Then you would agree to let me go?"

"No," he said, "I do not agree. But I will understand if that is the way of things. But do not ask me to agree to lose you."

"You promise you won't stand in my way?"

He sighed, but nonetheless, he said, "I will not."

Sierra dropped her gaze from him, feeling as though she had won the battle, but lost the war. However, when she looked at him again, she said, "Then so be it."

And with no other conditions to add, at least none for the moment, she propped herself up on her forearms and said, "Mr. High Wolf. Why do you hesitate?"

She loved him. Ah, yes. Make no mistake, she loved this man with all her heart.

As he fanned his fingertips over the soft skin of her belly, as he ran his palm down to her hand and grasped hold of it, as he leaned over her to take possession of her lips, the knowledge that she had once again committed herself to him settled deep within her. It didn't frighten her this time; it didn't demand anything of her, either. For he didn't rush her; he didn't push her. Instead, with his lips, his tongue, his embrace, all of him, he slowly adored her.

And she was left in no doubt that this man loved her still, as much as she loved him. Although, came a wayward thought, hadn't she believed that of him ten years ago?

She whimpered, the sound high-pitched and soft.

Perhaps he was right, she thought; perhaps she should let go of the past. Like unwanted baggage, the memory was soiled and secondhand. Why did she keep dragging it with her as though his mistakes were set in gold?

Was life not stirring within her at this very moment? And as he had said, there was no single, perfect human being . . .

At that instant, he shifted his weight, and coming up to his forearms, he leaned over her, his gaze serious, determined. And he said, "This is our wedding night."

Without thought, she shook her head.

"Yes, it is," he affirmed. "It is what we should have had. And we will have it . . . now."

"But you don't understand—"

"In my country, in my tribe, when a woman and a man spend the night together, they are married. And so we will be."

She let out her breath slowly, only now starting to realize the danger of what she was doing. And she said, as much for herself as for him, "I cannot marry you. You know this."

"I do not know this."

"High Wolf, do not say this to me. I have been quite clear on the subject."

"True. I have heard your words. But that changes nothing. After tonight, in my heart, we will be man and wife. And if you cannot accept that, then that is too bad. Perhaps you should pretend it is so."

"Pretend?" She stared up at him, shocked that he would suggest it, thrilled at the prospect. And with more aplomb than she felt, she reached out to take hold of a lock of his hair. And she said, "Is this another game, like the ones that you used to teach me long ago? For this is quite a proposition you present me."

"It could be a game, if you like," he said.

She smiled slightly as she twirled that lock of hair around her finger, and she said, "I suppose we could pretend—for today only—that we are married. I remember how well I used to love it when you would play games of observation with me and with Prince Alathom. Do you remember them?"

He inclined his head.

"As long as you realize this is a pretense only?"

"I do," he said at once, as he caught her hand in his. "But if we are to pretend, let us imagine that there is no one else alive this day, but us. No past, no future, no others to interfere. No upset, none of the problems that have afflicted us. There is only now. You and me. *Haa'he*, for today, let us pretend that we are an old married couple, who have many years of life yet to share with one another."

"Yes," she said. "Yes, I like that. And let us make believe also that we have lived with each other for many, many years already."

He grinned and remarked rather disdainfully, "If we have, I think I have missed out on something quite important."

"We're pretending," she said, her voice a mild scold. "And if we are imagining all this, then I shall make believe that I have every right to do with you as I wish."

His smile widened. "I am at your disposal."

"Truly?" She glanced up at him shyly.

And he squeezed her hand. "Truly."

"But after today, we will not be really married. You must remember that, won't you?"

"For you this will be so."

"But not for you?"

He nodded. "Not for me. If I make love to you to-night, from that moment on, you will be my wife."

She gave him a soft smile. "It seems hardly fair, does it? And yet I cannot marry you, not in actuality." She drew her brows together in a frown. "And this you accept?"

"No," he said.

"But I thought . . . didn't you say that—"

"I do not accept it. Perhaps I should warn you that I will do all I can to make you my wife in fact. But if, by the time you are prepared to return home, you cannot see fit to 'make an honest man of me,' I will not stand in your way."

"And this you promise me?"

He nodded. "This I promise you."

She exhaled slowly, saying, "Then let us begin. Where do we start?"

He groaned. "I think we begin with a massage."

"Oh," she said. "Yes, that's correct. You wanted me to massage you."

He shook his head. "Not this time. At the moment, I want to massage you."

"Oh."

"Since you are already lying down, it seems the right thing to do, does it not?" This he asked with a wink.

"Yes, I suppose so."

And without another word, he lay down beside her, and bending his arm at the elbow, he propped his head up against one of his hands, while he threw a leg over hers. Gently, he trailed his hands down over her arms, lightly rubbing. He massaged her torso down and up, rubbing her breasts in between, then moved his hands down one leg to the other and up again, massaging her calves, her thighs, her belly.

Leaning over her, he kissed her belly.

And Sierra shivered with ecstasy. "Hmmm," she said, "that feels good."

"Yes," he said, "doesn't it?"

He continued up over her shoulders to her neck, trailing caresses over her breasts. And where his hands led, his lips soon followed.

"We must remove your corset," he said softly. "It will feel better for you, then."

"Yes," she agreed, reaching up to help him with it. Carefully, they worked over the laces, pulling them apart until the garment slipped from around her. Breathing a deep sigh at the feeling of freedom, she lay down fully on the pine boughs, there beneath his gaze. And as she did so, she realized that in all these years, this was the first time she had ever presented herself to High Wolf in such a fashion.

And he adored her with his eyes.

"You are so beautiful," he said. "How I have missed awakening to this every day of my life."

"But I have never been here for you to miss it."

"I know," he said. "That is the point."

"But now you have me."

"Yes," he said. "Now I have you." And as he gently kneaded her softened mounds of flesh, he placed a kiss there, too, murmuring, "Let us pretend that we are deeply in love with each other."

She nodded.

"So much in love that when I place my hand here"—

he touched her on that spot most sensitive, at the junction of her legs— "you welcome the embrace."

Again she nodded.

"And of course, an old married woman like you would not object if I remove these drawers, so that you and I might enjoy our time together without the barrier of clothing."

"Yes," she said. "But if I do this, then you must remove your . . . ah . . . breechcloth, too."

He groaned, deep in his throat. "Yes," he said. "I will. All in good time."

With hands that were not quite steady, he removed her drawers. And for a moment, he stilled; his gaze caught hers. Unsteadily, he inhaled.

"I'm afraid that my illusions of you have not done right by you, my love. Now." He leaned over her, placing his hand low upon her tummy. "I am going to touch you here." He moved his hand lower, over her triangular mound of hair. "But being an old married woman, you will expect this, will you not?"

"Yes," she said. She sucked in her breath. "That feels quite good."

"*Haa'he*. I know." He massaged her gently. "Now, you must widen your legs to greet me."

She bowed her head in acknowledgement, realizing she was already accommodating him. Instinctively, her legs had already parted.

And using the touch of his fingers, he worshipped her.

All at once, every bit of her attention was drawn to what he was doing down there, and arching upward, she moved her hips in rhythm with his hand.

"Oh, my love," he said. "Do you feel it? Do you feel the magic between us?"

"Yes," she murmured. "I do. Oh, High Wolf. What is happening to me? I feel . . . I feel . . ."

"Do not think of it. Just experience it, knowing that you have my love."

"Yes," she said. "Oh, yes. High Wolf." Her eyes went wide. "I . . . I . . ." she moaned, as pure sensation overtook her, and gyrating her hips in rhythm with his hand, she came to a plateau of such overwhelming pleasure, she thought she might not be able to bear it. On and on it went, her hips rising and falling with the pulse of it, as pleasure swamped her.

And with her eyes wide, and staring straight up at High Wolf, she said, "Oh, my."

Chapter 16

If we had been together from the start,
If joy had followed us around the clock,
Would we have found the wisdom in our heart?
Excerpted from a poem by David Ziff
"Sonnets to a Soul Mate"

"**S**o that is what it means to make love," she said sometime later.

"It is a part of it."

"Hmmm. There is more. Of course there would have to be more . . . for you. Does a man seek . . . pleasure . . . similar to that of a woman?"

He concurred with a bob of his head.

"And is it obtained in the same way? Do you wish me to do this to you?"

"There are other ways, better ways, sweeter ways."

"Yes, yes, of course. And I'm sure I know these things. After all, I am an old married woman."

"Yes, you are," he agreed. "At least for today."

"So," she said, "what do I do now?"

He grinned, and grabbing hold of her hand, he

brought it to his chest. "This old married woman could kiss me for a start."

"Yes," she agreed, and leaning in toward him, she placed a peck on his cheek.

"A passionate kiss."

"Oh," she said, and sitting up, positioned her lips on his, her tongue sweeping into his mouth, much as he had done to her.

"Did you mean something like that?"

"Yes," he said. "Something like that."

"And now what?"

He grinned. "You will have to find that out for yourself."

"I will?"

He nodded. "A man's body is ofttimes sensitive in much the same places as a woman's."

"Really?" She reached over to place a touch against one of his flattened nipples, pleased to hear him suck in his breath. And she murmured, "Did that feel good?"

"Quite," he said.

"And if I trail my hand down your chest like this, does that feel good, also?"

He grabbed her hand, saying, "A little too good."

"And your neck and the lobe of your ear," she said, leaning upward to press kisses in these places. "Are these as sensitive as mine?"

He groaned.

"I think they are," she whispered, her breath blowing against him gently.

"Yes," he uttered, and it was all he uttered. Changing position, he came up over her, placing his body weight on his forearms. And he inquired, "I must know, Princess. Have you ever made love to a man?"

At first she nodded, but then, seeing his frown, she bit her lip.

"I want the truth."

"I . . . the truth?"

"*Haa'he.*"

"I . . ." She turned her head to the side. "I . . . in ten years, it would be natural to assume that I would have."

"That was not an answer to my question. The truth now, Princess. It's important."

"I . . ." She sent him a shy glance. "I have not."

She felt, more than heard, his sigh.

"I did not think that you had, but I had to be certain."

"Why?"

"If you were experienced, you would know why."

"I would?"

He nodded. "The first time for a woman is not always a pleasant experience."

"I have been told it is never a good experience for a woman. It has been said that sex is merely a thing to be endured. And only because men require it."

"Endured? Required?" He looked cynical. "Who has told you such a lie?"

"A lie? High Wolf, I believe this to be so," she said, casting him a wide-eyed glance. "Why many of the older, married women—those who attend me. They all speak of it in this way."

"Then they should know better than to try to scare a young woman. A union between a man and woman is a sharing experience, not a thing to withstand."

"Then these women, what they said, it is not true?"

"Not in the least. But," he said, leaning down to place a kiss on a ripened breast, "it is not always good the first time for a woman. It may hurt."

"Yes," she said. "So I have heard."

"Some say that the pain goes away quickly. Some never experience relief until after the first few times. But if one practices it, and attends to it, a woman should experience the same feeling that you felt only a few moments ago."

"Truly?" she said. "That was a good thing, was it not?"

He nodded. "That was a good thing." Then he grinned. "And so we should practice it often."

"Of course we should," she said. "We are an old, married couple, after all."

"Yes, we are. And now, my wife of many, many years, are you ready?"

With her gaze locked with his, she nodded.

"Then do what I tell you to do, and perhaps this first time will be memorable for you, instead of one filled with . . ."

She smiled at him. "I will try."

He gazed down at her, and in his look was such adoration, Sierra brightened.

"Princess, Princess," he said, "do you know how much I have loved you?"

"Even these past ten years?"

"Yes," he admitted. "Though I have refused to acknowledge it. But I am not lying when I tell you that you have haunted my dreams. For me, you are all I have ever known, all I have ever wanted. In ten years, there has been no one else."

Her look at him was mocking in the extreme. "And you expect me to believe that? You, a handsome, young man—in a country where a man can take more than one wife?"

"Why would I marry another when my every thought was harried by you? How could I give my heart to another when you were still living here within me?" He touched his breast. "I admit that there have been others who have tried to interest me in marriage. But always, when I would look at another, I would see you; I would remember . . . us. And when that happened, the sadness would return to torment me. No, unfortunately for me, when I lost you, I lost a part of myself, as well, for I died a little on the day I left. And nothing since has made me come alive . . . until now . . ."

Reaching out to him, she eased back a lock of his hair, as she said, "High Wolf, do you mean these things you tell me?"

He nodded. "Very much."

"Oh, High Wolf, I am sorry, so very sorry that things have turned out as they have, and were it in my power, I would forget my reason for being here, for needing to find the prince. But the die is cast. There are things a person cannot forget. Actions that can never be taken back. Reputations that must be upheld."

He grabbed hold of her hand, turning his head into it, and pressed kisses onto her palm. He said, "What are you saying?"

"That no matter what happens, I must return home . . . with the prince as my husband."

"No, you should let it go."

"I cannot."

"Then tell me why this is so." He eased himself into lying next to her, and with his head propped up by his hand, he said, "I think the time has come for you to tell me what has happened in these last ten years. What is it that gives you such a determined purpose, for I sense that there is much you are not telling me."

She inhaled swiftly, letting go of her breath slowly. "It is complicated."

He gestured around him, saying at the same time, "I have much time in which to listen."

"No, I cannot tell you. You might not understand, and I think you will condemn me, much as everyone else has."

"Who is everyone else?"

Again, she sighed. "The servants, the serfs, the housemaids, the kitchen maids, the butlers, the farmers, their wives. But mostly Prince Alathom's father and mother."

"They blamed you when the prince left?"

"Not at first," she said. "But when one year turned to three, four, five, and still he could not be found— despite envoys sent to discover him—it became apparent that he was not coming back because of me—or so they thought."

"And 'they' are all these people you mentioned?"

She nodded. "But mostly his father and mother."

High Wolf frowned. "I know his father and mother well. After all, I spent six years there myself, and I became close to them both. I cannot imagine them condemning you, unless there was ugly gossip that they began to believe."

"Of course there was gossip. From the lowliest servant to the highest. From the townspeople to the clergy. And it is a certainty that I do not even know most of what was said. All I am aware of is that no matter the problem, I became the reason for it. There were even those who began to say I was a witch, and this was the reason Prince Alathom left. Luckily Father Junipero defeated most of these rumors."

"Father Junipero did this?"

"Yes."

High Wolf frowned.

"But even Father Junipero could not put all the rumors to rest, and eventually I had to flee Baden-Baden. Soon after I left, however, the country was invaded, and the reason for the invasion was placed on me, as well."

High Wolf sat in silence for a moment, then said, "Why would you want to return there? If all this has happened, why would anyone be so determined to go back?"

"Because," she sat up, taking hold of her corset and drawers and placing them in front of her, much like a shield. "Because my family, as well as my country, bear the insult. And there is tension now between those who were once the best of friends. In truth, war threatens between my country and Prince Alathom's unless I can resolve this."

"*Saaaa*, now I understand. And so you hope to find the prince and take him back to the Continent in order to prevent a war?"

She nodded. "For a long time, no one knew where Prince Alathom was. But when, only several months ago, he was found at last, I began to make plans to come to America. I concocted the scheme, and Maria helped me design each detail. Arrangements were set;

all was in order. I had even obtained my parents' permission. But then, only weeks after learning of Prince Alathom's whereabouts, news came announcing his death.

"Well, as you might imagine, I refused to believe it. I refuse to believe it still. No, it is my conviction that his 'death' is simply another ruse on Alathom's part to keep from assuming the responsibility that is rightfully his. And he will be made to come home and take it, for it is only he and I together who can put an end to this threatened war between our two countries . . . if it has not already started."

High Wolf nodded. "Thus, you are honor-bound to return."

"Yes."

"And what if the prince is dead?"

"Then I will return and continue to help my country as best I can."

"And if the prince is alive and refuses to go back with you?"

"Then he truly will be a dead man."

High Wolf grinned. "Surely you would not, yourself, try to kill him?"

"And why would I not?"

"Because he is your friend."

"*Was* my friend."

High Wolf paused, looking as though he were deep in thought. "I could return with you. I was adopted by the prince's father and mother. Perhaps I could . . ."

She grimaced. "No, that would also make very little difference. Your relationship to the family is not a blood lineage. You cannot inherit the throne or rule. No, it has to be the prince or no one."

High Wolf nodded. "I feared as much. I must admit that I never understood all these rules and conditions that govern the royalty. I knew that you and the prince were bound by them, but they made little sense to me."

"Yes, but we are not bound by rules so much as we are by duty. Duty to do the best that we can for our people and our countries. Rules can always be changed; duty cannot."

High Wolf tipped his head to the side. "And so you cannot marry me because you and the prince must remain married in order to establish peace?"

"Yes."

Lost in thought, High Wolf rolled over onto his back, putting an arm onto his forehead, saying nothing.

And at length, she asked, "What are you thinking?"

He hesitated. "I am thinking that we had better find the prince as quickly as possible. And to that end we should prepare to leave immediately. I no longer believe we should wait until nightfall to prepare."

"But I thought you said it was unsafe to travel or even to venture out into the open by day."

"That is true. But it can be done."

"But weren't we going to finish . . . I mean, there is more to making love, and . . ."

"That can wait; I can wait. Besides, there will be other times, other places."

"Yes, I suppose there will be, even though we were pretending to be married only for today . . ."

But if he heard her, she would never know, for he didn't move or acknowledge her in any way. He lay there beside her, saying nothing, doing nothing, his mind obviously as far away from her as if they lived in different worlds.

At last, Sierra queried, "Does something else trouble you?"

"*Hova'ahane*, no. But I think I should warn you that, though you may believe that you *have* to marry the prince, I do not intend to let you go now that I've found you."

"There is no other way for me, for my country."

High Wolf grunted, the sound low in his throat. "There is always a way," he said after a moment. "It's simply that I have not yet discovered it. However, of this I am certain: You are my woman. Now, and for the rest of our lives. So perhaps I should warn you: I will not rest until the world knows that it is I who is married to you . . ."

Sierra opened her mouth to retaliate, but upon casting High Wolf a sidelong glance, she thought better of it. And, alas, what would she have said anyway? What could she have said when her heart had warmed to the very thought of marriage to High Wolf . . .

Chapter 17

Of more than bodies bound in harness and yoke—
Mechanics are a stage, technique ignites
A purpose senior to each breathless stroke:
Affinity's own golden, joyful mission,
Transcendence of the physical position.
Excerpted from a poem by David Ziff
"Sonnets to a Soul Mate"

"Ohhhhh! Is this truly necessary?"

High Wolf chuckled as he streaked yet another bit of mud on her face. "You must be covered completely with the mixture of this mud, for when it dries, it will become a gray color, which is similar to that of the prairie wolf. Thus, to any casual glance, you will look a natural part of the landscape, instead of like an enemy. I will even make ears of this mud to set on your head to complete the image."

"But to wear mud—on my face . . . in my hair . . ."

"It is clean mud—it is good for you."

"Somehow that isn't reassuring."

High Wolf merely smiled at her, choosing to remain silent. After their talk in the morning, he had left their camp posthaste, that he might scout out a safe place in which to prepare themselves for their coming journey. And he had found a good spot, one that was filled with timber and the much-welcome shade from the majestic willow, as well as the cover from the larger, more numerous cottonwood trees.

It overlooked a small lagoon. That it was nestled away from the Missouri River made it an even more secure spot. And the fact that it cut into the canyon walls above them provided a natural shelter, and made it fairly private.

Briefly he had tracked the circumference of the place to ensure its safety, had even set a few man traps, just in case. And at present, he was satisfied that, despite the daylight, the two of them could be there without too much worry.

But Sierra was continuing to complain, and she said, "I do not believe that there has been a day in my life where I have purposely tried to make myself appear ugly."

High Wolf shook his head. Did she not know? Was she not aware that her beauty needed no fancy trappings? It seemed incredible that she did not, and he said, "You could never be ugly. Even in this ruse, you are the loveliest creature I have ever been so fortunate to witness. Truly, your green eyes shine through this mud like stars against a darkened night, and I confess that no amount of dirt I cake on you hides your curves, for they seem to have a life of their own."

She grinned at him, then gave him a stern look. "I think you are a bit heavy-handed with your compliments, High Wolf. Look at me, I'm covered."

"Yes," he said. "I'm looking . . . and I like very much what I see." He smiled when she made a face at him, and he added, "My lady wolf."

No sooner had the words left his lips than her eyes lit and sparkled, reminding him of starlight, and she said, "*My lady wolf*. Yes, I like that."

"I will have to remember."

"Yes, yes," she said, "you will. Now, tell me, am I to paint my clothes . . . my undergarments in a similar fashion as this?"

He inclined his head. "There must be nothing about you to indicate that you are anything other than a common wolf. As we travel, I will do my best to initiate you into the manner in which a scout moves, that you might learn to blend your body—as well as your mind—to the force of nature. That will be your protection."

"But I don't know how to do any of this, let alone paint myself correctly."

"I know," he said. "That is why I will do it for you." *Even if it means pure torture*, he thought.

Perhaps, he conjectured, she could relegate their early morning rendezvous to the back of her mind; he, however, was more than unusually aware of her; of the bends and turns of her figure, her planes, her hollows and valleys, her sexuality. To touch her, knowing that he could most likely persuade her to his need . . .

And he could only think: *Was it really necessary that he rush?* Would a few hours, a day, perhaps two, set them back too readily? Yes, an urgency within him demanded that he set out at once, but another part of him longed to linger.

He exhaled slowly, saying, "Come close to me now."

She obeyed, stepping toward him, not stopping until she was little more than a hand's-length away from him.

"*Saaaa*." The low-pitched sound was centered deep in his throat. This was too much. Her scent engulfed him; her nearness bewitched him, and his head spun. Nevertheless, he said, "None of the white of your underclothes must show. Your body, as well as the things you wear, must blend into the colors of nature. I will pat mud on you, but it may not stick. We men put the mud on our nude body, but I cannot ask that of you. So I might add a bit of ash or charcoal to help it stick, as well as to hide the color of your clothes."

"Hmmm," she said, leaning in toward him.

And he clenched his jaw. "Now watch what I do," he instructed, "for you may be required to repair this yourself."

Ever so gently, and with eyes twinkling, she bobbed her head, while throwing back her shoulders to accentuate her breasts.

High Wolf grinned. She was flirting with him, actually flirting with him. The knowledge warmed him, made him want to sing. And perhaps, he thought, it might not be as difficult as he had thought, to have her longing for him, which would, of course, be a necessity. That is, if he were to keep her with him.

Hope sparked within him, but pretending indifference, he simply said, "It might be best to streak the material of your clothing with mud and charcoal. Like this . . ." And with his fingers dipped in the stuff, he smeared it onto her shoulders, his fingertips seeking out each hollow, each peak and valley of her body, that he might memorize it.

How soft was her skin, how radiant her glow, and he realized he wanted to stay like this, be like this for the rest of his life.

But he said not a word as he spread the earthen mixture over her, though he did massage each feminine inch of her flesh. As he bent slightly at the waist, his touch roamed lower and lower, down over one breast, to knead the silky skin beneath her clothing. Then over to the other breast.

Involuntarily, he groaned.

And she was quick to ask, "Is something wrong?"

"No," he said. "Everything is right, except perhaps the moment I have chosen to do this. To touch you like this, to feel your skin, to paint the outline of your breasts, causes me to think of other things besides scouting, other things besides duty, besides finding the prince. Yes, at this moment, my mind wanders onto many other pleasant things."

She remained silent, though he noted that as he spoke, she had drawn in her breath.

But he said no more, continuing his work down, over each of her arms, over to her flat tummy, lower still to the juncture of each leg.

And coming down onto his knees where he reached for more sludge, he said, "Spread your legs."

Instantly, she complied, without objection, without even a mild word of censure.

In response, High Wolf swallowed the knot in his throat before going on to say, "I am going to touch you once again, in the same place I did earlier. Do you understand?"

She acknowledged him with a nod.

And he continued, only this time his voice was no

more than a hoarse whisper as he said, "Earlier, however, you had no clothes to protect you."

Again, she bobbed her head, though no words escaped her lips.

But that was all it took to have him touching her, smudging the silted muck onto her clothes, there at the top of each leg. And his head spun.

Despite the binding of her clothing, her honeyed scent filled his nostrils, making him think, making him want other things. Even the feel of her hot skin beneath her clothing lured him to do what he knew he should put off until later. Worse, he was aware, without even inquiring, that were he to ask it of her, she would receive him. She was ready. He could feel it, could sense it.

And so was he.

Still, he picked up another piece of the sooty dirt to splatter on her, knowing that if he gave in to his desires, he'd only have the entire procedure to repeat.

But she tantalized him, her femininity only a touch away, and the knowledge that he could tug at those drawers to feel the supple flesh beneath, was almost more than he could bear.

She would let him make love to her. He knew she would. Why not reach out and take it?

At that moment, she leaned down to him and whispered in his ear, "We could spare an hour or so, could we not?"

He practically came apart right there. Even still, it was all he could do to utter as smoothly as possible, "Yes, my lady wolf, I think we could spare an hour or so."

And she smiled. She simply smiled at him, and in response, his world exploded.

Her drawers were the first thing to leave her body, though his fingers trembled with their work. Nevertheless, tugging them down her legs, he helped her to step out of them, leaving that place most private open, not only to his touch, but perhaps to his kiss, as well.

And as he knelt before her, he did touch her there, spreading her legs as she stood before him, until he could place himself between them.

And he whispered, "I am going to do something to help prepare you for lovemaking, for I worry that I might hurt you."

"Yes," she said, but she swayed unsteadily, and he caught her as her knees gave way and she swooned toward the ground. Holding her in his arms, he came up to his feet and carried her to a grassy knoll, upon which grew a large, old weeping willow. And pushing back its branches, he set her down on a soft patch of grass beneath it, the branches of the tree surrounding them as though it were nature's canopy.

"I will do something I think might make this more pleasant for you. It is only that," he muttered, "I want you so much that I fear I will not be able to long control myself."

Gazing up at him, her eyes were filled with passion, but also with love, and he thought he might surely cheer when she said, "Please don't hold back. I would have you experience what I did earlier this morning."

"Yes," he said, "however, I must rein myself in, if you are to have a pleasurable experience."

"But why? Have I not already—"

He shook his head, laying a finger over her lips. "A woman, unlike most men, can usually experience this sort of thing over and over."

"Oh."

But he barely heard her. He had already bent toward her, his fingers working over the corset, which was now caked in mud. And he found himself silently cursing this particular article of clothing, for the material and gook on it proved to be too much.

Luckily for him, she reached up to help him. And when she at last gave a tug and the garment fell away, he knew what it meant to crave something desperately.

And looking down upon her, he sucked in his breath.

What beauty. What treasure. What loveliness.

Her breasts were perfect, white mounds that spilled out into his hand, begging not only for his touch, but for his kiss.

And he complied, sampling first one breast, then the other, kissing her deeply, but listening, always listening for her response.

And when he heard her moan, his own breathing accelerated.

Her beauty engulfed him; her fragrance seduced him; her softness reminded him of the velvety petals of the wild rose. He wanted to lose himself in her, and for a moment he cursed the limits of the flesh, for if he could, he would merge his body with hers completely.

But such was impossible, and so he settled for something less and kissed his way down toward her belly button, the taste of her balmy and fresh within his mouth. Still he listened closely for her response.

And when she trembled in his arms, he went quietly out of his mind.

Ah, to be a part of her, to experience her warmth. The thought, however, made him slightly wild with excitement.

And he inched his way farther south.

But she was beginning to become suspicious of his movements, and she jerked upward, exclaiming, "High Wolf, what are you doing?"

"I am loving you," he said simply.

"Yes, but—"

"Sh-h-h. Do not stop me. Do not think. You will enjoy it, and so will I."

"But surely this is not love, this is not—"

Briefly he came up onto his forearms to look into her eyes, as he said, "If we have only a short time to be together—as you tell me we do—I would take every memory of you with me, including this."

"But I've never heard of such a thing . . ."

"It is no wonder," he said, "if all that has been told to you is that lovemaking must be 'endured.' Perhaps these women, who have declared this to be so, have deficient husbands."

The comment made her smile, and he returned the gesture, saying, "If you ever return there . . ."

"I will return there."

But he ignored her words, and went on to say, "*If* you ever return there, perhaps you should tell these ladies a bit more about lovemaking. Maybe you could make them envious."

"But, sir, it would be scandalous."

"Indeed," he said. "It would be all the more fun for that reason, and that reason alone."

And when she chuckled, he joined in. But there was so much more to be done, and without another beat of time passing between them, he returned to the business at hand.

Quickly, he resumed his former position, and just as quickly, he began to kiss her . . . there.

She sighed. She moaned. She whimpered. And he loved it all. She tasted of spice and river water, as well as the heady balm of feminine splendor.

Ah, he thought, the magic of her, the sensation, the excitement. Even the warmth of her body had him wanting more of this, more of her, more of them together. And quickly, in less than an instant, he became one with her, in soul, in spirit, if not yet in body.

How it happened, he did not know. Perhaps it was their physical closeness. Perhaps not. All he knew was that right now, there was no past, no present, no future. No space between them, yet all was space.

Indeed, he came to know her as well as he knew himself. And truth to tell, what he saw he knew to be utterly divine. In faith, he had never loved her more. And he realized in that moment that their love was a coming together not only of the flesh, but of the spirit. Truly, she was a part of him.

Which was why he had never forgotten her . . .

It was a moment of discovery, a moment of fulfillment, a moment of utter and complete joy. It was also an instance wherein he knew that he could trust her, had always been able to do so. For she was not only trustworthy; she *was* trust.

He stirred uneasily. So this, he thought, this is what the two of them had missed all those years ago. This coming together, this soul-to-soul camaraderie.

And he realized more: It had been a mistake not to make love to her back then, and to hell with what her narrow-minded society might have thought of it. For if he had known her in this way ten years ago, he could never have made the error that he had.

Well, she was his now. He was alive; she was alive. They had a chance.

It would be his task, and hers, too, perhaps, to nurture their love into becoming as real as the world around them: as real as the plains, the sky, the very air they breathed.

All at once, she whimpered, interrupting his thoughts. And he gave her body his full attention, only to see that she was beginning the dance that would forever belong to the two of them.

And when she muttered, "Oh, High Wolf, I had no idea," he merely nodded, but otherwise remained silent.

"I have never felt closer to you than I do at this moment," she said. "I . . . I . . ."

But no words formed on her lips as yet another cry escaped her, and he watched as she surrendered to the physical demands of their passion. And as she reached her apex, her soft cry made his heart swell to many times its size . . .

Sierra dipped a toe into the muddy water of the lagoon, the shock of the cold water making her shiver. Briefly she glanced over her shoulder, espying High Wolf beneath the branches of the willow, the tree that would forever be indelibly etched upon her mind. That he was still lying where she had left him, and that he was looking directly at her, should have shamed her, for she stood upon the brink of the lagoon, utterly naked.

However, it did not. Instead of the shame, she experienced a feeling akin to excitement.

"High Wolf," she called to him, "are you going to teach me to swim now?"

"Not today," he said, raising up onto an elbow. "We must repaint you with earth and sand."

"But surely not right away. There is still another matter to attend to."

"*Haa'he*. That there is."

"I will not be long. I simply need to dip myself in the water to wash this grime off my face and hair."

"Why?" he asked. "I will only have to repaint you, again."

"Then that is what you will have to do. For now, I must have it off me."

He inclined his head in acknowledgement, then lay back against the grass beneath him, his gaze seemingly intent on the branches above his head. And the thought occurred to her, as she watched him, that he must be tired.

Not only had he little to no sleep, he was also preparing for a journey across dangerous land, a fact that must weigh heavily on him.

Perhaps she should allow him a few moments alone to sleep—at least before they took up where they had left off. After all, she had her hands full. Imagine, a face and head full of mud.

She dipped down into the water and, submerging her head, hand washed her hair.

Something caught her around the ankle, and she would have screamed had she not been in water over her head. As it was she choked in liquid instead of air and surfaced at once, coughing.

"High Wolf," she screamed as soon as she had settled herself, "there's a monster in the water."

But when she looked back toward the willow, he was not there.

"High Wolf!"

Slowly, a head surfaced from out of the water, and Sierra bit back a scream.

But then she looked closer. The head materializing before her was human, sporting long, black hair.

High Wolf.

He came up smiling.

"You! How did you get there?" she scolded, frowning at him, yet unable to completely suppress the need to laugh. And her lips throbbed as though they might betray her. But she held her ground, kept her frown, and asked, "Where did you come from? You were under the tree not a moment ago. And I didn't hear you get into the water."

He chuckled. "That is because you were so involved in what you were doing that you did not pay attention to the rest of your environment. A scout never relaxes his awareness. Not even for a moment. A scout must always keep his senses listening to the forces of nature, and what they are telling him."

In response, she splashed him. "Well, I am not a scout," she said, "and you didn't tell me you might startle me."

"And neither will an enemy give warning."

"But why should I learn these things when I have you with me?"

"Because," he said, "I cannot be with you every second of every day. Or would you like me to come with you when you have feminine matters to attend to?"

She didn't answer, except to send him another splash. And he retaliated, but his splash was small in comparison to what he did next. Submerging, he swam around her until he was able to catch her around the waist. And standing up behind her, he pressed up close against her, leaving her in no illusion as to his need.

And he said, "If you wish this sand and ooze to be washed from your hair, you might have asked me to help. For I think that I should do it."

She nodded, willing at least to concede this.

And he began to massage her head. "If you were to try to do this alone, little bits and pieces of mud might remain."

"Then you most certainly must help me," she agreed.

"And alas," he said, "I see that there is silt and clay still clinging to your breasts."

She grinned, glancing down and seeing only cleanly washed flesh. But bending quickly, he brought up a handful of mud to splash on her there. And she said, "Goodness, yes, they are quite dirty. I must have done a terrible job of cleansing myself."

And he rubbed and massaged her chest. "Aren't you glad I am here to help?"

"Yes, sir, I am. But I think the job is hardly done yet."

"Then I cannot be remiss."

"Hardly."

"On my honor," he said, as he bent again to grab some more of the morass from the river bottom, smearing it over her belly and lower still . . . "I believe there is still some dirt down here. Tsk, tsk, what would you do were I not here to teach you how to wash properly?"

"Yes," she said. "What would I do?"

He nuzzled her neck with his lips. "Hmmm," he said, "river water and mud. What an enticing combination."

And she swooned backward, into his arms.

But she was not long in the embrace, for, bending, he placed an arm under her knees, and with a single flourish, he picked her up, cradling her in his arms. And then he began to tread back toward the shoreline, while Sierra clung to him, hugging him around the neck, cuddling her head into the crook of his neck.

And she wondered, how had she survived these past ten years without this? Without him?

Had she been only half alive?

The truth stung as its reality hit home. Yes, it was true. Her world, her very existence, had been empty without this man. In sooth, without him, the brightness of the day had faded into a dullness of pomp and formality. No, without him, life had become no more than something to be endured.

And now he was here, and the earth was again full of color, of adventure, of life and love.

Yes, love.

Oh, dear Lord, she prayed. What was she to do? For duty to herself, her family, her people, demanded certain actions on her part; while love . . . love gave and gave, leaving her with a happy glow of hope, awareness, beauty.

But it was also something she could not have. The

time when she could have easily reached out and taken it had long since passed her by.

But she wouldn't think of that now. For this moment in time, she had this man, this make-believe marriage, these memories. And at least no one could take these away from her. No, these were owned by no one, save herself; hers and hers alone to keep, to cherish, and to replay over and over again in some distant time . . .

He kissed the top of her head as he trod toward their bed beneath the willow. Quickly, efficiently, he pulled back its branches, and set her down, oh so gently, upon their grassy knoll.

And coming up over her, he said, "I think you are ready for me. Are you?"

"Yes, my love. I think so."

With his knee, he spread her legs, and she waited, wondering . . .

But he didn't rush her. Instead, he caressed her, there in that place most private. And he said, "Here, where my fingers touch you . . ."

She nodded.

"This is where I will place myself."

She looked up at him, drawing her hand over his back. "I know. This much I have been taught."

"Good," he said. "This is good." And then, supporting his weight on his forearms, he thrust forward, joining their bodies in the age-old act that would forever unite them as man and wife.

It did hurt. And she stiffened.

"I am sorry," he said. "It cannot be helped."

"I know."

He withdrew a small distance, then plunged inward again, this time a little deeper. Then once again.

Her fingernails dug into the flesh of his back. But he didn't appear to mind, if he, indeed, even noticed.

Over and over, he thrust inward and out, and Sierra bore it as best she could. And then it was over. They were joined.

"Is that it, then?" she asked.

He laughed. "No, I have but begun."

"Oh."

And without moving the lower half of his body, he kissed her lips, his tongue searching out hers, tasting, testing, mating. Slowly, so slowly she barely noticed, he began to move once again . . . there.

And she strained against him.

He said, "If you tighten your muscles there, and pull them in, it might help ease the pain."

She did so, and he groaned.

"Did I hurt you?"

Again he laughed. "No, the opposite."

"Oh."

"Do it again."

She did, receiving the same reaction from him, and she said, "You can feel it when I do that?"

"Oh, yes," he said. "I feel it very much." And with an easy maneuver of his body, he began to move.

Instinctively, she joined in with the motion, rejoicing in his low-pitched grunts and groans, enduring the tenseness in her body.

And then it changed.

Ever so slowly, instead of pain, sensation—intense

and consuming—began to build. The same sort of sensation that she had revelled in earlier.

"High Wolf," she whispered. "I feel something there . . . again . . ."

"I know," he said. "I feel it, too."

"But . . . again? And now?"

"You are, indeed, an incredible woman," he said, and he kissed her.

And they danced, and they danced, that ageless reel that has no steps, no rules and no regrets. She twisted beneath him; she gyrated, she wiggled. And remembering his comment from earlier, she tightened her pelvic region, each time glorying in his reaction to such a small movement.

The pleasure, indeed, the sensation built; it crescendoed, it became consuming and the rhythm of their movement increased. Rising up on his forearms, he gazed down into her eyes as the sweat of their bodies commingled, and he whispered, "I love you, Princess. I have always loved you. And I swear to you that I will make you glad to be my wife."

She bit her lip, holding back the emotion that was welling up inside her. To have said such a thing, and at such a time, moved her, truly moved her, and she thought at this moment that he might likely be the most beautiful being of her acquaintance.

And then he surged upward, once, again, passionately, and she followed him there, both of them attaining that plateau, as though they were of one body.

Over and over the pleasure continued, so intense, she thought she might not be able to withstand it. But she did; and he did.

And then, with a finale, he collapsed against her.

But it was far from over. Beyond the flesh, their spirits soared upward, up over the willow, up toward the sky above them, their very space, their lives joined irrevocably.

And so it was that she came to know him, as well as she knew herself, for there was nothing between them, only truth.

And at that moment, she found him not only beautiful, but worthy of . . . trust. Trust?

It was true. And she knew with a certainty that was uncanny that this man had not betrayed her. Not then. Not now.

The knowledge caused tears to well up in her eyes. *He had not betrayed her after all.* Despite all evidence to the contrary, he had remained true. She had been lied to, manipulated.

Oh, what had she done? What a waste of years.

And as the tears slipped silently from her eyes, she uttered softly, "I love you, High Wolf. I have always loved you." And truth be told, her words were a vow.

She would always love him, then and now. And no matter what the future held, it would always be so.

In response, he cradled her in his arms and hugged her. And then, with his head nestled upon her breasts, he fell fast asleep.

Chapter 18

I'm putty in your hands, a willing thrall
Devoted to your charming beck and call.
Excerpted from a poem by David Ziff
"Sonnets to a Soul Mate"

"**A** scout is expected to go naked into the environment, without tools or weapons, and to survive. And he should not simply survive, but should flourish in that environment as well. A scout knows nature's rules, he lives with them, and he knows how to go outside of them, thus becoming invisible."

"And you will teach me to do this?"

High Wolf glanced askance at her. "I will teach you a little. Enough to see you safely to the Mandan village, which is a little farther north. Here," he said, bending down to pick up a rock. "Do you see that deer?"

He pointed out the animal, which had come silently up to the lagoon, where it had stopped to drink.

"Do you notice how far away it is from us?"

"Yes, it must be . . . over one hundred yards away."

"Good, watch what I do. I am going to throw this

rock in the water, gently, so as not to make too much of a disturbance, but I want you to watch what happens with the deer."

"Yes, very well."

He did so, creating a minor splash. Then he said, "Do you see the concentric circles made by the water?"

"Yes."

"Good, now, look at the deer."

She did. Soon—much sooner than she would have thought—the deer stopped, looked up, and startled, it scampered away.

"What happened?" she asked.

"The deer felt the interruption of nature all around it. Notice that it had been quiet, and then, because of the circles spreading out farther and farther in the water, the deer became aware that something was not as it should be. It could not see us or detect us, but the disturbance told it that something else was there besides itself. And so it ran."

"Fascinating."

"Now, the air, the trees, the grass, the wind; all these things react in a similar way as this water does with a stone. In nature, movement and certain noises make up a constant backdrop. One must become aware of the background of nature. If something happens that is sudden or different, this disturbs the flow of nature. This, too, creates vibrating ripples that, like the circles, expand and spread out in all directions. But these ripples in nature are felt, not seen."

"Really?"

"Yes. Now, a scout knows how to detect these disturbances, and being able to do so, his awareness can extend far beyond his body's vision. This is the beginning of how he makes himself invisible. He learns how to walk so that he walks in the natural flow around him, so that he is often outside most people's awareness. Thus he becomes hidden to others."

"This is incredible," she said. "I always knew that you had ways of perceiving things differently than I did, but until now, I never understood it."

He nodded. "And now you know a little."

"Yes, but, High Wolf, if this is so, why do we need to disguise ourselves as we travel?"

"Because even if you can walk as a scout does, a man must still blend in with the environment, if he is to be secure in it. There is another reason, as well. All tribes have their scouts, and a scout can more easily spot you."

"Ah," she said, "I begin to understand. This is why we will have to disguise ourselves, wear this mud."

"*Haa'he*, that is true. However, for you, I have a surprise."

"A surprise?"

He nodded, giving her a wink. "I always carry my wolf skin in my parfleche."

"Your what?"

"My wolf skin. If one is going to be a wolf, one should look like a wolf, and this skin, when thrown over you, will help your disguise."

"A wolf skin?"

And to her look of utter disgust, he smiled and, taking her hand, said, "Come, I will show you."

"Twirl around," High Wolf instructed her, as he held a handful of softened earth in one hand and a piece of charcoal in the other.

And Sierra complied, having become used to these daily inspections of her camouflage.

At present, she and High Wolf were standing next to a small creek, heavily shaded, and rich in a predominance of mud. True to form, High Wolf missed not a spot in her disguise, and looking down at herself, she bit her lip: Her once white drawers and corset were hopelessly colored by the soot and charcoal. They would never be the same again.

But . . . complete with mud ears on the top of her head and a wolf skin over her body, she had managed to roam over the prairie safely and without detection. So perhaps one corset and a pair of drawers was a small price to pay, if it meant her life. Of course, the wolf skin had helped, but it didn't completely eliminate the need for the mud . . . unfortunately. And so it was that the two of them, often on all fours, had traversed over the territory of the dangerous Riccaree.

However, they weren't out of peril yet. Indeed, they would not be able to relax completely until they at last came to the Mandan village, those people who had been friendly to whites.

At present, the sun was beginning its descent over the western sky. Funny how she was coming to enjoy this time of day—the period when she had High Wolf to herself, if only to paint and scrutinize her camouflage.

Odd, too, how the early evening scents of the grass and prairie flowers, all mixed up with the smell of the muck, the greenery and the creek water, brought on a feeling of joy. It was hard to remember that at one time, these smells had been most disagreeable.

How she had changed.

And it was all because of this man.

There was nothing for it: Sierra had long ago admitted to herself that she was still very much in love with him.

Ah, what a wonderful feeling this was, too. And she sighed contentedly.

Was it because of him, she wondered, that the air seemed fuller, crisper; the grasses greener, softer; the fragrance of the wildflowers more exotic? And why did everything, even the air she breathed, give her such pleasure, such happiness?

Had the world always held this rosy glow? Or was it because of the change in her?

Whatever it was, Sierra was certain she wanted it to remain this way forever, although of course that could never be.

And the thought saddened her.

Try though she might to forget, there were some things that she could never put completely from her mind: things in the past that needed to be set right; reputations that had to be upheld, duties she must perform, countries to save.

Ah, yes, countries to save.

She gazed skyward and moaned. Perhaps High Wolf was right. Perhaps she should grab hold of this moment and keep it close to her, for it might be all the happiness she would ever know—and for the rest of her life.

It was not a pleasant thought, and it certainly didn't deserve any of her attention on this fine, summer evening.

But, though she loved High Wolf with every bit of her heart, she could never quite lose sight of the fact that this would all end—perhaps sooner than she might like.

She rocked back on her feet as she exhaled.

And immediately, High Wolf asked, "Is something wrong?"

"No," she said at first. Then she smiled. "Actually something is very wrong. Do you see this?" She pointed to a spot underneath one of her breasts, which was heavily caked with gook, and reeking of a dull, gray color.

He gazed at it closely.

"Tsk, tsk. There is not nearly enough mud there. Do you see how the white of my corset shows?"

He grinned. "How unobservant of me to have missed it. I shall have to fix it at once."

"Yes," she said. "Please."

"Of course," he observed, "there are other spots that are much worse." As he spoke, his fingers trailed down her stomach to that spot most tender between her legs. "I think I have failed you here, too."

"Oh, no," disagreed Sierra. "You have far from failed me there, my wolf prince."

He laughed; the sound was like music to her ears. Oh, that she might never forget, that she might hold on to this moment.

But alas, the world insisted on beating out time, and when High Wolf said, "Shall we dally here a little longer, and repaint ourselves later? Or shall we set out upon an early start this evening?"

"Oh." She let out a deep wail. "I say we dally, my dearest, dearest wolf."

How utterly beloved was his grin, she thought. And when he said, "Your wish is my command, Your

Highness," she thought she might likely burst with delight.

And she said, "Yes, my love. I would very much like to have my wishes granted."

"I will try," he promised, as he slowly bent to her. "I swear that I will try."

And Sierra moaned with pleasure, knowing that High Wolf was, indeed, a very honorable man, one who always kept his promises . . .

By the misty light of morning—that time before the sun first rises—the dark shadow hung over the Indian village, as though seeking someone, or something.

But the hour was early and the shadow went unnoticed by medicine man and mystic alike . . . except for one . . .

"There is the Mandan summer village."

High Wolf had raised up from all fours, onto his haunches, and was pointing to a high, western peninsula that overlooked the Missouri River. Directly atop this were situated fifty or more of the Mandan earth lodges. Sierra, throwing back the wolf skin that had become a second nature to her, looked out upon the view before her. A more beautiful—indeed, a more radiant sight—she had rarely seen.

Situated on the western side of the river atop sheer bluffs, the Mandan village looked to be a well-chosen spot, since its location alone would make it easy to defend. With a backdrop of blue skies, whimsical clouds and a gentle wind, the village basked under a morning sun.

It was a happy moment. For the village would afford her and High Wolf the opportunity to discover more about the prince's whereabouts. However, being here also marked the completion of this part of their trek. And Sierra was sorry to have it end. Alas, thinking back on it, she was certain she could not recall a happier time in her life than the past couple of days.

She caught her breath, and High Wolf immediately sent her a fleeting glance. He asked, "Are you not happy to see the village?"

"I'm very happy to see it. And yet," she said, "if I could, I would keep you with me a little longer."

"It will not set us back if we take a few moments to linger here. Your servants should be awaiting you at the Mandan village. And I will have to make inquiries about the prince there, as well."

"Really? Does that mean that—"

He nodded. "One more night spent together should not make a difference. In Indian country, I am afraid there are some things that cannot be rushed, and making inquiries is one of them. A man must show proper respect."

"Good," she said. "I am glad. Although . . ."

He raised an eyebrow.

"Although in some ways, I wish I could put the world off forever—to put it away from me and stop worrying about my home. After these past few days, I must admit that the prospect of staying here is . . . well, it is appealing." She sent him a surreptitious glance. "Here I would be. Here you would be."

"Yes." He reached out and took hold of her hand. "You could do it."

"Could I? Somehow I don't think so. Would I ever be happy if the demons that haunt me aren't put to rest? Always I would remember my obligations, I think. And I fear that if I do not act in a manner befitting my station, I would think ill of myself. No." She let out her breath. "It is an impossible situation for me, for us."

"No, it is not impossible," said High Wolf. "It only appears that way now. Together, we will find a way."

"Yes," she said, though little believing it.

"Come," commanded High Wolf, and with her hand held firmly with his own, he began to lead her *away* from the village.

"Where are you taking me?"

"To the water," he replied. "I promised to teach you to swim, I will do so now."

Her lips curved upward in a smile. "I would like that very much. Do you know of a private place?"

"Yes," he said. "Although their scouts must know of it, as well. But perhaps, since it is still early, we will have the spot to ourselves."

"Yes," she said. "Perhaps."

The swimming lesson had ended in the only possible way it could with two people so much in love . . . in each other's arms. And naked, they lay together, lingering by a shady lagoon, as though each were unwilling to be the one to end the embrace. At length, however, the sun climbed high in the sky, and even Sierra knew it was time to move on.

"Don't make me go back to St. Louis," she said. "I don't think I could bear to have come this far, learned so much, done so much, only to return empty-handed."

"I understand," he said, "And I won't. Those were conditions I had set for you in my ignorance. I am no longer unaware of your plight. However"—he trailed an eager finger from her breast to her stomach—"I will insist on painting you again as a wolf before we approach the village."

"Must you?"

"I must."

"Why?"

"Because it is safer. Because, although the Cheyenne and Mandan often trade, we are also often at war, and the Mandans may not understand that I am coming in peace. Therefore . . ."

"Ah," she said by way of acknowledgement. Then, glancing skyward, she inhaled and exhaled slowly, as though by doing so, she could catch her breath. "Well," she said after a time, "I suppose I ought to rise, then, and begin the lengthy process of becoming a female wolf."

"Yes," he said, winking at her. "And such a lady wolf you are . . ."

Chapter 19

. . . and it becomes my duty to say it; a better, more honest, hospitable and kind people, as a community, are not to be found in the world. No set of men that ever I associated with have better hearts than the Mandans, and none are quicker to embrace and welcome a white man than they are—none will press him closer to his bosom, that the pulsation of his heart may be felt, than a Mandan; and no man in any country will keep his word and guard his honour more closely.

George Catlin, *Letters and Notes on the Manners, Customs, and Conditions of North American Indians*

What an odd sight, she thought, giving the Mandan village a closer look, though her view of it was marred by several full-grown trees.

Their lodges—or perhaps what she saw might be more accurately described as huts—looked like many round pots turned upside down. Somehow, she had expected something different.

And glancing up toward High Wolf, as he finger-painted her with charcoal and earth, she said, "I thought Indians lived in tents made of the skins of buffalo."

High Wolf inclined his head in agreement, saying, "Many do. But the Mandans, along with the Minatar-rees and Riccarees, have made their homes on the Missouri River since"—he frowned— "since time out of mind. The Mandans do not live solely for the chase of buffalo and never have, but dwell in what the white man might call permanent villages. Here these people plant corn and squash and pumpkins which they trade with many of our roaming tribes."

"Indeed." Sierra quirked up an eyebrow. "I had no idea such Indians existed. I thought all the Indians were strictly hunters."

"Humph," he said. "There are many different kinds of American Indians. All are not the same." Bending, he picked up another piece of charcoal. "In faith," he continued, "it is said that the Mandans have been here, living along the Missouri, much longer than any other tribe. I have always known their village as a place of much Indian commerce."

"Have you?" She sent him a speculative look. "Then, if that is so, this must be a place where you have been many times before?"

Again High Wolf inclined his head, going on to say, "That I have. Now, look there, next to the village and situated farther away from the water. That is Fort Clark. Do you see it?" He pointed.

"Yes."

"That is the place where the Indians trade for things that only the white man offers. This is also where you will stay."

"Will I?" she said. "And you? You make that statement as if you will not be remaining there."

He shrugged. "I would not be welcome in the fort."

"Is that so? And why not?"

"Because I am Indian. Besides, outside of visiting it to see you, I have no wish to seek lodging there. The Mandan lodges are quite comfortable, and since I have some friends there, I will be happy to solicit my lodging with them."

What was this? Sierra cut High Wolf a severe glance. Surely he did not intend to become separated from her. Not now. Not after they had come so far, become close . . . again. And she said, "Then perhaps I shall stay there, as well."

"No," he replied at once. "You will be more comfortable at the white man's fort, where I believe you will also find your servants."

"Oh, yes," she remarked before falling silent. Although after a while she commented, "But I thought we would remain together once we reached the Mandan village. I mean, after all, are we not still pretending to be married?"

He glanced toward her, his look uneasy, and he said, "Yes, and no."

Dead silence filled the air. And the only thing to be heard around them was the lapping of the water in the lagoon, and an occasional squawk of a gull.

"What does that mean?"

He hunched his shoulders. "I would almost rather face the fieriest warrior in all the prairie than have this conversation with you."

"Oh?" Sierra frowned. But all she said was, "And what conversation would that be?"

He grimaced, and turning fully toward her—much as a man might do if facing a firing squad—said, "I will be leaving you at Fort Clark."

"Oh?" At this news, her stomach gave a queer pitch, and she stared up at him in surprise. However, all she did was inquire, "Leaving me? But didn't you say that . . . ?"

"I promised not to take you back to St. Louis. This is not the same thing."

"But—"

"Consider, Princess. How could I bring you farther into Indian country in all conscience? It is simply not safe to do so."

She stood there, her arms spread wide as he caked gook and mud onto them, too stunned to say a word. At length, however, she asked, "What do you mean, not safe? Have I not sneaked through Riccaree country with you? Have I not slipped through their scouts?" She stirred uneasily, her breathing becoming quick, short. "High Wolf, consider all that I have learned. I can disappear into the countryside, I can strike camp without leaving a sign, I can even read images upon the earth. And now, as I'm beginning to master the art of scouting, you say you're going to leave me behind?"

He paused, his brow furrowed. And there was a flicker of foreboding in his countenance as he responded, "It is true that you have done well, but there is so much more you do not know, have not mastered, and it will be easier and quicker if you remain here, secure—behind the wooden walls of the fort. In truth, knowing you are safe will allow me the freedom to travel farther north in search of the prince."

"Freedom?" Her look, underneath the scoutlike disguise, was incredulous. And she continued, "For a man who has been regaling me with promises of passion and talk of marriage, you seem anxious to be rid of me . . ."

At her words, High Wolf bristled, his manner at once brisk, and he said, "Do not twist my words. You know well that I do not wish my freedom from you. I require it only long enough to give service to you. There is a difference. I will either find the prince or not, and will bring the news of what I discover back to you, here."

"Ah," she said, as she put her weight on one foot, hand on her hip. "So that is your plan. To leave me and go about seeking the prince on your own."

When he didn't answer, Sierra stared up at him, boldly holding his gaze. And she inquired, "May I ask how long you have intended this?"

He looked away from her. "Perhaps since last night."

"I see," she said, wondering if her face mirrored the unexpectedness of this remark. Although, she thought, perhaps she should have been more prepared. And she commented, "How cleverly you have avoided telling me this until now."

He didn't answer.

But Sierra went on to say, "And what about the advice from your grandfather? Do you not remember telling me that he advised you to take your woman with you wherever you go?"

High Wolf hesitated, looking away from her, although at last he said, "Yes, I do. But look around you. Have I not done so?" he asked. "Have I not brought you here to the Mandan village and to Fort Clark, instead of taking you back to St. Louis? Princess, understand. I cannot put your life in constant danger."

For a moment, she looked sullen, then, "Well, I think you will have to change your plans."

"I think not," he answered at once. "There is little else I can do, and remain an honorable man."

"Because," she went on as though he hadn't spoken a word, "I won't stay put. Do you understand? We have had this conversation before, but it appears we need to have it again. Heed my words on this, I intend on going the entire way into Indian country. And I aim to find the prince, whereupon I will either gain his cooperation to return with me to Europe, or die trying."

At this last declaration, High Wolf sent her a lopsided grin. "Don't you mean that someone will die . . . if *he* doesn't cooperate?"

But Sierra was in no mood for humor, and she shot her chin into the air, saying, "I have no idea what you are talking about."

But High Wolf was not about to utter more on that subject. However, he did observe, "If I find the prince, I will bring him to you."

"No, no. This is not what you promised me. You gave me your word that you would help me, and that you would take me with you."

"Yes, that I did, and I have brought you here. And look here before you: I *have* helped you, and I will continue to help you." He paused. "Notice, however, that I do not, and did not say in the past, how I would give you that help."

"A fine concession. You know as well as I that I assumed we would go on together."

It was a legitimate point she presented, but High Wolf did not seem in any mood to be reasonable, and he said, "Then that is your error, and not my problem."

Not my problem?

Had he actually said that? As she straightened up, she began to wonder if this stubborn man was the same man who had taken her in his arms only hours ago? The same man who had declared his love?

After a short pause, she said, "I beg to differ with you on that subject. It *is* your problem. And if it isn't now, it soon will be, for I mean it. I will run away if these are your plans. As God is my witness, I will find the prince—if need be, on my own."

But High Wolf's reaction was hardly what she expected. Instead of retaliating, he merely tottered back on his feet. And he said, "You know you will not do so."

"Yes, I shall."

He raised an eyebrow at her. "Am I to understand that after only a few days, you believe you have learned enough about scouting to accomplish this on your own?"

She scowled at him.

"Do you? Tell me true."

"Oh!" She was caught. Truly caught, and she knew it. "You . . . you . . ."

"Come," he said, taking hold of her elbow. "There is only one thing for us to do that is sensible. Keep in mind that I am not your enemy. I am the man who loves you, and I have pledged myself to help you. And I will help you, but in my own way. Now, perhaps it is best that we go forward, to the fort, where you will be secure. Then I shall go on to discover what I can from the Mandans."

But Sierra was far from finished, and she pulled her arm out of his grip. "If I go there, to Fort Clark," she declared, "I swear I shall find another guide to lead me to the prince."

"No, you will not," he said, "for I will ensure that the scouts know better than to take your bribe."

"Oh!" she sputtered. "Oh!"

But High Wolf seemed unaffected by her temper, and with a speculative look in his eye, said, "When we arrive at the fort, you must also pretend that there is nothing between us. To them, I will be no more than your guide. There can be nothing familiar; no touching, no unnecessary talk."

Sierra shot her chin into the air. "Good. That is very good, indeed, for that is exactly how I feel at this moment."

He nodded, becoming silent. But when he didn't offer a word, not even to comment on her sulking, Sierra asked, "Why is it that we must act that way? As though we have no relationship? It seems a little ridiculous to me."

He gazed away from her, the air about him tense. "I know," he said. "And it is. But you have not experienced yet the dynamics at play here in the West. There is much prejudice. Why this is so, I don't know. Suffice it to say that it is there—much more so than anything you witnessed in Europe."

"Ah, I see," she said. "So great is the prejudice, then, amongst your friends, that you do not wish it known that you have married a white woman? Is that it?"

From beneath his own disguise, High Wolf gave her an astounded look. "Princess, again you twist my words into misunderstanding. It is not for myself or the Indian people that I worry. In sooth, there is little prejudice from my people against yours—except that they believe that all white men are liars . . ."

"Do they?"

But he ignored her, and said, "There is, however, great bias from the white man toward the Indian in this country."

"What makes you think that? I have seen very little of that myself."

"Yes, I am certain this is true. But you must ask yourself, have you been here long enough to observe it?"

She shrugged.

He continued, "If you stay here, you will see that this is so. It is to be observed in the way the white man does business, in the way he treats the Indian customer."

"Humph." Her nose shot into the air. "I'm not certain I believe you."

"I invite you to look, then. Once you are at Fort Clark, observe how the white man acts: that he does not allow the Indian into his fort except during certain hours of the day. Witness that though the white man marries into the tribe, he holds himself apart, never participating in the ceremonies of the people or becoming part of the tribe. He has even been known to desert his wife if he has to leave the country. No, heed this advice, Princess. It is best to keep the white man in ignorance of us. Besides, you and I have problems enough without adding long explanations to them."

"What do you mean, long explanations?"

He clenched his jaw before saying, "If it should become common knowledge that you and I are together as more than guide and princess, I fear we shall be forced to do nothing more than spend our visit explaining to the proprietor, James Kittridge, and his company, why you prefer being seen with a red man instead of a white man. Are you ready to do that?"

"Yes, of course."

"Yes, I'm sure that you could. But I think it best to avoid a problem before it begins. No, Princess, while we are within the realm of the fort—even within the Mandan village—we will give others the impression that I am no more than your guide."

"Will we? Will I? You forget, High Wolf, that as a princess, I am entitled to act in any way that suits me. Do you really think these people would question me because of my taste in friends? Besides, what does it matter to me what Mr. Kittridge and his friends might think?"

"It matters not in the least, except for one thing."

"Oh? What is that?"

"That a scout functions better if undetected. Hear me on this," he said, raising a hand in protest, when she might have interrupted. And he continued, "It is the scout who tells his people where it is safe to camp, where is the enemy, where is the buffalo. It is the scout who tracks down the enemy, the scout who tells the others when and where are the best places to stage an attack. It is the scout who can enter an enemy camp undetected, thus bringing back valuable information for his people. This is why we wear the wolf disguise and why we paint our bodies to blend in with the environment; it is why we sneak into enemy territory, rather than ride straight into it. Our warfare is mostly of the mind and of the senses. When undetected, one can learn many things about an enemy. When detected, we fail."

Sierra, although listening intently, was, however, in no state of mind to be moved by a speech, and she said, "I fail to see why—"

"Because if we act in the manner that we have these past few days, we will be found out; my business will be laid out for all eyes to see, like an open hand. This, and this alone, would make it difficult, if not impossible to glean news about the prince."

"Humph!" That bit of information caused her some speculation. Perhaps it was true. Maybe.

Defiantly, she met his cool look with one of her own. However, at some length, given the logic of his reasoning, all she said was "Very well. If that is how it is to be, so be it. But I still think it monstrous ill that you have decided all this without consulting me. Or without even giving me a chance to relate my own opinion on our predicament."

"I have."

"No, you have not."

He quirked his brow at her. "Have I not?"

"No, you have dictated to me what I am to do, without finding out what problems, if any, I might have."

"But I know your problems."

"No, you do not. You *think* you know them. That *is* the problem."

"Is it?" He stared at her for several seconds, then, reaching out toward her, he touched her face, his graze gentle upon her.

But she pulled back from him. "Keep away from me," she said. "I am very upset with you."

"I know," he said. "And I am sorry. Truly, I am, but it cannot be helped. I am doing what I think is best."

"Yes, I know you are, but I disagree with it."

He breathed out on a sigh. "Then, tell me, Princess, if my plan is not to your liking, what do you suggest?"

Sierra threw caution to the wind, deciding to tell him exactly what she thought. And she said, "You do me an injustice. I am a princess, and used to having my own way. Now, when I told you I was going with you, I wasn't asking you, High Wolf. I was telling you."

He shook his head. "Now who is ordering whom?"

"But I, at least, have every right to do so."

"As do I, when you are in my country," he said. "But tell me, why do you object so strongly? I am thinking only of your safety. Is there some problem that you know of that I have not considered?"

From beneath her lashes, she shot him a covert glance, saying, "There is."

"And that is?"

"If you understood me at all, you would know."

"I am sorry that I do not. Please tell me."

She blinked, slanting him a frown. "Well, the truth is," she capitulated, "that if you left me behind, not only would you upset me, but I would worry about you. And if something happened to you, how would I discover it? I already have one man I am seeking. I have no wish to make it two."

For a moment, High Wolf seemed taken aback. At last, however, he concurred, saying, "You are right. I had not considered this."

And although this might have mollified her a trifle, she was hardly in a mood to give quarter, and she added, "Anything, even danger, is preferable to sitting in some dark fort, alone, worried, wondering."

Again he acknowledged her with the tilt of his head. "I know of women who feel similarly. They often go with their husbands on the war trail, for they would rather die with him than live without him."

"Yes, not knowing is worse than . . ." She glanced up at High Wolf, as his meaning became clear to her. For a moment, she brightened. "Does this mean you will let me go with you?"

But he shook his head, effectively erasing the smile from her face. "I cannot promise you that yet. What I shall do is consult with an elder, and I shall tell him all we have spoken of. He will give me wise advice."

"Oh." Her voice, even her look, must have carried her disappointment.

And she wondered, what good was this? A tribal elder would surely relegate her to the fort.

"But I will promise you this," High Wolf went on to say. "In the future, anything that concerns us both will be discussed by us both before I again tell you what to do . . . that is, unless it is an emergency."

"Oh," she said. "Yes, that is good, then, I suppose." Briefly, she gazed toward the village once more, before she said, "I would still rather stay with you in the Mandan village."

"I know, Princess. But James Kittridge is most likely expecting you. Your servants should be there, also, and, if I am correct in what I have seen, Kittridge has scouts out looking for you."

"Oh? Has he? Have you seen any?"

"There have been one or two. But we have avoided them."

"And they didn't see you?"

"No," he said. "Those men sent out by the white man to scout are not the same as those of us in the wolf clan. Those men, under the direction of the whites, are not trained in the same manner as we of the clan, and they do not know of the most intricate knowledge that is kept only to a wolf clan scout. Such men are easy to fool, easy to avoid."

"Oh," she said. "Then there are differences amongst scouts?"

He nodded. "All Indian men of all tribes know how to track and how to find game. But the knowledge of the clan goes beyond this basic tracking; the clan takes it further, and a scout learns to become so much a part of the environment, he cannot be seen in it. There is great difference between the two."

"Ah," she said, "and have I been learning the true method?"

"*Haa'he*, I have been teaching you the way of the wolf clan. But there is still much you do not know. Now, if we wish to arrive at the fort while the sun is still up, we should start out now, for the white man bolts his gates, and no one, particularly an Indian, is admitted after dark. Come, your disguise is complete, and the way is not far."

And so it was that the two wolves—one male, one female—approached the fort with great stealth, and not once were they seen for who they truly were, until they were well upon the gates.

Chapter 20

❦

*And I recollect well that Governor Clarke (sic) told
me, before I started for this place, that I would find
the Mandans a strange people and half white.*
> George Catlin, *Letters and Notes on the
> Manners, Customs, and Conditions
> of North American Indians*

Sierra awoke to the din of high-pitched whoops,
the running of what sounded to be thousands of
feet, battle cries and children's laughter.

Laughter? Were they being attacked? By children?

Rousing herself from her bed, she pulled on her robe
and stepped to the crude window in her room. Throwing back the wooden barricade, Sierra looked out upon
a scene of much beauty and curiosity. Before her was a
most luscious view of the prairie. Between Fort Clark
and the Mandan village itself was a beautiful mixture
of green valleys and hills, with thousands upon thousands of swells and rises extending as far as the eye
could see. At present, the sun was bathing the ground
with a fresh, morning glow, and the grass fairly twinkled with dew, waving under a gentle, majestic wind.

To add to the excitement, out upon that prairie were hundreds of young boys, playing, who were all, except for a belt around their waist, completely naked. In his left hand each boy toted a bow, and in his right many arrows—or were they arrows? In truth, these objects looked as though they were no more than long blades of grass.

Sierra smiled. What a pleasant sight.

It was then that she espied an older man, two of them, each leading hundreds of these boys.

Why, this was no more than a mock battle, she thought. Training for the boys, as well as exercise for the youngsters' bodies. She smiled and yawned, all at the same time.

Best to arise as quickly as possible and see what this day was yet to hold for her.

Of one thing she was certain, however: She would not remain long under the roof of Fort Clark. For, though James Kittridge, its proprietor, had been most gracious and had tried to make her stay here as comfortable as possible, her quarters were unbearably hot, shabby and dirty. Plus, the bed housed tiny creatures, so many that Sierra feared to ask about them. Worse, the previous evening, her dreams had been haunted by the sound of the Euro-American's drunken brawl.

And she couldn't help but wonder if High Wolf knew of these matters, deciding that he, in most likelihood, did not.

Well, regardless of what High Wolf said should be so, Sierra would seek out the Mandan village and decide for herself if there might not be more pleasant accommodations there.

As to her maid and steward, Sierra had quickly

learned that the two of them—unable to determine what had happened to her—had travelled farther north, toward the Minatarree village, where, according to Mr. Kittridge, the two hoped to learn more of the whereabouts of Prince Alathom.

But alas, rather than comfort her, that piece of knowledge only served to upset her. If Maria could travel in this country, why was *she* to be denied?

But these questions would have to wait until she saw High Wolf, whom she hadn't laid witness to since yesterday afternoon.

And despite all reason to the contrary, she missed him. She might be upset with him, she might disagree with him, but she could not deny that she yearned for his presence. Truth be told, she missed his kindness, his helpful suggestions, his patience with her mistakes . . . his love. But most of all, she missed—of all things—his trustworthiness.

But High Wolf had said he would come for her when the time was ready. In the meantime, she was to wait for him.

Wait for what?

Was she some lackey to cower to him? Some servant to bide her time, awaiting his leave?

Certainly not. She was a princess—mistress of her own destiny.

And so, High Wolf's mandates or no, she would go visiting. For, truth be known, the Mandan village beckoned, her curiosity aroused by the beauty of the prairie surrounding it, by the children's games and by the strangeness of what she could see of their village.

Fortunately for her, either Maria or Mr. Dominic

had salvaged one of her dresses from the ship and, had left it and a few other things stored here at the fort.

And so it was that Princess Sierra emerged from the fort a few hours later, dressed in a lightweight forest green redingote, which fell down and almost completely covered a highly embroidered white dress. White knit gloves, black boots, cashmere shawl, a white straw bonnet, and hair dressed in spiral curls at the side of her face completed the image.

Perhaps it had been her utter lack of apparel, and her disguise as a wolf, that had made dressing all the more pleasant. Or perhaps it had something to do with an urge to impress High Wolf.

Whatever the reason, opening up her green and white parasol, she stepped onto the open prairie. And she vowed that she would find High Wolf this day and make arrangements to continue her arguments on her behalf, forthwith.

Hand up, palm outward to show that he held no weapon, High Wolf walked into the Mandan village. Almost immediately, dogs, children, women and the most pleasant odor of smoke and cooked food wafted toward him. And while the crowd of people surrounded him, the smells tantalized him.

Inhaling pleasantly, he had scarcely taken more than a few steps before a man emerged from the crowd, a man High Wolf recognized as Running Coyote, Mandan scout and friend. Briefly, the two men exchanged silent greetings, until at last, Running Coyote stepped toward him. And then, as was custom, Running Coyote passed his arm through High

Wolf's, and thus led High Wolf safely though the village, toward what was most likely his own dwelling.

Meanwhile, the crowd, seeing that High Wolf was well known by one of their own, dispersed.

Pulling High Wolf with him, Running Coyote strolled through the southeastern side of the village, into and then past the main, circular courtyard, which was surrounded by earth lodges, these being spaced so closely together that there was walking or riding room between them only. Onward Running Coyote trod, until they reached the northwestern side of the village.

With a flourish of hand motions, Running Coyote indicated his own earth dwelling, which was round and covered by earth that had been packed and worn down so that it practically shone. Upon entering, High Wolf was at once comforted by the delicious fragrance of cooking meat. And though his stomach growled and his mouth watered, he said not a word.

Truth be known, his mind was set, not upon the concerns of his appetite, but rather upon the Mandan lodge itself; looking at it with "new eyes," he was attempting to view it as the princess might. Spacious, comfortable and orderly, the lodge was about sixty feet in diameter, making it quite comfortable for a family of perhaps twenty people. The floor of the Mandan interior was sunken about two feet into the earth, and although made of dirt, was so hardened by use, it presented a polished look. In the center of the dwelling was the ever-present fire, quietly smoldering in a round pit, around which reclined members of Running Coyote's family. And, suspended from wooden poles over the fire hung a clay kettle that was at present boiling over with roasted buffalo meat, the source of the mouth-watering scents.

But High Wolf was in no hurry, and he took his time gazing around the lodge.

The interior was completely circular, and around the edge of the lodge were beds, which had much the appearance of the white man's beds, although perhaps not constructed so high. With buffalo skin stretched over four small poles on the ground—each about two feet high—the bed consisted of the buffalo robe, which when dried would harden, thus becoming the bottom of the bed. Over this then was placed another buffalo robe, serving as a bottom sheet, with other robes drawn over this, or rolled up for a pillow. And covering these beds were casings, resembling curtains, these being ornamented with hieroglyphics or quills or paint.

On the right-hand side of the dwelling were tools and other necessities of the Indian life: lances, war shields, bows, arrows. On the left were pottery items belonging to the women. But what would be most unusual from Sierra's point of view, High Wolf thought, was that, since the lodge was large enough to accommodate animals, two horses were at present housed within.

At length, without disturbing High Wolf's scrutiny, Running Coyote led his friend to the edge of the fireplace, which was surrounded with stones. And gesturing toward a beautifully garnished buffalo robe, he invited High Wolf to sit.

High Wolf waited as Running Coyote chose another robe, then, did as bid and sat down. And by the language of gestures, Running Coyote requested High Wolf to "Eat."

At once, one of the women in the lodge set a bowl of pemmican before High Wolf. In Indian country, this was the equivalent to "bread and butter."

Soon another woman set another dish before High Wolf, this one consisting of those tempting, well-roasted buffalo ribs.

Drawing out his knife—for no utensils were ever given to guests—High Wolf commenced to eat, while his host sat ready to serve him, waiting on him as he, the host, prepared his pipe for an after-dinner smoke.

In due course, High Wolf finished and, with his appetite sated for the moment, sat up. No sooner had he done so than Running Coyote lit his pipe, inhaling its fragrance deeply, and then with another series of hand motions, passed the pipe to High Wolf.

At length, again by sign language, Running Coyote said, "It has been many seasons of the moon since I have feasted my eyes upon my friend from the Cheyennes. I am happy to see my Cheyenne friend."

"And I, you," said High Wolf, also in sign.

Both men lingered there in silence for a while, though after a bit, Running Coyote grinned, signing, "My sources tell me that my friend is still an unattached man, though he is beginning to climb higher in age. Has my friend come to our village to select a wife? If so, he has come at a good time."

High Wolf smiled. "I am not as unattached as you might think," he responded.

"Humph," said Running Coyote. "Then, if not to select a wife, tell me what brings my friend to our village?"

"I have come," High Wolf began, "to seek an elder from our clan. I am to embark upon a duty of some importance, and as is custom, I would confer with an elder from our clan before I set out upon it."

Running Coyote nodded calmly, obviously understanding the reason now for the visit, for it was not an unusual request. Tradition dictated that a scout confer with an elder before beginning a task, no matter how great or small. That High Wolf was away from his own people would matter not in the least. A member from the Mandan tribe would be happy to meet with him.

After a moment, Running Coyote said, "This I will be able to arrange soon. I will talk with the others, and I am certain there will be one who you will be able to visit."

High Wolf nodded. His purpose now stated, he relaxed a bit, at least enough to say in sign, "I see that there are many of the white items of trade here in your home."

"Yes," signed Running Coyote in return. "My woman likes the glass beads, which are easier to use than those blue ones that she can make herself."

"Ah," said High Wolf. "I see, too, that the fields are dry. Has anything been done to cause it to rain?"

"Not so far, though the women are begging the medicine men to try," said Running Coyote.

"That is good," said High Wolf. "That is good. It is to be hoped, however, that it will rain without the ceremony."

"Yes," said Running Coyote. "Although there are many young men who would like to try their hand at making rain."

"*Haa'he,*" said High Wolf. "I am certain this is so."

"Do you plan to be here very long?"

"Only as long as I need to consult with an elder."

"Ah," said Running Coyote. "Then you must stay with me while you are here, as my guest."

"I would be most honored," replied High Wolf in sign language.

And thereupon, Running Coyote emptied the pipe and the two men arose.

"Where is your other?"

Astonished at the request, High Wolf actually looked around him, as though another person might be standing there. "Other?" he asked with sign motions.

"There are two of you, are there not?"

"Yes," said High Wolf to the old man, Shining Arrow. And though High Wolf might be surprised by the elder's question he was not in the least astonished that this particular wise man would have knowledge of the princess. High Wolf continued, "Yes, there is another, but she is a woman, and because she is white, she will be staying at the white man's fort while I go into enemy territory."

The old man nodded. However, in sign he said, "You must bring her to me. For, though you may have little knowledge of it, she is involved in all you do. Bring her to me. Then I will talk to you about your scouting party."

High Wolf acknowledged the old man, though he would have loved nothing more than to argue the point. However, High Wolf, as well as most other Plains Indian people, held the greatest respect for his elders, and this kept him quiet.

And so it was, at some length, that High Wolf signed, "I will bring her here this afternoon, if you would be able to receive us then."

The old man said, "*Shusu*," and making the sign for "good," closed their meeting.

As High Wolf rose to leave, he was mystified by the old man's request, but he knew he would eventually understand his reasoning. There was no need to rush. And so, with his palm down, arm at chest length, High Wolf made a sweeping motion with his arm from left to right, saying "good." And with this, he took his leave.

Accompanied by James Kittridge—a drab-haired man of German descent—Sierra heard the drumbeats from the Mandan village long before she stepped foot within the village. And with each footfall, those drums became louder, differences of pitch giving the cacophony of noise the appearance of being strewn everywhere in the entire village.

"Careful, Your Highness," said Kittridge as Sierra tripped over an unlevel piece of ground. "Stay to the path." With a gap-toothed smile and breath reeking of whiskey, Kittridge made a motion toward her, as though he might grab hold of her to steady her. But when Sierra stepped away, out of arm's-length range, his hand dropped back to his side.

Involuntarily, she shuddered. Though the man had been cordial in terms of hospitality, she had, perhaps, never been so close to a man so vile. His person reeked of unwashed body odor; his clothes—made mostly of buckskin—were soiled and stained. His teeth were yellow, tarnished and rotting. And his beard housed what Sierra feared might be unmentionable. Worse, there was evidence of certain debauchery left lying about the fort; broken whiskey bottles, clerks found half asleep and in various states of undress. Too, the Indian maidens under this man's care—and there were several of them—did not look as though they fared well.

Still, until High Wolf returned for her, she was under this man's influence. And so as politely as possible, she said, "I don't remember hearing these drums last night. But I have noticed since arising this morning, that they are quite steady, and seem to continue endlessly."

"Yep," said Kittridge, his dry lips cracking into a smile. "Once we're inside the village, you might be careful to observe the Injuns' dancing and drumming, since the darned savages sing and dance most of the day through."

"Oh?" said Sierra. "Really?"

"Yep, this way, ma'am," he said, and once more he made to grab at her.

But Sierra easily thwarted the attempt, and with a sidestep, moved out of the way.

It caused Kittridge to rock on his feet, and with his hand still in motion, he made a grand gesture toward the wall that surrounded the village, as though that, and that alone, had been his intention all along. He said, "Looks like a white fort, don't it, ma'am. But you wait. Jest wait. Here we go."

"Thank you, Mr. Kittridge. I am looking forward to seeing the village," she said, as she walked over the lush, rich buffalo grass. "It is good of you to escort me into the village."

"Think nothin' of it, Your Highness," he said. And then, strangely, he laughed.

Not that his mirth was directed at her, but rather he was found to be chuckling at the antics of the people they were passing. Many of these Indians had stopped and stood completely still as the two of them walked by. They stared at Sierra as if she might be some mystical being. Some—many of them women and youngsters—held their hands over their mouths, which Sierra assumed was their way of showing surprise.

And she asked, "Have these people never seen a white woman before?"

"No, ma'am." He coughed, "I mean, Your Highness. Well, now let me correct that," Kittridge said, and scratching his beard, he seemed oblivious to the dirt stirred up by the action. He continued, "They ain't never seen a white woman like you. Your maid was here before you, 'n' she was white, but she declined visiting the village. But even if she had taken an interest in it, she wasn't dressed as you are."

"I see," said Sierra. "Then perhaps you would be so kind as to introduce me to various members of the society, so they might talk with me, and become more at ease with me."

Kittridge acknowledged her by inclining his shaggy head. Then said, "I will introduce you." It was a good-humored remark, or so it would seem. However, he giggled inanely, causing Sierra some concern, before he commenced to carry on, saying, "If you beg pardon, Your Highness, I think it might be some time afore these people are at their ease. Nope, don't rightly believe they'll forget a sight such as you."

Sierra smiled, and though she hardly felt complimented, she said, "If it is your intention to flatter me,

Mr. Kittridge, I thank you. If it is not your intention, and you are merely being factual, I thank you anyway. I am most happy to have the opportunity of seeing this village. I don't imagine many white people have been here."

"Now there I think you're right, Your Highness. Here, this way," he said, and they passed along the Mandans' fortified walls.

Sierra stopped for a moment, taking stock of what she was seeing. And a more novel place, a more unusual people, she could not have imagined.

At a distance, because of its position on the river, the village had appeared to be a more cultivated place. But this was spread out before her, and was hardly what one might call a European civilization.

The village sat on a bluff that rose up from the river at a ninety-degree angle; its cliffs—about forty or fifty feet above the river—were of sheer rock, making them impenetrable. The site was also protected by the river and cliffs on three of its sides, the river changing course at a right angle. The remaining side of the village, which was unprotected by nature, had a large wall built around it, composed of wooden posts, some eighteen feet high and about a foot across. And inside the wall was a rather large ditch filled with water.

Strange. The moat was on the inside, not the outside of the village.

Also interesting was the fact that there were bastions stationed at each end of this wall.

She said aloud, "How curious."

"Yep," agreed Mr. Kittridge. "That it is, Your Highness. That it is. A very odd place, even at first glance. But as you get to know the Mandans, you will see that

they are even more peculiar than you might at first
have believed."

As they advanced farther into the village, the hum of
conversation, of children's laughter, of the high-
pitched giggling of young girls, caught up to them, reminding Sierra that this was, after all, a village of
people, and their customs aside, not much unlike various villages in her own kingdom. There were some
things, she decided, that were most likely held in common to all people.

As she and Kittridge stepped through the village,
the barking of the dogs added to the sounds of the
drums, the singing and the resonance of differently
toned voices. And as she glanced around her, several
dogs ran toward her and Kittridge, making Sierra
suddenly glad to have Kittridge at her side.

But the dogs did no more than wag their tails enthusiastically, sniffing at Kittridge's boots, then at
hers. And all were strange-looking; being half wolf,
half dog.

No one said a word to these animals, however. Not
to claim them, or even to restrain them from leaping
upon their guests.

Sierra tried to rescue her dress from the muddy paws
of several of these animals. But after many unsuccess-
ful attempts to keep them away, she gave up in disgust.

The wind suddenly changed direction, bringing
with it the smells of roasting meat, of smoke and an
indefinable scent of sweet herbs. Ah . . .

"Mr. Kittridge," said Sierra. "What is that smell in
the air? The one of herbs?"

"Herbs?" said Kittridge, "Oh, I reckon that's probably the wild sage. The Injuns use it for everythin'; for

prayin', for deodorizin' their homes, for bathin'. Though why the Injuns are so fond of bathin' is hard fer a civilized fella to understand."

Sierra gave the man a long look, before commenting, "Hmmm. It's quite exotic, isn't it? Exotic and . . . exciting."

"Excitin'?" He scratched his head, while Sierra, raising a hand to her lips, hid a merry smile. But he was continuing to talk, and he said, "Well, Your Highness, come with me. Reckon I'll introduce you to Bear-that-runs, a chief of the Mandans. His women will help you to feel at home." Kittridge pulled on his beard, and practically talking to himself, said, "Don't see how the women'll take to ya." And then with more intonation in his voice, he said, "Well, follow me, Your Highness." And he pointed toward a lodge that faced out into an open, circular area, an area that looked much like a plaza.

"Mr. Kittridge, did you see that?"

The proprietor looked around quickly. "What?" He pulled his rifle into his grip.

But Sierra brushed the gesture away, and said, " 'Tis not dangerous. Only that the person over there to my right," she whispered. "She had blond hair . . . and there's another with golden hair, with brown, with . . . Mr. Kittridge, that youngster over there has a full head of gray hair."

But Kittridge only smiled that odd gap-toothed smile. "I told ya the Mandans was a strange people. You're also goin' ta find that many of the Mandans have blue and green and gray eyes, as well as brown. Yep, Your Highness, they sure are a peculiar people."

"Indeed."

"But don't make the mistake of thinkin' they are any less savage because of their hair color, light skin and light eyes."

"But how do you account for it? Do any of the other Indian tribes have these characteristics?"

"Nope. None that I've seen, Your Highness."

"How bizarre."

"Yep, that it is."

At that moment, they came to one of the earth lodges, and as Sierra looked up, she realized the immensity of these earthen huts, for she felt quite small in comparison.

"How big are these lodges, Mr. Kittridge?"

He shrugged and frowned. "Well now, I reckon they might be anywhere from forty to seventy feet in diameter, Your Highness, dependin' on the family. A moment, please, while I see if Bear-that-runs is home."

"Yes. Please."

She turned away, while Kittridge scratched on the entryway, and she glanced around the village. On the tops of these earth lodges sat groups of people, the roof of the hut affording them a bird's eye view of the rest of the village, and perhaps of the prairie, as well. And such a wild group of people she had rarely seen.

Children, chiefly naked, rushed through the village, laughing, or riding ponies; men stood in dignified poses with their colorful robes wrapped around them and their heads adorned with eagles' feathers or plumes. Women passed by in groups, whispering, giggling, many of the young women quite pretty. And everywhere about her were shades of blond and golden hair, as well as a startling number of young gray-hairs.

And as she gazed out at all this strangeness, she became aware that there was one who didn't seem so unusual; one who stood apart, watching her; one very beloved.

High Wolf.

He was probably some fifty yards away from her, but his face, his person, so dear to her, stood out from the rest.

Ah, how her heart reached out to him. In faith, at this moment, espying him, she felt as if she might burst, so strong was her adoration. And there, amidst the wildest of possible environments, amidst people so strange, time ceased to exist, for her, for him, too, perhaps. There were only the two of them. No space. No time. Nothing.

She smiled. He returned it. And though neither made a motion to move, it was understood that each was content with simply staring at the other.

And on that thought followed another: Somewhere, somehow, they two would be together. Yes, though seemingly impossible now, somehow . . .

"Your Highness."

Sierra didn't hear, didn't understand.

"Your Highness, this way."

She felt a pressure at her elbow, and sighing, Sierra realized that, indeed, the world around her still existed. More's the pity.

Reluctantly, she broke her gaze with High Wolf, and turned toward Kittridge.

"Yes?"

"Your Highness, Bear-that-runs is ready to receive you. Best you come this way, now."

"Yes, Mr. Kittridge. Thank you." And turning away, Sierra started to enter the lodge as requested, but before she did so, she glanced back, over her shoulder.

And there he was. Still standing motionless, still watching her, still smiling.

She grinned back at him. And she knew at that moment that she had never loved anyone more, and probably never would again. They were irrevocably intertwined.

She rocked back on her feet as the realization hit her. How was she ever to leave this man?

Chapter 21

The here and now dissolves and we're alone,
A world's created that we call our own.
Excerpted from a poem by David Ziff
"Sonnets to a Soul Mate"

"**M**y friend," signed Running Coyote. "Look there. Have you ever seen such a sight?"

High Wolf, who had been watching the archery games off in the distance, turned in the direction that Running Coyote indicated.

That's when he saw her. Standing in the middle of the village, she looked a vision in green and white, her beauty stunning, even amid the Mandan village of pretty women and colorful dressing. And High Wolf stopped where he stood, for the moment enthralled by her.

"Is that your woman?" asked Running Coyote.

High Wolf's first inclination was to answer in the affirmative, to stake ownership of her at once. But he stopped himself short, recalling that, while in the village, he was supposed to remain separate from her—a condition *he* had imposed.

Saaaa. What had he been thinking? Had danger blinded him to his own need? Caused him to be out of his mind?

Or had he grown complacent? Certainly, Sierra's charms had been hidden beneath the disguise of mud and a wolf skin. But his love for her had transcended all that; these past few days with her had drawn him to her in a way that was not tied to the physical. In sooth, he had come to appreciate her character, her companionship, her gentle humor; the physical side of her appearance becoming unimportant.

But seeing her here like this, a radiance amid people whom he admired, impressed a point upon him. And he stared at her as though he might never be able to satisfy himself with her.

And then she turned toward him, and looking up, her gaze caught his.

And in that moment, something happened. Something strong and powerful.

Love bloomed. Alas, she was his; he was hers.

Despite what the world around them might think, might do, he realized that they were a perfect match for each other, she being his other half. And he knew in that moment that for the rest of his life, if he were to live without her, he would be only half alive.

His eyes felt curiously wet, for indeed, this was a truth that he had not fully realized.

And then suddenly she smiled at him, and a multitude of stars suddenly lit up his world. His stomach dropped. And he wondered, had anyone ever had more cause for happiness?

He returned her smile, of course. How could he not? And truth be told, at that moment, he felt as though he were an adolescent again, enraptured by first love.

It was an intense moment, for he knew he was caught up in her spell. A spell he had willingly submitted to.

And more. He wanted to give her all of him that there was to give. It was odd, because less than a few weeks ago, he had thought he'd reason enough to act out his frustrations on her, as though having once loved her gave him that right. In truth, he had even heard others swear that this *was* love.

But in a quiet moment of sanity, he knew that this was simply not true.

No, love desired to give. *He* desired to give. Love, he thought, induced a man to become all he could be . . . because of her. And love strove to master one's baser impulses, that he might make the other person happy.

And so, still staring at her, he silently vowed to himself, and to her, that he would do everything within his power to make her happy.

Yes, *this* was love; and this was what he and the princess had once shared, long ago. Moreover, this was what they would have again in the future.

He vowed it would be so.

Somehow . . .

When High Wolf realized where James Kittridge intended to escort the princess, it had required little effort to gain an invitation to the lodge of Bear-that-runs. And with this now accomplished, High Wolf seated himself around the fire with the others, although truth to tell, his attention was centered not on his host—as manners dictated it should be—but upon her.

Because of her notoriety, the princess had been given a seat within the council of men, a novelty in itself. Sitting with her legs to the side—as naturally as Indian women did—with her long, full skirts puffed out around her, she appeared to be the embodiment of beauty, floating in a sea of green and white.

And High Wolf, despite himself, could hardly keep his eyes from her.

And of course, amidst a people adept in the art of perception, this was not something that could long remain a secret. And soon, Bear-that-runs brought the subject to a head, speaking and signing to High Wolf at the same time, "Perhaps you should take your woman to your lodge. Have you been long separated?"

Although High Wolf might have been surprised by the directness of the question, he denied nothing, and said, "We have been apart ten years, and yes, perhaps it would be best if we were to leave, but not to be alone. In truth, Shining Arrow has requested we both visit him, for he wishes to speak with the princess."

"Humph," said Bear-that-runs, making the sign for "good." And he continued, "Then you should take her there while the sun is still high, for to my knowledge, Shining Arrow's habit is to retire early."

High Wolf nodded. "Yes, perhaps that is best."

But Bear-that-runs grinned, saying, "And if there are any lingering moments, maybe you might have a moment or two to be alone with your woman."

High Wolf returned the smile. "Yes," he said, still using the language of sign. "Perhaps we might. Forgive my ill manners in being so obvious."

But Bear-that-runs merely widened his smile. "There is nothing to forgive. Seeing you thus reminds me of my youth, brings back memories of my own anxiety to be alone with my woman—each one of them. Ah," he said, "Those were happy days."

"*Haa'he*, yes," said High Wolf. And then turning toward Sierra, High Wolf said in English, "There is a man of some worth amongst the Mandans who has asked to see you. He has requested that I bring you to him. Bear-that-runs has agreed that we may leave his counsel in order that we seek out this man."

"Has he, now?" Kittridge spoke up before the princess could say a word.

For a moment, High Wolf did nothing but stare at the other man. In truth, he had practically forgotten that Kittridge, the man the Indians called "Dirtybeard," had brought the princess there, that he still remained; and that, despite Kittridge's many encounters with the maidens in the village, he might feel he had a right to stake a claim on Sierra. But this attitude was not something High Wolf could easily indulge.

And though he wished to warn off the other man with threats if need be, courtesy dictated that he say simply, and in English, "Yes, he has given us leave. This man who wishes to see us is Shining Arrow, and as you know, he is a man of some wisdom and knowledge."

But Kittridge, seemingly intent on arguing, countered, "How'd he know the princess is here, since she only just arrived?"

At this, High Wolf could barely resist raising a sardonic brow, as he said, "Need you ask? Have you not been amongst these people long enough to realize that many men know of things, of happenings, long before their event?"

A long silence followed the question, both men apparently intent on pressing their point.

And when it seemed that tensions might deepen, a soft voice spoke up, saying, "Mr. Kittridge." It was the princess. "I see your concern over my welfare, but do not worry yourself over this. This man High Wolf and I are well acquainted, having met one another first in Europe. And as you know, he saved my life when I was aboard the steamship, and brought me here. I trust him completely." Her gaze—soft, intent— lingered not on Kittridge, but on High Wolf.

And then she smiled at him, a heavenly, tender affair.

And High Wolf took heart. It was as though, with these words, with her look, she uttered a vow, as though she were saying: *The past be damned.* She would place her trust, her very life upon his integrity . . . much as she had in the past. And High Wolf was not unaware of the immensity of the honor she paid him.

In response to her declaration, however, Kittridge muttered an oath, and with barely concealed resentment, arose and left. Such was the height of bad manners. But then, for good or for bad, the Indians were becoming more and more accustomed to the illbehavior of the white man. And in response, not a word of censure was spoken.

However, in Indian country, it was an oddity that a woman would speak up without invitation during a council of the men. But if Bear-that-runs were in the least disturbed over the lack of formality—or the familiarity in Sierra's manner—he made no mention of it either in his address to her, or in his bearing. Instead, emptying his pipe, he indicated with his arm that their meeting was at an end. And as further proof of his goodwill, he said, "You are always welcome here—both of you."

"Thank you," said Sierra, and rising, she followed High Wolf to the entryway.

High Wolf took her arm as he led her through the village. And when he did so, even Sierra was aware that this show of affection was an unusual circumstance— since she saw no other men and women walking or even talking together. And she observed, "In Indian country, aren't the women supposed to walk behind their men?"

"You are not Indian," he said.

"True," she agreed. "But I am here. And that being so, shouldn't I follow the local custom?"

"Perhaps," he said. "But the custom arises from the need of the man to protect the woman when out on the plains, or when traveling. I see little cause for that here in the village."

"Oh," she said. "Very well, then. And may I ask, where are you leading me?"

"To the lodge of my friend Running Coyote."

"Ah, very good," she said. "Is that the friend whom you have mentioned several times?"

"Yes. We will wait there until Grandfather can see us."

"Grandfather?" she asked. "Your grandfather lives here?"

He flashed her a grin. "Yes, he is here, and no, he is not my blood grandfather," explained High Wolf. "To address a man as Grandfather means simply that the man is an elder of the tribe, and that he is helping you in some way—either to accomplish a dream or to impart some knowledge."

"Ah, I see," she acknowledged, and then fell into silence. Although, after a time, she looked down at High Wolf's hold on her arm, and observed, "If it is your intention to hide our relationship from 'all eyes,' sir, I fear you are going about it the wrong way."

He shook his head. "I was wrong to impose those conditions. How could my love for you harm our purpose? No, you were right to question me. I have no wish to hide our love beneath a stone, as though it were as slimy as the creatures that live there. On my honor," he said, "were I to have my way, I would announce our attachment to each other from the tops of each Mandan lodge."

Sierra smiled, and despite herself, she practically beamed. "Really?"

"Truly," he said.

Perhaps it was the way he spoke the words. Or maybe it was simply his intent. Whatever the cause, her heart pulsed erratically, and tiny sparks seemed to ignite all over her body. Inanely, she grinned up at him, only to discover him doing much the same.

And gradually, so happy were they, they began to laugh. Alas, however, so caught up were they in each other, they passed by Running Coyote's lodge without even realizing it.

In the evening, before the sunset hour, the council among Shining Arrow, High Wolf and Sierra commenced. The place was to be Shining Arrow's lodge.

A courier had brought the message, and as soon as it arrived, High Wolf and Sierra had taken their leave from Running Coyote and his family.

At present, the three of them were seated around the small fire that was lit in the center of the lodge. It was a cool evening, and the presence of the fire was most appealing, giving off its warmth to every part of the lodge. Inhaling, Sierra could almost taste the savory scent of the smoke and the sweet odor of sage, as well as a few other aromatic herbs. And a feeling of comfort, of being at home, came over her.

Perhaps it was the soft feel of the robe beneath her, or perhaps it was the kindness that radiated from the old man before her. Whatever it was, Sierra suddenly realized she liked this place; she liked this man a great deal—without having yet spoken a word to him.

It was strange, she thought, how a person could know so much of another by simply looking at him. And she wondered if Shining Arrow could do the same with her.

Shining Arrow had lit a pipe, its fragrance adding to the already smoke-filled atmosphere. After sending the smoke in the four directions, Shining Arrow passed the pipe to High Wolf, then going so far as to give the pipe to Sierra.

This was something unexpected, yet, with barely a pause, and with as much dignity as her position afforded her, she took a whiff. For a moment, she sat stiffly, with what was most likely a silly smile upon her countenance, willing herself not to cough.

However, none seemed to realize her strife, and soon they all fell into silence. After a time, Sierra decided to take the moment and gaze around the lodge.

At once, her glance alit upon Shining Arrow's wife. He had only one wife, she had discovered from High Wolf after arriving here. And according to High Wolf, contrary to what written accounts might have one believe, the taking of only one wife was a more common practice among the Indians.

At present, however, much to Sierra's disappointment, Shining Arrow's wife sat quietly off to the side of the lodge. Disappointed, Sierra briefly frowned. She would have appreciated the company of another woman.

It was not to be, however, and so she brought her attention back to the matter at hand, wondering what this man had to say to her. It was, indeed, strange.

However, truth be told, here in Indian country, as peculiar as things might seem, they were, nevertheless, complete reality to the people who lived here.

At present, both High Wolf and Shining Arrow seemed to have little need for her, as they attended to the formality of opening the council, and glancing once more about the lodge, Sierra took even greater stock of her environment. Amazingly, she was pleased by what she saw.

Mandan lodges were certainly clean, she decided—which was a welcome relief from the rotten stench of Fort Clark. The floor of this lodge—as well as that of the dwelling of Bear-that-runs—had been swept clean and was matted down from perhaps so many feet treading over it, that it practically gleamed. In truth, she doubted if white linen would have come away dirty, even if trailed over it.

Here and there, to her right and left, were objects of work, which were placed neatly against the sides of the lodge, away from the fire. Indeed, the effects of Indian life lay all around her. And if it could be said that the condition of the possessions of a people indicated their emotional state, she had to admit this lifestyle, then, should lend itself to a pleasant, happy life.

And why would it not? Was it not free from the restraining force of propriety, from the ever constant scrutiny of public life? Was it not a life with no worry over tomorrow, no rush for the golden coin? In truth, why would anyone want to live differently?

Perhaps this was why the trader and the trapper— even the scholar and the occasional prince—who, once having tasted the free life—never wished to leave. Or if they did do so, they forever lamented their loss.

No, this was a land of living legends, a land of freedom, a land where a man could make the most of himself.

And yet once upon a time, High Wolf had been willing to leave here, to give it up. Why? For her?

Was that possible?

She frowned and was so lost in her own thoughts that when the old man spoke to her, she barely registered his voice.

But Shining Arrow indulged her, and repeating his advice, said, "*Ne megosh, etta hant tah.*"

But Sierra didn't understand the words or the signs, and not until High Wolf said, "Shining Arrow says that you are seeking the wrong man."

Wrong man? Aloud, she said, "High Wolf, you can't be speaking to me."

"But I am."

"And this is what this old man had to say to me?"

"Yes."

"But I fail to understand what he means. Is it possible that you might ask him to elaborate?"

"Yes," he said, and High Wolf, now acting as translator, relayed her question.

The two men spoke on and on and Sierra listened intently, wishing she had taken the time to learn the sign language that all these Indians seemed to use. But wishing did not make it so, and she had no choice at present but to wait impatiently, while High Wolf and the old man conversed.

At length, High Wolf settled back and said to her, "He says that the man you seek is the man who has placed the curse on you."

Curse? Sierra sat stock-still. Although after a long moment, she queried, "What . . . curse?"

"I have been trying to determine that, Princess. But I have no more information to give you than what I have already said."

"A curse?" she spoke softly, and mostly to herself. "Surely there has been some mistake."

"There is no mistake," said High Wolf. "It is why Grandfather has wished to speak to you personally. Perhaps if you ask him a more specific question, he might be able to tell us more."

"Yes," said Sierra. "Oh, yes. Please ask him if he can tell me if I am the only one cursed. Is it a curse passed down from my family?"

And nodding, High Wolf turned toward the elder, whereupon a lengthy conversation followed between High Wolf and Shining Arrow. At last, however, High Wolf turned back to her and said, "He says that you alone carry the curse—from a man who is living, and it is not something that originated with your family. You were specifically cursed, and he assumes you and I are traveling together so we may discover its source and break it."

Sierra could barely breathe. She had often heard that Indians were a superstitious people, but until this moment, she had never been close enough to their culture to observe it.

She had just done so.

She cleared her throat, saying, "Tell him that I have no conception of what he speaks. I am here to find my husband, if he is still alive. That is all. It has nothing to do with a curse, or being cursed."

Again, she awaited the translation, this particular interlude seeming to take longer than the others.

But then suddenly, the talking ceased, and High Wolf didn't speak, didn't move, didn't do anything except sit beside her silently. In truth, he seemed at a loss.

What was wrong?

At length, however, High Wolf said, "Grandfather says he does not know why you are here, except to break the curse. If you are here for some other purpose, you are on the wrong path. The curse must be broken, he says, before happiness can be found."

Again, Sierra had little option but to stare at High Wolf dumbfoundedly. "I know not of what he speaks."

"Grandfather also wants to know why, if you are married, you have taken me as a husband, as well. And he wishes to know if women in your culture may have more than one husband."

If it hadn't been for the seriousness in the old man's face, Sierra might have laughed. But glancing upward, she could see that Shining Arrow was completely serious.

"Did you tell him," she said, "that we are not married?"

"But we are."

"No, we are not."

High Wolf frowned, and leaning toward her, he whispered, "We have lain together. In my country, that makes us man and wife."

"Oh, yes," she said, glancing down toward the floor. "That's right."

Again the old man spoke, and once more, he and High Wolf spent some minutes in conversation.

At last, however, the old man motioned toward her, and High Wolf, turning to her, said, "I have explained that you think your husband is dead and that you are trying to determine if this is true or not. I have also told him that you and I were in love long before you married the prince. He says that you must determine the truth or the untruth of this before you take another husband. To do otherwise you stir up rancor between brothers."

Sierra gulped. It was one thing to know this within the limits of her own heart; it was another to be told so by a man she had barely met.

How did he know so much about her? And why would he care enough to tell her these things?

Drawing a deep breath, Sierra said, "Please convey to the old man my thanks for his wisdom. It is a wisdom beyond my comprehension. Could you ask him how he knows of this curse?"

High Wolf shook his head. "One does not ask a wise man his secrets."

"Oh, I see," she said, "Then might you ask him, if you

please, if he is aware of the identity of this man who has placed a curse upon me and what sort of curse it is."

High Wolf proceeded to do so while, again, Sierra waited.

And quickly he turned back to her. "He says," High Wolf began, "that the curse is to keep you from having anything that might make you happy. It uses your deepest fears, and acts to bring these about to your own detriment. He does not know the identity of this man."

Your deepest fears.

It seemed to fit. She had feared losing her friends: one by one she had lost them. She had feared ruling the country without the prince, and yet this, too had come to pass.

And she said, "You don't suppose that if there is such a curse, that it might have contributed to our own troubles, do you?"

High Wolf hesitated, his faced marred by a frown. At length, however, he said, "It is hard to know what to think. I believe that if Shining Arrow thinks this curse is worth mentioning, then it is strong enough to do most anything."

"I see." She coughed. "And did he say how to break it?"

High Wolf nodded. "He says we must stand strong and together in a time of much turmoil. He also says there are three of us—"

"Three? The prince?"

"It could be."

"Then we must find him."

"Yes," said High Wolf. "We must. However, if the prince is alive, you understand that there is yet another, deeper problem?"

Of course she did, but she was loath to be the one to express it in words.

And High Wolf went on, "Even in Indian country a woman is only allowed one husband. If he is alive . . ."

"Please do not say it."

"And yet I must. You know it."

Sierra looked away from him.

"If he is alive, I must let you go."

Of course. It would naturally follow. However, she couldn't help asking, "Why? If the prince, as you have said, has not staked a claim in ten years—"

"Because he is my brother," said High Wolf. "And because Shining Arrow has reminded me that, while one might steal and marry the wife of a man from an enemy tribe, one must not do so to a man's brother."

"But did you explain that—"

"I did not. He is right. Prince Alathom is my brother, no matter what else he might be. If he is alive, I can no more take you for my wife than I could take his, yours or my own life."

"But—"

"Grandfather reminds me that I have forgotten my duty as a scout. My honor."

He couldn't have looked more serious, or more crest-fallen, and Sierra didn't know what to say, deciding that silence might be, perhaps, best in this circumstance.

But the old man had something else to add, and thereupon followed another lengthy conversation between the two men. Sierra sat as though dazed, watching the flow of talk, the gentle and graceful hand motions, but she observed it as though from a distance; as though what was taking place had nothing to do with her.

At last, the talking ceased, and High Wolf turned once again to her. And this time, his countenance was determined. And he said, "Grandfather tells me also that as I go to search for the prince, I must take you with me. In this search, we are of one mind, and my going alone would be as to enter into a marriage with oneself, alone. A silly proposition. He reminds me that our problems were forged together, and thus together we must solve them."

But on this account, Sierra held no qualms, and she said, "On this, he and I concur. I couldn't agree more."

High Wolf, however, obviously did not share such sentiments. His manner, his whole being emanated it.

And after a time, he said, "Grandfather has said all he has wished to say. Now we must give Grandfather something for his time and wisdom. I think a gift of tobacco would be greatly honored, if we might induce James Kittridge to part with some of his stock at the fort."

At this, Sierra smiled. "I think that can be arranged."

And upon these words, the old man emptied the pipe of its ashes, thus ending the council. But as they made to rise, the old man caught Sierra by the hand, and with High Wolf translating, said, "This man"— he gestured at High Wolf—"is your true love. But you must console the anger that troubles your spirit before you are free to be his. No man or woman can make his or her happiness upon a bed of hatred."

And with this, Shining Arrow nodded and sat back, indicating with a wave of his hand that their council was at an end. Thus Sierra and High Wolf, promising to bring tobacco in the morning, took their leave.

Chapter 22

Each boy had cut his wrist, and High Wolf, gesturing toward Alathom, invited the prince to place his wrist against High Wolf's own.

"This makes us blood brothers," said High Wolf, who, although the younger of the two boys, was yet the taller.

"Yes," said the prince, his blue eyes shining, a striking feature since they were set against his dark hair. "From this day forward, we will be brothers."

And arms held high, they placed their wrists together, their lifeblood flowing from one to the other.

"He is well remembered here," said High Wolf, "and is known by the Minatarree people as Eyes-of-the-sky, or Blue Eyes."

Sierra grinned easily, that particular reminiscence

of the prince a happy one. She had forgotten, completely forgotten how blue Prince Alathom's eyes were.

She said, "Were they able to tell you anything of him—whether he lives or is dead?"

High Wolf shook his head. "He has definitely been living with a band of the Mountain Crow, though. There are three Crow warriors that just arrived here, and perhaps I might be able to discover something from them, if they will talk to me."

"Why wouldn't they talk to you?"

"Because I am Cheyenne, and the Crow and Cheyenne are traditional enemies. But because I am here in peace, they might be willing to talk to me . . . or perhaps to you."

"To me?"

"The Crow and the Minatarree have long been friends of the white man. They might be more willing to give you the information that they would withhold from me."

"Do you really think so?"

"*Haa'he,* I do. The Crow and Cheyenne have been enemies too long to give their trust to one another."

"Very well, then," she said. "What must be done to call a council?"

"Come," he said, turning away from her to trod in the opposite direction, as though expecting her to follow—which, of course, she did. Over his shoulder, he called, "We will see if we might counsel with the Crow."

"Yes," she said, and looking down at the sorry state of her clothing, she heaved a deep sigh. Both she and High Wolf had once more donned a wolf disguise to traverse the eight miles upriver to the Minatarree village. And though they had washed off their disguise to enter the village, Sierra longed for one of her morning dresses, perhaps one of lace. Better that than her corset and drawers. Of course, she had now in her possession a Mandan dress of white elk skin, and though it was comfortable, and was worn over her undergarments, she would have preferred her own clothing.

Resigning herself to the feminine hardship, she exhaled, glancing around the village as she followed High Wolf. It was interesting to note how much the Minatarree village mimicked the Mandan town, though the people were as different as spring is from fall. Here were none of the European features, so prominent among the Mandans.

There were no gray-hairs, no light eyes. In fact, these Minatarree people had an entirely different look about them, one that was even distinct from . . . well from that of High Wolf, for instance.

A tall, proud-looking people, there was a distinguishing mark about them—a low receding forehead—that would immediately identify them, she decided. And the men—though very handsome and distinguished-looking—had a wild look about them, many of them cultivating their hair to great lengths, she noted, some with hair trailing the ground as they walked.

But she digressed from her purpose, and noticing that she was lagging far behind High Wolf, she quickened her step, if only to keep the pretty, voluptuous women in the tribe from forming groups around High Wolf.

Another problem. It seemed that the men of this

tribe were constantly at war, making the numbers between the fair and the rougher sex rather disparate. Oh, how she wished she had her finery with her that she might at least compete on the same level with these beauties.

Shrugging, she bemoaned her situation and rushed to High Wolf's side.

It had taken them little effort to reach the main Minatarree village, she remembered. This town was the largest of their three villages and sat high on a bluff of the Knife River, a small, winding tributary that fed into the Missouri. Occupying a high position, it overlooked their other two villages, which were located below and almost swallowed up by their numerous corn and vegetable fields.

She and High Wolf had left the Mandan location soon after their council with Shining Arrow, and disguising themselves once again as wolves, had set out early in the morning, skulking along the shores of the river, unnoticed, unseen by the casual eye. Still, Sierra had been astounded to watch as, even miles from the Minatarree village, numerous groups of men, women and children were out upon the water in the early morning, all to be seen in riotous play.

Indeed, she and High Wolf had passed by bathers, children, even lovers. And throughout their journey, she saw the most rambunctious swimming, the Indians using a stroke that Sierra had never seen until only a few days ago, when High Wolf had taken it upon himself to teach her water safety.

Instead of shooting the hands out in front of the body in a semicircle, and drawing the legs up to the body and out, as the Europeans did, the Indians lifted one arm out of the water at a time, their body perpendicular to the water, propelling themselves smoothly. And Sierra, watching them, longed to swim with them, for the spirit of play these people engendered was most contagious.

Upon their arrival, Yellow Moccasin, a very ancient-looking chief, had kindly taken High Wolf and her into his home, welcoming them and inviting them to make his home theirs while they stayed. Curiously, upon learning that Sierra was white, he had asked after Lewis and Clark, calling them by their Indian names, Long Knife and Red Hair. It seemed that the two men had made Yellow Moccasin a chief of the tribe thirty years ago—a position he had held ever since.

After he made them comfortable in his home, and passed around the ever-necessary pipe, the two men began to speak with one another, Sierra noticing that after a while, neither man deemed it necessary to use words, but rather continued conversing by way of hand gestures. Quick, fast and smooth, the motions held a sort of beauty, and Sierra soon found herself bewitched by the movements, deciding that it was like watching a dance of the hands, though she knew well that every gesture held a meaning.

After a time, Yellow Moccasin waved toward one of his wives, asking her to come to his side, where he spoke quietly to her. Presently, she gave the old man a quick nod and disappeared, off toward a side of the lodge.

In the meanwhile, High Wolf leaned close and said, "Yellow Moccasin says that he will invite the Crow warriors to his lodge, so that you may speak with them."

At first Sierra could hardly register the words, so caught up was she in watching the dynamics at play within the lodge. But when the meaning of the message—and the fact that she understood the words—took hold of her, she straightened up, looking toward High Wolf.

"Yellow Moccasin will send his son, Blue Thunder, to find these men and bring them here."

Again, Sierra nodded and smiled.

"While we wait, Yellow Moccasin has instructed one of his wives to bring forward a gift that he hopes you might present to his friend Governor Clark."

"Really?"

"Yes. Wait, here she comes."

Looking up, Sierra espied the young woman—a woman much younger than her husband—returning with something in her hands. Why, it was a pistol, a firelock pistol, and a beauty, too.

In due course, Yellow Moccasin handed the pistol to Sierra, via High Wolf, who stared at it, turning it over and over in his hand, as though testing its balance. Made of silver, with beautiful engraving, it was a slender thing, its barrel long and shiny.

"It is primed," he said, smiling at Sierra, "and the flintlock looks in good repair. A very good weapon. Look at how long the barrel is . . . for accuracy. Beautiful."

Presently, High Wolf relinquished the thing to Sierra, saying, "Yellow Moccasin tells me that this weapon was given to him by Red Hair many years ago. It was not his to keep, as Red Hair said he would

return for it. But he has not done so in all these years.
Yellow Moccasin has had it in his possession all this
time. But he wishes to return it to Red Hair now, who
is its rightful owner. He gives it to you, if you would
take charge of it, that you might give it back into Red
Hair's care once more."

Sierra stared at the weapon, admiring the beauty of
it, for it was as pretty as the finest jewelry. "Yes, yes, of
course I will," she said, her eyes still trained on its en-
gravings. "This is, indeed, a great honor."

The old man nodded.

"And please, High Wolf, tell Yellow Moccasin that
I am pleased by his trust. However, I fear that harm
might come to so pretty a gift, were I to take it with
me now, as we are traveling north, not south. Tell
him, however, that I will come here on our return trip,
and at that time, I would be happy to pick up this
charming firelock and carry it back to Governor
Clark."

With a quick nod, High Wolf turned back to the old
gentleman, and once again Sierra was treated to a display of their communication skills.

After a moment, the old man bobbed his head up
and down and reached out toward her, making hand
motions at the same time. And Sierra needed no in-
terpreter to tell her that this arrangement was fine
with him.

She smiled, whereupon after a few moments, another one of Yellow Moccasin's female relatives set a
bowl of pemmican before both her and High Wolf.
And with another smile, the two of them commenced
to eat.

* * *

"Tell me again why we did not ask at least one of those Crow warriors to accompany us."

"Because," High Wolf said, stopping behind a bush to glance back at her, "I do not trust them. They are Crow. I am Cheyenne, and our tribes are not on friendly terms. Besides, I could see that at least one of them was considering how well my scalp would decorate his tepee."

"Hmmm. You think he would threaten you even though I am with you?"

"*Haa'he*, most likely because you are with me. You would make some man a good wife."

"I already have a husband."

"I know," he said, flashing a wink at her. "I am that man."

"Yes," she said, "you are that man, I think."

High Wolf grinned. "I am glad you finally admit it."

"But," she said, "you know, as well as I do, that there is still much in the way of our becoming married. There are my country, my people . . ."

"All things that can be solved with time."

"Yes, however, I'm not certain why we are going to the place where the prince supposedly died."

High Wolf looked askance. "Because in that place there will still be clues that might tell me what happened."

"Will there?" said Sierra. "But I am still uncertain that I understand this. Didn't you say that the Crow warriors related the entire incident? And that the prince did indeed die there?"

"*Haa'he*. They did. But again, I do not trust the Crow warriors. They would as easily lie to a Cheyenne as they would to an enemy. No, I would go and see for myself what clues are there."

"Then you think, after all this time, there will still be clues?"

"I do," he said. "If it were a battle of great strife, then there will still be signs that might tell me what happened. It is true that the tracks will long be gone, but that is not all that a scout can read from the earth. You will see."

"Yes," she said. "I would like that. But I don't understand why you insist on distrusting the Crow. They were kind. Besides, they were talking to me. What would they have to gain by lying to me?"

High Wolf frowned. "I am uncertain," he said. "Yet my instinct tells me that they were lying. At any rate, I would see it for myself."

"Very well." She sat back against her heels, pulling the wolf skin away from her body. "I still don't see why we have to travel in the middle of the night, however."

Again High Wolf grinned. "Are you pouting?"

"I am not pouting. I would just like . . . a few feminine things, that's all. I am tired of wearing mud and looking like a wolf."

"Although I find you a very attractive wolf."

"And I am glad that you do, but I will be happy to be back at the Mandan village, where I can once again wear my own clothes and look . . . pretty."

He put his arm around her. "You are a very pretty wolf."

She grinned, and losing all argument, fell into his embrace. Glancing up at the sky, she sighed. "What beautiful clouds these are. And it will soon be night, the time when we can once again be moving."

"Yes."

"High Wolf, I've been wondering, do you believe Shining Arrow? Do you think, truly think, that I am cursed?"

"I believe it is possible."

"And do you think that I should be frightened?"

"Not very much," he said. "If you are truly so, you have most likely been cursed for many years, and yet you are still alive."

"Well, I must admit that it does frighten me."

"That is understandable. But we are doing something about it. If three of us are needed to be present to break the spell, and if Prince Alathom is still alive, then we must find him and do all we can to break the curse."

"But if he is dead, as the Crow have said he is, how will we break the spell?"

"I do not know. We can only try."

"Yes," she said. "We can try. But what I have a difficult time understanding is, if I have been cursed, why haven't I been haunted by it? Until Shining Arrow told me, I was unaware of it."

High Wolf turned his head toward her, frowning. And he said, "You have perceived nothing? Not anything that might have indicated it?"

"No. Nothing . . . except a few times, I have seen a figure in a fire, but it's always been at a time of great turmoil, for instance, when the boat caught fire. But it was probably no more than my imagination."

"Hmmmm."

"Yes, do you think that is something?"

"I truly don't know," he said. "We can only keep alert and watch for other signs that will tell us something."

"Yes," she agreed, falling silent. Then, "Do you think we are being unfair to the prince's memory? That is to say, he was a friend once. Should we not be mourning his loss?"

But High Wolf, far from showing any grief, chuckled. "And this from the woman who was once determined to have his life." He drew her head down to his shoulder, and then more seriously, he said, "I do not mourn him yet, because I have not settled in my own mind that he is gone."

"But the Crow said—"

"I know. But we have already discussed this. Those warriors were not being completely truthful. I am certain of it."

"Very well." She sat up on her knees to pull the wolf skin more closely around her. Not only did it provide adequate disguise, it kept her warm. "Did you notice how much the Minatarree Indians and the Crow Indians are similar in facial characteristics?"

"*Haa'he*," he said. "That is because they were once part of the same tribe. The Crow split off from them long ago, but they still remember their kinship, and so you will often find the Crow in the Minatarree village, visiting relatives. It was one of the reasons I wished to go there myself, as I thought I might find word of the prince there."

"And you were right. How much longer do you think it will be before we will get to the site of the fight?"

Again, he grinned. "You sound like a small child, anxious to get to camp."

"I am eager to put this behind me."

He nodded. "The way is not far. Perhaps in a few days."

"A few days," she said. "Yes, that would be good."

The dark shadow shifted ever steadily northward, using the night as its cover. Briefly, at dawn, it hovered over the Minatarree village, but not finding what it sought, it kept on.

The place of the fight was a stunningly beautiful spot. Set against a backdrop of jutting stone cliffs and gentle sloping hills, it was a mixture of dry, golden grass and fresh, green pastures, which continually blew in the wind. A river or stream had once flowed here, and was still trying to do so, for the landscape was spotted with pools of water and sand bars.

It was quiet here; too quiet, she decided, without even the sound of a cricket or a horny toad.

Still, the place was certainly not without its merits. A few willow trees and cottonwoods dotted the cliffs directly above the water line. But mostly the area was surrounded by bush and shrub.

"Stay crouched," High Wolf instructed her as they hid among a lush growth of bush. "And stay close to me. The Crow might determine that we are coming this way and might have a party hidden here, awaiting us. Do not make any moves without my permission. Do you understand?"

She inclined her head once, in agreement.

"You are to stay here, while I scout out the area and

see what I can find. If you hear or see something, or have a problem, you know what to do?"

"Yes," she said. "I howl like a wolf."

"And how many times?"

"Two."

"Good," he said; "If I find it is safe, or if I discover something of interest, I will come and get you, that you might also see it."

"Yes," she said; then, "High Wolf, do be careful. If there are Crow warriors . . ."

"They will not see me. I promise you. And I will not announce my presence until I am well sure it is safe."

Pressing his lips against his fingers, he brought them to her lips. "It's the best I can do for now. I fear, if we attempt more than this for a kiss, we will end up a muddy mess."

"True," she said, a half smile pulling at her lips. "So true. I will wait here."

And with that, he was gone.

She heard singing—low, baritone singing. Softly at first, and then louder and louder, it came to her on the breeze.

High Wolf. High Wolf was singing?

> *Hey yah. Hey, yah, yah,*
> *Ne-ve'-ea'xaame.*
> *Hey yah. Hey yah, yah.*
> *Ne-sta-va-voomatse.*
> *Hey yah. Hey yah,*
> *Ne-ve'-ea'xaame.*
> *Hey yah. Hey yah.*
> *Ne-sta-va-voomatse.*

The song was beautiful, yet mournful, as though High Wolf were pouring his soul into it. Why was he singing like this?

And then she knew. He had found something. Dear Lord, he had found something.

But was it safe for him to be singing? Or, like a bad omen, was this going to bring on danger?

Slowly, she rose up from behind the bush.

And there she saw him . . . and more. Kneeling in front of a pile of rocks that was topped by a cross, she realized that he was crying over a grave.

Prince Alathom's?

So the prince was dead, after all.

She stopped still, barely breathing, as though she had become suddenly numb.

But then what was she supposed to feel?

Elation? No, the prince had once been a friend—a very good friend. On the other hand, he had ruined her life. And she had been quite prepared either to take him home with her, or, if he refused, to commit murder.

Should she grieve? No. How could a person grieve for a man she had meant to harm?

And yet she did feel something . . . but what?

Nostalgia?

True, once, long ago, the three of them had been close, so close they each one would have died to honor the other. But surely she was past all that, wasn't she?

Funny, she hadn't thought of Prince Alathom with any degree of affinity for a long time, such a very long time . . .

But, as though the memory had been sitting there all along, she recalled it now.

* * *

The three friends had stood together, toward the back of the ballroom, as His Serene Highness and His Royal Highness, the grand duke, had gained position on the platform of honor.

"Your Majesties, Noblemen, Friends and honored guests," began His Royal Highness, Grand Duke Colheart. *"It is my pleasant task this evening to make an announcement."*

"Come," whispered Prince Alathom, as he came up behind Sierra and High Wolf, taking hold of both their arms. *"It is time. Let us take our place beside our fathers."*

Both the princess and High Wolf nodded as they followed Prince Alathom through the crowd.

"Tonight," continued His Royal Highness, *"we are announcing a long-awaited decision, and without further ado . . ."*

Prince Alathom, Princess Sierra and High Wolf together stepped up the stairs. The princess and High Wolf exchanged smiles.

". . . I would like to announce the engagement of my daughter, Princess Sierra Morena Colheart, to His Highness Prince Alathom of Baden-Baden."

It took a moment for the declaration to secure an effect upon the three friends, for, indeed, it caught them all in the throes of well-wishes, engaging smiles and happiness. But within moments, the horror of the proclamation took its inevitable toll. And all three of them—the prince, princess and High Wolf—stopped as though of one body.

Stunned, no one could utter a word. It was as though the world had suddenly ceased spinning on its axis.

But alas, time waited for no mortal man, and it marched forward with a certain vindictiveness. And when His Serene Highness, Prince Eric, at last spoke, saying, "A toast, if you please, to the happiness of both the prince and princess," together the three friends stared straight ahead, not one of them able to do more than gape.

From afar, Sierra heard murmurs of glad tidings, and all in the room, except these three, took up their glasses and drank.

"Come forward, Prince Alathom and Princess Sierra," said His Serene Highness, "for I hold in my hand the engagement ring passed down from each monarch in our family. Come."

Neither the prince nor the princess moved, not even a single motion. At last, servants came down the steps toward them to help the prince and princess.

For, as though they were both caught up in the same nightmare, they had to be escorted forward. The ring was produced, shoved into the prince's hand. But instead of placing it on her finger, he whispered to her, "I knew nothing of this."

"Nor did I."

"It must be a mistake."

"Yes," said Sierra. "Let us smile at our friends and leave here at once that we might speak with our fathers."

"Put it on her finger," His Serene Highness ordered, interrupting them.

"But Father . . ."

"Put it on her finger."

Alathom did as ordered, jumping back from the princess as if he had been burned by doing so. Dazedly, they stared at each other, as though they had committed the ultimate sin.

In a moment, however, the prince took heart, and grabbing hold of Sierra's hand, he helped her descend a few steps to where High Wolf waited, and tapping him on the shoulder, he said, "We must all go and talk to our fathers, away from these people and this madness. Come."

High Wolf remained silent, while Sierra bowed her head, also unable to utter a word. And she wondered if her countenance mirrored the look of horror she espied on High Wolf's face.

"Come," said Prince Alathom. "It is a mistake. I am certain of it. Let us go and see what we can do to repair it."

Still, neither High Wolf nor the princess said a word, but rather they both turned glibly around and followed their friend up the stairs, glad for the moment that one of them had their wits about him . . .

Yes, at one time, Prince Alathom had been one of her best friends. Both had argued with their respective parents, Prince Alathom's voice being the loudest. Meanwhile, High Wolf had stood toward the back of the room, listening, but not joining in, not speaking at all.

In time, however, it became clear that neither set of parents would relinquish their point of view. And that was when the three of them had hatched another plan.

All three would leave and sail to Scotland, where Sierra and High Wolf could be married quickly. And with the deed done, then and only then would they return to Baden-Baden.

The rest was a matter of the past.

But now the prince was dead . . . dead . . .

And instead of crying, Sierra wanted to damn his soul. How dare he leave her, once again?

Hey, yah, yah. Hey, yah, yah,
Ne-ve'-ea'xaame.

Hey, yah, yah. Hey, yah, yah
Ne-sta-va-voomatse.
Hey, yah, yah. Hey, yah, yah,
Ne-ve'-ea'xaame.
Hey, yah, yah. Hey, yah, yah,
Ne-sta-va-voomatse.

And yet, there was High Wolf, grieving for his friend, his brother. And as she listened to him, to the beauty of his voice, his grief, his tears; a wetness at last filled her eyes.

What had happened to the three of them? Why had Prince Alathom left, refusing his responsibilities? Leaving her to fend off the wolves, alone?

Could his departure, too, like hers and High Wolf's, have been the subject of mistakes? Had he been unable to correct the deed, once done?

Had she been judging him too harshly?

Perhaps, she thought. And yet, he could have returned at any time. He could have stopped the rumors. He could have helped her, saved their countries.

Dear Lord, help me to understand.

Silently, slowly, she trod toward High Wolf, aware of the soft sound of the grass bending with each step beneath her feet. The wind blew gently in her face as she slowly walked forward.

Why was she so aware of the day? she wondered. Of the sun beating down on top of her head, the dry feel of the air with each breath, the squawk of a hawk from high overhead?

She said not a word to High Wolf, but rather, kneeling next to him, placed her arms around him.

He didn't move at first, but then reaching around

toward her, he took her in his arms, and together, they cried.

Alas, she did grieve. Perhaps it was because High Wolf's heartache reached out to her, and she found herself responding in kind. Perhaps it was because she had remembered Prince Alathom's undying devotion to both herself and High Wolf. Yes, he had once been loyal to them . . . once.

And as though it were someone else speaking, she found herself saying, "I know you loved him. I did once, too. But at least he lived his life as he desired, and he died an honorable death, amongst the people of his choice."

High Wolf raised his head, and placing a single finger beneath her chin, brought her face up to his, saying, "You are mine now. And no one in either heaven or earth shall come between us again."

"Yes."

"The prince could not give this to us in his own country. And it is my belief that he stayed away from you because he could not, he *would* not place himself between us. I think he believed you and I would somehow end up together."

"Yes, you are probably right," she said, reserving her own opinion on the subject.

"You know that this is his gift to us, do you not?"

Again, though Sierra had her doubts, she kept them to herself.

"I would never have had him give up his life for us."

"I would not, either."

"And yet he has done it."

"Yes."

"I love you, Princess. I swear that here, this day, before my friend, before the Creator, I vow I will stand by you. Whatever your problems, they will become my own. Whatever your dreams, those, too, are mine; mine to help you."

Then looking toward the heavens, he said, "Do you hear me, my brother? I swear that I will make your death have meaning . . . by loving the princess as we both have loved her."

And then looking back at her, he said, "I surrender my heart to you, and by doing so, I fully intend to help you make your peace with the prince, with your own people. This I promise you, Princess; this I promise him."

Listening to him, with tears streaming down his face, had its effect on her. And without knowing why, moisture filled her own eyes. Alas, how could she have ever thought High Wolf an enemy? How could she have been so blind?

And without another moment passing by, she cried.

How she wished she could speak so eloquently, how she wished she could express herself so well, but not a single word came to her lips.

Instead, she took hold of High Wolf's hand, and pulling him to his feet, led him toward a thicket of bushes, which stood off to the side. Once there, she pushed High Wolf down, forcing him gently backward until he lay on the ground. Tenderly she removed the parfleche bag he always wore, and the little bit of clothing upon him, which was no more than breechcloth, moccasins and weapons of bow, arrows and a knife.

"Are we safe here?" she asked.

He nodded. "Indians stay away from gravesites."

And she said, "Then let us seal this pact between

ourselves and the prince in the way that we should have done ten years ago."

"Yes," he said.

"I have been so lonely. Did you know that?"

"I, too, although I barely realized it."

She ran her fingers down his chest, glorying in the way he shivered beneath her touch.

"How I have loved you," she said. "I begin to think that the hate I felt when I first came here was strong only because we once loved so well."

"Yes." He groaned when her touch lingered over his groin. But in his eyes were tears. "It took the prince's death to bring us together. I think it was his plan."

"I, too, begin to think so," she said, though still, there was doubt within her own mind.

And then she touched him there, much in the same way as he had done with her.

He caught his breath immediately.

"Does that feel good?"

He grinned. "You know it does. But I fear that if I am to please you, you must not keep doing that."

"Perhaps," she said. "But, this day, beneath the eyes of the Creator, I am here for you alone. You have made a pledge to me, and I mean to make one to you. But the words do not come easily to my lips, so I think I will show you the depth of my promise to you."

"But you already show me in so many ways."

"No," she said, "you don't understand." And with this said, she began to kiss him, not on his lips, but in much the same way, and upon that same portion of his body, that he had once done to her.

And she gloried in his every groan, in his every

whimper, and when he at last could stand it no more, and took control of their lovemaking, placing her beneath him, she knew she needed to tell him. Now, this minute, before he became the master, she had to communicate, and she said, "And with my body, I do thee adore."

"*Haa'he,*" he said. "Oh, yes."

And there, beneath the sun, they proceeded to show one another their devotion in oh, so many ways . . .

Chapter 23

I think I have said that no part of the human race could present a more picturesque and thrilling appearance on horseback than a party of Crows rigged out in all their plumes and trappings—galloping about and yelping, in what they call a war-parade.

George Catlin, *Letters and Notes on the
Manners, Customs, and Conditions
of North American Indians*

High Wolf left sweet sage on the gravesite, scattering bits of the herb in the wind. Sierra, on the other hand, honored the man she had once called a friend by placing flowers on the stones of his grave.

Golden rays of sunshine shone brightly down on them, a most welcome sensation, and truth to tell, Sierra did feel as though the three of them were together again. Meanwhile, High Wolf said another prayer; Sierra did the same, and then together, they spoke their good-byes.

"What should we do now?" Sierra asked, as they started to leave.

High Wolf placed his arm around her waist, pulling

her in close. "I think," he said, "that we should make haste to the Minatarree village, where you can visit Yellow Moccasin and pick up that pistol. Then, perhaps we should rethink our plans. We will probably find safe lodging at the Mandan village. And there we could discuss what problems you are having in your homeland. It is my hope that together we can decide what is the best thing to do."

"Then you really are willing to go back there with me?"

He grinned at her. "Of course. You are now mine; I am yours. I meant it when I said that your dreams, your aspirations are mine now. Together, we will make them come true. Unfortunately, my problems are now yours, as well."

She gave him a lopsided smile. "And do you have many?"

He tilted his head, looking at her obliquely. "Mostly my dilemma has been how to forget you." He laughed. "On my honor, I look forward to putting to rest the rumors spread about you in your homeland. It will be my pleasure to find them and destroy them. I plan to devote myself to the task."

Sierra threw herself into his embrace. "I'm sorry. I'm so sorry that I have harbored such malice for you these past ten years. It has been very wrong of me, and very unnecessary."

Again he shrugged. "I think you were deceived."

"Yes, perhaps."

"Come, whatever the truth is," he said, "let us make our way back to the Mandan village, via the Minatarrees. Once there, we can decide what we should do first. Perhaps we might attempt to find your maid and steward before our return to your country."

"Yes," she said. "Oh, yes, we must do that."

"Then, come, let us leave our friend here and make our way downriver. Perhaps at Fort Clark, we might be able to discover more clues about what has happened to your servants."

"Yes," she said. "And will we be traveling openly, or once again as wolves?"

A flash of amusement crossed his face, and then he grinned. "Traversing the countryside as a wolf is the safest way to get from one place to another."

"Well, then, I believe we should retire to the river, my husband, where you shall paint me with earth, sand and charcoal."

"It will be my pleasure," he said. "My utter and complete pleasure."

As they approached the Minatarree village, they were at once treated to the sight of a horse race in full swing. The track was set upon the prairie and a good deal of the village had turned out to watch.

From a distance, unobserved, unnoticed, High Wolf and Sierra sat and watched the race for several moments, before deciding to go on.

At last, they approached the main Minatarree village, and Sierra was the first to note the sounds of many drums from within the village.

"There seem to be more drums beating there than what I remember. Do you know why?"

"Perhaps the Minatarree are having a dance. Or maybe, if my vision is correct from this distance, we might find that there are Rain Makers on top of the council house."

"What?"

"Rain Makers."

"I have never heard of such a thing. What are they?"

High Wolf, who had been crawling through the shrub, stopped and turned toward her, his manner relaxed and full of good humor. And he said, "Have you seen that the Minatarree raise a great deal of corn and vegetables?"

"Oh, yes."

"Have you also noticed that there has been no rain since we have been in this country, which is almost three weeks? That is a long time to go without rain, if one is raising crops."

"Ah," she said, "I begin to understand."

"Do you? Here is what happens. When the crops are failing, the women, who raise the corn, appeal to the medicine men of the tribe to help. And if the women's cries are sufficient, these wise, old men will parley in the council lodge. Here they will burn sage and other medicine herbs, and then they will appeal to the Creator for help.

"Now, this lodge is closed to all but a few—perhaps fifteen young men. These are the young men who are willing to risk their reputations against the force of nature. And with their own medicine, they appeal to the spirits to make it rain.

"If one of them fails, he will, then, never become a medicine man. But if he succeeds, he will become a man of some importance. Now, if I am correct, this could be the source of the drumming. Would you like to go and see?"

"Yes," she said. "Most definitely. But if this is a ceremony, won't we interrupt it?"

"No one will notice our coming and going. There is too much taking place here today, and people will be watching other things, not us. But hurry, let us go there quickly and find a good location where we could sit and watch, for I believe you will find it interesting."

Slowly, he turned around and started in the direction of the river, where they might wash the mud from their bodies before approaching the village. But Sierra tapped him on the shoulder and asked, "Tell me, have any of these young men ever made it rain?"

"If their medicine is good."

"Oh, really?"

"Yes, really."

"And do you believe that one of them will do so now?"

"I do," he said.

"And all because they implore the Creator for help?"

"Yes," he agreed, "and because some of them have much medicine of their own, and can talk to the spirits. I have known such people."

Her eyes filled with humor, and she laughed. "Well, I, for one, don't believe it."

"Don't you?"

"No."

"Would you like to make a bet?"

"Hmmm. Perhaps," she said. "What would we be betting?"

His eyes twinkled as he said, "It is my opinion that a good, long back rub would be in order."

"Very well." She raised an eyebrow at him. "I seem to remember you asking for a massage once before. However, I feel that in this case, I will be the winner." She gave him a merry, lopsided grin. "What do you think?"

He stretched, yawning. "Ah, I've always loved a good back rub . . ."

Entering the village as unobtrusively as possible, they made their way toward Yellow Moccasin's lodge. Once there, they were able to quickly find a seat atop the earth lodge, sitting directly at the hut's apex. That they shared their seat with several of the youngsters made it seem to Sierra as though she were on a picnic.

"Now there"—High Wolf pointed to a particular earth lodge—"is the council lodge, and inside are the medicine men who are singing and beating the drum. Do you smell the herbs? They are burning them, so that the Creator will be pleased and will take pity on them."

"And the man on top of the lodge?"

"That is one of the young men, who is determined to test his prowess. This man I am told is Gray Elk. Look, he is about to start."

Gray Elk was certainly an extraordinary man, Sierra decided. Tall, big-boned and well built, he wore a most beautiful costume of what must be elk skin, for it was bleached white. He also carried in one hand a war shield, and in his other, his bow and two arrows.

And brandishing his bow and arrows toward the skies, he began to sing, as though the very air were filled with spirits.

"What is he saying?" she asked.

High Wolf leaned close, and said, "At present, he is telling the crowd that on this day, their woes are at an end. He is here to sacrifice himself to the task of making it rain, for he knows well that if he fails, he will be disgraced. He says that his shield will draw a great cloud, which will give them all rain."

Sierra glanced around her, at the cloudless heavens overhead, and said, "Is he a dreamer?"

"Perhaps. But he is given all day to make the rain fall from the sky. We have happened upon the fourth man to try."

"The fourth?"

"Yes, and Gray Elk will be on top of that lodge most of the day, pleading to the heavens."

"And do you think he will make it rain?"

"Perhaps."

Again, she smiled. Such strange customs. Still, she glanced right and left, noticing that behind her, arising, from the west, was a small cloud.

"High Wolf," she said, "look there."

He did so, and then slanted her a look of delight. "Ah, I will enjoy that back rub very much."

She chuckled, her glance skimming over the heads of the villagers, who had also spotted the cloud. And as Gray Elk's pleas became more urgent, Sierra suddenly caught sight of something . . . someone on one of the other rooftops. An image of someone familiar . . . someone with dark hair, hair that was liberally sprinkled with gray, an oddity for one so young.

But it was not a Minatarree man. It was a white man. A white man she recognized . . . the prince.

Prince Alathom? Here?

But wasn't he dead? Hadn't they sung songs over his grave?

Was he a ghost?

No, he looked real, for he was talking and laughing with some children, who were gathered round him.

Dear Lord, what did this mean? Or more importantly, what was she supposed to feel? Relief that a friend was still among the living?

Or remorse?

And that's when it happened. The reality of what this would mean to her, to High Wolf, to them, took hold of her.

"Someday, I will have to leave this place, and when that day arrives, there will be no room in my life, nor in my heart for you. If you would love me, then you must do so knowing that this day will yet come."

It had come. She would lose High Wolf.

No!

This could not be. She could change her mind, couldn't she?

She shut her eyes, rubbing her forehead as her words came back to haunt her.

"We are not bound by rules so much as we are by duty. Duty to do the best that we can for our people and our countries. Rules can always be changed; duty cannot."

No!

High Wolf could return home with her. High Wolf would become her prince. Not . . . not Alathom.

"I was adopted by the prince's father and mother. Perhaps I could ease the situation between your countries."

"I'm afraid that would make little difference," Sierra had said. "Your relationship to Alathom's family is not that of a *blood lineage. You cannot inherit the throne or rule. It has to be the prince or no one."*

No!

She and High Wolf had at last found happiness, had at last obtained peace with themselves. Hadn't they only realized that they would have the rest of their lives together?

And yet her duty would be to . . .

Perhaps it didn't matter. Hadn't she and High Wolf decided that Alathom had done what he had for them? So that the two of them could spend the rest of their lives together?

"A man can steal the wife of an enemy with little regard for his actions. But not so a brother. If your brother lives, you must give her up."

Even Grandfather's words came back to consume her. No!

Perhaps she could pretend she hadn't seen him. Could she sneak away? Or was that a coward's way out?

Surreptitiously, she glanced to the side, where High Wolf still sat beside her, unaware of the momentous occasion so unceremoniously thrust upon them. She caught him in the throes of a great deal of humor, as, leaning toward her, he said, "Would you like to start that back rub now?"

But then he looked at her, *really* looked at her, and he must have sensed something in her countenance, for he said, "Princess, are you all right? You look pale. Is something wrong?"

It took Sierra a few moments to speak, and even then, she had no idea what to say. And so when she at last spoke, saying, "He is alive," it was no wonder that High Wolf frowned, gazing at her as though she had taken leave of her senses.

What was wrong with her? she wondered. Surely she could talk, although her tongue seemed oddly thick for her mouth. And she found herself stumbling over her own words. However, at last she managed to utter, "The prince . . . he's alive." And that's when she pointed . . .

High Wolf glanced in that direction. Blinking against the sun, he frowned. But alas, he did see him.

Indeed, it was Prince Alathom. And this was no ghost. The prince was very much alive.

High Wolf stared, willing his body to show no reaction, though confusion engulfed him as surely as if he were being swept away. On one hand, he loved the prince, had honestly mourned his passing.

On the other . . .

The princess.

Did this mean she was no longer his?

High Wolf let out a deep guttural sound, so deep in his throat it was barely audible.

No!

"A true scout puts duty before all personal objectives. Honor and trust are the qualities that distinguish a scout. No, my son, if your brother still lives . . ."

High Wolf shut his eyes for a moment, as though simply wishing would make it different.

But it would not; even he knew it would not.

No!

Sierra loved him. Him. Surely she wouldn't leave him, not now . . .

"If you are unable to 'make an honest man of me,' I will let you go."
"Do you promise?"
"I promise."

But so much had happened. Things were different now. *He* could go back there. He wanted to go back there, if only to help her.

"I cannot marry you. Only the prince can help to establish and keep the peace between our two countries. If I find him, I will bring him back with me or die trying."

Or die trying.

And that's when he made his decision.

Grabbing Sierra around the waist, he propelled her down off the roof.

"Where are we going?" she asked.

"We are getting out of this place; we are going somewhere where we can talk. I will make a camp for the night. For, if on the morrow, I must lose you because of this, we will have this night to ourselves."

"Yes," she said. "Yes. Let us at least have that."

And with no more to be said on the subject, they quietly faded out of the village, out onto the prairie.

In a hidden cove just off the water's shore, he made their bed of willow branches and soft prairie grass, sprinkling sage and other sweet herbs over the "floor" of their camp. A small, smokeless fire had been built to ward off the cold, and Sierra crowded around it now, if only to chase out the chill of her thoughts.

She stared straight in front of her, almost afraid to look High Wolf in the eye, and she said, "We don't have to go back there."

He didn't speak for some moments, and when he at last did, his voice was almost devoid of emotion. He took a deep breath, let it out slowly, and without looking at her, said, "We do. You know we do. What good would come from running away?"

"Our happiness, perhaps?"

He laughed, but choked on the sound. And shaking his head, he said, "I think not. This would always hang over us like a heavy weight, marring our happiness."

"But could we not in time forget it?"

"I think not," he said. "Besides, what would you think of yourself if you went back to your home without the prince, knowing he was still here in the West? What would you think of me if I let you? No, sooner or later a person must confront his demons. For us, the time has come now."

"But I don't want it to be now."

"Neither do I. But come, perhaps we depress ourselves for nothing. Do you remember my thoughts when we were at the grave site? That the prince had staged this so that we could be together?"

"Yes, then do you think there's hope for us?"

"There is always hope, I think. But just in case, let us have this night."

"Yes."

"Perhaps we should appreciate that our friend is still alive, and we will see him tomorrow."

"Perhaps."

"But tonight we will not think of him anymore, I believe. No matter what happens, tonight is ours. If I must lose you tomorrow, I will have this night to remember for the rest of my life."

"Yes, for the rest of our lives."

"*Haa'he.* This night, let us still be married; we, the old married folk, do you remember?" His voice caught as he attempted another laugh. And softly, almost beneath his breath, he said, "Hold me, my love. Hold me so that I know you are real, and not merely another of my wild dreams."

She scooted toward him and took him in her arms at once. "I am here."

"Love me," he said. "This night, I have great need of you. Let us make love to each other so well that we will have memories to last a lifetime, my fine wife. Just in case."

She nodded, her voice caught somewhere between her throat and her tongue.

And he went on, "Do you remember once, we used to pretend that there was no one else alive, only you and me?"

"Yes," she said. "Oh, yes."

"Then let us pretend this again. Only this time, let us make believe our marriage is real, is true; that on the morrow, there will be no prince to account to, no kingdom to rule, no one but you and me."

"Yes," she said, shutting her eyes, as though the simple action might ward off the lump forming in her throat. She swallowed, hard, but before she lost her voice, she wanted him to know, and she said, "I love you, High Wolf. Never forget that. My love is real."

"I know."

"Hold me tightly," she said, as she fell in against him.

"I promise you that I will . . . all through this night."

He touched her face, then, his fingers trailing down over her cheek, to her neck, lower still, and a million tiny sparks of pleasure cascaded over her nervous system. She inhaled deeply, as though she would fill her lungs with his fine, musky scent.

And he said, "Do you recollect the game we used to play when we were young?"

"The 'remember everything' game?"

"Yes," he said. "Let us play it again, for I would memorize everything about you, about the universe around us, about the world, how it was this night, how we responded to it, to each other."

Placing her hand in his, and gazing up at him with adoration, she nodded.

And he continued on, saying, "I will always want to keep close to me the memory of you. There are little things that make me think of you. Did you know that?"

She shook her head.

"Your scent, for instance, your sweet, feminine perfume, even though it might be all mixed up with mud and the odor of a wolf skin."

She tried to laugh, but the gesture was beyond her, and so she contented herself with a grim smile.

"I love the way your lips twitch when you try to smile, the slightly crooked grin you have."

"Crooked?" Again, she attempted a turn at humor, but no words of amusement came to her. And so instead, she said, "Now it is my turn. I think that I will always want to remember your humor, the feel of your skin, warm, pliant beneath my fingers."

"Pliant?" he said, himself chucking. "I will have to increase my physical exertion if this is your thought. And do you smell the warm air all around us?" he asked. "It is scented with the wild rose—do you smell it?"

"Yes."

"That is because there are rose bushes growing outside this small cove. Now, when I smell the rose bush, I will remember you, my love. I promise you it will be so."

She bowed her head, so he could not see the tear falling down her cheek. And that's when she heard the raindrops outside their cave. "It is raining."

"Hmmm. So it is. Do you see? Even the very heavens grieve with us this night."

"Yes."

He fell into silence, and looking toward him, she saw that he, too, was fighting back a tear or two.

And placing a hand on his arm, she said, "There is more. Do remember ten years ago, I had confided to you that storms frighten me?"

"Yes," he said, "we were together that night, on a balcony, if I remember correctly. We had been talking of our love for one another."

"Yes," she said, "And do you remember what you told me, then? That I should think of you, whenever it stormed, and be comforted because it would remind me of you, and to recall that you loved me. Do you remember that?"

"Yes."

"Do you know that, from that moment forward, storms no longer had the power to frighten me? And do you know why?"

He shut his eyes, as though to hide an overpowering emotion.

And she continued, "Because I promised to think of you, instead of my fear. I have done that, my love. With each and every storm."

She reached out and touched his face, her finger tracing the tear that he tried to hide. She said, "It was a good thing."

And he caught her hand. "It was a very good thing."

"Why?" she said. "Why must we part? You tell me. Why can't the world favor us, instead of . . . ?"

He didn't answer. Instead, he took her in his arms and hugged her tightly. "I don't know," he said, "but I do know this. I love you very, very much. And this time, though we may have to part, we will have a moment we can cherish so long as we exist. This time, when we part, there will be no anger between us. This time, there will be only understanding and the knowledge that we both will stand by our duty. Perhaps this is the meaning of being honorable to one another."

"Oh, High Wolf." She couldn't help herself. She, too, cried.

And he kissed away every tear.

"I will remember," he muttered against her cheek, "the salty taste of your tears. Perhaps I will begin to salt my food."

She laughed, though it came out more as a croak. "I don't want to say good-bye."

"Neither do I," he agreed. "And maybe we won't have to."

"Yes, perhaps." She sobbed, and couldn't speak for a moment. But now was not the time for silence, and she said, "High Wolf, kiss me. Kiss me so that I may commit to memory the feel of your lips against mine; the taste of your breath as you steal away my own. Kiss me so I don't have to think of tomorrow."

And he complied, ever so willingly.

They kissed and they kissed, as though they might never have the opportunity again. And perhaps they wouldn't.

A deep, low groan escaped from his throat. "I don't think I have ever heard a more pleasant sound," she whispered against his lips, "than the little noises you make when you are excited. Always, I will recall this."

"Truly?" His fingers had made their way to her corset, and, as he fumbled over the ties and buttons there, he said, "I have hated this garment and the way it confines you. But as I gaze at it now, I will always remember the look of you in it, covered in soot and charcoal, wrapped in a wolf skin." And then as if he couldn't help himself a second longer, he said, "I love you, Princess. I think I have from the first moment I ever saw you. And I promise you, sometime, somewhere, we will be together. It may not be here and now. But a day will come. I promise. I will not rest until I make it so."

Pursing her lips together, she sniffed, as yet a fresh set of tears crept up behind her eyes.

And then he began to nibble at her breast, and arching her chest toward him, she invited each and every embrace. Briefly, he looked up to her and said, "Do you feel the fire between us?"

"I do, my love. I do."

"Say it will always be so."

"It will always be so," she said.

And he moaned.

"I will never think of mud in the same way again,"

she said, eliciting a slight chuckle from him. "I believe I will even miss creeping through each and every crevice of the prairie."

"As well I hope you will, for these are the effects of my domain," he commented, his lips nibbling at her again, causing a fresh set of goose bumps to form over her skin.

And gradually he moved lower, down to her belly. "Did you see the moon tonight, before it began to rain?" he asked.

"Yes," she said. "It was large and bright, it was almost a full moon."

"Another commemoration of our night. Let us make a pact that whenever we see a moon such as this, we will think of each other, knowing that somewhere in the world, both of us are alive. At those times, it will be as though we are together. Do you agree?"

"Oh, yes," she said. "Oh, High Wolf, I can stand it no more. Please make love to me."

"I will, my love. I will," and drawing her in his arms, he came up over her, giving her another one of those wonderful groans. And reaching down, he pulled her drawers over her legs, not missing a chance to massage her limbs as he pulled off first one, and then the other leg of the drawers.

"Oh, that feels wonderful," she said. "But am I not supposed to be doing this to you?"

"What? A massage? Perhaps, but I think it is I who would have this memory, if you will allow me."

"Yes."

And then he removed her shoes, which had become

of late moccasins, and he gently massaged her feet, her toes, her instep.

"You are so beautiful. I wish I were a painter that I might set your naked image to canvas. As it is, I will have to rely on my poor memory, which does you no justice whatsoever."

The statement brought too clearly to mind this man's ability, and casting him a rather dubious look, she said, "You, a poor memory? You, who can memorize everything in a room within mere minutes? This is an extraordinary memory, my love."

"But even that is not enough to fill the lonely nights ahead of me."

The statement made her sob. And it took a moment before she was able to utter a simple "Yes."

"I think I will always remember your rounded hip, your rosy nipples, your tiny waist that you try to make smaller with that horrible corset."

She attempted a smile, but the effect was nothing more than the trembling of her lips. "Like your strong shoulders that remind me to unburden my heart to you. Your slim hips, so powerful that they give me pleasure after pleasure."

A low grunt met her declaration.

"I would have you now, my dear," she said.

"Yes," he agreed, as he came up above her, taking her hands in his grip and placing them over her head. And keeping hold of her gaze, he entered her slowly, so very, very slowly.

"Hmmm. That feels good," she said.

He shut his eyes, as though his feelings were too intense to be shared.

And she commented, "I will remember the feel of you inside me. All my life I will carry this memory. And I hope that this night will make me a present that I might cherish for many days of my life."

He gulped. "If this happens, no matter where you are, you must tell me. Somehow you must get a message to me. It's important to a man to know these things. You will promise me this?"

"I promise."

"Good. And now, my love, I surrender myself to you." And then he began to move within her, Sierra following his every lead.

She drew her legs around him, as though she might keep him there forever. How she wished she could.

And hugging him, she began a series of the internal muscle squeezing that she remembered he had loved so well, pleased when his low-pitched sounds filled her ears.

She pushed him onward, and he melted into her. And then he thrust upward farther, as they began their dance.

She whispered, "Let me look at you, my darling. I would like this memory, as well."

And coming up onto his elbows, he stared down into her gaze, as they each one moved in time with the other. It was as though their dance were pure magic. It was not a taking, but rather a giving experience.

But nothing remains the same forever, and soon, his strokes became stronger, more intense, his guttural sounds more wonderful, as though he would give her all within him that there was to give.

And then he was there, meeting his release, his gaze caught and held by hers.

My Lord, he is beautiful.

"I love you," he said. "Always you will have my love."

And crying, sobbing, loving him, she met him on that plateau, one on one.

Sweat stood out on her body, his, too, and as their body fluids commingled, he fell against her. And she, closing her arms around him, held him. Just held him.

She could sense his loss, and the extent of his pain brought on fresh tears. And yet, he was here now, and hugging him tightly, she said, "You are mine. Don't you dare forget that."

She felt his lips flutter against her shoulder, as he attempted a smile. And then together they drew close, so close to each other, it was as though they were one. And lifting up above themselves, they floated into the very heavens.

For in that moment, she was not only next to him; she was he; he was she. Alas, she knew this man, she understood this man as readily as he knew and understood her. And his desires, his strengths, his weaknesses were hers, as well.

Lifting up onto his elbows, he trailed a wayward lock of her hair through his fingers, and he whispered, "Take heart, my love. We will always be together. Perhaps not physically. But as long as I live, you have only to think of me, and I will be there for you. Let us also join our minds as we have joined our bodies."

"Yes," she said. "Oh, yes. Let us."

And together, they shared a tender smile.

Chapter 24

I celebrate with you each new success,
Your battles mine as well, I fight them too.
We'll face together what the future holds,
Be there for one another as life unfolds.
Excerpted from a poem by David Ziff
"Sonnets to a Soul Mate"

The sun had barely made its appearance in the sky when two people, one male, one female, approached the Minatarree village. Both figures strode with great reluctance, as though each step were an effort.

Neither High Wolf nor she had slept through the night. At first, Sierra had thought they might catch tiny interludes of sleep, but neither one had been willing to surrender a single second to unconsciousness.

No, they had made love to one another over and over, each time bringing a new perception to mind, something else that would keep them close in spirit.

And then the time had come for them to make their preparations to meet whatever fate might hold. Sadly, they had plunged themselves into the river, washing each other, splashing each other, and for a time, acting as if they were children who had the rest of their lives to play with each other. Neither one had been willing to admit that the time when they would have to part was approaching all too readily.

But then, much too quickly, it was there. As soon as the sun had shown itself on the eastern sky, they had both known what they had to do.

They had helped one another dress, he assisting her with the corset he hated so much; she admiring him as he drew on his breechcloth, moccasins and weapons.

Odd, thought Sierra as they approached the village. Something was missing. What was it?

Stopping for a moment, she listened to the wind, which was blowing directly in her face. It was a fragrant wind, filled with the scents of morning, of dew, of prairie grass. It was also quiet.

She had become quite accustomed to hearing the mock battles of the boys in the morning; their drums, their singing. But this morning, no one was about.

It was as though even the village mourned the couple's loss.

"Come," said High Wolf. "I have an idea where the prince will be."

"You do?"

He nodded. "A white man almost always stays with the chief. It is expected that the chief will entertain him. Therefore, I think we may find him in the lodge of Yellow Moccasin."

"Yes."

But before they entered the camp, High Wolf stopped, and turning toward her, said, "You know that

I would do most anything not to give you up. And yet there are some things I cannot prevent."

Sierra glanced away. "Yes, I know."

He sighed. "Maybe in some other lifetime distant from this one, we will at last be together."

She didn't look at him. She couldn't.

However, she did utter, "I do not believe as you do about such things, but perhaps this once, I will make a wish that it will be so. Let us, then, make a pact that somewhere, somehow, we will be together."

She saw him swallow, hard.

And the knowledge that he was holding back his grief was her undoing, and without her conscious will, the tears came to her eyes.

But no further words were spoken between them. Instead, when he turned, taking a few steps forward, she simply followed.

They found him in the lodge of Yellow Moccasin, as High Wolf had predicted.

And there, reclining around the fire was not only Yellow Moccasin and Prince Alathom, but Mr. Dominic.

Glancing up, Prince Alathom seemed to recognize the two of them at once, and came up onto his feet, stepping toward them. He was not a tall man, perhaps not much over five feet. But what he had lacked in height, he had always made up for in personality, which was usually sunny and bright.

"High Wolf. Princess Sierra," he said with a big smile. "Mr. Dominic has told me that you have been searching for me, Princess. I have come here to end your exploration. Actually, I was on my way to the

Mandan village, as I thought you might be at Fort Clark. But seeing you here is a good thing."

Sierra didn't answer. Instead, she nodded toward her servant, saying, "Thank you, Mr. Dominic. You have done very well."

"Yes, Your Highness."

"But might I ask where is my maid Maria?"

"Lost, Your Highness."

"Lost? But were you not able to rescue her?"

"Yes, Your Highness," said Mr. Dominic. "I saved her from the ship, only to lose her after we left the Minatarree village. We were raided by the Assiniboine, and she was carried off. One of our men followed her, but soon returned without a clue as to where she had been taken. It looked as though I had lost both of you. It was then that I decided I should go on and complete my search for the prince, and if I could, bring him to you."

"Yes," said Sierra. "You acted in the best way you could. Thank you."

The prince crossed his arms, then, and grinning at them, said, "Well, if the two of you aren't looking as though the world has suddenly come to an end. You could act a little happier to see me. But where are my manners? Please, won't the two of you be seated?"

And gesturing behind him, he offered his own buffalo robe to the princess.

And if Yellow Moccasin wondered at the strange actions of these people, catering to a young woman, he diplomatically said nothing. Instead, he signaled to one of his wives to place breakfast before his new guests. And he waved forward another wife, bearing the gift of the silver pistol. Then, settling down upon his own robe, he looked as though he might be preparing himself for a siege.

Sierra received the gift of the pistol with all due grace, and smiling at the chief, said, "I will carry this to Governor Clark. I assure you."

And after the old man nodded his assent, she turned to Alathom.

Princess Sierra was nothing if not forthright in affairs of state. She had been taught to be so, and she came directly to the point, saying, "We had thought that you were no longer alive, Alathom. Word came from the States saying that you had met with an accident."

The prince had the presence of mind to cough. "And so I had," he said. "But as you can see, I am still amongst the living."

"Yes," she agreed. "Though I must admit that you did a grand job making a grave for yourself at the battle scene. What was the purpose of that?"

Prince Alathom hunched over, his sights for the moment not on them, but on some other unimaginable thing. And he said, "I can see that formalities are useless here."

"Yes," said Sierra. "They are. Now, if you would be so kind, I would like to know what has been your purpose in sending us notice, and faking your own death?"

He fidgeted. "There are some places on this earth that are more precious to me than my homeland, I fear. I did not, and I do not wish to return to the place of my birth. In truth, I had only received notice from my father that certain persons from his guard would be coming here to escort me back across the seas. I decided I did not want to go . . . On my honor, Princess, it seemed the only thing to do."

Sierra was at once the monarch she had been groomed to be, and her chin shot into the air. "Well, I'm here to inform you that you *will* be coming back with me, whether you like it or not."

"I won't."

"You will."

"Are you intending to make me?"

What she did next was more from instinct than anything else. Slowly, without eliciting a glance from either man, she rose to her feet and grabbed hold of the beautiful silver pistol. And standing, she pointed it directly at the prince. And she said, "Yes, I am. Either you come back with me now, and take up your responsibilities, or you will truly be a dead man. It's either one or the other. Your actions have proven treasonous to the state, and if need be, I am prepared to be your executioner. Mr. Dominic, take any weapons away from him."

Mr. Dominic rose to do exactly that.

But once done, no one moved. Not the prince, not Yellow Moccasin, not High Wolf. Not even Sierra.

"Princess," said Alathom, "it has never been my intent to rule the country. Nor was it my desire to come between you and High Wolf. I thought my actions would have shown that."

"They have shown me that you are an irresponsible prince, not worthy of the title."

"Yes," he said, "that is true. I have never been worthy of the title, unlike yourself. I would have thought that you and High Wolf should have married by now."

"High Wolf left the country shortly after you," she said. "I have been coping with things as best I can.

The affairs of state, servants, gossip, and war. Yes, war. Your absence has caused a war between our countries. Now, I am prepared to either escort you home, where you will end this war, or I am completely ready to shoot you. The choice is yours."

"Well," said Prince Alathom. "Checkmate."

"What do you mean?"

"I'm not leaving."

"Then I'm afraid I will have to shoot you . . ."

High Wolf glanced at the princess as though he had never seen her before. He had become used to thinking of her as his lady wolf, crawling beside him across the prairie. But here before him was a sovereign. Here was a woman worthy of all the laurels associated with that position. And she was wielding it with authority.

Somehow, he had never taken her threat to murder the prince seriously. He had teased her about it, thinking it no more than an empty boast.

But he took it seriously now.

Luckily, she paid very little attention to him, and he was able to scoot away from the fire and sneak up behind her.

But not to stop her.

No. If she chose to kill the prince, he would not stand in her way. Brother or no brother, this was between the two of them.

But perhaps he should make her aware of other things. Other very important things . . .

Someone touched her shoulder, and Sierra jumped. "It is I," whispered High Wolf in her ear.

"Do not stop me. This does not involve you. I am

prepared, Prince Alathom, to have Mr. Dominic put you in chains if need be."

"I would rather be dead," said Prince Alathom.

"That can be accomplished," she said.

"Princess," said High Wolf. "Do not brush me aside. I have no intention of holding you back." He paused dramatically, then said, "But I think you should be aware of something."

"What is that?"

"Look to the fire."

"I will not take my eyes off the prince, for he might—"

But the prince had turned his attention to the fire, and stared at it as though he might be confronting the devil himself. And perhaps he was . . .

A brief glimpse told her something, some image was reflected there.

"Do you remember Grandfather's words to us, Princess? Remember our true mission. United, together. Stand together in a moment of grave danger. Only in that way can you break the curse."

"No," she said. "You are trying to sway me. The prince has betrayed me. He has betrayed his people. He will either—"

Pull the trigger, came a low voice.

Sierra shook her head. "Did you say something?"

Kill him. Kill the Indian. Kill the prince.

And then came words from High Wolf, whispered softly in her ear, "Look to the fire, Princess. Look there now."

She did.

It was a face. The face of Father Junipero.

It was Father Junipero.

And suddenly, like the right cards in a good hand, the pieces fell together. It was Father Junipero who had told her that High Wolf had left her. Father Junipero who had convinced her of High Wolf's guilt, of Alathom's.

There it was. Without fanfare, without ceremony, without formality, the truth stared at her full frontal. She had been used, had been molded and crushed like a piece of putty to do Father Junipero's will.

It was Father Junipero's advice that had seen her married by proxy, just as it had been his advice that had kept her from searching for the prince all these years. How could she have been so blind? It was Father Junipero who had ruled the country—through her.

Ten years. For ten years, she had been used and had nursed hatred in her soul . . . for the wrong man.

Good Lord, what was she doing? The prince was here. He could be reasoned with. He didn't want to go back across the seas; he even wanted a marriage between herself and High Wolf.

"Alathom," she said, beckoning him toward her with the pistol. "Come here."

The prince came to his feet, walking toward her, while she turned the weapon toward the fire.

"High Wolf, tell Yellow Moccasin to get his wife and children from the lodge. Mr. Dominic, you help him."

High Wolf complied, and together Yellow Moccasin and Mr. Dominic quickly gathered together the family, ushering them out of the lodge.

And then turning fully toward the blaze, she spoke to it, as though the man were standing there with them. And she cried to it, much as the Rain Maker had wailed to the skies, "Do you see that we are united, Father Junipero? Do you see that your curse has failed? We are together. The three of us. Look at us."

As though of one mind, both men put their arms around her, and the image in the fire shot up, sparks shooting everywhere.

Hatred. You all have reason to hate, spat a low voice.

The only reaction of the two men was to hug her even closer.

And she continued to speak, "Look at us now. Your evil has come to nothing. Do you see? Whatever you have sent us, we have bested. And do you know why? Because the three of us together are more than you have ever been. Your best, your very, very best has failed. And it will always fail."

No, if you don't do as I say, all is lost.

But Sierra continued talking as though the shadow had said nothing, and she hollered, "And do you know why it will fail? Because we love one another. We love one another, and we forgive one another. And that is greater than any hatred. It has always been so."

No. I am your only friend. Kill them. Kill them now, those who have betrayed you.

"Yes," she said. "Yes, I will kill the one who has betrayed me." And as much to her surprise as to anyone else's, she cocked the firelock, pulled the trigger, and aimed it straight at the fire.

But although the image was not made of flesh, and could not be injured, an eerie cry issued forth, not only from the fire, but from within the lodge. Worse, a black shadow rose up from the ashes, enlarging itself as though her action had made it ten times stronger. At the same time, a wind kicked up, stirring the contents of the room as though a whirlwind had been let loose within it.

Both men stepped in front of her.

"His weapons are fear, hatred and secrecy," shouted High Wolf over the noise. "Show no fear. Show no hatred, even of him."

But Sierra was not about to be relegated to the background, and she pushed both men out of her way, coming to stand once more between them.

And she yelled at the image, "Your scheme has been found out, Father Junipero. You, who sought to control us with hatred and fear, your plan has failed. For we have discovered your curse. And why? Why did you curse us? Because you can't stand to see anyone love one another as much as we did each other. But look closely. Despite your influence, we love, we are together. So go away, old man. You have no power here."

But the winds inside the lodge howled, storming as though it might create thunder and lightning within this very lodge.

Objects flew everywhere, but the two men sheltered her, and at last, High Wolf, catching her gaze, much to her surprise, began to laugh. Slowly at first, but then with more gusto, the three of them seemed to find something very, very funny about it. And together, they began to rock back and forth with mirth, as though this were a tremendous joke.

No words were necessary. It was as though an unspoken bond between them sheltered them from harm.

And there, amid a seething storm, the three of them embraced. And when the prince said, "Indeed, I can't tell you how glad I am to see you both," the wind lost a bit of its power.

High Wolf grinned back. "My brother has certainly put some gray in his hair since I have last seen him."

And Sierra, with tears in her eyes, threw herself into both their outstretched arms. "We're friends," she said. "We have always been friends. It's gone. Whatever hatred I have felt is gone. In fact, I don't know when I've loved any two men more."

And the shadow, black as it had once been, strong as it had once appeared, simply faded away, as though it had never been . . .

. . . Leaving only the laughter and camaraderie of three friends who had discovered, after all, that the bonds of friendship are, indeed, stronger than any evil.

In the aftermath, the three of them together began the task of setting Yellow Moccasin's lodge back to rights, as though each piece they placed were a part of their growing friendship.

After a moment, however, Prince Alathom spoke up, saying, "Is anyone else hungry?"

And when the question was met with a round of laughter, Sierra felt as though their bond had brought back to life a part of her that she had thought died long ago.

Truly, had anyone ever had more cause for rejoicing?

"I never had any intention of coming between the two of you," said the prince. "Do you remember our original plan?"

"Yes," responded Sierra and High Wolf in unison.

"Well, when neither of you arrived at the ship, as we had schemed, I suspected that there was trouble. I waited and waited until I could wait no more. It was then that I had to make a decision. Did I go back, and possibly complicate things? For I realized that someone at the castle would be insistent upon us marrying, Princess."

"That was certainly true," said Sierra.

"Right." Alathom smiled. "Or did I leave, and allow things to work out for themselves? I'm sorry that my choice has caused you such pain, Princess. It was never my intention to cause you trouble, for I had always thought that you and High Wolf would have stayed together, that once the confusion had blown over, you would marry. I was quite shocked when my father discovered my whereabouts and informed me that you never had married High Wolf. He even insisted I come home. And after so many years, to threaten to send a guard after me . . ."

Alathom shuddered. "And so, yes, I faked my own death and sent home word of it. But also, within me was the hope that if there was trouble, the two of you might follow me and try to find me. And I hoped that you, High Wolf, would locate the grave and decide that whatever the state of mind of our parents, you now had every right to marry. In fact, if you would be so kind, it is my pleasure to present to you my family, if you would like to meet them."

"Your family?" This from both Sierra and High Wolf.

"Yes," he said with the same sort of giggle she recalled from their past. And he continued, "My wife and my two children. Unlike the two of you, I have been quite busy. Come. They are staying with relatives in one of the other villages."

"I would be pleased to meet your family. Pleased and honored, sir."

High Wolf simply smiled.

And together the three friends sauntered out of the main Minatarree village, out onto the prairie, where they found, to Sierra's surprise, horses. The prince's horses.

"We are going to ride to their village. But it's only a short distance."

Prince Alathom merely shrugged. "What can I say? I have been amongst the Crow for so long now, I don't walk anywhere. Not when I can ride."

There was a moment of stunned silence, then laughter.

Sierra glanced up at High Wolf then, and taking hold of one of the animals, began to lead it away.

But Prince Alathom soon caught up with her. "The idea is to ride the horse. It does save time."

"Save time?" she asked. "Well, then by all means, we must save time. After all"—and here she gazed critically at High Wolf—"if we are to give Alathom any competition at all, my love, we will have to become very, very busy. What do you think? Are you up to the task?"

"Up to the task?" For an answer, High Wolf trod toward her, picked her up and began walking back toward the village, away from the horses, away from Alathom. Over his shoulder, he flung to Alathom, "I think I had better show my wife just what I'm made of. We will catch up to you later."

And Alathom, grinning, saluted them.

Epilogue

"'Tis said she brought our own prince back to life."
"Yes, she is certainly a princess worthy of all our
good wishes. But then, have I not always said so?"
Gossip between servants at
Prince Alathom's castle

And so it was that peace was finally established between the two kingdoms in Baden-Baden.

Never were parents so glad to see a son, welcoming him and his Indian family to their home with open arms, even before the legal annulment of marriage between the prince and princess. Further, it is certainly a matter of record that Princess Sierra and the wolf prince ruled a just and equitable reign, and that matters between both families became as harmonious as a lovely melody.

And if several trips were made by the three friends to the American West that they might remember the time when they had all renewed their lives, it was understood by the citizens within their kingdoms that the countries owed their peace to more than simple matters of state.

As for Father Junipero: He had disappeared long before the two couples returned home. And no matter how many inquiries High Wolf made into the matter, not a single soul seemed to know the whereabouts of the man.

Perhaps he had, truly, simply faded away.

Or perhaps he had simply been unable to stand the qualities of love and friendship. For indeed, friendship had proved to be stronger than even the fieriest of hatreds.

After all, didn't they three have living proof . . . ?

Historical Note:
The Steamboat *Diana*

⌒〜◯◯〜⌒

It is my hope that you will forgive my weaving a bit of fiction with history. The steamboat *Diana*—built in 1834—did not sink due to fire. She snagged and sank on the Missouri River on October 10, 1836.

In truth, it was the *Assiniboine* that sank due to fire on June 1, 1835. The *Assiniboine* was built in 1833, and was a historic, as well as a very important steamboat, in that it carried Prince Maximilian and Karl Bodmer into Blackfeet country, a journey that furnished us much information, as well as many paintings of that time and people.

Now, truth to tell, I could have used the *Assiniboine* steamboat in *The Princess and the Wolf*. However, I'm afraid I liked the name of the *Diana* so much that I found myself using her instead of the *Assiniboine*.

Besides, I had already used the *Assiniboine* to carry another heroine in yet a different, earlier book. Do you know which book that was?

At any rate, I hope you will forgive my stretching the boundaries of history a little.

Glossary

~~~ ⤾⤿ ~~~

For your ease in reading this story, the following glossary is added to help understand a few of the words used that might or might not be familiar.

Mandan Indians—as noted in the story, these were a sedentary group of Indians who made their home on the upper Missouri River. Their origins puzzled many of the early explorers. And it has been speculated that they might be descendants of a fourteenth-century prince: Prince Modoc of North Wales, who set sail with ten ships, never to return. According to George Catlin, Welsh history and legend tells of the prince settling somewhere in North America. Unfortunately, these Indians were almost entirely wiped out due to the smallpox infection brought to them by the traders.

Medicine—a word used to denote something of spiritual power, or someone who has obtained this power.

Minatarree Indians—these Indians are also known by the name of the Hidasta Indians, who were a sedentary group of Indians, and like the Mandans, did much trade with other plains tribes. According to George Catlin, the Minatarree Indians—or People of the Willows—were a small tribe and were found living next to the Mandans, who at one time had given them shelter.

Riccaree Indians or **Arikara (Aricara) Indians**—according to George Catlin, these Indians were also sedentary Indians and were related to the Pawnee tribe of Indians farther south. Having been attacked by Colonel Leavenworth of Fort Leavenworth fame, these Indians were hostile to all white people in their vicinity. Even George Catlin did not dare to set foot in their camp.

Saaaa—this is an expression used by the Cheyenne Indians denoting an exclamation, much as we might say, "darn."

Voyageur—at this time, a voyageur was a man employed by one of the fur trading companies to transport goods to the far outposts on the American western frontier. This was done by means of boats. At this time in history, they were often of French descent.